PRAISE FOR LI

"Author Regan keeps the tension al̶i̶v̶e̶ ̶f̶r̶o̶m̶ ̶t̶h̶e̶ ̶f̶i̶r̶s̶t̶ ̶p̶a̶g̶e̶.̶ ̶H̶e̶r̶ psychological insight into her characters makes the story as intriguing as it is real as today's headlines. This is a well-written and thought-provoking novel that will keep you riveted until the conclusion."
—*Suspense Magazine*

"Readers should drop what they're reading and pick up a copy of *Finding Claire Fletcher*."
—Gregg Olsen, *New York Times* bestselling author

"*Finding Claire Fletcher* is truly a story of our times and magnificently told . . . it is superbly written and moves with intense, page-turning speed."
—Nancy S. Thompson, author of *The Mistaken*

"The writing shows a maturity and control that many far more experienced writers lack. The characters—even the minor ones—are well developed and three-dimensional. Expect to hear a lot more of Lisa Regan."
—David Kessler, author of *You Think You Know Me Pretty Well*

FINDING
CLAIRE
FLETCHER

OTHER TITLES BY LISA REGAN

Aberration
Hold Still
Cold-Blooded

FINDING CLAIRE FLETCHER

LISA REGAN

THOMAS & MERCER

Published by Thomas & Mercer, Seattle

www.apub.com

Amazon, the Amazon logo, and Thomas & Mercer are trademarks of Amazon.com, Inc., or its affiliates.

ISBN-13: 9781542046107
ISBN-10: 1542046106

Cover design by Damon Freeman

Printed in the United States of America

For my husband, Fred, and daughter, Morgan—
everything I do is for you!

CHAPTER ONE

I still saw her sometimes—the girl I used to be. She lived behind a locked door in my mind. The door that protected the last secret part of me. The final bastion I had that no one else could infiltrate or overcome. It was locked so securely that no one but me could force or tease it open.

Behind the door, the girl stood on the street corner waiting to cross, shielding her eyes from the sun with one slender hand. She was in the tenth grade and was on her way to school. She wore jeans and a yellow cotton shirt with a backpack slung over her left shoulder.

Behind that door in my mind, I liked leaving the girl suspended on the street corner for as long as I could. Sometimes I just watched her stand there, guarding her eyes, vaguely aware of the cars whizzing by in front of her, a slight smile on her face. I wanted her to stay right there on the street corner forever, frozen in her peaceful beauty and teenaged innocence.

But she couldn't stay there forever, not even behind the locked secret door in my mind. Eventually she crossed the street, walked the thirty feet or so . . . however, in my mind, she didn't stop when she saw the man crouched next to his car, his neck craning to peer beneath it, the back-seat door hanging open next to him. No. In my mind, she just kept walking.

She never knelt down beside him to look beneath the car just as he did, in his attempt to coax an imaginary but frightened kitten from underneath it. In my mind, the man didn't smash her head on the door-jamb and stuff her stunned, slack body unceremoniously into the back seat. No. These things never happened to the girl I used to be behind the locked secret door in my mind.

I envisioned two alternatives for that girl. The first was that she stood on the corner, shielding her eyes with one hand, and when she stepped off the curb into the street, certain that the way was clear, she was crushed by an oncoming truck and killed instantly. There she lay in the street, limbs twisted and bent at odd angles, her thick red blood congealing on the pale asphalt. Her eyes were fixed upward, blank, and unknowing. I liked this scenario because it did not involve the man who unmade her and took everything pure away from her.

The second alternative was that she did not cross the street at all; instead, she turned left and avoided the man altogether. The girl went on with her life, knowing nothing about the abject horror she had escaped—and she was still innocent in that way.

This girl from the second scenario lived a parallel life. I imagined that she was still out there, living out my existence. She went to her proms and high school graduation. She had a boyfriend and went off to college. And at the very second I thought about her, she was out there living the life I was supposed to live.

Maybe she was making plans to get married or have a child with someone. I liked to think of her that way, as if she still existed in some other dimension. I liked to think that someday I'd run into her and see in her face that, in spite of what I've been through, the girl I used to be is all innocence and light.

That when she smiles, it's beautiful and not broken.

CHAPTER TWO

"First time in a bar?" the woman asked. She smiled at Connor in a way that made him feel like prey. A meal waiting to be devoured. He almost sighed.

Ten years on the job and his first thought was *She must be a prostitute*—except she wasn't dressed like one. She wore a simple cotton V-neck shirt that was just small enough to show the pertness of her breasts without being tight. Straight-legged blue jeans and plain black shoes. Her face was fresh and unlined, but when Connor looked into her blue eyes, he saw something worn down and leathery from use. Her long, untamed brown curls tumbled over her shoulders and down her back.

She almost looked like somebody's wife. Almost.

There was something undone about her, though. She couldn't be somebody's wife, he decided. And thank God, because if she was trying to pick him up, he wasn't so sure he'd refuse.

"Connor," he said, releasing his scotch long enough to extend a hand.

She arched an eyebrow but accepted it, her grip firm and dry.

"Claire," she responded.

He downed the rest of his drink and motioned to the bartender for another.

"Scotch?" she asked.

He smiled. "Perceptive."

She caught the bartender's eye and signaled for a second one. Connor stared straight ahead. When the scotch arrived, he swiveled to face her.

"Claire," he said, holding his glass aloft. "What should we toast to?"

She half smiled, and he noticed just how wide and full her lips were. "Let's toast to being found," she said.

"Found?"

She leaned into him, and he caught a whiff of lavender. Her blue eyes were flecked with green, and they looked even older than he'd first thought.

"Yes," she said. "To being found."

He clinked his glass against hers. "Interesting," he said.

"Indeed." She sipped her scotch without taking her eyes from his.

"Which of us has been found?" Connor asked.

She set her glass down and put her hands in her lap, studying them. "That remains to be seen."

"Enigmatic."

"Maybe."

"So, are you picking me up, Claire?"

She looked at him again, unruffled. "Why do you ask?"

"Because I'm already having a pretty rough day, and if you are picking me up, I'd just as soon dispense with the formalities and go to my place."

She smiled wryly. "Charming."

He pursed his lips and nodded. "Honest," he replied.

She gazed at him thoughtfully. "Connor, what do you do?"

"I'm a detective," he said.

"Are you any good?"

He laughed. "I was."

"Was?"

He bit his lip and tightened his fingers around his glass.

4

"Oh," she said. "The bad day."

"Some of it."

"Want to talk about it?"

"Not really."

"Fair enough," she said. "The rest?"

He took a moment to study her. She had her elbow propped on the bar, one hand playing absently at her curls. She was appraising him. He shuffled his bar stool closer to hers and leaned his face into hers so that their mouths were nearly touching. She remained still, relaxed.

"You *are* interesting," he said.

"Are you picking *me* up?"

"I don't know," he said, backing away. "Would you like me to?"

She ran a finger around the rim of her glass. "That depends."

"On what?" he asked.

"On the rest of this conversation."

"Formality," he said, waving a dismissive hand.

"Maybe. Maybe not," she countered. "Tell me the rest."

"The rest of what?"

"Of what made today a bad day."

Suddenly, Connor felt like hurling his glass against the wall. Instead, he gritted his teeth and replied, "So, what is this? What? I have to buy you a drink *and* pour my heart out to you just for some sex? Or do I have to buy you seven drinks *while* I pour my heart out so you'll be good and shit-faced when I take you home?"

Claire continued to eye him with a calculating look that slowly began to unnerve him. She stood and slid a twenty-dollar bill across the bar. She put her lips to his ear. Her voice was calm, even. Her breath felt cool on the nape of his neck.

"I'm buying," she said. "Three minutes ago, you thought I was a hooker. Then, for about ten seconds, you thought I was a bored housewife. After that, you wondered if I was a bar hag, hitting on the fresh meat. None of those things are the truth."

With a single finger, she turned his chin so that he was looking directly at her. For a fleeting moment, staring into her bottomless eyes, Connor felt terrified. "Not a very good detective, are you?" she said.

She sauntered away from him and out of the bar, her supple behind swaying. She carried nothing. No purse, no jacket. Connor's stupefied jaw hung where she'd left it.

Before he realized what he was doing, the bar door was flapping behind him and the cool night air rushed at his face like a hard slap. He caught up with her a block later, tugging on her arm from behind. She snatched it from his grip, a flicker of something in her eyes. "Are you crazy?" she said. It was the first sign of emotion he'd heard in her voice. Anger.

He huffed but stood in front of her, blocking her way. She tried to move around him, but he followed her. She spun on her heel and began walking back toward the bar.

"Wait," he called. He ran again and planted himself in front of her. "Divorce," he said.

She folded her arms and glared at him, but she didn't leave.

Connor threw his hands up in surrender. "My divorce went through today, okay? That's the rest of it. I fucked up at work—botched an arrest—and then came home and there was this letter in the mail from my attorney saying my divorce was final. It's been coming for a year, you know, but to get the news today of all days. I mean I fucked up my marriage, I fucked up my job. I just . . . I don't . . ." He floundered and fell silent.

A smile crept across her face. "So, what you're saying is you're a fuckup?"

He laughed. "Well, yeah, okay. I guess I am. I fucked up with you."

Her eyebrows knitted together. "Well, you're starting to repair some of the damage."

"I guess that's something," he said.

"You're much cuter when you're honest and vulnerable."

He shot her a quizzical look. "Yeah. I was honest in the bar and that didn't go so well."

"I said honest *and* vulnerable," she clarified.

Connor looked at his feet, then back at Claire, feigning shyness. "So you think I'm cute, huh?"

This time, she laughed. The sound surprised Connor, both because he liked it and because there was a harshness to it he hadn't expected.

"Can I give you a lift?" he asked.

"No."

"Okay. Can we get another drink? Something to eat?"

"No."

"How about a walk?"

Claire considered that. "How far do you live from here?"

"Like ten blocks, but I have my car."

"I'll walk you home," she said.

Connor studied her for a moment. "Well, all right," he agreed. "It's that way."

He pointed over her shoulder and she turned. They walked the ten blocks in silence. Connor glanced at Claire repeatedly, but she did not look at him.

"This is it," he said when they reached his house.

It was a simple white one story with black shutters and a small but neatly kept front lawn. There was a brick path leading from the sidewalk to the front door with large clusters of yellow flowers crowding the path on either side.

Connor watched her take it in. "Not very masculine, I know," he said. "My wife's touch. Ah, my ex-wife. Sorry. First day."

"You have a yard" was all Claire said.

Connor took two steps onto the walkway and gestured toward the house. "Uh, yeah, there's one in the back too."

Claire was mesmerized by the flowers—their long, muted stalks rising and leaning in unison toward the direction of the next morning's sunrise.

Connor clapped his hands together awkwardly. "Look, Claire, if you don't want to come in, that's okay. I just wanted to meet you—properly, that is. I don't expect anything."

The spell broken, she stepped onto the path with him and extended a hand for the second time that night. "Claire Fletcher," she said.

Connor smiled and shook it. "Connor Parks."

"Are you going to invite me in?" she asked. "I'm getting cold."

He laughed. "Yeah, okay. Come on."

They entered the house, which was just as silent as it had been for the last two years since Denise left him. Connor was automatically attuned to the small sounds that filled his ears like a cacophony. Sounds no one else noticed. The ticking wall clock in the living room, the steady hum of the refrigerator in the kitchen. The drip-drip-drip of the leaky faucet and the nearly inaudible whir-clink-clink-whir of the fluorescent light above the kitchen sink that he always left on.

"It's quiet," Claire said as he closed the door behind them.

"Yeah."

He went to turn on the lamp beside the couch, but she stopped him, her hand at his elbow. "No," she said. "I like it this way."

"Okay."

Connor wondered if he should kiss her, if that was his cue. He pictured her full lips curving when she spoke. Claire slid her hand down over his and led him toward the dimly lit kitchen. She sat at the table and looked at him. Now it was she who looked vulnerable, and he really did want to kiss her.

"A drink," she said.

"Scotch?"

"Of course."

He got two glasses and an unopened bottle of Glenlivet from the cabinet above the sink. Claire watched him. "Take off your jacket," she said.

Connor obeyed, and she reached over and pulled out the chair diagonally across from hers. "Sit," she commanded.

Again he obeyed and let her pour the scotch. He picked up his glass and for the second time that night asked what they should toast to.

Claire's grin was catlike. "Let's toast to fuckups," she said.

Connor laughed. "To fuckups," he said, and drank.

"Tell me about the arrest."

Connor sighed. "You don't want to hear this."

"Don't be shy, Detective."

He lifted his palms and let them fall back to the table. "This guy," he began. "We were on him for rape, five counts, and armed robbery, two counts. We'd been on this case for two months. We thought we had him cold twice before, but when we went to arrest him, he wasn't there. Either our information was bad or he was tipped off.

"Anyway, we had him today. We went to this house where we knew he was hiding out, and we went in. We get up to one of the bedrooms, you know, and the whole house was clear; so we start looking under beds and in closets and shit. So one of the other guys opens the closet door in this bedroom, and there's this fucking guy. He's crouched there and he's got something in his hand. I thought it was a gun."

"So you shot him," Claire said matter-of-factly.

"Yeah," Connor replied, meeting her eyes.

"It wasn't a gun."

"Nope. It was a lead pipe."

"You killed him."

"Yeah."

"Feel bad?"

"No. I don't know."

"Were you glad?" she asked.

"Yeah, in a way," Connor admitted far more easily than he would have liked.

"But now you're in trouble."

"Oh yeah." Connor smiled at her and ran a hand through his hair. Fatigue and scotch were beginning to slow him down. "Are you from IA?" he asked.

She cocked her head slightly to the side. "IA?"

"Internal Affairs," he said. "Are you from Internal Affairs?"

Claire smiled. "Ha. No, I'm not."

She poured them more scotch. "Your turn to toast," she said.

He picked up his glass. "Okay. To mysterious women. No, no. To beautiful, mysterious women."

Claire smiled and touched her glass to his.

"Why'd you pick me?" Connor asked. "Tonight. In the bar."

Claire looked into her glass and swished the amber liquid around thoughtfully. "Well, if I'm right about you, you'll figure it out eventually."

"Is this a trick?" he asked.

"No," she said, looking suddenly tired. Her eyes moved from the glass to his face. "Connor, do you have a room in this house that was, you know, mostly your wife's room? One you haven't really gone into since she left?"

Connor blinked. His heart was a tiny pinging ball in his chest. "Yeah," he croaked.

"May I see it?"

"Um, sure. Okay."

He guided her into the formal dining room, which was opposite the living room. Connor flicked the light on and they both squinted. He stood in the doorway, which was as far as he ever got, and watched Claire.

She moved slowly, as if walking through a museum. She studied the smooth flow of the mauve wallpaper to the mauve drapes with mint-green sashes hanging above them. The small cherry writing desk with its two drawers and seven cubbyholes. Impractical. Connor had always thought so.

Claire ran a hand over the hard-backed chair tucked under the desk before moving on to the large cherry china cabinet with glass doors. It stood empty like a faceless sentry looming over the room.

"She took the dishes," he explained.

Claire nodded. She turned to the dining table, which still held the tabletop calculator, their joint checkbook, a pen, and a pile of two-year-old bills that Connor had finally paid when the late notices came in. Denise had always paid their bills at that table. Connor had not touched it since she left.

Claire ran a finger over the table, making a shiny, thin streak through the accumulated dust. She turned to look at him, her gray-smudged index finger in the air as though she were checking the direction of the wind.

"She met someone else," Claire said.

Connor smiled grimly. "Yeah."

"Come here," Claire said.

He locked eyes with her and let a moment pass before walking toward her. She stepped so close to him, her breasts brushed against him. He was almost a foot taller than her. He breathed on her forehead, trying not to tremble. He wanted her, but again felt that terrible second of panic she'd inspired in him at the bar. She tilted her head so he could look at her.

"Who are you?" Connor asked.

"I told you."

"Claire Fletcher." He shook his head. "That doesn't—"

She didn't let him finish. She stood on the balls of her feet and closed her mouth over his. Connor melted into her as his body sagged to wrap around hers. She put both hands in his hair, pulling him into her so furiously their teeth clanged together.

He pulled away. "I'm sorry," he breathed.

"Don't stop," she said.

Their mouths met again. Connor squeezed her tightly around the waist and scooped her up, holding her against him. Her feet dangled above his. He felt like he was holding a live wire. Her whole body buzzed with electrical current.

Claire gripped a handful of his hair and yanked his mouth from hers. "The bedroom," she said.

Connor carried her through the doorway, holding her lengthwise against him, past the living room and down the hall to his bedroom, kissing her, knocking their fused bodies against door frames and walls.

When they reached the bedroom, he freed one of his hands to flick the light on. He set her standing at the foot of the bed and dropped to his knees. He slid her jeans down gently. She put her hands on the top of his head like a saint granting benediction and stepped out of her pants.

Claire's legs were smooth and well muscled. Connor kissed her thighs and the front of her plain black cotton panties where they lay over her hips. He lifted her shirt to kiss her stomach. Claire's hands slid down his back and tugged insistently at his shirt. As he hurriedly pulled it over his head, she sat on the bed and pushed herself back.

Claire's eyes were ablaze, but in the little green flecks, Connor saw a deep sorrow. "Claire," he said.

She pulled his shoulders, guiding him over her, opening her legs. "Here," she said. "I want to feel you."

Connor crouched over her, and she ran her hands down his chest. She lifted her head to kiss him. Her tongue teased his neck. She reached for his fly, but he brushed her hands away. "Claire," he repeated.

"Here," she said again. She pulled her shirt over her head. He looked down at her, naked except for her underwear. She was exceptional. Mostly angles and taut muscles, which only served to accent the curves of her breasts and hips. He bent to kiss her breasts, and she bucked impatiently beneath him, lightly scratching his shoulders and arms in her effort to draw him closer.

Connor slipped his arms under hers, his hands curving over her shoulders, his fingers resting on her collarbones. As he lowered himself onto her, her legs scissored his waist. He stopped, face-to-face with her, and watched her. She tried to kiss him, but each time he buried his face in her neck to avoid her mouth. Finally, she lay still.

He looked into her eyes again, wanting to look away but training his gaze. "No," he said softly. "I don't want to do this."

She bucked her pelvis against his. "I think you do," she said.

He laughed. "Well, you are very compelling." He kissed the tip of her nose. "But I don't think I want to do this tonight."

For once, she was at a loss for words. Connor kissed her face—forehead, eyes, chin, and finally her mouth. "I know nothing about you," he said.

"Tell me about the man you shot—about his victims," Claire said.

"You have to give me something, Claire," Connor replied.

"Tell me about them," she insisted.

Connor sighed and rolled off her. He lay on his side. Claire wiggled up against him, curling her back into his chest. He pulled her in and wrapped her in his arms, settling his chin on the top of her head.

"Okay," he said. "There were five—five that we know of. The first was a fifteen-year-old girl. She was walking home from a party with a friend. A guy no less. The perp—that's the rapist, the perpetrator—he came out of nowhere and grabbed her. They were walking past a convenience store. He held a knife to her throat and told this kid that if he didn't do what he said, he'd kill her. So he takes them behind the store, puts the kid in a dumpster, and throws a bunch of crates on top of it. Then he rapes the girl right there behind the store. Leaves her there. Eventually the kid gets out of the dumpster and goes for help."

Claire shivered in his embrace, goose bumps rising along her arms. "You sure you want to hear this?" Connor asked.

"Yeah."

"The second two were college girls. They were sitting in a car out-side this guy's house—one of their boyfriends. I guess they thought the boyfriend was cheating and wanted to see if any other chicks were coming or going. They had the windows rolled down. The perp comes right up to the passenger-side window, same thing, knife to the throat. Makes them drive out to this abandoned factory. Makes them take off their clothes. Binds them with the clothes and rapes them one by one.

"The fourth was a thirty-six-year-old housewife walking home from a PTA meeting. Perp grabbed her on the sidewalk, bashed her head on a tree, stuffed a sock in her mouth, and raped her right on someone's front lawn. The last one was a twenty-two-year-old bank teller. She left work at six, was walking to the bus station, and the perp came out of a doorway to an apartment building. Grabbed her, put the knife to her throat, and raped her in the stairwell."

"You killed him," Claire said.

"Yeah."

"How did it feel?"

Connor shifted and nuzzled her ear. "It felt . . . strange. I mean in a way it felt really good knowing what he'd done, but still—I shot an unarmed man. And after all that these women went through to get this guy and then—bam—he's dead. No reckoning. No day in court."

"You think you denied those women justice," Claire said.

"In a way."

Her voice was edgy. "He's gone. He can't hurt them again. He can't come back or go after them or the people they loved. That's justice."

"Maybe," Connor said.

They were silent for a long time. Claire nestled deeper into his arms and sighed. Connor moved one hand up to cup her breast and felt himself stir for the second time that night. Claire moaned and moved her rear against the front of his pants.

"Now would be a good time," she said.

"Yeah?"

She squirmed in his arms. She reached behind her for his pants, but again he stopped her. He held her against him. "No," he whispered.

Connor moved his fingers downward from her breast, sweeping his hand along her thigh and back up, gently stroking her skin. He trailed his fingers along her neck and collarbone, down her arm, across her stomach, and over her hip. He caressed her skin until his arm ached, and he felt Claire's frame relax. Finally, he loosened his grip on her body.

She turned into him, her curls tickling his bicep. She smiled languidly with a smile of pleasure, her eyelids at half-mast. "That feels so good," she whispered.

Connor pushed her wild brown hair away from her face and traced her jawline with his fingers. "Now tell me something about you," he said.

Claire closed her eyes, her smile lingering as Connor continued to run his fingers lightly along the contours of her body. In a voice growing heavy with sleep she recited, "Claire Fletcher likes peanut butter and hot dogs made on a grill. She has a great sense of humor. She likes to read all kinds of books. She loves animals. She's great at math, and one day she wants to be a veterinarian. She's kind. Her favorite color is purple. She loves summer the most. She's a really good swimmer . . ."

Claire drifted off to sleep in Connor's arms. He watched her face go slack. He wanted to ask her why she referred to herself in the third person, like she was reading about herself in a high school yearbook, but he didn't want to wake her. Once more, he ran his hand down the smooth whiteness of her skin from shoulder to hip. She sighed softly and nestled deeper into his arms.

He watched as she slept deeply and peacefully. When he could no longer feel his left arm, he disentangled himself, trying not to rouse her. He brought a blanket from the closet and draped it over her. Then he brought a chair from the kitchen and turned it backward so he could lean his arms on the back of it. He set it next to the bed and watched her sleep.

Connor had never watched a woman sleep before, not even Denise. He'd never felt compelled to do so. For some reason, he didn't want to go to sleep and let this beautiful, enigmatic woman out of his sight. He chuckled softly. The day hadn't been so bad after all. It ended with a naked woman lying in his bed.

Connor rested his chin atop his folded arms and began to doze.

In the early morning hours, Claire called to him. He opened his eyes and saw her holding out a hand to him. "Come here," she said.

Wordlessly, he climbed into the bed alongside her. She snuggled her long body into his, and he held her against him, pulling the covers over both of them. Connor tried to stay awake, but soon her scent and the delicate warmth of her body lulled him into a deep, peaceful sleep.

CHAPTER THREE

It took me exactly fourteen minutes to walk from Connor's house back to the bar where I had left the truck. The sun was coming up. I rolled the window down and sped toward the highway. The cool morning air was a salve. I felt like all of my skin was laid open, sliced neatly from my scalp to my little toe and then pulled gently from my body. I gulped the air in as it rushed through the window, trying to calm my nerves. My heart beat wildly, like a washing machine off balance, threatening to careen through my breastbone with an annoying bang.

When I got to the highway, I pushed the truck as hard as I could. It was at least twenty years old. It had been painted so many times, there was no telling what the original color might have been. Now it was a dull camouflage green, laced with rust. I pushed it to sixty-five but dared not go any faster. At that speed, the old beast shimmied and swayed, the springs blaring an operatic melody as if the truck might break apart at any second.

Although it was futile, I pounded the steering wheel with the palm of my right hand. "Shit," I said through gritted teeth.

I was dangerously close to not making it back on time and astonished to find that I didn't know what felt more frightening—not getting back on time or leaving Connor behind forever. I knew that leaving again was a risk. My first attempt at escape and my previous three outings had cost peoples' lives. But I'd never stayed out this long. I'd never fallen asleep before, certainly not with one of them.

I felt something that I'd never felt before, although I often watched the girl I used to be experience the phenomenon in her parallel life. I felt something for Connor.

I had a crush.

I was both relieved and disappointed. I thought for certain that men were ruined for me, but last night I wanted to sleep in Connor's arms. I wanted to stay there, nestled in that space against his warm torso. I never imagined feeling that way about a man. A tiny sapling of hope shot up in my heart only to be immediately crushed by the reality of my life.

My hand met the wheel angrily in time with my muttered words. "Stupid! Stupid! Stupid!"

I had to return before he realized I was out of town. He would find out. He always found out. Then sooner or later, he would find out about Connor. A flashbulb memory lit up my brain: stubble on Connor's chin, his lips weaving a sleepy smile as I tickled his neck, a kiss.

He would track Connor down and kill him.

The word *no* strangled itself round the lump in my throat.

Again, the bulb flickered: Connor's face. His short brown hair standing in all directions after he ran a hand through it. Blue eyes betraying his constant assessment of everyone and everything. His mouth turned up more on the right side when he smiles. A hard jaw. Long, lean body. Toned muscles beneath lightly tanned skin.

I chose Connor because I'd sensed something in him that would be smart enough to avoid any danger or repercussions that followed my visit. He was a police detective. He shot a man. Surely, Connor could survive *him*.

Like the others? asked a spiteful voice in my head.

I chewed my lower lip, wishing that Connor didn't fill every ounce of my mind. I'd never felt attracted to a man before. I'd never actually wanted to have sex with any man before Connor. He surprised me by not giving in. I'd never been treated that way before.

The other three had not been like him at all. There was Rudy—he was first. I didn't actually pick him; I stumbled upon him. He was kind of nerdy, his loneliness palpable. I felt badly for using him, but I was much younger then and not as skilled at reading people.

The second man was far older than me, which was precisely the reason I chose him. He was unmarried and childless, lonely and bored with his life. The third man, Jim, was just a regular guy, also a little lonely and down on his luck. I picked him because, like Martin, the older man, I knew he could be manipulated easily. I knew that within a week he would do what I required.

Now it was Connor's turn. I knew that he too would do my bidding, and sadly, I knew it wasn't because I manipulated him to do so. I wanted to see him again. I wished I could explain things to him, and this was a compulsion I'd never been rocked by before. I wanted to kiss him again and feel his arms around me.

Something was breaking inside, and I wasn't sure I could handle it. I didn't know there was anything left inside me to be broken, but there it was. It was too late, though. I had already set things in motion and there was no turning back. Maybe Connor would be smarter than the others.

"God, please," I murmured.

My mind was so consumed with thoughts of Connor that I nearly missed my exit. I swerved madly off the highway, over the gravel median, and onto the exit ramp. The truck tires squealed indignantly, and the entire vehicle lurched right to left before I was able to correct it. I was grateful there were no vehicles close behind.

As I drew nearer to the lonely, rural road and tiny trailer I inhabited, the air became dirty and heavy in my lungs. I was loath to breathe it in. I didn't want to return, but if I didn't, there would be consequences. There always were.

I had to come back. This was my ugly life. My name was Lynn now. He had christened me Lynn, and I could not escape him.

CHAPTER FOUR

Connor slept so soundly that he never even heard Claire leave. He woke up alone in bed, bare chested, his pants still on. He didn't need to check the house to know she was gone. He rolled into the blanket they'd shared and inhaled deeply. He could detect the faintest scent of her body mixed with lavender.

"Claire Fletcher," he said aloud, letting the name roll off his tongue. He glanced at the bedside clock and realized he'd have to be at work in a half hour and his car was still at the bar.

Don't want to be late on the day I get fired, he thought grimly.

He sat up and ran a hand through his hair. He looked around the room for Claire's discarded clothes, knowing they wouldn't be there. The kitchen chair still sat next to the bed. The morning sunlight cast a golden glow over the chair's sleek wooden frame.

Connor sighed and headed for the shower. As he readied himself, he began to wonder if the mysterious woman from the bar was a ghost. Then he went into the kitchen and saw the two scotch glasses sitting on the table from the night before. He smiled as he struggled with his tie. She had been there. He had kissed her and touched her luminous skin. As he drew closer, he noticed a small square of paper beneath one of the glasses. He pulled it from under the glass and read it, his heart thumping at the sight of her neatly printed letters.

Claire Fletcher, 1201 Archer Street, Sacramento, CA

There was no phone number, but that didn't matter to Connor. He didn't want to talk to her on the phone. He wanted to see her. He slipped the address into his pocket and left for work.

Connor was barely through the dingy, scuff-marked double doors of the Major Crimes Unit when he heard Captain Richard Riehl yelling, "Parks! Get your ass in here."

As he made his way to Riehl's office, there were no glances from his colleagues. They were all behind him, but they knew as well as he did that there were rules in this line of work, and one of them was that you didn't shoot an unarmed man, suspected rapist or not, and get off easy. It was almost as if looking directly at Connor might jinx them.

Riehl was busy clearing files off the chair in front of his desk. His office had the perpetual look and feel of a disaster area. There were books, files, photos, statements, and other miscellaneous paperwork piled in stacks on the desk, chairs, the floor, even the filing cabinets, which were already bursting. Somehow Riehl always managed to find what he was looking for and navigate his stocky frame throughout the room without displacing a single sheet of paper.

The captain plopped down in his own chair behind the desk and eyed Connor with a look that was both severe and carefully blank. A minute passed. Riehl leaned back in his chair, picked up his glasses, and held them under his chin. "You shot an unarmed man," he said pointedly.

Connor shrugged. "He had a lead pipe."

"Which he might as well have thrown at you. You had a firearm. You failed to identify yourself and give him the option of surrendering the, uh, weapon."

"Okay, yeah," Connor conceded.

Riehl put his glasses back on the desktop. "You're on the desk," he said.

"The desk?" Connor was surprised but pleased. He'd expected to turn in his badge and his gun that morning.

Riehl leaned forward and propped his elbows on his desk. "Yeah," he said. "The desk. Paperwork. That's it. No active investigative work. Nothing on the street. You'll go before the review board in two weeks. Until then, you keep your head down and your trap shut. Got it?"

"Got it," Connor agreed eagerly.

Betraying no more emotion than he had since Connor entered the room, Riehl said, "The guy was a scumbag. Had it coming. But there are rules, Parks."

Connor lowered his head. "I know, sir."

"And when you break those rules, there are consequences."

"Yes, sir."

"I'll see what I can do with the review board. We'll see if you can't keep your badge. But you might have to go on unpaid suspension," Riehl warned.

"Yes, sir," Connor said.

Riehl nodded. "Good man. Now get the hell out of my office, and unless you save a hundred school kids from a burning building, I don't want to hear your name for two weeks."

Connor nodded, flashing the captain a lopsided grin, which was not returned. The day was starting out better than he'd expected.

◆ ◆ ◆

Three days later, Connor pulled up in front of the address Claire had left for him. He'd wanted to see her right away, but he'd been out of the dating game for eight years and didn't want to look desperate.

Yesterday, thoughts of her had led him into Denise's formal dining room. He wanted to throw out all the dust-covered cherry furniture, but the impractical writing desk was all he could carry out alone. He brought it outside and threw it on its side with a clatter. He stood looking at it next to the rest of his trash with a half grin of satisfaction. He felt more liberated than he had since Denise had left.

The two-story single home at 1201 Archer Street was set on a tiny piece of land. It looked as if it had been beautiful at one time, but now paint peeled in uneasy strips from the siding, and the front yard was overgrown with weeds. The two concrete steps leading to the front door were cracked and crumbling.

Connor paused a moment before knocking. Maybe he should have called her first, he thought. He could have easily found her number using her name and address. *No,* he decided quickly. He opened the screen door and knocked three times on the storm door. Claire left only the address. If she meant for him to call, she would have left a number.

The door was answered by a tall, wiry woman with short black hair cut in a shapeless style. Her face bore a striking resemblance to Claire's, though she was certainly older—not old enough to be Claire's mother—perhaps a sister. Her eyes were shaped similarly, although their blue shade was lighter than Claire's. She had the same narrow, delicate nose, the same chin.

"Can I help you?" asked the woman.

Connor shifted his weight from foot to foot. "Hi," he said. "I'm here to see Claire Fletcher."

The woman's face paled. She hesitated before opening the door wide with one trembling hand. "Come in," she said.

Connor stepped inside the foyer. The woman turned to the flight of stairs opposite them and yelled, "Tom!"

Connor felt a prickling sensation in his arms and legs. Unconsciously, almost of its own volition, his right hand slipped inside his jacket to rest on the butt of his pistol. "Is something wrong?" he asked.

The woman ignored him, her eyes fixed on the steps. Waves of raw, scarcely contained energy rolled off her. A disembodied male voice barked back from somewhere above them. "What?"

"Tom! Get down here right now." The woman's voice rose an octave, and, as she realized it, she covered her mouth with one hand. She did not look at Connor.

His palm was dry and steady, resting on his weapon, though the logical part of his mind could divine no possible danger at hand.

Tom came trotting down the steps in blue jeans and a long-sleeved, button-down shirt. He looked to be in his thirties, about Connor's age, although his brown hair was thinning at the top. His eyebrows rose quizzically at the woman, but the rest of his face smiled kindly at her. Connor eased his hand out of his jacket.

"Brianna?" Tom said, taking her elbows.

She nodded her head toward Connor but did not look at him. Tom turned his bright smile on Connor and extended a hand. "Hi," he said. "Tom Fletcher."

Connor blinked but shook hands with the man. "Connor Parks," he replied.

Tom clapped his hands together. "What can I do for you, Connor?"

Before Connor could answer, Brianna said, "He's here to see Claire."

Tom was obviously someone whose face lacked the ability to hide emotion. Whereas Brianna's face had paled, Tom's flushed a deep red at the mention of Claire's name. Shock and confusion played havoc with the man's features. *He wouldn't make a very good criminal,* Connor thought.

Tom stared at Connor as though he'd shown up holding Claire's decapitated head in one hand. "Claire," Tom gasped.

Finally, Brianna's eyes were on Connor, but he did not like the look of them at all. "Yeah," Connor said. "Claire Fletcher. She gave me this address."

Tom's hands flew to his chest. "When?"

Connor shrugged. "Um, jeez, a few days ago. Wednesday, I think."

"That's not possible," Brianna said icily.

"What?" Connor said.

Tom stepped toward him, a look of wounded pity on his open face. "Connor—Mr. Parks, our sister disappeared ten years ago. She's never been found."

CHAPTER FIVE

I woke to the insistent rattling of the trailer door. I rolled onto my back and nearly fell out of the bed. The flimsy door shimmied. I groaned and pushed a mass of tangled curls out of my face.

The rattling changed to banging, only it sounded like the angry *tink-tink-tink* of someone flicking their finger against a tin can. That was not very far-off. The trailer felt like a tin can. It was almost small enough to be one.

It was his gift to me. Pseudo-freedom. The trailer sat lopsided on a plot of unattractive land, overgrown with weeds like a carcass on the shoulder of the road. Still, it was mine. As much mine as anything could be while I was still his captive.

Tink-tink-tink. Tink-tink-tink.

I sighed and squeezed my eyes shut. What would he do if I just didn't answer? If I stayed inside the tin-can trailer, tucked into my tiny bed, and never came out again? I could stay here. I would just stop getting up. I'd get hungry but I could take the hunger pangs. I was sure of that. I would only get up to pee until I was too weak from hunger to do so. Eventually I'd drift off to sleep and never wake up. It would be so easy. So blissfully easy.

Except for him.

I opened one eye and looked at the door, which rattled with a whole new intensity. The hinges wouldn't hold much longer. I got up and wrapped my robe around me, hugging the lapels to my chest.

I opened the door and, without a word, he stepped past me. I waited as he searched the trailer. It didn't take long.

"There's no one here," I said flatly.

He stood in the middle of the trailer, in my combination kitchen/dining area, and glared at me. His fists were clenched at his sides and his steel-wool eyes bore into me.

"Why was the door locked?" he asked.

As always, his tone was calm, matter-of-fact, as if he were asking merely out of concern or curiosity. But there was a disturbing edge to his face. A nebulous tension surrounded his frame.

I crossed my arms. "Because I don't want some stranger walking in here while I'm asleep," I said.

"You mean you don't want me walking in here," he said, his voice betraying a hint of petulance.

I rolled my eyes and plopped onto the couch, one leg folded beneath me. "What does it matter? I let you in, didn't I?"

"I have to be able to trust you, Lynn," he said.

I felt tired, so tired. "Well, you're not in prison, are you?"

He bristled but didn't move toward me. "You were fifteen minutes late coming home last night."

"Oh my God. You woke me up at six a.m. because I was fifteen minutes late getting home from work? You're fucking crazy. Why don't you just go home to your little pet and fuck with her head some more?"

Slowly, he sat beside me, arranging himself carefully. He tangled a hand in the curls behind my head. Then he jerked my head back. I gasped and reached for him, but he quickly wrapped his other hand around my throat. I winced as he applied pressure. My windpipe sagged beneath his grip.

"Lynnie," he said softly, his voice almost soothing. "You know Daddy doesn't like it when you talk that way. So be a good girl." He squeezed harder. My eyes watered. "You want to be a good girl, don't you?"

I did my best to nod. "Good. 'Cause you know what happens when you're bad, and we wouldn't want anything bad to happen to the Fletchers, now would we?"

I shook my head as vigorously as I could. He smiled. He released the back of my head and stroked my hair. "Now, are you going to tell Daddy honestly where you were after work last night?"

I nodded. He loosened his hold on my throat but didn't let go. I coughed, trying to draw in air. "I took some of the large dogs for a quick walk before I locked up," I said.

He studied me. I reached up and pulled his hand away from my throat. Finally, he said, "Okay, Lynn. That's okay. I just worried."

"Yeah," I said, massaging my neck. "Sure."

He smiled at me, the loving smile of a father. It made me want to retch. He stood up and straightened his clothes, stroking the lapels of his jacket repeatedly until he could look at me again.

I made a conscious effort to keep the look of disgust from my face. I had to remain carefully neutral. It was the key to my survival.

His face was bright red. "Well," he said. "Okay."

He fidgeted with the buttons on his shirt. I stared at him blankly. Silently, I urged him to go. It seemed like an eternity before he moved to the door. He stepped outside and, once again, flashed his beneficent smile. My stomach twisted into a knot. He hopped down the front steps. Quickly, I pulled the door shut after him.

I let out a sigh and my body relaxed back to its natural state. Mentally, I coaxed my pulse to slow, perspiration to cease, and the sound of blood rushing in my ears to ebb. I willed my muscles to loosen and my stomach to stop churning. I went to the window over the kitchen sink and pushed aside the curtain. I watched him walk briskly across the deserted road and disappear into the tiny clapboard house opposite my trailer.

Then I locked the door again.

CHAPTER SIX

Connor had no recollection of being invited into the living room, but there he was minutes later, ensconced on the Fletchers' couch, a cup of coffee in his hand, staring at the two remaining Fletcher siblings.

"It can't be," he blurted.

Not even his skills as a detective had prepared him for this kind of shock. This was a woman he'd seen—touched—in the flesh. In all of her flesh. He'd kissed her, smelled her. She was real.

Brianna Fletcher sat across from him, arms folded tightly across her thin chest. Her cold blue eyes chilled him. He was glad looks couldn't kill, because from the glare he was getting, only the coffee table between them stopped her from castrating him and leaving him for dead.

"If this is your idea of a sick joke, I'm calling the police," she spat.

Tom rested a hand on her knee. "Brianna," he said softly.

"I am the police," Connor muttered.

"What?" Tom said.

Connor set his coffee down and fished his ID and badge out of his pocket. He tossed it onto the table. Brianna snatched it up and studied it before handing it to Tom. The harsh lines of her face softened somewhat. Tom looked at it and slid it back to Connor. "Detective," he said.

"Connor. Please."

Tom smiled grimly. "Connor. Our sister, Claire, has been missing for ten years. The woman who gave you this address was mistaken."

Connor shook his head. "No," he said. "She said her name was Claire Fletcher."

"Maybe she just didn't want to see you again," Brianna sneered.

The wheels in Connor's head started turning once more, slowly. "But why give me the name and address of a missing woman? She could have just given me a fake phone number."

Claire's face flashed in Connor's mind.

"I think we should call Mitch—before Mom gets home," Brianna said to Tom.

"Let's toast to being found," she'd said.

"Interesting," he replied.

"Indeed."

"Which of us has been found?" he asked.

"That remains to be seen."

"No," Connor said abruptly. "She sent me here." He looked beseechingly at Tom.

Tom shook his head. "It wasn't her."

Brianna rose. "Dammit, Tom. Call Mitch right now."

"But she talked about being found. She said—"

"Stop it!" Brianna screamed, putting her hands to her ears. "It wasn't Claire. It wasn't."

Connor swallowed and looked at Tom. "Could I just see a picture? Please?"

Tom nodded and left the room. He returned with a framed five-by-seven photo. He handed it to Connor. "She was fifteen," he said. "On her way to school. There was one witness who said she saw a man pushing a girl who matched Claire's description into a blue station wagon about the time she should have been arriving at school. They never found any man or the car or Claire. I'm sorry, Mr. Parks."

Connor held the photo with both hands. He needed only a glance to recognize that the girl in the picture was indeed the woman he'd spent the night with. In the photo, the face was rounder, the skin more pristine. The hair was much shorter but had the same color and the same unruly curls. The fifteen-year-old smile was brighter, but it was the same curvy, wide mouth.

"Her eyes were different," Connor mumbled, almost to himself.

"See!" Brianna said. "It wasn't her." She snatched the photo from his hands.

"No," Connor said. "She looked just the same—well, older of course—her eyes were the same color and shape, they were just different."

Her eyes had lost their innocence. Connor had felt panicked looking into them, as if he might fall in and get trapped on the other side. If the world had had eyes since the moment of its creation and witnessed all manner of natural and man-made violence and destruction, its eyes might never match the despair Connor had seen in Claire Fletcher's eyes.

"Call Mitch," Brianna demanded again. She hugged the photo to her chest and eyed Tom fiercely. "Mitch will deal with him, just like he did with the others."

Connor's head snapped up. "The others?"

Tom pulled a business card from his wallet and handed it to Connor.

"That number is for Mitch Farrell. He's a private investigator. He's worked on Claire's case as a favor to my family for years," Tom explained.

Connor stood and looked from Tom to Brianna and back. "What others?" he asked.

Tom ushered Connor to the door. "I'm sure you can see why this is difficult for us to discuss, but Mitch will want to talk to you, check out your story."

They were now standing on the broken-down front stoop. Connor looked at Tom. "What others?" he asked again.

Tom glanced back at the door to be certain his sister couldn't hear him. He sighed and drew closer to Connor. "Over the last eight years, there have been three other men, and like you, they showed up here out of the blue to see Claire. They all said they'd recently spent the night with her and that she left them this address."

CHAPTER SEVEN

In the shower, I made the water so hot it scalded my skin. I scrubbed my neck raw where he had touched me. When I finished, I put on a pair of sweatpants, two pairs of socks, a T-shirt, and an oversized sweatshirt. I climbed back into bed and pulled the blankets all the way over my head.

"Five minutes," I whispered, and, as always, my actual voice sounded much calmer and more controlled than the voice in my head. As if it were not really me speaking but some other woman who knew what to do, knew how to handle things, knew how to live in the strange wasteland of Lynn Wood's life.

"Just five minutes," she said.

I concentrated on my breathing, inhaling deeply through my nose and exhaling through my mouth. I put one hand on my abdomen and felt it rise and fall with each breath. "Five minutes," the woman said again. "All you need is five minutes. The door is locked. You're safe. For the next five minutes no one can hurt you. No one can get to you. You don't exist except right here where it's warm and cozy and no one can get to you."

I breathed deeply and slowly and tried to make my mind as blank as possible. This was an exercise I'd done for years. My way of coping. I had to smuggle my freedom and security secretly in small five-minute increments.

Sometimes I did it at the local veterinarian's office where I worked. All I really did there was grunt work, but the animals soothed me. Sometimes I took my five minutes with them. Sometimes it was in a bathroom or the truck. But it always worked best when I was under the covers. It was here where I felt truly hidden from the world—from my bereaved family, my broken life, the memories I almost couldn't bear, from whom I'd become, and most of all, from him.

I still remembered those first months as if they had just occurred. I snuggled deeper under the blankets, shivering. Those first months I would have done anything for a blanket. I was so cold, so scared.

CHAPTER EIGHT

1995

He took me right from the street. He used some clever ruse. When I walked by, he was crouched beside his car, looking underneath it, the back door ajar. He said there was a cat under the car.

I knelt beside him and almost immediately felt rough hands at the back of my head. My face met steel, and the world faded to black as he pushed me inside the car.

The next thing I remembered was being in the room. It was dark and I was lying on a bed. He'd stripped me naked and tied my hands and feet to the bedposts. I must have looked like a four-point star in the stifling darkness. I was cold, and there was no give to the ropes he had bound me with. Instinctively, my body tried to curl into itself but could not. My head ached.

Before I was even fully aware of where I was or that I was awake, I struggled violently to break free. My voice took a long time to come. My throat was dry and my mouth felt like it was filled with cotton. My voice finally came to me after a lot of gasping.

I cried out for help. I screamed for what seemed like days. I screamed until my throat was so raw and swollen that I could barely breathe through my mouth.

Then came his disembodied voice in the blackness, cooing and issuing soothing words. He touched my face and my hair. He kept saying, "It's okay, Daddy's here."

It confused me because I knew it was not my father's voice or his touch, although he sounded every bit as sincere as any adoring father.

That was one of the things that came to sicken me most—he really believed he loved us. It wasn't just an act. He wasn't trying to manipulate us. He didn't have to. He had ropes, duct tape, and handcuffs.

The first several times he came to me, I begged him to let me go. I swore I would never turn him in, without ever thinking about what that really meant. Would I return to my family and never speak a word of what had happened to me?

I tried everything I could think of, but he didn't respond. He just kept stroking my hair, telling me it was okay. "Daddy" was there and he was going to take good care of me. It was like pleading with a tape recording.

I don't know how many days or weeks it went on, but he came and fed me, gave me milk and water. He untied me so I could relieve myself in a large bucket he kept in the corner of the room. I was stiff and unable to move well from being bound. He had to help me because I was too weak to sit up or clean myself. Sometimes I thought that was the worst humiliation of all.

I begged for clothes—for a blanket—but he said nothing.

He gave me sponge baths, and I sobbed with shame because the hot water and his gentle touch felt wonderful after being so cold for so long. He always whispered, "It's okay. Daddy's here."

I tried to keep track of the days, but there was no window in the room; he kept it dark except for when he was there. Whenever he came, he turned on a single lamp on the scuffed table beside the bed. It didn't light the room very well, but I could see that the room was mostly barren. It held only my bed, the table, the lamp, and the bucket.

He was relatively young. I didn't know it at the time, but he was only thirty-seven when he stole me. He was thin and wiry but tall with sandy-brown hair. He looked so average. The first time I remember seeing him, really seeing him, was the first time he raped me.

I heard him come in. I began squirming earnestly against the ropes that bound me. By then my wrists and ankles bore deep welts that were scabbed over and bled anew each time I struggled.

He turned on the light.

I began my endless entreaties. "Why are you doing this to me? Please. I want to go home. Let me go. Please just let me go."

He ignored me just as he always did. Then he started taking his clothes off. A new terror gripped me. I was suddenly aware of my own stink and the fear that rose from within me, popping out on my skin as fat beads of sweat. I stopped protesting and watched him with growing alarm. He undressed slowly and carefully. I was young, and while I'd kissed boys and fooled around, I was a virgin. I'd never seen a naked man before.

"No," I said, but he climbed onto the bed with me.

Tears leaked from the corners of my eyes. I begged. Oh, how I begged him not to do it.

"Shhh," he murmured. "It's okay. I won't hurt you."

"Don't do this," I said.

"It will be okay. I'm going to make you feel good. You'll see."

I started to gag. It was involuntary. He sat up quickly and watched until I had control of myself.

I opened my eyes and looked at him. He stared at me differently. Up to that point, he'd been gentle, adoring, even tender. This time there was something else. Something raw, something explosive barely held in check.

"You're going to be mine now," he said. "You will do as I say. You will give yourself to me and you will enjoy it."

Through clenched teeth, I replied, "I will never enjoy it. I hate you."

Then he slapped me, hard, across the face. My arms strained instinctively to cover my face, but they were bound tight.

What I remember was how quiet it was. Eerily so. I turned my head and focused on the lamp beside the bed. The sound of the bed squeaking was like a sonic boom.

When he was done, he collapsed beside me, his head on my shoulder. "You're mine now," he whispered. "I'll take care of you and we'll be together forever. Your name is Lynn now. That's what I'll call you." He stroked my skin. "My sweet Lynn."

Afterward, I turned my head and vomited. He dressed slowly, as carefully as he had undressed, and without a word left the room.

CHAPTER NINE

Beneath the covers, my whole body recoiled. I had tried so many times to expunge that memory from my mind's record, but I never succeeded. Maybe it didn't really matter because forgetting wouldn't make it unhappen.

I got out from beneath the covers and wedged a chair under the handle of the trailer door. It was about as flimsy as the door itself, but it made me feel better. It might not stop him from coming back, but it sure would piss him off.

I padded into the kitchen and peeked out the window again. Across the road, I saw him standing on the porch of the brown house, facing off with Tiffany. It was an unusual sight to see her outside of the house. Something was wrong. I could see only their profiles, but I could tell by the rigid lines of their bodies and Tiffany's crossed arms that they were arguing. The car keys in his hands jingled nervously.

I leaned over the sink for a better look, as if getting closer to the glass panes would enable me to hear them. But I didn't need to hear what they were arguing about. The arguing was not my concern. Tiffany's incessant whining and clinginess caused daily disagreements between them. He had created his monster, and the consequence was to put up with her every day.

It was the fact that their argument had carried itself outside that concerned me. I watched his keys drum against his thigh. A tingling began in the pit of my stomach, always a precursor to another beating or some violation—trouble.

He was a nervous type. He had reason to be after all the things he'd done. But this was his domain. This tiny stretch of road that lay between my trailer and his dilapidated shack was the kingdom he had created, and here, he was in total control. He made sure of that.

He moved off the porch, gripping his keys with both hands and fumbling with them, glancing back over his shoulder at Tiffany. She stomped her feet on the wooden floor of the porch, her face caught between a pout and a scowl. A familiar sight. He had stunted her growth literally and figuratively the day he brought her to live with us.

Tiffany had the emotional acumen of a thirteen-year-old, and even though she was now twenty years old, she still looked like an adolescent. Clothes hung on her bony frame. Her skin was pale and sallow, her dark hair lank and dull from poor nutrition. She starved herself to stay so thin. She ate so little that she'd ceased to menstruate, a fact for which he was grateful.

Unlike me, Tiffany was a runaway whose mind he filled with delusions of grandeur. It didn't matter to Tiffany that she had to perform disgusting sexual acts with a man who could conceivably be her father. In the house of "Daddy," Tiffany was number one, and no matter how he mistreated her, she would not trade all that attention for anything—not even an innocent person's life.

Repulsion washed over me like a cold wave of stinging ocean water. He flew off in his old car, obviously relieved to be free from Tiffany's cloying presence. He'd fidgeted with the buttons on his shirt this morning while he questioned me for being fifteen minutes late getting home from work. Something he no doubt found out from Tiffany, who loved to make my life even more hellish than I imagined it could be under the circumstances.

I turned away from the window and got a drink of water from the tap. I tried to think of the last time he'd barged in on me the way he had this morning, suspicious to the point of being flustered. It had been months, a year perhaps.

My heart pounded as Connor Parks filled my head. I still smelled him—sweat, cologne, and scotch. In the last few days, I had tried without success to banish him from my thoughts. Had my abductor found out about Connor? Had Tiffany somehow realized that I wasn't home that night and ratted me out? I had taken every precaution. I had been so careful.

Connor's sleepy smile played on a film screen in my mind. I ached in places I never knew I had and in places I thought were long dead. Flashbulb memory: He sighs in his sleep. His feet twitch. His arms tighten around me. Sleep without nightmares.

The illusion of safety I had when I was with him was almost too real to turn away from. If only my life were normal. If only I were normal, I could see him again, date him, and talk to him. The girl I used to be could do it. She could call him on the telephone and say something trivial like "I had such a good time with you the other night."

Maybe she could cook him dinner, barbecue in his backyard. She could curl up easily in his arms as they lie together in a foldout lawn chair, soaking up the last rays of sunshine, maybe reading a book together, drinking wine, or whatever it was that normal people did on a date.

I was not that girl any longer. I was not normal nor would I ever be. This was my life, and it did not have room for someone as beautiful as Connor.

Still, if something happened to him as it had the others, I would be responsible. I was already responsible for so many lives that I could not bear another murder on my conscience. I had to find out how much my abductor and his pet knew, if they were on to Connor. I dressed hastily in jeans and a sweatshirt and stomped across the road to the little house.

CHAPTER TEN

Mitch Farrell's office was located in a small pocket of an old strip mall whose former businesses had moved on to more highly trafficked areas of the city. The square block of storefronts was dilapidated, most of the windows yawning empty, the signage above them leaving ghostlike letters of businesses past. All that was left was Farrell's office and a Laundromat, which was unoccupied at the moment.

The only sign that Farrell did business among the empty shops was simple gold lettering on the front door bearing his name and title. A waiting room held a few scruffy chairs and a battered table with some very out-of-date magazines. There was no receptionist, just a small hallway to Connor's right.

"Hello?" he called. "Mr. Farrell?"

"You must be the detective." Farrell's voice arrived a split second before he did.

The man was in his sixties with salt-and-pepper hair and worry lines surrounding his dark-brown eyes. He was tall, dressed casually, but with the posture of someone who'd spent time in the military.

"Connor Parks."

Farrell eyed him from top to bottom. "The Fletchers called me. Come into my office."

Connor followed the man down the hallway and took a seat in the chair opposite Farrell's desk.

Farrell's office was the polar opposite of Captain Riehl's. It was neatly kept and smelled like Pine-Sol. There were two large filing cabinets and a large oak bookcase lined with books. Not a single scrap of paper littered any surface in the room. The walls were decorated with framed photos, various certificates, and Farrell's private investigator license. Farrell's desk offered only a phone, computer, and ink blotter. The office was simple and well organized.

Farrell arranged himself behind the desk and folded his hands, regarding Connor with an air of skepticism. "So you had an encounter with a woman claiming to be Claire Fletcher."

"I saw Claire Fletcher," Connor corrected.

Farrell sighed, pulled a notepad and pen from one of his desk drawers, and said, "Tell me what happened."

Connor recounted the salient points of his encounter with Claire, leaving out the intimate hours they'd shared in his bed. Farrell did not look at Connor while the younger detective spoke. He kept his eyes on the notepad. His pen moved slowly, as if he were doodling, wholly disinterested in the story, while Connor talked.

"She left me a note with the address 1201 Archer Street on it. So I went to see her but—well you know the rest," Connor concluded.

At this, Farrell's eyes rose to meet Connor's. "A note?"

Connor shook his head. "No. Not exactly. Just a piece of paper with her name and the address on it."

"Do you have it with you?" Farrell asked.

Irritated, Connor replied he did not, although the piece of paper in question rested in the inside breast pocket of his jacket. He just didn't want Farrell to have it, although he wasn't sure why not.

Farrell nodded indifferently. "Did you sleep with her?"

"What?" Connor said, more loudly than he'd intended. He felt an uncharacteristic flush rise from his collar to his forehead.

Farrell eyed him. "Did you have sexual intercourse with this woman?" he asked.

Connor shook his head. "No."

Farrell seemed genuinely surprised. "You didn't?"

"No," Connor repeated.

"You meet a woman in a bar. She hits on you. You chase her outside, take her home, ingest large quantities of scotch, and the two of you don't have sex?"

Connor shrugged, affecting the same indifference Farrell had displayed until then. "No, we didn't have sex."

Farrell stared at him for a long time. Finally, he said, "And you expect me to believe that?"

"Look," Connor said coolly, sitting up straight and giving Mitch his best imposing glare. "I don't give a shit what you believe. I'm not here to sell anything. I'm here as a courtesy to the Fletchers, who wanted me to speak to you, and because I want to know what the fuck's going on."

A slow, appreciative smile spread across Farrell's face. He put his pen and notepad away and leaned toward Connor. "Well, all right," he said.

Connor did not let his hard exterior slacken. A moment passed between the two men. Then another. And another. Farrell smiled and Connor glared. Neither spoke, but in the air between them, an intense and invisible flood of communication roared. This had happened to Connor before. Indeed, his mastery of this unspoken language between men was one of the things that made him a good detective—that is, when he wasn't firing off his weapon indiscriminately.

They were like two alpha wolves scenting each other warily, testing the ether for any sign of threat or weakness. Pushing each other, nipping collars, baring teeth, circling. Each one assessing the other's strength and trying to draw out the other's true intentions without expressing his own.

Connor played the game well and got his way, as he usually did. The next words out of Farrell's mouth were: "Do you want something to drink?"

Connor relaxed and smiled. "God, yes," he said.

Both men laughed, dispelling the tension in the small room.

"Come on then," Farrell said.

He led Connor into another room much the size of his office, although in slightly more disarray. It looked exactly like someone's living room, though it was evident by all the surveillance equipment stacked along the far wall that this was not Farrell's home. There was a midsized black leather couch and a small coffee table, which faced a large television and VCR ensconced in a modest entertainment center. Behind the couch was a larger table with some files neatly stacked on its surface. Beside the table was a small refrigerator from which Farrell plucked two bottles of Corona.

He motioned for Connor to sit. Connor perched on the edge of the couch and removed his jacket. Mitch popped the caps off the beer bottles while Connor studied a framed photograph in the center of the coffee table. It was a young woman, probably midtwenties, with long red hair, delicate features, and a wide smile.

"My daughter," Farrell said, handing Connor a freshly opened beer. "Holly Louise. She's on the East Coast in medical school now. I can't believe it. My little girl in medical school."

Connor smiled. "Is she why you took the Fletcher case as a favor?"

Farrell frowned at the photo, his bushy gray eyebrows meeting above the bridge of his nose. "Yeah," he said. "In part. Holly was only a couple of years younger than Claire, but I'd known the Fletchers—Mr. and Mrs.— for quite some time. It was terrible, you know?"

The older man shivered but not from cold. "I can't imagine what it's like, losing a child and never knowing what happened. The department here did good work on the case, and I didn't interfere. I told Jen and Rick to let them do their job. But after a year or so, the trail gets mighty cold and the police have lots of other crimes piling up. Cases with better leads and tangible evidence. You couldn't blame them for backing off."

Connor sipped his Corona slowly, enjoying the taste. "You used to be on the payroll?" Connor asked.

Farrell kicked one foot onto the coffee table and took a long swig from his bottle. "Yeah," he answered. "But not here. I worked homicide in Atlanta for twenty years. Ten on Special Victims in Oakland after that. Then I moved to Crescent City. I met the Fletchers when I moved there.

"Rick was a public relations guy for some local corporation, and he and Jen came to all kinds of functions—banquets and benefits and the like. They were a great couple. Real down-to-earth and funny. Rick and I used to fish together. Our kids were near the same age—I have a son too; he's in college in Colorado. So I used to bring mine down sometimes and they'd hang out with Claire, Bree, and Tom while me, Rick, and Jen shot the shit. My wife died shortly before I came out here, and Rick and Jen were great friends to me. I needed it then. Jen helped me a lot with Holly. With her mother gone, someone had to do the woman-to-woman stuff, and I wasn't exactly fit. A few years after I met the Fletchers, I retired, went private."

"Then Claire went missing," Connor said.

Farrell drank the rest of his beer and rose to get another. He glanced at Connor's bottle, which was still half-full. "Help yourself if you want more," he said as he resumed his seat on the couch.

Mitch continued. "Like I said, after a while the police backed off. Jen begged me to keep working the case. She would have paid me, but I wouldn't let her. You see, all this time, even to this day, Jen has never given up hope that Claire will come home. She still believes with all her heart that Claire is alive. Even keeps her bedroom exactly the way it was the morning Claire left, right down to the dirty clothes strewn on the floor."

Connor smiled. Then his heart gave an uneven thud. Quickly, he sucked down the rest of his beer and rose to get another. He thought of Claire, of the Claire he'd met and spent the night with. She'd asked to see Denise's room. Well, the dining room, which Connor had always considered Denise's territory. A room he hadn't gone into since Denise left him.

He remembered the way Claire had walked around the room. So slowly—taking in everything, skimming her fingers over the furniture, the lines of her tensed body a mixture of curiosity and sadness.

Had she wondered if her own bedroom remained in the same fashion, ten years' worth of dust lying heavily on all of her old things? She must have known the Fletchers still lived there. She'd given him their address.

Mitch popped the cap off Connor's second beer and Connor took a sip. "Go on," he said.

"Well, I couldn't turn Jen down. I mean what if it had been my Holly?" Mitch smiled lovingly at the photo of his daughter.

"So I agreed to do whatever I could, which hasn't been jack shit in the last ten years, I'm sorry to say. But me doing it seemed to give Jen some peace, so I kept on. Rick, on the other hand, he couldn't hold out day after day the way Jen could. Hoping like that every day. After a couple of years, he kind of gave up. He really believed Claire was dead, and he just wanted to grieve her and move on with his life. That didn't suit Jen.

"Eventually he left. Took off to Maryland. Been there ever since. He looks after Holly for me now and then. They never did get a divorce, Rick and Jen. I think they still love each other. They just can't live in the same reality, I guess."

Mitch snorted. "The kids, they're the same, you know? It's funny that way. Tom sticks by his mother, never says a word to dampen her hope. Brianna, on the other hand, is just like her father. She can be a real wrecking ball, that girl."

Connor gave a little humph of understated agreement, remembering Brianna's unholy glare.

"She thinks Claire is dead. In a way I think she even wants Claire to be dead so they can all move on. She won't hear a single word on the possibility of recovering Claire alive. It just pisses her off."

"You don't say," Connor interjected.

Mitch laughed. "Oh yeah, I forgot you'd met her."

"God save me from her wrath."

Mitch laughed uproariously, and his genuine affection for Brianna, wrecking ball or not, was evident.

Connor set his beer down and looked curiously at Mitch. "What do you think?" he asked.

Visibly sobered by the question, Mitch turned his brown gaze toward Connor. "I don't know," he said.

Connor pressed on. "You're a professional. You must have some theory."

Mitch sighed and heaved his other foot atop the table, crossing his legs. "Everything about this case points to Claire Fletcher being dead. Long gone."

Connor hunched forward, elbows on his knees, head turned to look at Mitch. "You don't think she is," Connor stated. A flutter of excitement took hold of his stomach. "Tom told me there were others."

Mitch looked at him sharply. Farrell was a professional. Connor recognized that he carried with him the uneasy burden of all the men and women like him who worked horrific cases of murder, violence, and unexplained disappearances. When you dealt with families of victims or even the victims themselves, it was often necessary to hide your gut instincts behind a cool facade of neutrality. You didn't want to lend too much hope to the loved ones of victims of violent crimes.

Farrell had remained carefully neutral about the subject of Claire Fletcher for so long, he wasn't immediately able to discuss his own theories.

"The others?" Mitch echoed carefully.

"Three men in the last eight years. All approached by a woman claiming to be Claire Fletcher. All given the Archer Street address, same as me," Connor said.

Mitch said nothing for almost a solid minute. Connor waited. Then the older man asked, "You really didn't sleep with her?"

Not what Connor was expecting, but he answered nonetheless. "No," he said. "Well, yes, I literally slept with her, but we didn't have sex."

Mitch's eyebrows rose. "You slept with her?"

Connor hid his irritation by finishing off his beer. "Yeah. I went to sleep with her."

Mitch turned his whole body toward Connor. "Where?"

"What?"

"Where did you, ah, go to sleep with her?"

Connor's brow wrinkled. "My bed. Where else? What's this got to do with anything?"

Mitch stared at him, awed. "You're not like the others at all. But why? Why you? Why now?"

"What are you talking about?" Connor demanded.

"What did she look like?" Mitch asked instead, his more practical manner returning.

"She looked exactly like the picture of Claire Fletcher that I saw at Archer Street, only older, longer hair and—" Connor broke off, deciding it best not to try to explain about her eyes. "I know it was the same person," he concluded instead.

Mitch considered this. Then he asked, "So why are you here?"

"Because I—" Connor began but stopped abruptly.

The shock of the scene at Archer Street and all he'd found out had sent him racing to Mitch's office with no consideration of why. Claire Fletcher was a ghost to all who'd known her. Connor had spent a single night with a woman he believed in his gut to be exactly who she said she was—Claire Fletcher. Yet *the* Claire Fletcher had vanished ten years ago without a trace. There was indeed a mystery. But for Connor it was much simpler than that.

"Because I want to see her again," he said.

CHAPTER ELEVEN

Connor went home shortly after nightfall with a moderately thick copy of Claire's file under his arm. He didn't bother turning on any lights. Tonight he needed the quiet and the darkness to let the strange events of the day sink in. He plopped down onto the couch without taking his jacket off and watched idly out his front window. The curtains were white, almost sheer, so he could see the occasional car pass or the figure of one of his neighbors walking a dog. He could watch the small square of world beyond his home without being seen.

Faces, conversations, and random words from the day tangled in Connor's mind. A confusing mass of revelations. He fingered the file under his arm, running his index finger over the corner of the pages. If he got into this, there would be no turning back. Mitch had searched for Claire for ten years with no luck.

But Connor had met Claire, walked through this very room with her, her hand in his. He pictured her long limbs and creamy skin. He'd heard her laugh, saw her haunted eyes in his mind. She wasn't a naive teenager anymore. She was a woman whose eyes had secrets to tell.

Connor would find her again.

He stood and strode into the dining room, switching the light on. He took a small trash can from the living room and swept the contents of the dining room table into it, calculator and all. He opened Claire's file and began spreading the pages across the table. He froze when he noticed the quarter-inch-wide streak where Claire had run her finger through the dust.

She had been there. It wasn't his imagination. He wasn't creating invisible women to distract his mind from his failed marriage or the stress of his job.

Careful not to disturb the streak Claire had left on the table, Connor sat down and began reading Mitch's first reports on Claire Fletcher's case.

On the morning of February 21, 1995, Claire left 1201 Archer Street at 7:30 a.m. to walk to school. Her high school was six blocks from her home. She never arrived. At 8:15 a.m., her homeroom teacher reported her absence to the school's main office. At 9:00 a.m., the school secretary called the Fletcher home and left a message that Claire had not shown up at school that morning. Rick and Jen Fletcher did not receive the message until Jen returned home from work at 4:00 p.m. that day.

Jen Fletcher searched her home and then called all of Claire's friends. No one reported seeing Claire that day. Jen Fletcher called her husband at his office and then contacted the police.

Connor made a note to himself to get all the police reports on the case. They likely said the same things as Mitch's reports, but one never knew. Sometimes the outcome of a cold case depended on some small, seemingly insignificant detail that had been overlooked.

Connor turned to the second part of Farrell's initial report. The morning of Claire's disappearance, there was a 911 call made by a thirty-six-year-old housewife named Dinah Strakowski. Strakowski reported seeing a white male, approximately five foot ten, 180 pounds with light-brown hair, pushing a girl into a blue station wagon just outside her home at 656 Miller Avenue.

Connor went to the kitchen and pulled out a city map from one of the drawers. He brought it into the dining room and spread it out on the opposite end of the table. He found Archer Street and circled the

1200 block. He did the same with the 600 block of Miller Avenue. It was roughly four blocks from Claire's home.

"So close," Connor muttered to himself.

He'd known of children being abducted right in front of their homes, sometimes without a single witness. Vanished into thin air, as if a great void had opened up in the ground beneath them and swallowed them whole. One moment they were there, the next moment they were gone.

The thought chilled Connor. He knew that stranger abductions were rare. The majority of missing children were either taken by their noncustodial parent or had run away from home. He also knew that most stranger abductions ended in the worst-case scenario. The children's bodies would later be found abused and violently killed, as in the cases of Polly Klass, Megan Kanka, Samantha Runnion, and Danielle Van Dam. Few stranger abductions actually remained unsolved. Even fewer saw the children returned alive to their families.

Both the police and Mitch had interviewed Dinah Strakowski. In fact, emergency responders arrived at Strakowski's residence five minutes after she placed her 911 call.

"Not bad," Connor said.

Strakowski said she looked out her living room window and saw the man forcibly push a young girl into the back seat of his car. She estimated the girl to be about twelve or thirteen years old. She saw neither the man's face nor the girl's. She didn't get the plates on the car.

Police canvassed the area, four miles in every direction, but turned up nothing. They gave up after that. They had no corroborating witnesses, and no child had been reported missing so far that day.

That evening, of course, Jen Fletcher would report her fifteen-year-old daughter missing.

There were no leads in the case. Nothing at all. Missing child posters went up statewide. The press got involved. Claire's abduction was featured on all the local news channels. Nothing. Not a single legitimate lead. It was as if Claire and her abductor had driven off into a black hole. There was no composite of the abductor because Strakowski never saw his face. She wasn't even certain of the make or model of the vehicle.

Then, almost three years later, twenty-two-year-old Rudy Teplitz showed up at 1201 Archer Street and asked for Claire Fletcher.

Teplitz claimed to have met her at a bar the previous night, gone with her to a motel room, and slept with her. He claimed she left the address while he was asleep. Teplitz was interrogated, investigated, and cleared as a suspect by Farrell. Whether the woman Teplitz met was really Claire Fletcher or not, she disappeared as if she had never existed.

Connor flipped through the pages of the file, checking the dates on each report. The trail picked up every two to three years. Always with a man arriving at 1201 Archer Street, expecting a romantic interlude with a woman he'd just spent the night with. Instead, like Connor, he found himself an unwitting participant in the Fletcher family tragedy.

The second man, Martin Speer, was older than Teplitz. Speer was forty-six, unmarried, and marginally employed. He was looked at much more closely by Farrell as a suspect in Claire's disappearance. Eventually, he was cleared. The third guy was a twenty-six-year-old auto mechanic named Jim Randall. He was also cleared as a suspect.

All three men had gone with Claire to a motel for the night, and on all three occasions, Claire slipped out while they slept, leaving only her address. Prints were never taken because of the highly trafficked nature of the motel rooms.

Connor ran his hand through his hair. He slipped back into the kitchen for a drink. He sighed with relief as he saw the two scotch glasses next to his sink. He hadn't taken care to wash them.

Gripping Claire's glass carefully by the rim, he slipped it into a large Ziploc bag he pulled from the cabinet over the sink. Before he got any deeper into this case, he had to be certain.

CHAPTER TWELVE

I banged on the door because I knew she hated it. Tiffany took her time answering, although I was certain she heard me approaching.

"What do you want?" she asked when she opened the door.

"What's going on?" I said without preamble.

We stared at each other, the raw hatred between us palpable. She twirled a thin strand of hair around one finger and looked through me. "I don't know what you mean," she said.

"You know damn well what I mean. Something is going on, and you're going to tell me what it is."

She smiled wickedly and met my gaze. She thrust her tiny breasts my way. "You've been banished, little Lynnie. What goes on in this house no longer concerns you," she said.

I placed a palm on the door. "What goes on in this house concerns me when that psycho deviant bangs down my door at six a.m. What are you up to?"

She sucked her teeth. "Wouldn't you like to know. You haven't been a very good girl lately, have you?"

His words dripped from her phony pubescent mouth. I wanted to punch her in the face. "Don't play games with me, you little twit. It's getting old and so are you. If you think making trouble for me is going to keep you on his good side, you're wrong. You're already past your expiration date."

I said it because I wanted to hurt her, although it was true. I was cast from the fold like garbage at nineteen, never more grateful to him. For Tiffany, however, that was her greatest fear.

"He's always loved me more than you," she spat. "Now go away."

"Tell me what's going on. I know something is up."

"You don't know what you're talking about. Go away or I'll tell him what you've done."

Fear tickled the back of my neck, but I tried not to show it. "Which is what, exactly?" I challenged.

She did her best little-girl-playing-coy act and looked at her feet. "Well, I don't know, but I'm sure I can come up with something."

"You're pathetic."

"No, I'm not. He still wants me," she replied tartly. And with that, the door slammed in my face.

I stomped back to the trailer, feeling her beady eyes on my back. I couldn't shake the image of him fidgeting with the buttons of his jacket as he stood in the run-down living/dining room of my trailer. I knew those motions by heart. He was hiding something. Tiffany was helping him, as she always did.

Back in my trailer, I shoved the chair under the doorknob once more and peeked again out the kitchen window. The slight shift in the curtain in the front window of the house mirrored me. As always, she was watching. My heart beat faster as Connor's face floated through my mind, all exquisite lines accentuated by a broad smile. I felt his skin on mine again, and my lips tingled with the memory of his mouth on mine. I should warn him. It was a risk, but it was the least I could do. I pushed the curtain back in place and got back into my bed, deep beneath the heavy pile of covers. My mind searched for some tattered remnant from the battery of tricks it had used over the ten years of captivity to keep me sane and alive. I closed my eyes, welcoming thoughts of Connor and then pushing those same thoughts away.

CHAPTER THIRTEEN

Connor let himself into the vestibule that led to the doors of the Sacramento County District Attorney's Crime Lab. It was late. Except for the guard in the front lobby and one or two lab technicians, the building was unoccupied. He buzzed the intercom outside the locked double doors to the lab.

Lena Stark's voice came back to him, a grainy twitch. "Yeah?"

"It's Connor," he said. "Buzz me in."

"What do you want?" the box demanded.

"Stark, just let me in."

"This better be good," she said.

The doors buzzed and Connor slipped through. The lab was dark, most of its crew had gone home for the day. Only Lena remained, mostly to log evidence and process what she could of the overworked lab's backlog.

Lena emerged from a dimly lit room to his right. She wore her long white lab coat over a plain white blouse and black slacks. Her blonde hair was pulled back and smoothed away from her face by the wide black band of a set of goggles. Her hands were on her hips. "What is it, Parks?"

He smiled as charmingly as he could. "I need a favor," he said.

Lena rolled her eyes. "A favor? Now?"

"Do you think I'd be here this late if it wasn't important?"

Lena frowned and bit the inside of her cheek. It was an endearing little tic he'd loved while they were dating. They'd only gone out a few times, but it had been too soon after Denise left for Connor to put any energy into developing a relationship. They'd parted amicably and remained on good terms.

"Heard you were on the desk," Lena said.

"Oh man," he groaned.

Lena stepped toward him, a smile playing at the corners of her delicate mouth. "Well, are you?"

"Yes."

"Wanna talk about it?"

"For God's sake, no," Connor said.

Lena shrugged. "Okay."

Clearly, she did want to talk about it. Connor leaned against a nearby table. "Look," he said. "If you already heard from someone that I'm on the desk, then you already know why, and in two weeks you'll know the decision of the review board too."

She moved in front of him and touched his hand. "I'm sorry," she said.

Connor gave her a lopsided smile. "Well, it's not over yet."

"Not by a long shot."

"So about that favor?"

"What have you got?"

Connor pulled the Ziploc bag with the scotch glass in it from his pocket. "Can you pull prints from this?" he asked.

Lena took it from him, all business now. She held the glass up to the overhead light to examine it. "This is it?"

"Yeah," he said.

"Do you need a chain of custody voucher?"

"No," he replied. "I said this was a favor. It's a cold case. I only need the prints for confirmation. They're not evidence." He cleared his throat. "Some of them will be mine."

Lena looked at him, one graceful brow arched in curiosity. "You aren't in any trouble, are you?" she asked.

Connor laughed. "No. I mean no more than usual. It's just that— well, I think the other person who touched that glass is someone who's been missing for ten years."

Lena's brown eyes widened. "Really? Wanna talk about that?"

"No. Not yet, anyway. Maybe when I've got a little more of it figured out."

Lena dropped the glass into the side pocket of her lab coat. "Fair enough. Want me to run it while you're here?"

"That would be great," Connor said.

Two hours later, Connor and Lena huddled together in front of her computer, picking at the Chinese takeout they'd ordered.

"Are you sure she's in the database?" Lena asked. The mouse moved in concert with her hand. Her eyes were trained on the large glowing screen.

"Yeah," Connor said. "She'll definitely be in the National Center for Missing and Exploited Children database. Her parents had all their kids fingerprinted. Part of some safety program at their school."

"Well, at least our tax dollars are going to good use," she said.

She sat back and they watched the computer zip through thousands of faces, looking for a match to the fingerprints Lena had taken from the scotch glass. It took only a few moments. The computer emitted a low ding, and a photo of fifteen-year-old Claire Fletcher flashed on the screen—her school photo, the same one Tom Fletcher had shown Connor.

Connor already knew what the prints would yield, but the cold confirmation sent another wave of shock through him. His stomach, which had been blissfully full a moment ago, suddenly felt hollow.

Lena was staring at him. "That her?"

"Yep."

Lena squinted at the screen, reading the information that scrolled beneath the photo and set of matching prints.

> Claire Bridget Fletcher, abducted 02/21/1995, from the 600 block of Miller Avenue. Last seen wearing blue jeans, yellow cotton shirt, and white tennis shoes. Hair: brown. Eyes: blue. Approximate height: five foot four. Weight: 122 pounds. Scar on left elbow. DOB: 10/22/1980. Age at time of disappearance: fifteen. Age now: twenty-five.

Lena made a low sound under her breath. "Holy shit."

CHAPTER FOURTEEN

1995

During those months I spent in the dark visited only by him, my body laid open for his use, I had this fantasy that any moment a SWAT team would break down the door. Men swathed in black armor, wearing black helmets, and bearing huge guns would storm in and rescue me. They would untie my hands and feet and avert their eyes from my nakedness. Gentle hands would lift me into the air and wrap me in a heavy blanket, finally covering me.

They would spirit me outside. My eyes, so accustomed to darkness, would hurt from the daylight. There, on some lawn in front of some house, would wait my parents, huddled together, looking anxious and hopeful. My mother would be wringing her hands and leaning away from my father's embrace, her eyes searching for me. My saviors would deliver me into their arms, cradled in blankets like the day I was born. I would feel my parents' tears raining on my face, their arms closed around me until the three of us were a single, compact unit.

Seconds later, burly SWAT members would emerge from where I was being held, dragging him along between them, his hands cuffed so tightly behind his back that the metal nipped and chaffed his skin. They would throw him down on the ground, face in the mud, and step on the back of his neck with their heavy black boots. Triumphant, my saviors would nod solemnly at my newly unified family, as my abductor squirmed like a garden snake under their oppressive feet.

From there, I added variations. Sometimes my parents would take me home, and my mother would draw me a steaming bubble bath and stay with me while I soaked away the dirty injustices committed against my body. I wouldn't have to go to school for a long time. My mother would take me and Brianna shopping.

Other times, my parents, Tom, Brianna, and I would celebrate my return with a barbecue, after which we would play softball in the backyard. Brianna would sleep with me at night. My body curled into hers while she stroked my hair in the dark. And I would never have to tell her about the things he did.

In some scenarios, my brother would escort me every place I went, like a bodyguard, and when I was frightened, he would throw an arm around my shoulders like he always did and say something to make me laugh. Sometime after I had arrived home, we would get a dog, and my family would let me choose its name.

I sustained myself on these fantasies, stories I told myself while I waited in darkness. Whenever he came to touch me, to screw me, I would go away in my mind, to the day when the SWAT team arrived and I was delivered from that cold black womb.

I don't know how long he kept me in that room. He came many times to feed and wash me and allow me to relieve myself. Then he would come for the other. One day he arrived to find that my period had begun. I hadn't given it much thought, but when he realized what it was, he was infuriated. He slapped me, and my arms tugged mercilessly to cover my face.

"What is this?" he asked.

"My period," I said with difficulty, my right cheek stinging.

"How can this be?"

I didn't look at him. I actually considered launching into the biological mechanics of a woman's body, a lecture I'd heard from both my mother and my health teacher at school. Instead, I said, "I'm fifteen. I've had it for years now."

"Fifteen," he said, but it was not a question.

I hazarded a look his way. His face drained of color, his eyes widened. He met my eyes. "How long does this last?" he asked.

If I could have shrugged, I might have. "It depends," I said, forming each word carefully so as not to aggravate the ragged tear inside my right cheek where my teeth had cut into the impact of his slap. "Sometimes four days, sometimes seven, or anywhere in between."

He looked down his nose at me. "You're soiled," he said, and his voice was the quiet of a knife's edge.

He turned on his heel and left, his jacket flapping against his sides. I thought he would not return for several hours, as was his habit when something about me displeased him. But he returned within minutes, flying into the room, face twisted into an ugly mass of creases and lumps, like scar tissue. His fists were working before he even reached me, and I had a split second of terrible awareness of what was coming before his hands descended on me.

He beat me. Fists, knuckles, and open hands beating a staccato rhythm up and down my body. I was literally like a drum, my body like rubber stretched taut over the mattress so that some of his blows glanced off me. I turned my head from side to side, frantically trying to avoid the worst of what was directed at my face. At some point, I realized he was speaking. His voice came in appalled gasps. "Fifteen," he said. "Fifteen. Fifteen. Fifteen."

As quickly as he entered, he was gone.

It was difficult to catch my breath. I panted, my head still turning wildly from side to side, the muscles in my neck not yet conscious of the fact that the beating had ceased. My skin stung and later my body ached and swelled. Blood dried at the corners of my mouth and in my teeth. I yearned to touch my own face.

It was a long time before he came back. He did not look at me. I felt his hands releasing first my left hand and then my feet. In spite of my pain, I felt wild with anticipation, like a person wandering the desert without drink for days on end, spying an oasis on the horizon. He untied the bindings on my right hand and used handcuffs, which he pulled from his pocket, to secure my right hand to the head of the bed. But still, three of my limbs were free.

Curling into myself was not as easy as my body wanted it to be. I was stiff and terribly bruised. He did not release my right hand and take me to the bucket, however. Instead, he set a bucket of soapy water next to the bed. One washcloth and one towel beside me. A bowl of soup on the table beneath the lamp.

"Clean yourself" was all he said. Then he was gone.

The pain of my body wilted under the glare of my new freedom. To be able to move three of my limbs, curl up my body, touch my swollen face! To be able to wash myself and feed myself privately! I had to move gingerly, but I reached the washcloth into the bucket and came up with a handful of warmth. I started with my face, then my shoulders, breasts, and stomach. I washed and washed, gently rubbing the washcloth over my skin again and again until the water in the bucket cooled.

I stuck my feet in it and let them soak for a while. Then I ate. The soup was bland, but in that moment it was the best soup I ever had because it did not come directly from his hands. I lay down curled on my side, my right arm stretched awkwardly above my head, still cuffed. I pulled the towel over me and slept.

He did not come back for a very long time. I knew it was several hours because I had to urinate, and the waste bucket was far from my reach. I debated on using the wash bucket since it was already dirty, but I didn't. I held it until it seemed as if the slightest movement would cause my bladder to burst. Finally, I went on the floor. I realized it would likely garner another beating, but I did not care.

Time stretched on. The rosy glow of my newfound freedom fell away with the hours. Hunger pangs came and went, replaced by weakness and what felt very much like delirium. I began to worry that he had abandoned me or that something had happened to him and that no one would ever know where I was. I would die in the barren room.

I didn't know whether I wanted to live or die. I thought that if he returned, I would wish I had died. But if I wanted to live, I had to do something because I knew it had been days since I'd had anything to eat or drink. I remembered reading about people who drank their own urine to survive while trapped in the wilderness or under collapsed buildings in the rubble left by earthquakes. I wondered if I really wanted to live badly enough to do something that my fifteen-year-old mind could only describe as *so gross*. But my fantasy of SWAT rescuers and being reunited with my family had been my sustenance for so long that I could not let go of that one last, ragged thread on which my will to live dangled.

I drank the wash water.

The water was gone by the time he returned. I was too weak to move or speak. I saw him from beneath heavy eyelids. I wondered if he was really there or if I was hallucinating. He said nothing. He simply went about his business and left.

The next time he came bearing food. He fed me and stroked me as if I were a pet. He talked in that soothing voice, telling me it would be okay. He was here now. He would take care of me.

"There now, love," he cooed. "My sweet Lynn. From now on we have to be careful. We can't get you pregnant, you know. You're much too young for that kind of responsibility. From now on we'll have to use contraceptives." He spoke as if I were a coconspirator, a willing party, a partner.

I wish I could say that those weeks were my lowest point.

CHAPTER FIFTEEN

Mitch held the fingerprint report in his hands for several moments before he let out a low whistle. "My God," he said, his voice betraying the amazement and excitement he felt. He continued to stare at it until Connor could no longer tell if his eyes were even in focus.

"Farrell?"

"I don't believe it."

Connor grinned. "I know."

Mitch looked at the younger detective, and Connor thought he saw tears welling in the corners of the older man's eyes. "This is . . . I don't know what to say."

Connor plopped down in the chair in front of Mitch's desk and folded his hands across his middle. "Say you'll help me."

Slowly, Mitch sank into his own chair. He looked again at the fingerprint match. "I will," he mumbled. Then he caught Connor's eyes, and his composure began to return. "Are you sure this is right?"

Connor rolled his eyes. "Of course it's right. I had Lena take three prints and they all match. This is it, Farrell. She's alive. I wasn't hallucinating." Connor leaned forward, unable to contain his eagerness. "I want to find her."

Farrell placed the report on his desk and leaned back into his chair, swiping his hair back with one hand. "I just never expected this," he said.

"Something like this is very rare," Connor concurred. "But we have a chance here. We could find her."

Farrell frowned. "But maybe she doesn't want to be found. I mean, why, after all this time . . . ?"

"She makes contact every two to three years," Connor said. "She wants to be found."

"But if she can just walk into a bar and pick up a man and send him to her house, then why doesn't she just come home?"

Connor had not thought that far ahead. He was silent as he mulled over the question. Claire had made contact two and a half years after she was abducted. She was obviously free to come and go as she pleased, and she had chosen to stay lost. It didn't make sense. She came back again and again, but she never returned to her family.

"She wants them to know she's alive," Connor said suddenly, thinking aloud.

"What?"

"She comes back every two or three years, right?"

Mitch nodded.

"She makes *contact*, but she never comes home. She disappears again. If she didn't want to be found, why go to all the trouble of picking up a stranger in a bar, sleeping—um, spending the night with him—and sending him to her family's home? Why not just come home? Reappear on the doorstep and say, 'Hey, I'm back.' Yeah, she goes back to wherever it is she's been, but she wants her family to know she's alive."

Farrell considered this. "Do you think she's under duress?"

Connor thought of Claire Fletcher's haunted eyes. In the last twenty-four hours, he'd been looking at the case from the objective eyes of a detective, trying to fit the pieces together. The word *abduction*, the reality of it, had not hit him.

Maybe he didn't want to think about it. This was a woman he'd held in his arms. A woman whose scent lingered on his bedcovers. A woman he wanted desperately to find and not just to return her to her family or to solve a cold case. He just wanted to see her again.

Someone had snatched fifteen-year-old Claire Fletcher right off the sidewalk. God only knew what had been done to her in the intervening years. Maybe she was too ashamed to come home.

"You have thirty years on the force, right?" Connor asked.

Mitch nodded. "Yeah."

"You worked Special Victims, right?"

"Yeah."

"What happens when you get an abduction? A teenage girl, abducted from the street or her home or wherever it happens?"

"Parks, you know what happens," Mitch said.

"Yeah, I do. So where do we find them if we find them at all?"

"Dead," Mitch replied flatly.

"What else?"

"Sexually assaulted."

Connor sat back in his chair, pain creeping across his face.

"So what are you saying? Claire was abducted and sexually assaulted, but clearly she wasn't killed."

"Maybe she's too embarrassed to come home," Connor suggested.

Mitch shook his head. "No. No way. That's not the Claire I knew."

Connor stared hard into Mitch's eyes. "Yeah, but we don't know what she went through. Things—things like that change a person."

Connor thought of the rape victims from his last case, the case that might end his career. He remembered their eyes. Sometimes the only thing that made it possible for him to do his job without going crazy was thinking that he might prevent someone else's eyes from looking like that. Broken, helpless, shamed.

Claire's had been worse. Beautiful, bottomless pits of despair. What had she seen? What had her abductor done to her?

Mitch changed tacks. "What about the abductor? What happened to him? Ten years. Did he just let her go one day?"

"I don't know. Look, we have a chance here. Claire Fletcher is alive, and I want to bring her in. Are you going to help me?"

Mitch nodded solemnly. "I just hope we can find her," he said.

They started with Mitch's files. Connor had Farrell take him through them line by line. It took a whole day. Farrell had been pretty thorough; there wasn't much he had left out of his files. Connor decided to go through the police files next, and then he would interview both Dinah Strakowski and the other three men that Claire had sent to her family's house.

He didn't know why Claire had chosen to stay lost for ten years, reappearing every few years to make contact but never returning home, but he would deal with that when he came face-to-face with her again.

Connor spent the next two days at his department desk, poring over the police reports from the Fletcher case. His eyes were tired at the end of each day. He went to sleep with visions of suspects and car descriptions dancing in his mind. He didn't have time to think about the precarious position of his job. He left a message for Strakowski.

The third day, he looked over the vehicle search, which had yielded nothing. Strakowski had said it was a blue station wagon. She couldn't tell the make or the year. She had looked at hundreds of photos of station wagons, and the closest she could come up with was a Chevrolet Caprice station wagon manufactured sometime in the late eighties. They had done a county-wide search of owners registering that make of vehicle but had come up with no suspects. Strakowski had even driven around with the responding officers, looking for the car, but they never found any trace of it.

It didn't make sense. No one reported seeing any blue Chevrolet Caprices within a ten-block radius in the hours after the abduction. There were reports of station wagons, but they all checked out. If the department had missed something, if they had in fact interviewed the abductor in those first hours and not realized it, it would take Connor months to track down all those witnesses and vehicles again and check them out.

Connor put the report down and rubbed his eyes. Mitch's words rang in his ears. Before Connor had left Mitch's office the other day, Farrell said to him, "How do you plan on doing this? Yeah, we know she's really alive, but we've still got the same cold leads we always had."

Again, Connor had not thought that far ahead. It was true. Connor had nothing more to go on than the investigating team had had ten years prior. He just hoped that he would find some detail that the rest of his colleagues and Farrell had overlooked. It was his only chance.

"Parks! Hey, Parks!"

One of the other detectives in the division interrupted his thoughts.

"Yeah," he answered.

"There's a Dinah Strakowski on line four for you. Says she's returning your call."

"Thanks," Connor said, snatching up the phone.

He spoke with Strakowski for five minutes and arranged to meet her at her home the next morning. As he hung up, he glanced out the window. He watched the last dim shades of daylight sink into the horizon. It was evening. He could go home. He'd been laboring over paperwork all day, and his eyes were weary. He lingered at his desk, dreaming about home, his bed, and a blanket smelling of lavender from the soft skin of Claire Fletcher.

CHAPTER SIXTEEN

1995

My captivity didn't take place entirely in that dark, windowless room. I don't know how long I was there, but at some point he saw fit to move me.

I was so excited the day he arrived carrying a T-shirt and pair of shorts. I had been naked, uncovered, without so much as a blanket or sheet for so long that the prospect of clothes made me weep. After nearly starving me to death, he had left me handcuffed by only my right wrist. That day he unbound me completely and ordered me to put on the clothes. Before I could think of anything besides the luscious feel of fabric against my skin, he cuffed my right hand again and left, returning moments later with a bowl of soup and a plain piece of white bread.

"Eat" was all he said before leaving once more.

I ate hungrily, slopping the soup onto the floor and mattress. I subsisted on soup since it was all he ever brought me. The bread was new and tasted like rich chocolate cake to my starved tongue. I curled into a ball when I was finished, my body nearly purring over the treats.

Minutes later, drowsiness—heavy like a winter coat—seeped into every limb and finally into my center. My heartbeat slowed. I tried to keep my eyes open, but my eyelids felt too weighted. Sleep came. I dreamed of my mother.

What seemed like days later—and for all I know it could have been—I woke disoriented to find that I was no longer in that room. The weight of sleep hung on me. I had to think about my arms and legs to get them to move. My eyelids were pasted together, my mouth parched.

When I opened my eyes, I was temporarily blinded by the daylight streaming through a single window in the room. It had been so long since I'd seen natural light that I wanted to open my mouth and drink it in.

The room was barren except for an empty closet, which stood open. I was lying on the hardwood floor, both hands bound together above my head. I was still wearing the clothes he had given me, and now I had a blanket, although it lay beneath my body.

I looked up over my head to see what I was tied to. It was an old cast-iron radiator, and my hands were bound to one of its claw feet with heavy rope. I squirmed and rolled side to side, using my feet to pull the blanket from beneath me and cover myself up as best I could. I watched the daylight filter through the curtained window.

He came later, closing the wooden door behind him. He smiled at me benevolently.

"You're up," he said softly. "Well, I hope you'll like it here. I haven't got all the furniture yet, but don't worry, Lynn. I'll have your room fixed up in no time at all."

"My name is not Lynn," I said. "Where am I?"

"You're home, darling."

"This is not my home."

"Oh, Lynn," he scoffed, the painted smile never leaving his face. "Your home is with me now."

"Let me go," I tried, although I knew he would not.

He made a tsk-tsk noise and shook his head. "Now I can't untie you until I know you're going to be a good girl."

"That's not what I meant. I want to go home."

"Oh, I know it doesn't look like a home now, but once I get some furniture—"

I cut him off, shouting, "I don't care about furniture! This is not my home. My name is not Lynn, and I want out of here."

He looked at me for several minutes, silent. Then he arched his eyebrows and his smile grew. "I know what you need," he said.

"I need you to let me go."

He went on as if I hadn't spoken at all. "You just need some attention."

I began to squirm, and my shouts were so loud they bounced off the walls and ceiling, echoing back to me. When he knelt beside me, I began kicking at him.

My legs worked furiously, hitting his chest like a drumroll and knocking him back onto his behind. I kept kicking. He got up on his knees and grabbed for my legs, catching my feet after several tries.

We struggled wordlessly until he straddled me. His hands closed around my throat. I tried to stave off the pain, cling to consciousness, but blackness descended on me and I slid gratefully into the dark oblivion.

When I woke, my feet were bound. When he came in again, I heard only his voice.

"I know what's best for you, Lynn. I'm sorry you can't understand that right now. I don't like being hard on you. I wish you wouldn't make me do such things. I want us to make a home here."

He untied my legs and left my hands bound together but untied me from the radiator. He pulled me up, but my legs still didn't work properly. Just like a baby deer trying to walk for the first time, my legs folded beneath me. I stumbled along as he half carried me out of the room. Everything was dark and fuzzy.

When I felt the cold hardness of porcelain on the backs of my legs, I realized we were in a bathroom. After I relieved myself, he took off the ropes and my clothes, and showered me. The water scalded my face. I did not fight him.

He dressed me again and returned me to my new room, tying me to the same place and securing my legs together tightly. That is where I remained. I began to count the days by the waning and waxing of the delicious daylight. When the count reached 102, I began weeping each day in time with the sunrise.

Surely, I could not have been his captive for so long. I was disoriented. My defiance of him and entreaties for freedom earned me beatings, but I could not stop. I no longer cared about the fists flying at me or the heavy feet impacting my sides. I just did not want to go willingly.

CHAPTER SEVENTEEN

Dinah Strakowski had lived in the same house since 1995. In ten years, she had had no desire to move. In fact, she had had a new roof installed and cut back the foliage around her home. She had also replaced one water heater and all of the tiles on her kitchen floor. So she told Connor when he visited her.

She was forty-six now. Her two children had recently left for college and she lived alone, which she liked because it was quieter and there was less laundry to do, but still she missed the sounds of her children moving around the house at all hours.

Her hair was badly dyed a coppery red. She was round and pudgy, which she attributed to the effects of aging. She was so pleased to have a guest—even if he was there to talk about the awful thing that happened to that poor little girl so long ago—that she made cookies and lemonade just for Connor's arrival.

Dinah chattered while Connor sat on her couch and fished a notepad and pen from his pocket. He tasted the cookies and lemonade to be polite, and despite the fact that he had already been there ten minutes and found out nothing useful, he discovered that he liked Dinah. She had a lovely, off-center charm about her that had mostly to do with her open, gracious manner and her effusive offerings.

"Mrs. Strakowski," Connor said when he could finally snatch a moment of silence. "As I said on the phone, I'm investigating the abduction of Claire Fletcher as a cold case. What I'd like to do is take you through that morning again, and I'd like you to tell me everything you remember. I know it's been ten years, but I'd like you to try to recall every detail, no matter how insignificant it may seem."

Mrs. Strakowski nodded solemnly. "Oh, Detective, I haven't forgotten that day at all. Something like that is hard to put out of your mind. Why, I've thought about that poor girl and her family quite a bit. I even kept one of those missing flyers on my fridge for a couple of years because I felt so bad about it. I still second-guess myself today. Maybe if I had run out there with my broom or my son's baseball bat instead of calling 911, I could have saved her."

"You did the right thing, Mrs. Strakowski," Connor assured her. "You can't blame yourself. You did exactly what anyone would have done. You called the police and reported it immediately."

She twisted her hands in her lap. "I felt so bad," she repeated.

"Now, could you just take me through what happened? What you saw?"

Strakowski looked upward, as if the contents of her memory were visible on the ceiling. "Well, I had just got the kids off to school maybe twenty minutes before. I was in here in my bathrobe just straightening up. The phone rang so I went into the kitchen to get it. It was a cordless, so I came back in here and was talking to my sister—she had one bastard of a husband back then. She was always crying to me over that one. Almost every morning she called like clockwork. 'What'd he do now?' I'd say as soon as I picked up."

Connor caught her eye, and she smiled sheepishly. "Well, anyway, I was on the phone, just puttering around in here. It was a real nice day so I went to the window and pulled the curtains. I was listening to my sister go on and on and standing at the window, just looking out at the day. There was a man parked in his car right out front. Just sitting there in the driver's seat. Looked like he was reading something. He had brown hair, but I couldn't see him too good from here. I didn't pay him no mind 'cause this is a busy street. Lots of people park out front. Sometimes they block the driveway, though."

"Did you leave the window?" Connor prompted, so he didn't lose her again.

"Well, yes, I went back into the kitchen for something, my coffee cup I think. I wasn't in there for more than a minute or two. My sister was just jabbering away, and I went back to the window because I was thinking I'd like to get out there and work on my garden, seeing as it was so sunny.

"By that time, the man had got out of the car, but his back was to me. He was kind of squatting down next to the car, and the back door was hanging open. I still didn't pay him any mind. I thought maybe he was just fixing something. Maybe he had been sitting in there reading a repair manual or something and had just got out to fix something, even though it was a strange place to be working on your car in front of someone else's house."

"Did he turn around at all? Did you ever see his face?" Connor asked.

Dinah shook her head. "No. He never did turn around. I only ever saw the side of his face, even after, when he got back into the car. But I did notice he didn't have any facial hair."

"That's good," Connor said, jotting on his notepad. "Can you describe what he was wearing?"

"Mmm-hmm. He had on khaki pants with a belt and a navy-blue collar shirt—short sleeves," she said.

"Good. Was he tall, short, fat, skinny?"

"He was tall but not as tall as you. And he was real skinny. I mean he didn't look like a weakling, but he was kind of wiry, you know?"

Connor nodded. "Okay, you saw him squatting next to the car, and then what did you see?"

"I saw this girl coming down the street toward him. She wasn't really looking at him. I didn't even realize that they were talking until she stopped because he didn't turn around or anything. He didn't stand up or approach her. She stood there looking at him for a minute, and then she got down next to him on her hands and knees and was looking under the car.

"I thought maybe he dropped something but couldn't get under there far enough to get it and that's why he asked a young girl 'cause she was kind of small. But then the next thing I know, he puts a hand on the back of her head and just bam! Smashes her head right off the car, you know where the door was opened, right where you'd go to step into the car. I couldn't hardly believe what I was seeing.

"I froze for a minute 'cause it was just so unexpected to see. Then he smashed her head again and again, and he kind of scooped her up from behind and rolled her into the back seat. Just like that."

"Approximately how long did that take from the time he assaulted her to the time he pushed her into the vehicle?" Connor asked.

Dinah cocked her head to the side. "Oh, not more than ten seconds, for sure. That's what was so shocking. It was so fast. Before I had an idea of what was happening, it was over. I hung right up on my sister and dialed 911, but my hands were shaking pretty bad and I had to dial twice. By the time they answered, he was back in the car and then he just drove off."

"Did you go outside when he drove away?"

Dinah nodded. "Yep. I took the phone right with me and ran out there to the sidewalk in my robe. I was hollering at him and trying to talk to the police dispatcher all at the same time."

"You didn't see the license plate?" Connor asked.

Dinah's mouth drooped. "I'm sorry, Detective, but no, I didn't. He was too far down the street by then. I couldn't think what to do, I was so shocked. If I had thought about it, I would have chased the car and tried to see the plate."

"That's okay. You did fine, Mrs. Strakowski." Connor smiled at her. "I'm just required to ask. Now, in your earlier statements you said the car was a station wagon and that it was blue, is that correct?"

"Yes, sir. That's right," Dinah said.

"You could not identify the make or model of the car?" Connor asked.

At this, she became agitated. Her thick brows came together over pained eyes. "Oh, I just felt awful about that, you know? And they were so good about that particular thing. The police were so thorough. They took me around in the car that day. They drove me to dealerships and showed me photos. I looked and looked and looked, but I couldn't find one that looked like it. They came back a few times too to show me pictures. I think they narrowed it down to three makes it could have been, but I don't think they ever did find it."

"Was this a vehicle you had seen around the neighborhood a lot?" Connor asked.

"Well, I saw some blue station wagons around, what with the school so close and everything, but I don't ever recall seeing a man who looked like him driving one like that before. Plus, they all looked the same to me. I was never so good with telling makes or models of cars. I just knew station wagon, van, that kind of thing. Although last year I was flipping through this magazine, just some trendy housewife magazine, you know, and I saw this picture of one that looked just like it."

Connor felt his heartbeat rise steadily. He tried to tamp down his excitement and keep his voice calm and controlled. "What kind of picture?" he asked.

Dinah waved a hand, gold bracelets tinkling on her wrist. "Oh, it was some human-interest story about a girl surviving some terrible disease. There was a picture of her standing next to a car, and I'll be damned if it wasn't the exact same kind that awful man had that day. The thing that struck me is that it had that little thing sticking up right on the front of the hood that the Chevy model didn't. Exactly the same car but for the hood ornament. I wish I had seen it nine years earlier."

Connor could not stop his body from inching to the edge of the couch. "Mrs. Strakowski," he said, amazed at the reserve in his voice. "Did you keep that picture by any chance?"

Dinah looked at Connor like he had just grown another head. "Well, of course I did," she said. "I couldn't ever get that day out of my mind and always feeling so guilty about not being able to identify that car. I don't even know why I kept it after all this time, but I sure did. I tore it out and tucked it away in my—"

"Can I see it?" Connor asked, unable to let her finish.

"Why sure," Dinah said.

It took her ten minutes to find the picture in one of her kitchen drawers, during which Connor's stomach felt as if he'd just ingested a large quantity of molten steel. He was so relieved when she handed it to him, he almost hugged her. He thanked her profusely and gave her his card in case she thought of anything else. Strakowski walked him outside to his car, which was parked in the same spot the mystery station wagon had been on the day Claire Fletcher was abducted.

"Have I been of any help, Detective Parks?" Dinah asked.

Connor smiled broadly. "You certainly have," he said. "I really appreciate your time."

"Oh, it's nothing," she said, her face flushing and nearly matching her hair. "Glad I could be of help."

Connor turned to go but looked back abruptly. Dim shapes moved in the back of his mind. He chased them, trying to discover their import but could not catch them. "Mrs. Strakowski," he called.

Dinah was nearly to her front stoop. She turned. "Yes?"

"Which direction was the car facing? Do you remember?"

She nodded. "Why, yes. It was facing the same way as your car."

"When he drove away, which direction did he take?"

"Well, he pulled right out and went that way," she said, pointing in the direction Connor's car faced.

"Thank you," he said.

Connor stood beside his car for several minutes. Something was working its way up from his gut, but he couldn't yet put a finger on it. Finally, he pulled out his cell phone and dialed Mitch.

Farrell picked up on the second ring.

"Farrell? I'm at the Strakowski residence. Could you come down here?"

CHAPTER EIGHTEEN

1995

At some point, I realized that my SWAT fantasy would not become a reality. It was up to me to escape, and up to that point, I had not made the conditions optimal for escape. Slowly, I decreased my verbal and physical struggles with him, although I could never bring myself to be silent. This earned me privileges, which came first in the release of my limbs, starting with my feet, until I was bound by only my right hand again. Then I got a pillow, socks, and different kinds of food.

Each time he brought something I so desperately wanted, I had to remind myself not to feel grateful. He kept me so starved for even the smallest amenity that I could not see past the next privilege or what my deathly thin and battered body thought of as treats. I forced myself to focus on one thing—escape. Even when he slid the white cotton socks over my feet and my whole body shuddered with pleasure, I repeated the word like a mantra in my head so I would not lose sight of my ultimate goal—escape.

Escapeescapeescapeescapeescape.

My pseudo-cooperation allowed my body time to get stronger. The first time I escaped was not well thought out. The prospect of freedom was too big, and I rushed at it, head down, body sprung forward like a bull charging a red flag.

He had my single hand bound with rope, with several layers of duct tape over the knots, to discourage me from simply untying them with my free hand. It took three days, but I gnawed through the middle of the rope, slicing and gnashing through the thin threads with teeth and fingernails. When he was there, I covered it with my pillow or blanket.

The second I was free, I leapt up and the room spun wildly around me. It took me a few minutes to gain my balance and work my legs. The door was locked and so was the window. Outside, all I could see was grass and trees. I tried to unlock and open the window, but it had been painted shut.

Wrapping the blanket around my foot, I broke the glass, pushed the shards out of my way, and climbed through. When my feet hit the soft grass, I ran without looking back. In fact, my mistake was that I did not look around at all. I simply ran toward the trees, hyperventilating, wheezing with the effort and the overwhelming sense of freedom, of escape.

He tackled me from the side before I reached the tree line.

That night he beat me far worse than he ever had before.

It was weeks before I was strong enough to try again. He rotated me from room to room. The house was sparsely furnished with second-hand furniture. After my failed escape attempt, he used a chain instead of rope and duct tape. The chain had two feet of links, and I actually preferred it because it granted me more mobility, although it took me a while to figure out how to get my hand out. He usually chained me to a heavy piece of furniture, a pipe, or the radiator.

Being out of my room enabled me to study his activity—when he left the house, when he came back, how long he was gone. It seemed strange that he left me there. I could not imagine him going to some job and acting normal, making idle small talk with coworkers or salesclerks. Could no one see that he was a monster? Was there nothing about him at all that alerted the outside world to his depravity?

When he came home, he talked at me in that effeminate, sing-song voice. The thread of his one-sided conversation never deviated, no matter what I tried to interject. It did not matter what I said, how I objected, or how many times I pointed out the reality of the situation, in his mind I was "Lynn," and I was his. This was "our" home, and we would be together forever.

When he looked at me, he did not see a shrunken, dangerously thin girl with hatred in her eyes, literally chained in place. He saw his fantasy. In his eyes, I was a willing party, and my face was always aglow with my eternal, flaming love for him.

The second time I escaped, he had left the house. I was chained to a metal bar in the bathroom. Bracing my feet against the wall, I grasped the chain with my left hand. I pulled and pulled until my body was slick with sweat. I kicked the bar several times in an effort to loosen it. Eventually, it tore out of the wall, leaving two nearly perfect gashes in its wake.

I scurried, dragging the chain and the bar with me, right out the front door. There was a porch, and a gravel area where he must have parked. But nothing beyond that. No road, no houses—nothing but trees. I ran to the right, straight at them. I stayed in the trees but parallel with what looked like a driveway, though it was only a narrow clearing in the trees, wide enough for a car to pass through.

He caught me as he drove past, returning sooner than I anticipated. My heart beat wildly as the car slammed to a halt and he got out, not even closing the door behind him. I turned and began running away from him, barely cognizant of anything but my own labored breathing. I glanced over my shoulder and saw that he was closing in easily. I was too weak, and he overtook me with little effort.

When he reached me, I pulled the towel bar up and swung at his head. He caught it in his hands, pulled me into him, and pressed the bar against my throat. With my neck sandwiched between the bar and his body, sharp pressure on my carotid artery, I passed out in seconds.

Again came the beating and, along with it, days of starvation until hallucinations set in. Endlessly I babbled to myself, looking for something—magic words. *Magic words, magic words*, sung a voice in stereo just outside my left ear.

He gave me only water and kept me bound to the radiator, this time with handcuffs. My body felt weightless and nonexistent. After several days, I found the words I was searching for and began an endless litany that carried into my sleep.

"I hate you," I said, over and over again. "I hate you. I hate you. I hate you."

I said it until I did not know how to stop. I said it as he raped me, fed me, and bathed me. I said it while he was gone and tried to infuse more fervor into it when he returned.

Weeks passed without me trying to escape, and he began to return some of my privileges. I stopped speaking. The day he freed my left hand, leaving my right cuffed to the radiator in the living room, I made my third attempt at escape.

The moment he left the house, locking the door behind him, I wet my right wrist and hand with saliva and dislocated my thumb, pulling my hand free. Skin scraped off the top of my hand in long strips. The pain only spurred me on. I cradled my hand at my stomach and unlocked the door with my other hand, which quaked and trembled.

He was waiting outside, arms crossed in front of him. He stood in the center of the clearing out front. His eyes narrowed as I emerged.

"You fucking bitch," he said, his voice low but hard.

I tried to evade him but could not. He dragged me, kicking and screaming, back into the house. He pushed my face into the toilet until my chest burned and my mouth opened against my will to breathe in deep lungfuls of water.

I woke on the bathroom floor on my side, spluttering, coughing, and choking. Water poured out of my mouth, and my body snapped shut on itself, spasming to bring up the remaining water.

He sat across from me, back against the wall, limbs folded neatly like a Buddha prepared to meditate. His eyes were dark but calm. When my body settled into quivers and intermittent coughs, he spoke.

His voice was quiet, even. "I don't know how to make you understand, Lynn. You are not leaving me. We will work through this for as long as it takes. I wish you wouldn't make me hurt you. I love you so much, and then you go and try to leave. I'm trying to make a life for us. I don't know why you insist on fighting me every step of the way. After everything I've done to make sure we could be together, you still don't appreciate it."

A voice in my head said, *I appreciate that you're fucking crazy and I wish you were dead.*

He shook his head sadly. "I made sacrifices for us. I wish you could see that. I really thought that once we had a home together, you would turn around, but you disappoint me, Lynn. You really disappoint me."

I stared at him with aching, itchy eyes. He crawled toward me, and my body recoiled involuntarily. He did not notice. He stroked my hair and touched my cheek. "Because I love you," he said, "I'm going to give you another chance. I know you want this to work just as much as I do. Don't make me do anything we'll both regret."

I had been beaten, raped, and starved so many times that the drowning, though new and terrifying, had almost no effect. I did not care what he did to me. Even when he reset my thumb, popping it back into place and wrapping it in an Ace bandage, I let out a single, short cry of pain and nothing more. Again, I began the long, tedious process of healing my body, gaining strength, and earning privileges. It was a long time before I considered escape again or how I would do it.

CHAPTER NINETEEN

Twenty minutes after Connor's call, Mitch stood beside him, listening as Connor recounted his interview with Dinah Strakowski. Connor showed him the picture of the blue station wagon. Mitch studied it and looked back at Connor. They didn't discuss it, but they both knew that a tiny detail like that could be the key to solving a cold case.

"I'll get on the car," Mitch said.

Connor nodded and stepped off the curb. He stood in front of his car, facing the direction the abductor had gone when he drove away with Claire Fletcher's body in his back seat. Farrell's mouth turned up on one side, half smile, half scowl.

"What are you working on, kid?" Farrell asked.

Connor flashed him a smile and ran a hand through his hair. It felt good to work with someone who could follow his thoughts, even when Connor himself could not. He gestured down the street, trying to articulate the fusion of gut instinct and shapeless suspicion in his mind.

Mitch walked toward him. "Start at the top," he instructed.

Connor nodded. "All right. The guy is sitting here in his car, right? Before she even comes down the street, he's sitting here. Waiting."

"Premeditation," Farrell said. "You think he stalked her first?"

Connor pursed his lips together, took another swipe at his hair. "No, no I don't. I think this was just prime hunting ground. The school is two blocks away. These guys, they look for a type, right?"

"Yeah, assuming he's a sexual predator. Most stranger abductors are," Mitch agreed. "They generally don't deviate from their type."

"So this guy is looking for a teenage girl, dark hair, probably between the ages of thirteen and fifteen. He had to have picked the spot beforehand, though," Connor said.

Mitch crossed his arms and leaned against the hood of Connor's car. "Yeah, probably. I mean some of these guys are really impulsive, reckless, but those are the ones who have their fun, kill the vic, and dump the body. We know this guy didn't do that. To pull off the snatch-and-grab without getting caught, there's got to be some planning."

"Right," Connor said. "So he chooses this spot, which means he had to be doing some surveillance, but Strakowski said she doesn't recall seeing a blue station wagon parked on the street before, at least not with a driver fitting this guy's description."

Mitch, sensing Connor was onto something, said, "Okay, we'll get back to that but go on."

"He can probably see her coming for a block or so. He doesn't know if she's going to keep coming this way or cross the street, turn the corner or what, but he's betting she'll come his way, so he gets out, comes around the side of the car, and sets the trap."

"Man having trouble with car," Mitch added.

"Right. A lot of these guys use the same type of lure to get the vic close enough to grab them. So what does he say?"

Mitch rubbed his fingers over the gray stubble that covered his chin. "Well, the puppy or kitten is a popular one. Strakowski said he was down there looking under the car, right? So he sees Claire, when she gets close enough, he says, 'Hey, I got this cute kitty under the car and she won't come out, will you help me?'"

"Yeah," Connor agreed. "She gets down there next to him, right by the open door, which he's laid out for his own convenience. He knocks her out, tosses her in, and drives off."

"Okay. We've got that. So what else?"

"Well," Connor mused, surveying the street in both directions. "He drives off in that direction, right?"

"Yeah?"

"Police units are here in what? Five minutes?"

"Yeah."

"They set a perimeter, canvass the area, stop all the blue station wagons, and drive Dinah Strakowski around the neighborhood looking for this guy, right?"

"Yeah," Mitch repeated.

"This is a residential area. No highways. School zone, eight o'clock in the morning. The average speed limit within the surrounding eight to ten blocks is gonna be twenty-five to thirty-five miles per hour. There's gonna be a fair amount of traffic this time of day with kids going to school and people going to work."

Mitch stood up, fully erect, and looked Connor in the eye. "This guy is not going to want to draw attention to himself with an unconscious minor in the back seat. If we say ten minutes to start the canvassing, how far is he really going to get? He can't break the speed limit, can't drive erratically. Far enough to elude the police?"

"Exactly," Connor said. "This fucker disappears. Totally. Him, the car, Claire. Vanish into thin air. But how? Everything in this case was done according to best-case-scenario conditions and damn-near-perfect police response. So how did he do it?"

"Holy shit," Mitch said, the realization nearly exploding between them like a ball of flames. "He lives in the fucking area."

"Yeah. He has to, probably within a ten-block radius. He won't want to be too close because he'll be easily recognized but close enough to pull into a garage, close the door, and act like nothing happened," Connor said.

"Holy shit," Mitch said again. "But wait, they went door-to-door and didn't even come up with anything suspicious."

Connor waved a hand dismissively. "That won't turn up anything unless he's got her tied up in the foyer."

"What about the station wagon? Sure, they didn't know the make or model, but they did a search of all blue station wagons registered to people inside the perimeter. Why didn't this guy show up? Did he take off by then?" Mitch said.

At that moment, the gods of investigative insight smiled on Connor. The dim shapes in his mind revealed themselves. "No," Connor said. "The station wagon wasn't registered to him. It was registered to a woman. They probably went to the house. She's probably right there on the goddamn list. He's a son or a brother or something, maybe even a boyfriend. That's why he's not easily recognized in the neighborhood, but he still has access. He's transient. She was probably at work. He had the whole day to stash Claire while he figured out what to do next."

"You think he kept her in the house with this other woman?" Mitch asked.

Connor shook his head. "I don't know. At this point, I don't think it really matters. If we can find her, we can get an ID on him."

"She may have moved by now," Mitch said, but he emanated the same excited energy that presently made Connor unable to stand still.

Connor met the older man's eyes once again and could not suppress a smile. "You work the car. Narrow the make and model. I'll check the list again and go from there. It might take a while to get addresses from information that's ten years old, but I still want to track down the other guys Claire saw after she disappeared."

Mitch beamed at him from beneath bushy eyebrows. "Fine work, Detective," he said. "Damn fine work."

Connor drove back to the division, feeling heady and buzzed, the same high he felt whenever the job was going well, when an investigation hit a turning point. It was one of the things he loved about his job. It wasn't an easy thing to deal with the bad guys day in and day out and face the things they had done, shouldering the responsibility of bringing them to justice. He had to fit all the pieces together, make sure the evidence was viable, and that all the procedures were followed meticulously so that when he handed a case over to the district attorney, they could look forward to a conviction. But when things came together, he felt exhilarated in a way nothing else in his life provided. His wife used to say he was "in the zone."

Connor parked and walked toward the door where two of the detectives from his division were standing, smoking cigarettes, and talking shop. Boggs and Stryker. He'd worked with both of them on different cases, although they usually worked together. Where you found one, you'd find the other. The rest of the division liked to joke that they were together so much, they were practically married.

Connor smiled at them when he approached. "Hey, if it isn't my favorite couple," he said.

Stryker said, "Fuck you, Parks," but smiled back.

"Hey," Boggs said. "Good luck next week with the review board."

Connor jammed his hands into his pockets. "Thanks," he said.

"That's a bum rap," Stryker said. "That fucker got what was coming to him."

"That's a popular sentiment around here," Connor replied. "But I'd hate to lose my badge over him."

Boggs took a long drag on his cigarette. "It'll work out," he said. "Worst case, they'll put you on the desk for six months."

"Nah," Stryker said. "Unpaid suspension."

Connor rocked back and forth on his heels. "Either way it sucks," he said.

Boggs grinned at him. "You're a good egg, Parks. Riehl will go through the roof if he loses you. You had that piece of shit on five counts. The convictions would have gone through. You'll never get out of here."

"Don't go all sappy on me, Mrs. Stryker," Connor said.

"Hey, fuck you, Parks," Stryker said again in Boggs's defense.

Connor laughed.

"What are you working?" Boggs asked.

"Cold case," Connor said with a shrug. "Something to do besides typing reports for your pansy ass."

"Well," Stryker said. "Let us know if we can help you. We got our last one in the bag. We're about to go get the fucker now."

Boggs looked at his partner with disdain. "Good God, Stryke. You kiss your mamma with that mouth?"

Stryker narrowed his eyes. "No, but I do kiss your wife with it."

The two detectives flicked their butts to the ground in unison and started a pushing match as they sauntered off to their car.

"Fucking jerk," Boggs muttered.

Connor waved and made his way up to his desk. He pulled the vehicle registration list from the Fletcher file and got to work. Two hours later, he had narrowed the list of female owners of any blue station wagon within the four-mile radius of where Claire had been abducted down to twelve women. He'd have to get the last known addresses on all of them, but the list could be narrowed further if Farrell positively identified the make and model of the station wagon from the picture Strakowski had provided. Next, he would look for addresses on Teplitz, Speer, and Randall in his files at his house.

Connor ordered a pizza and picked it up on his way home. He changed into a pair of sweats and a T-shirt and worked over the file Mitch had given him in Denise's old formal dining room. He still hadn't gotten rid of the large furniture, but he'd taped a map on the wall as well as several items from the file. With the space effectively turned into what would pass for a task-force room in law enforcement, a half-eaten pizza box, and beer bottles on the table, the space was beginning to feel like his own.

He thought about Boggs and Stryker, the odd couple, and decided he could invite them over to help him get rid of the rest of the furniture.

He was thinking about how well a pool table would fit after he tore down the mauve drapes when his doorbell rang.

Expecting Farrell to be taking up the greater part of his front stoop, Connor was surprised to find a petite woman smiling up at him, bearing a Tupperware container filled with something that smelled delicious.

"Detective Parks?" the woman said.

Connor raised an eyebrow. "Yeah?"

"Hi." She extended a hand. "I'm Jenny Fletcher. I'm, uh, Claire's mother."

Connor grasped her hand. "Mrs. Fletcher, hi. Come in."

He ushered her into the living room. Jen Fletcher smiled, her eyes taking in the place. "Uh, make yourself comfortable," Connor said.

She took a seat on his couch, her dish resting neatly on her knees. "Can I get you anything?" he asked. "Something to drink?"

She smiled. She was an attractive woman. She didn't resemble Claire in any strikingly obvious way, but she was still lovely. Her hair was salt-and-pepper, curly, and pulled back with a shell barrette. She was short, probably only five feet, but she exuded a strength that belied her stature. Worry creases enclosed her mouth, and when she smiled, laugh lines accentuated the deep blue of her eyes.

"I'm fine," she said. "Thank you." When Connor said nothing for a moment, she added, "She always looked more like her father. Claire, I mean."

Connor swept one hand through his hair and sat in the chair opposite her. "I'm sorry," he said. "I didn't mean to stare."

"It's perfectly okay," she said. Her voice was soft and genuine, almost musical.

"I wasn't expecting you," he said.

"Mitch called me. He told me you'd been to the house, and then he explained about the fingerprints. I hope you don't mind that he gave me your address," she said.

Connor smiled. "Not at all. I'm glad to finally meet you. I didn't receive a very good reception when I visited your home."

For the first time, uneasiness crossed Jen Fletcher's face. "I'm sorry about that," she said. "Normally the kids aren't even there. Any other day you would have gotten me, but I had asked them to meet me there for dinner, and then I ran late at work. Brianna, she can be very, how can I say this? She was always a challenge, but she feels very strongly about Claire, or rather, what happened to Claire."

"People deal with things in different ways," Connor said.

"Yes. They do."

Silence drifted between them like dust motes floating through the air. Finally, Jen said, "Detective Parks, I have always known that my child is still alive."

Connor nodded but said nothing. She continued, "I don't know how. I don't know why. A lot of people tried to tell me that I was only saying that because I needed hope to survive—that I could never face the possibility of Claire being dead, so I clung to that hope to get me through the days."

"Mrs. Fletcher, it takes a tremendous amount of energy to hold on to that kind of hope over many years," Connor pointed out.

Her face lit up. "Yes! That's what I've always thought. Sometimes I envied Rick—that's my husband—because it seemed easier for him to mourn our daughter and just move on with his life. I could never do that. I just knew"—she placed a hand on her heart—"in here, that she was still out there."

Tears glistened in the corners of her eyes. "When Mitch told me you'd found proof, I felt . . ."

"Vindicated?"

She smiled. "Yes. But also more hopeful than I've ever felt. I wanted to thank you."

"That's really not necessary," Connor said.

"It is for me."

"Well, okay. You're welcome. But this is my job, and when I met your daughter, she, ah, she made an impression."

Jen laughed, and Connor was impressed by the ease with which she held both the loss of her daughter and the joy of having Claire as her child so close to the surface. Clearly, her pain did not eclipse the love she held for Claire.

"Yes," Jen said. "She always did."

She held out the Tupperware container. "I brought you something. Mitch said you were a bachelor."

Connor took it and thanked her. "Divorced," he said. "She left me, but that was two years ago."

Jen nodded. "I was wondering if you could tell me about Claire," she said. "The other men . . ." She made a face of revulsion. "Well, for one thing, we were never sure if they were telling the truth. The whole thing was so strange. But I never felt comfortable talking with them. Now that I know"—she motioned toward Connor—"Claire is really alive, that you saw her, it would mean a lot to me if you would tell me what she's like."

Connor stretched back into the padding of the chair and cradled the warm container in his large hands. He sighed. Claire's image was permanently seared into his mind. He had only hours of time with her from which to draw on, but from that short time he'd managed to collect about a half-dozen mental snapshots. How she looked the first time she spoke to him in the bar—a puzzle. The hard lines of her face when she told him off and left. Her wide mouth turning up slightly as she considered him in the street. Her blank, almost dazed wonder at the flowers framing his walkway. Her head thrown back slightly, corners of her eyes transforming her face when she laughed. The intense crease of her brow as she studied the dining room. And his favorite mental picture of her was her face as she slept, brown curls resting on her cheek.

"She's beautiful," Connor said.

Again, as if he'd flipped a switch, tears gathered in Jen's eyes. "Is she? Is she really still beautiful? He didn't—he didn't destroy her?"

Jen's voice trembled, and Connor joined her on the couch. She slid one hand easily between both of his. A single tear made its way down her cheek. She wiped it away quickly with her free hand. "I'm sorry," she said.

"Don't be sorry," Connor murmured. "Listen, Mrs. Fletcher. I don't know what Claire has gone through in the last ten years. Since she was abducted, it's a pretty sure bet that she's seen her fair share of torment."

Jen nodded and put her other hand atop their joined hands. The skin on her face pulled tight as she tried to rein in her emotions. Connor thought of Claire's anguished eyes. He wondered if he could prepare this mother for the sight of those eyes.

"When you see her," he tried.

He hadn't been comfortable talking with anyone about those eyes that, at moments, had provoked unmitigated terror within him. But Jen Fletcher deserved to know. He could not imagine what it was like for a mother to lose her child and not know, year after year after year, what was happening. Was she being tortured? Raped? Beaten? Neglected? Deprived? No matter what had happened to Claire, Connor sensed that it would not diminish Jen's love for her daughter in any way.

He started again. "When you see her, there might be moments, looking into her eyes that you can tell. You can see that she's been"—he searched for the right word but could not find one so he settled on—"hurt."

"Ten years is a long time," Jen agreed. Tears slid down her cheeks. "I understand."

Connor squeezed both her hands gently. "But you know, whatever happened to her is not all there is to her," he said. "I mean she's interesting and funny and witty."

Jen looked up at him and smiled brightly through her tears. "She was always like that."

"Tell me about her," Connor said.

Jen sank back into the couch and wiped her tears away. "Claire was always extremely persistent. Very stubborn but in her own quiet way. She was not one to give up easily when she wanted something. She loved animals. Over the years we had so many different pets. She always wanted a dog more than anything else in the world, but my husband is allergic so there was just no way we could have a dog. That didn't stop Claire from lobbying for one. Every time a new allergy drug came out, she'd ask Rick to try it. She did so much research trying to find a way around Rick's allergies."

"What about cats?"

Jen nodded. "Yeah, we had a cat. Actually, it had just gotten out of the house and run off a couple of months before Claire went missing. We never did find that cat."

Connor thought of the yearbook recitation Claire had given when Connor asked her about herself. "She was a good swimmer?"

Jen's eyebrows shot up. "How did you know?"

"She told me."

"Yeah, she was a great swimmer actually but she had no real interest in it. Rick was so disappointed. She could have done something with that, but like I said, she was more interested in animals. She wanted to be a veterinarian. I was always glad that she had found her calling so early in life. My other kids never really knew what they wanted to do, and now they are both approaching thirty and have changed careers twice already.

"Claire loved to read too. She always read way above her grade level. She was never without a book to read. She was your typical teenager too. She loved to go to the mall or the movies. She didn't have a ton of friends, just a few that she hung out with. She idolized Brianna. They're only two years apart, you know. They were really best friends. So it has been very difficult for Brianna."

Connor pictured Brianna's glare. "I'm sure," he said.

"Do you have brothers and sisters?" Jen asked.

"I have a brother. He's three years older than me. He teaches seventh-grade history in Elk Grove. My mom died of cancer when we were teenagers so it was just us and my dad."

"I'm sorry to hear that. Is your father still living?"

"Yeah. He lives in Elk Grove too, near my brother. I don't see them as much as I should. Losing our mom was horrible. I can't imagine what it would have been like if something had happened to my brother."

Jen nodded. "Brianna is a wonderful person underneath all the hurt. She just misses Claire. We all do. I just want my baby back, Connor," she said with a sigh.

"I know," he said. "I'll do my best to try and find her."

Jen Fletcher spent more than an hour at Connor's home. They talked easily, and Connor felt as if he had known her for years. He gave her his card and wrote his home number on the back, instructing her to call or stop by with questions at any time.

When she left, she pulled him into an embrace that seemed impossible given her size. She held him close and squeezed him tightly for a long moment. She kissed him on the cheek with dry lips before she left.

Once she was gone, Connor phoned Farrell. "Jen Fletcher just left," he said. "You could have given me a heads-up."

Mitch's hearty laugh came through the line loud and clear. "Why? What were you doing?"

"Nothing," Connor said. "I just wasn't expecting her."

Connor could see Mitch waving a meaty hand dismissively. "Oh, Jenny's a sweetheart. She's all good stuff, that one. It's Brianna you have to watch out for."

"Watch out for?" Connor said.

"Oh shit," Mitch said.

Connor's eyes widened, and he stood up in the middle of his living room. "You gave her my home address too?"

"Hey," Mitch said, voice rising defensively. "There's no talking that girl out of something once she's got it in her head to do it. You have a gun, right?"

"Very funny, Farrell," Connor said humorlessly. "So when can I expect her?"

"Don't know," Farrell said. "Just let her do the talking."

"You mean the yelling."

Farrell ignored that. "You'll be fine. It has nothing to do with you anyway. She's just . . . bitter."

"Is there anyone else you plan on sending to my door? 'Cause my dance card is full," Connor said.

"Women beating down your door, huh?" Farrell said, laughing again.

"Something like that," Connor said, thinking about the one woman he'd like to beat down his door.

Farrell changed the subject. "I got the make and model on that car," he said. "She was right, you know. The Chevy Caprice from the late eighties is almost identical to the car Strakowski gave you today. Write this down. A Pontiac Parisienne, probably eighty-seven or eighty-eight. Only difference between that and the Chevy is the hood ornament—well, from the outside anyway."

Connor took down the information. "A Parisienne? What the hell kind of name is that for a station wagon? Okay, thanks. I'll check it against the list; see if I can narrow it down some more. Listen, see if you can get last knowns on Teplitz, Speer, and Randall. I want to talk to those guys."

"I'll have 'em tomorrow," Mitch said.

They hung up, and Connor took Jen Fletcher's Tupperware dinner to the fridge. He looked over the vehicle registry again and found a single woman who had owned a blue Pontiac Parisienne station wagon and lived several blocks from Strakowski at the time Claire was abducted. Her name was Irene Geary. He locked his front door and went to bed. Tomorrow he would find the car owner and break the case wide open. He hoped.

CHAPTER TWENTY

In his dream, Connor stood in the doorway from which he had shot the rapist nearly two weeks ago. Except this time, Boggs and Stryker were smoking cigarettes outside the closet door, joking irreverently about each other's wives; although in reality, only Boggs was married. Connor maintained a shooter's stance. His Kevlar vest pulled heavily on his shoulders. His gun was aimed at the sliver of closet door between the heads of Boggs and Stryker. They didn't seem to notice he was there or that he had a gun aimed in their direction.

Behind him, a gruff voice said, "Come on, kid. Let's go." It was Farrell. Connor wanted to turn and look at the older man, but he could not. It was as if his body were frozen in place, but he could feel every nerve ending, every small twitch of muscle. He yelled for Boggs and Stryker to clear the way, but they did not acknowledge him. It was as if a massive block of soundproof glass separated them from Connor and Farrell.

Connor yelled and yelled. Beads of sweat formed along his hairline and popped, sending hot drops down his face. He felt an urgency he could not explain. Finally, he sighted and aimed between the heads of the other detectives. He fired off a shot. Boggs and Stryker disappeared. Farrell rushed into the room past Connor and opened the closet door.

A man whose face had been blown off fell to the floor at Farrell's feet. But it wasn't the rapist Connor had shot in the chest. It was Claire's abductor. Even though Connor had never actually seen the man, in his dream he knew with certainty that the body before him was that of Claire Fletcher's kidnapper.

Mitch looked at him, eyes burning intensely. "Where's Claire?" he asked.

"I don't know," Connor said.

"Where's Claire?"

"I don't know."

The dream shifted and Connor was running through the halls of his house. They were elongated, stretching before him, the distance from one end to the other infinite. There were more doors than his little house could hold, but he checked every one, yelling Claire's name and getting no response. Every room was empty.

Then he heard sirens. He kept running, bursting from room to room. The sirens got louder and closer. As he moved through the endless maze of halls, he realized the sound was not that of sirens but of a phone ringing. His dream self started searching the rooms for the ringing phone until his body began to wake—and somewhere between sleep and waking, in the haze of unreality and confusion, his mind told him that he was dreaming; he had to wake up because the sound was actually his phone ringing.

Connor rolled to the side of the bed and thrashed in the general direction of the phone. He opened his eyes the moment his hand closed over the receiver, the glowing green numbers of his alarm clock greeted him. It was 2:27 a.m.

"Yeah," he said, his voice husky and raw with sleep.

There was nothing. Air.

"Parks," he said.

Silence. Then, "Connor?"

"Yeah?"

More silence. Then his body jolted fully awake as a rush of adrenaline surged through him. His upper body sprang from the mattress.

He sat on the edge of the bed. He wanted to say her name, but he was afraid that if he did, he would suddenly wake up to find that the phone call really was part of his dream. He felt dizzy.

"Claire," he said.

Still no response, but he could hear her breath moving in and out of her body in ragged gasps.

"Claire? Don't hang up. God, whatever you do, do not hang up."

"Connor," she said again.

"Where are you?"

"I can't tell you that. I just called because I . . ."

"Claire, tell me where you are, and I will come and get you. Just me. I'll bring you in."

"That's not possible."

Connor's body pulsed, his blood rushing so furiously it sounded like a tsunami in his head. He wanted to swim through the phone wires and capture her. He had never felt so powerless in his life. She was there on the other end, and he couldn't get to her.

"Claire, I know what happened."

There was a sharp intake of breath, and her voice went up an octave. "No, no you don't. Listen to me. What I did—coming to you—I may have put you in danger. I'm not supposed to see or speak with you again, but I had to warn you."

Connor gripped the receiver so hard his hand ached. "What are you talking about Claire? Are you in trouble? Let me bring you in."

Her voice was throaty, as if she were about to cry, and Connor felt a tightness in his chest. The woman he met was so self-possessed. Damaged, but very poised and in control. He could not imagine her crying.

"I can't," she said. "Please. Just be careful. I have to go."

"Claire, no," he pleaded. He must have sounded as desperate as he felt because she did not hang up right away. He listened to her breath, which had become even more irregular. Connor lowered his voice. "Just wait," he said. "Don't do this. I can help you."

"No one can help me," she said. "You don't understand. Please, just be careful. You could be in a lot of danger."

She didn't speak for a long moment. Then, "I have to go."

"No." The word came out much more forcefully than he anticipated. She didn't speak, but she didn't hang up either. Connor didn't know what to say, yet he did not want to sever the connection. He knew what he was about to say would sound ridiculous, but he forged ahead anyway. "I just want to see you again."

He heard a muffled sound, and her voice was barely a whisper. "I know. I want to see you too."

Silence. He carefully listened to her breathe, taking in every little part of the sound. Finally, he said, "Just tell me what to do."

"You can't help me," she said. "It's too late for that."

"You don't know that," he said. "Give me a chance. Please."

"I wish I could." She was definitely crying now, and the sound of it made Connor sick to his stomach.

"Claire," he said softly. "Tell me what to do."

"Be careful," she said. "Don't come after me. I've already put you in danger. Just protect yourself."

He waited for the click and dial tone, but she stayed on for another moment. "Connor?"

"Yeah."

"I—" She stopped. He waited. He could hear her gulping air. "I'm sorry," she said, hanging up.

CHAPTER
TWENTY-ONE

I hung up the pay phone and wiped the tears from my eyes before turning away from the narrow booth. My body trembled; I couldn't control it. I gripped the grimy edges of the small shelf below the phone. Tears streamed down my face. Fear tickled my throat and the backs of my knees. The shivering and the tears came unbidden. I tried to breathe, but all that came out were strangled sobs. It was as if I were no longer in my body. I felt the emotion physically taking over, but my mind no longer had control. I hadn't felt like that for many years.

My nose ran, and I fumbled in my pants pocket for a tissue. Of course I could not find one. I never carried anything on me. I settled for my shirtsleeve. I squeezed my eyes shut and concentrated as hard as possible on my breathing. I listened to the cars pass by on the street, focusing on the sound. Air swishing, tires moving over the asphalt. If I did not get control soon, the world would start to spin and I would pass out. I couldn't draw attention to myself, and I couldn't be late getting back to the trailer.

"Get a grip," I muttered to myself.

Let me bring you in.

For a split second, I had thought that if anyone could bring me in, it would be Connor, and that thought made me cry. As if it were that simple. No one could rescue me, and if Connor tried, he would be sorry in more ways than one.

I wiped my eyes a final time and walked unsteadily back to the truck. I made it to the trailer moments before he pulled up to the house across the road, but I felt Tiffany's watchful eyes on me as I hurried inside.

When I had visited her the other day, it seemed as though she really didn't know anything. I had spent the last couple of days trying to convince myself of that, but maybe she did know that I had taken one of my ill-fated trips home, and she was just waiting to tell him—waiting until she had something to gain by telling him or until his attention waned.

I didn't bother with the lights. I moved into my tiny bedroom and changed into my pajamas, which consisted of a pair of sweatpants and an old, oversized T-shirt I bought at a thrift store. I swiped a sweater from my closet and pulled it around me. The door of the house across the way slammed shut, but no rattle on my own door followed. I had only made Tiffany suspicious with my visit, although I sensed that she was hiding something.

In the last seven years, I had waged many small battles with her in this fashion. She had increased the torture of my small life exponentially from the day she arrived, making my days more difficult in new and unexpected ways; although before she arrived it had been no picnic.

I climbed into bed and closed my eyes. My imagination conjured the heady scent of Connor and the smooth balm of his skin heating my own. The words seemed to come from another part of the trailer rather than from my memory. "Tell me what to do, Claire."

I had tried to tell him what to do, even though it scuffed and scraped a part of me that still yearned for sweetness. I hoped he would stay away. He had to. I couldn't bear to think of what would happen to Connor if he didn't let me go forever.

I had witnessed my captor's revenge for my sins firsthand.

CHAPTER

TWENTY-TWO

1996

One day after he had left me cuffed in the living room, I spied a newspaper on the floor by the couch. It took a lot of wiggling and squirming, but eventually I pulled it toward me with my feet, losing half of it in a trail of pages. I looked at the date on the paper, and my world tipped to the side.

He'd had me for a year and a half.

I was sixteen, almost seventeen. I had been missing for a year and a half.

I cried then. Great wracking, sucking, gulping sobs that I had held in up to that point. I let something go inside me that I had been holding on to for all those months. It hurt the way I imagined giving birth might. Great floes of denial floated and idled out of my reach, solid masses I had been clinging to, sleeping upon, pressing my face into.

It was real. It was all real. This wasn't a temporary state of affairs. It wasn't a nightmare I would wake up from. It was really happening, and there would never be a SWAT team on the other side of the door. Even left to my own devices, I had been unable to break free. This was actually my life, all of it, and it was just going on, working scrupulously through the days, indifferent to my pain and my hope.

That day, without rushing, without even breaking a sweat, I carefully worked my hand loose from the cuff once more. My thumb popped more easily out of joint this time. I gritted my teeth and reset it with a gasp.

I walked to the door, unlocked it, stepped outside, and walked toward the trees. At a slow, steady pace I picked my way carefully through ferns, thorny branches, fallen tree trunks, and rocks. I walked and walked.

Finally, I came to a stretch of road lined with trees on both sides. My mind acknowledged the fact that I was actually free. All I had to do was flag down the next car that came down the road in either direction, and I could go home. But my body continued along the shoulder of the road without notice. No rushing in my ears, no pounding in my chest, no short breaths coming so quickly atop one another that my throat whistled. I walked, my ears pricked for the sound of a car.

When I finally heard one approaching behind me, I did not even turn. The car pulled up in front of me onto the shoulder of the road. When he emerged from it in a huff and flurry, I was not even surprised. I didn't run, did not even look at him. I kept walking past him, past the car. He grabbed my arm, but I wiggled it loose and continued my balanced pace. Again, he took my arm and pulled me, but I bent my body forward, moving with my hips, gaining fewer steps but gaining nevertheless. When he plucked my entire body off the road and carried me back to the car, my legs kept working calmly, slowly, still walking toward home.

We reached the car, and he clutched the back of my head. The door frame rushed toward my face as it had the day he snatched me, and I thought dryly, *One for old times' sake.*

Acceptance came later that night. I don't think he ever really wore me down. No, he broke me with one swift and irrevocable act. All those months of pain, torture, and deprivation were almost for nothing. I was not tethered to him by any of those things or even the length of time he had kept me prisoner. It was his retribution, his punishment for my walking escape that finally broke me.

Both my hands were cuffed to the living room radiator. I sat cross-legged, waiting for his return and the beating that would inevitably follow. I felt numb, indifferent. I was ready for the blows, the slaps, kicks, and punches. Ready for them in the same way I would be ready to take a trip in a car or sit down to dinner.

Without a word he had brought me back, bound me, and left immediately. The only evidence of his anger was the gash above my left eyebrow where my head had met the car door frame hours earlier.

I had made my ill-fated walking attempt in daylight, and when he came back, it was night. Before the door opened, I heard scuffles, grunts, and gasps. Before I saw him, a body landed with a crack and a thud on the floor in front of me.

She had blonde hair. Her hands and feet were tied. There was something stuffed deep into her mouth and taped there, although one tantalizing edge of the duct tape peeled away from her skin. She was thin and slightly older than me. She squirmed, her body jerking up and down like an inchworm on speed.

I came to full consciousness. Suddenly jolted into reality, I could feel every inch of my body. My vision filled with the sight of her. I looked around as if seeing the place for the first time. All the colors and shadows became sharp and fast like a slap to the face. My voice rose out of me, strong and high. He stood above the two of us, looking down his nose with the smile of a predator about to tear into a very tasty meal.

I got up on my knees. I tried to reach her but could not. "What are you doing?" I said. "Oh my God, what are you doing?"

She was there on the floor—just inches out of my reach—and she would not stop seizing. Her face was turned away from me.

"What are you doing?" I repeated.

He pulled her across the room by the hair, and she squealed in pain—her legs pushing furiously to keep up with him, to keep her scalp from being torn off.

"I'm sorry it had to come to this, Lynn," he said, his tone as quiet as ever. "But you're impervious to all of my efforts to help you get comfortable here. I'm afraid I have to teach you a lesson."

He hefted her up and slung her over the arm of the couch. Her legs dangled on the floor, and her upper body curved over the arm. She turned her head and saw me. She had brown eyes. Big brown eyes with luxuriant lashes. Her eyes were so wide it looked as if someone was literally squeezing them out of her head. I pulled and pulled against the cuffs. My body drew toward her like a magnet. She screamed as much as the gag would allow. She spoke to me with her eyes that said, *Help me, oh God, please help me.*

My eyes on him, I stretched toward her. "No," I said. "I don't need a lesson. I don't need a lesson. Please. Let her go. Leave her alone. I'll do whatever you want. I'll never leave again. I'll be good. Please."

Her eyes filled with a mixture of horror and relief. I tried with my own to tell her that I meant every word. I would do anything to get him to let her go.

He shook his head sadly, sighing. "I'm afraid it's too late for that, Lynn."

"*No!*" I screamed. My body squirmed futilely against the cuffs. "I swear to you. Please. I will do anything you say, anything you want. I'll do it, I'll do it. Just let her go. Don't hurt her. Please."

I used his language. "I'll be a good girl. I'll be such a good girl, and we can forget all about before. I'll be so good you'll forget I was ever bad. Please. Just let her go."

"Yes," he said. "I know you will, but letting her go will not help us. I have to teach you a lesson, Lynn. I have to prove my love for you because it's obvious you don't believe how much I love you."

"No," I said. "I do believe you. I believe you. You don't have to do this. I don't need a lesson. I get it now. I get it, okay? Just let her go."

The girl blinked her eyes rapidly. Tears dripped from her face, and a thin strand of snot hung from her nose. Her face twisted, and I could smell both of our sweat and fear commingling, filling up the air between us.

"This isn't about her," I pleaded. "She has nothing to do with—us. Please. Oh, please."

His lips pressed into a thin line, and he took off his belt. I did not want to watch. I thought he would rape her, and I did not want to see it. I did not want to watch the violation he had perpetrated on my own body so many times.

I could not reach her. Nor could I look away. My eyes, my frantic gaze, and empathetic tears were all I had to offer her. But he did not rape her. Instead, he wrapped the belt around her neck, looping the end through the buckle.

It was over in a few minutes, and it was silent except for my screams, which ended abruptly when he released the belt that had become embedded in her delicate neck. Her skin was like clay, the belt cushioned in its purple mass. My voice cut to silence as if it were my own throat being constricted. I slumped, staring as sightlessly as the dead girl before me.

I had killed her. I had done this. My stubbornness, my sheer and unyielding furor to be free of him had led her to this place. A lonely wooden shack in woods unknown, bound, stinking of putrid fear like a compost of freshly slaughtered animal carcasses. A man on her back, tightening the strap.

When he approached me, he seemed to come from miles away, a dot on the horizon, even as I felt his leg brush against me. His voice seemed low and muffled as if he were talking to me from across the room.

"Now," he said breathlessly. "Tell Daddy how sorry you are, and we can forget this whole thing."

And God help me, I did.

CHAPTER
TWENTY-THREE

Connor prowled around his bedroom like a large cat, its hackles raised. He glanced at the phone on every turn as if looking at it would make it ring again, but after an hour, it didn't.

Claire had slipped from his grasp again, leaving him more agitated than ever.

He had tried to use his callback feature to get the number she'd called from, but the damn thing said the number was unavailable, which probably meant she used a pay phone.

Without a subpoena for calls to and from his home telephone, Connor could not access the number. He couldn't get a subpoena because he wasn't working on the case with the approval or backing of his division. He'd promised Farrell that he'd use all of his police resources to find Claire, but he never brought the case before Captain Riehl. Until he met with the review board, Connor was on the desk, and even then there was a chance that he might not be able to keep his job. He wasn't supposed to be doing any active investigative work.

But all that bothered him little compared to the fear and regret he'd heard in Claire's voice. Acid roiled in his stomach at the stark reality of not being able to help her.

Clearly, she was under duress as he and Mitch had theorized. Connor had not even felt this helpless two years ago when Denise announced to him over breakfast that she had fallen in love with someone else and would be leaving him within the week.

Her tone, which was the same as the one she used to tell him to take out the garbage or mow the lawn, should have alerted him that refusing to sign the divorce papers and trying to reconcile with her would prove futile.

The first year of their separation, as he tried to win her back, he'd felt as powerless as a man standing unarmed before a firing squad. Eventually, he accepted the fact that the marriage was over, and it had taken another year to sort out the details.

But in all that time, he had never felt as useless and ineffective as he did now. Silently, he had dismissed Claire's plea for him not to come after her the moment it left her lips, as he had her sorrowful insistence that she was beyond help.

He'd spent a single night with a woman he knew nothing about, but he wanted to see her again—her broken eyes and razor-edged laugh—more than he had ever wanted his wife to stay and work on their marriage.

He had to help her. Even if it meant going expressly against Claire's wishes to be left alone.

At 5:30 a.m. Connor woke Farrell, calling first his cell phone and then his home phone. The soft edges of sleep left the man's voice quickly when Connor recounted the phone call.

"How did she get your number?"

"I'm in the book," Connor said.

"She said you're in danger?" Mitch asked, focusing on a part of the conversation that had barely registered with Connor.

"Yeah," Connor said.

"You got a security system over there?" Mitch asked.

Connor grunted. "Yeah, it's called a lock and a dead bolt. I can't sleep."

Mitch grumbled words Connor could not make out, then said, "Okay, first things first. You said it sounded like a pay phone?"

Connor paused before responding. He'd been so intent on Claire, on her voice, on convincing her to let him come to her, that he hadn't listened for ambient noise or automatically tuned in to things his detective's mind would normally listen for. He explained about the callback, from which he drew the assumption that Claire had called from a pay phone, and that he could not get a subpoena for his phone records.

Mitch sighed. "All right," he said. "I'll see what I can do with that. Might be able to call in a favor or two. In the meantime, keep your eyes open for anything unusual. We can meet at your place later. I'll check it over for security measures."

Connor felt no calmer after hanging up with Farrell. It was too early for him to make any calls, so he pulled on a pair of sweats and went out back, where a heavy punching bag hung from the awning over the patio.

From the large storage bin he kept on the patio for gardening implements, Connor pulled out some hand wraps. After wrapping his hands and wrists tightly, he went to work on the bag, his fists slamming into it from all directions, springing off on angles as the bag swung back toward him.

Connor barely felt the cool morning air or the sting of his knuckles against the coarse material of the bag. There was only the hard, muted thud of his fists pummeling with satisfying impact into the bag. The image of Claire Fletcher's face, untouchable and out of reach, burned in his mind.

CHAPTER

TWENTY-FOUR

1996

The night my captor strangled the life from the blonde girl with the terror-stricken eyes, my voice left me. Even when my mouth worked, no sound issued from my throat. My body shook most of the time though I was not cold. My eyes stared straight ahead, and I could not force them in any other direction. They didn't see what was in front of me, though. My vision was filled with the entire room. I was looking down on myself—a small, huddled mass of bones and tatters with tangled, matted brown hair. I watched from the ceiling as the days blurred past. He took the girl outside. I had named her Sarah in my mind because she was every bit as real as me, only now she was dead, and it was my fault.

I watched, perched in a tree, as he buried her behind the house. I watched him return to the quivering body that still breathed, drank, ate, shat, and struggled blindly against his advances in silence, but was minus me, severed from me, because now I was on the ceiling. Sometimes I floated out back and sat beside the mound of dirt that formed Sarah's hard-packed coffin. I sang to her, though no sound came from me or the body within the house.

He no longer bound that body, and sometimes it called me back, tugging at me, unraveling me in long skeins and tightening me around it like a bandage. I could not stay in it long because of the panic attacks. My chest grew heavy as if I were the one lifeless and crushed beneath the dirt in his backyard. I felt the dirt filling my mouth. I couldn't breathe.

The room began to flash around me, a disconcerting strobe effect. I clutched at my throat, dug my fingers into my mouth, trying to scoop the invisible dirt out of my throat. A high-pitched buzz assaulted my ears, rising in pitch with my panic. Somewhere deep in my bowels, I screamed soundlessly. I was dying. Dying, dying, dying.

The body would pass out, not able to hold the panic, which was hard but slick, and I would leave again.

He was not pleased with me, with this body that was dead but still thrashed and tried to pull itself out of its own throat.

He did not beat me, though. Instead he came home with small green pills, which he put in the body's mouth, pressing his hand over its lips until it swallowed. Every day a green pill until the body began reeling me in more and more. Until I could lay in it quiet, formless, and unmoving for a few moments before the panic began again.

After many more weeks, I could feel myself breathing with the body again, could feel its cracked lips, cool sweat on the back of its neck. The panic lay just outside of us, ebbing and pulsing dangerously close but hesitating around our borders, uncertain, squeamish. I began to hear sounds again but still could not speak.

One day he returned home with a bed frame, box spring, and mattress. He had a dresser and several boxes. It was all packed into a stout rental truck. He unpacked it himself, sweat soaking the back of his shirt in an inverted V. I watched from the couch as he passed back and forth for hours. I heard the clangs, thuds, and the rustling of him working in my room.

At nightfall, he took my hand and guided me from the couch to the room. There was a bed with a pink floral comforter, pillows, a table beside the bed on top of which sat a delicate lamp. A dresser sat across from the bed, its wooden surface shiny. A vase filled with fresh flowers burst from the top of it. The closet was packed with clothes dangling from hangers. He had affixed a full-length mirror to the inside of the closet door. He said nothing and left me standing just inside the room, closing the door softly behind him.

I looked dumbly at all the things I had desired for almost two years. In the dresser drawers were bras and panties, socks, a pair of slippers. Beneath the clothes in the closet were two pairs of shoes. A pair of sneakers and a pair of black shoes, which were slightly dressier. I fingered the clothes and inhaled the scent of the flowers, feeling heady from the smell of something besides death and my own stink.

The table beside the bed was equipped with a single drawer just beneath its surface. It held a hairbrush, antiperspirant, and a towel and a washcloth, neatly folded. I lay down on the bed, sinking into its plush softness. I curled on my side and stared at the clothes hanging in the closet. I stayed there for hours. The night changed colors, and the sun came and went again.

I wanted to enjoy these things. The feel of shoes, socks, and undergarments. Real clothes, pretty clothes that fit my shriveled body. I wanted to shower by myself, wash the unending grime out of my birdnest hair. I wanted to comb my hair, smooth deodorant under my arms.

I wanted these things with a sultry blue ache, but how could I enjoy them? I deserved nothing. How could I revel in my ablutions, brush my hair, and put on new clothes when Sarah lay beneath a mound beyond my window, her pretty face peeling away?

Indulging myself would seal my complicity; I would be taking a step through the door I thought I would rather die before entering. I would really be Lynn. I would have taken candy from his hands, from the devil's own hands. Sold my infinitesimal soul to him, handing it over in tatters and shards.

I thought of killing myself. I had enough access to the rooms of the house to find something, some way of doing it. Surely that would be most prudent. But that seemed selfish. Beautiful, lithe Sarah lay dead in the ground while I lived. My life held nothing, not a single joy, not even the silly joy that came with relieving a full bladder after holding it indefinitely. But I was still alive, and she was not. I kept on in contrition and penance for her—the dead girl in the backyard whose real name I did not know.

I did wash myself, comb my hair, and dress in the new clothes. Some of them fit, some of them didn't. There were dresses, skirts, blouses, and slacks. Even a pair of jeans, which I wore the most. Sometimes I put on everything that would fit and slept that way.

I was not sure why I still lived, but a part of my brain, still partially hidden from my view, was working, trying to figure something out. Perhaps another bid for freedom. I began eating at the kitchen table with him, and he cooked full meals, though I rarely tasted the food I shoveled into my mouth.

One day I looked at him and said, "I want books."

"What?" he said, momentarily startled since it was the first time I had uttered a word in nearly six months. It surprised me a little too. It was strong, firm—a woman's voice.

"I want books," I repeated. "To read. Lots of them."

He set his fork down carefully on his plate, dabbed the edges of his mouth, and looked at me.

"Please," I added, though my tone was flat.

"What kinds of books?" he asked.

"Any kind. I don't care. Whatever you can get." Then, because I knew it would flatter him to think I deferred to his judgment, I said, "You decide. You pick them out. I would just like something to read."

This brought a smile to his face, and he blushed like a young girl. "Very well, my darling. You will have books."

I said nothing and resumed eating.

The next day my room was filled with books. Volumes. In spite of himself, he had chosen well. They were mostly classics: the complete works of Shakespeare, Jane Austen, the Brontë sisters, Dickens, Joyce, Twain, Faulkner, Hawthorne, and Thoreau. There were several newer novels, which he pointed out had all won prestigious literary prizes. There were a few history books, some biographies of legendary American figures, and *National Geographic* magazines from the past year.

I did not thank him because I could not get my mouth to voice the words, but I felt full with anticipation. For two weeks I read without sleeping, one book after another. I could not get enough. He seemed pleased, and while he still saw fit to touch me—to soil me over my objections and the thrashing, whipping resistance of my body—the days passed unremarkably.

Then one day I was sitting on the porch reading in a wicker chair he'd provided for just such a whim. My eyes drifted off the page as I watched dusk settle around the house. He had bought an old truck weeks before, in addition to his car. It sat there like a jilted lover, brown, stained with rust and dirt. He was gone for the day, although he would likely return within the hour.

I didn't give it much thought when I went into the house and retrieved the truck keys from the hook in the kitchen. I climbed into the truck, which smelled vaguely of cigarettes and gasoline. Before I was taken, my father had been giving me driving lessons. Had I not been stolen from the street, I would have had my driver's license within months. He taught me first how to drive a manual because, for some reason, he thought it was important.

"You never know when you might have to hop into a car that has a manual shift," he had said. "Could be an emergency."

Indeed it could.

The truck was a manual. I pressed the clutch to the floor and turned the key. It roared to life, hacking and gurgling like it was about to spit up a hair ball. It took me several stalls and starts before the art of driving came back to me. I turned the truck to the narrow trail and drove.

CHAPTER
TWENTY-FIVE

At 7:30 a.m., Connor showered, changed into a suit, and drove to the division. It was Saturday, but several detectives were there. Unfortunately, criminals never took time off. They worked weekends and holidays too, which meant that law enforcement investigators not only matched them hour for hour in work, but usually went overtime trying to clean up the carnage left in their wake.

Connor walked by Riehl's open door, greeting him in passing with a mock salute. Riehl barely nodded. Stryker, looking oddly like an amputee without Boggs, sat at his desk, which abutted his missing partner's, talking on the phone. The younger man leaned back in his chair until it looked like it might tip and send him feet over head while he twisted the phone cord around in his fist.

Stryker raised his head in acknowledgment as Connor leaned against the edge of the desk, waiting for him to finish his call.

When the detective hung up, he took a moment to disentangle himself from the phone cord, muttering expletives under his breath before grinning at Connor. "Hey Shoot-'em-up, what are you doing here so early on a Saturday? Thought you desk jockeys went fishing on the weekends."

"Cute," Connor said. "Where's the wife?"

"Fuck you, Parks," Stryker said without malice. He bobbed his head toward Boggs's desk. "Fucker's doing some family shit this weekend. Left me to follow up on these damn witness statements. It's all right, though. I'm saving the real combative ones for him. What's up?"

Connor pulled a sheet of paper from his pocket. "I need a last known," he said, handing it to Stryker. On it, Connor had written the name of the woman who had owned a blue Pontiac Parisienne station wagon and lived in Dinah Strakowski's neighborhood in 1995. "That's where she lived ten years ago. I need to know where she is now."

Stryker placed the sheet on his desk and turned to his computer. "Irene Geary," he said, manipulating the mouse with small but swift movements. "You might get more than one—name isn't real common like a John Smith or something, but there's probably more than one. You want to search the whole country or just the state?"

"Let's start with the state," Connor said.

Stryker moved silently and quickly, absorbed in the task. His hands worked as if they were extensions of the computer. Connor grinned as he watched. Stryker was the division's technology guru. Short but stout and well muscled from a daily regimen of running and weight lifting, Stryker looked more like he belonged in front of some trendy bar serving as a bouncer or acting as bodyguard for some important public figure, rather than behind a computer.

But the rest of the guys came to him when their own computer skills failed them. If anyone could find what they were looking for, it was Stryker. Connor could have done the search himself, using his own computer, but he knew Stryker would have an address within minutes, whereas it might take Connor a couple of hours to get the desired information from his own temperamental machine.

"Two in the state," Stryker said. "What the fuck are you grinning at?"

Connor laughed. "Nothing. It's just that you're gonna make a damn fine receptionist someday."

"Fuck you, Parks," Stryker said. He printed out the names and addresses and widened his search to include the rest of the country.

Connor pulled the printout from Stryker's printer tray and looked over the other man's shoulder. "The Internet?" he said. "Jeez, Stryke, I could have done that."

Stryker grinned. "No you couldn't. You dumbshits are lucky you can get a computer to boot up, let alone navigate the Internet. It's always, 'Stryke, I can't find this,' or 'Stryke, this file won't come up,' or 'Stryke, my computer took a shit.' I oughta give seminars. That way I could spend more time cracking down on shitwad perps instead of doing everyone's goddamn work for them."

"Yeah, we're so lucky to have you," Connor responded.

Stryker printed out another sheet of paper. "Fucking Internet Whitepages, baby," he said appreciatively. "Now I'm gonna use another database to see if I can get a social security number to go with that vehicle registration, and we'll just see which one of these Irene Gearys is the lucky winner."

Connor waited, tapping his fingers against the edge of Stryker's chair.

Fifteen minutes later, Stryker had a winner. The Irene Geary that Connor was looking for now lived in Arizona. Stryker printed out her address and phone number and handed it to Connor.

"I'm gonna start keeping a jar on my desk for tips," Stryker said. "Least you fuckers can do is give me a little extra scratch for all the shit I find for you."

Connor smiled as he walked to his own desk. "Here's a tip, Stryke," he said. "Don't piss in the wind."

As Stryker threw back his typical response, Connor mouthed it along with him. "Fuck you, Parks."

Stryker was all bark and no bite. Most of the guys in the division bantered with each other crudely and traded cruel insults in jest. Inappropriate humor and affected pit-bull personas were their strongest defense mechanisms. When you had to look at all the grievous sins that human beings committed against one another day in and day out, finding a way to cope with it, however crass, became a priority.

Connor settled behind his desk and booted up his own computer, which he was far more adept at handling than Stryker surmised. It took him another hour to run a full background check on Irene Geary. She had no criminal record, although she had been arrested twice before moving to Arizona—once for shoplifting seventeen years ago and once for disturbing the peace shortly thereafter. Neither arrest had resulted in charges being filed. She'd also been involved in several domestic disputes in which various boyfriends were charged with beating or harassing her, all of which took place prior to 1995, when, presumably, she was living with the man who would later abduct Claire Fletcher.

She had one child, a daughter named Noel, who, according to the records Connor found, would now be twenty-three years old. Connor found one local listing for a Noel Geary and jotted it down next to the contact information he had on Irene.

He phoned Irene Geary first. He would have preferred to drop by in person, which would provide her little opportunity to give him the brush-off if she was at all apprehensive about discussing a ten-year-old relationship.

A female voice that cracked under the strain of years' worth of smoking too many cigarettes snapped, "Who is this?" at Connor after he said hello.

"I'm trying to reach Irene Geary," Connor said.

"Yeah, who wants to talk to her?"

"My name is Connor Parks," he replied. "I'm a detective with the Sacramento Police Department's Major Crimes Unit. I need to ask you some questions."

"What kind of questions?"

Connor heard the flick and hiss of a lighter, followed by a deep, sucking breath and then a heavy exhale. "Ms. Geary, did you once reside at 1653 Larkspur Road?"

Another drag on the cigarette. Then, "Yeah."

"You lived there from 1992 to 1996, is that right?"

"I moved out of there in '95," she said. "What is this about?"

"In '95," Connor said, "what happened that precipitated that move?"

"Whose business is that? You tell me why you're calling or I'm not saying squat. How do I know you're a real cop?"

Connor offered her his badge number, the name of his captain, and the phone number for both the city police and his own extension. He instructed her to call the information line for the police department and confirm that he was indeed a detective there.

Instead she said, "I had a problem with a tenant. I left. Took me a while to get rid of the house. That it?"

"Can I have the name of that tenant?" Connor asked, excitement spiraling up from his gut.

"Don't remember," she said.

"Do you have some written records of that?" he asked.

"No," she said flatly.

"What was the nature of your problem?" he asked.

"Don't remember," she said again.

"Ms. Geary, does the name Claire Fletcher sound familiar to you?"

"Claire who?"

"Claire Fletcher. Have you heard that name before?"

"Don't think so," she said.

Connor would have had a better read on her had they been face-to-face, but she didn't sound as if the name struck a chord. "Ms. Geary, Claire Fletcher is the name of a woman that we think may be in grave danger. We're investigating the possibility that your former tenant may have something to do with her disappearance."

There was a long silence. "You don't even know his name," Irene Geary said. "How do you know he's involved?"

"I can't discuss the details of the investigation, but it is very important that we find out everything we can about this person," Connor said. "Are you still in contact with him?"

Irene Geary coughed and spluttered, hacking like a veteran smoker. "No," she said. "No way. I told you, we had a problem. I never saw or heard from him again. I don't know anything about any woman or anything else. Is that all?"

"Just a few more questions," Connor said. "Did you allow your tenant use of your Pontiac Parisienne station wagon in 1995?"

"Look," she groused. "I told you I don't remember. I'm done talking. Now leave me alone and don't call back."

Abruptly, Irene Geary ended the call, leaving Connor with the sound of a steadily buzzing dial tone pressed against his ear.

Connor redialed her number three times, but she did not answer, nor did an answering machine pick up.

CHAPTER
TWENTY-SIX
1997

When I hit road, I turned right. I didn't know where I was going. I was not experiencing conscious thought. I was numb and eerily calm, as I had been since I took on the part of Lynn, the pet who wore pretty clothes, slept in a bed unchained, and asked for books to read.

I drove several miles. Cars passed in the opposite direction, and it seemed strange that I should be out in the world, seen even fleetingly by others, and that nothing happened. There were no shouts, no pointing, and no masses of people rushing to my rescue calling, "There she is! That's the girl who was kidnapped! Call the police."

I didn't exist anymore, and that realization left me hollow. There were signs on the road that alerted me to the fact that I was a mere ten miles outside the city I had called home for the first fifteen years of my life. I pulled into the first place I saw, which happened to be a bar. Glowing neon signs promising various brands of beer bracketed the door. I got out, still with no particular plan in mind. The careless, ignorant fingers of the world that no longer saw or looked for Claire Fletcher scraped the last of the soft tissue from the hollow place inside me.

I walked in and took a seat at the bar. There were maybe ten people inside. Some playing pool, some at the end of the bar engaged in a secretive conversation with the bartender. I sat for some time, the cool, smoky air rubbing my arms lightly. I did not notice the single form nursing his beer at a corner table until he came to sit next to me.

He smiled at me, and the sight almost knocked me off my stool. My throat closed up with the realization that I had not looked at a single face besides my captor's and Sarah's in two whole years.

He was young and slightly overweight with shaggy brown hair and wide brown eyes. His smile was kind and a little nervous. Shy, I realized. He extended a hand.

"Hi, I'm Rudy," he said.

"Claire." The voice seemed to come from somewhere just behind me, startling me. I shook his hand.

"I haven't seen you here before," he said.

"I don't get out much."

"Can I buy you a drink?"

"Okay."

"What would you like?"

I looked at the beer in his hand. "Whatever you're having is fine," I said.

He smiled again and signaled the bartender, who hardly glanced at me and returned to the conversation at the end of the bar almost before he set the beer down in front of me.

I picked it up. It was wonderfully cold in my hand. "Thank you," I said.

"No problem."

I drank almost all of it in a single gulp. Rudy put his hand on my wrist, laughing. "Hey," he said. "Slow down."

Some of it dribbled down my chin and I swiped it away with the back of my hand. "Sorry," I said.

"Nothing to be sorry about," he said. "I just don't want you to get sick is all."

I nodded.

He studied me. "Are you okay?" he asked.

"Sure," I said.

I drank more slowly after that, and he bought me another beer and then another. He talked, and I surfed on the sound of his voice. A new voice, a different voice, a kind voice. His laughter suffused every part of my body. I closed my eyes, and my body cooed as Rudy's voice reverberated through me.

He told me about his life, his parents, and how he had dropped out of college last year and taken a computer repair job at a small office just miles away. Occasionally, he asked me general questions about myself, like where I was from, had I ever been here or there, which I answered monosyllabically when possible.

I stood up to use the bathroom and swayed from the alcohol. When I returned, Rudy's face was lined with concern. "Claire," he said. "Are you okay?"

"Sure," I said again. "I just—I haven't had anything to drink for a while."

"Then you definitely shouldn't have any more," he said. He placed another bill on the bar and gently touched my elbow, guiding me toward the door.

The air outside was hot and thick. The parking lot spun a little.

"Did you drive here?" Rudy asked, glancing at the vehicles in the parking lot.

"No," I lied.

"Well, can I give you a lift home?"

I looked at him for a long time. "No," I said. *I don't have a home,* I added silently. "I want to go somewhere with you."

His eyebrows shot up in surprise. "That's not why I was buying you drinks, you know, Claire," he said.

I smiled, something that felt unnatural to the contours of my face after the last two years. "I know that," I said. "Please. I want to go somewhere with you."

"Um, well, okay. But where? My apartment?"

I shook my head, and the ground tipped up ninety degrees and back. Rudy caught my shoulder so I wouldn't fall. "No, not your apartment," I said. "Where else can we go?"

He didn't say anything for a while, and before he spoke again, it was obvious the suggestion was couched in much hesitation. "Well, there's a motel just down that way, past those trees about a quarter mile."

I smiled again and leaned my body into his. "Let's walk," I said.

Rudy wrapped a hand around my upper arm to steady me as we walked. The motel was small, with shabby brown siding and ten identical doors. I waited outside as Rudy paid for a room. We were in number six. The room had only a bed, a nightstand, and a small bathroom off to the side, hardly bigger than a closet. I peed with the door open, and when I came out, Rudy stood awkwardly at the foot of the bed, hands thrust into his pants pockets.

I went over and stood in front of him. I smiled and pulled my dress over my head, dropping it beside us. I unhooked my bra and he flushed deeply.

"Wow, Claire," he said.

"Kiss me, Rudy," I said, enjoying the sound of a stranger's name on my lips.

He held my face and kissed me sloppily, his tongue flopping around in my mouth. I plopped onto the bed and kicked off my shoes. He looked down on me in raw amazement. "Come on," I said. "You have something, don't you?"

"Well, yeah, I . . ." He reached into his back pocket, pulled out a wallet, and from that a condom, which looked as if it had spent the better part of its shelf life in his wallet.

I had only to gesture for him to come closer, and he was fumbling at the front of his pants. He did not take off his clothes. He climbed on top of me, making a haphazard attempt to feel between my legs and graze my breasts with his hands. It took less than a minute. I felt nothing.

He lay beside me afterward, panting. "Wow, Claire," he said again. "Wow."

I said nothing, did not even look at him. I looked at the water-stained drop ceiling and felt the full satisfaction of my betrayal. Another man had touched me—finally. Another man had been inside my body. I was no longer only my captor's reluctant treasure.

In minutes, Rudy was snoring beside me. I pulled my clothes back on, not bothering to wash the smell of his sweat or sweet-and-sour breath from me. I watched him sleep for a while and wondered what I would do next. Some part of me realized that I could go home now. I was free. But the prospect of taking that road terrified me almost as much as returning to the shack in the woods with the dead girl in the backyard. I couldn't tell why.

I tore a page from the Bible that sat on the end table and fished a pen out of Rudy's pocket. On it, I wrote only my name—my real name—and my former address. Perhaps he would go there and look for me. Perhaps he would tell my family he had seen me, and they would know that I was alive, even if I could not return home.

I walked out into the cool night air, my feet padding silently along the road. I sauntered back to the truck, embraced and tightly held by the darkness all around me, filled with the sounds of cicadas and night-flying birds. I was almost to the door of the truck when I saw him. His car was on the other side, and he was pacing back and forth between the vehicles, his face set in angry lines, fingers drumming madly against his thighs.

He flew around the front of the truck and grabbed the back of my neck. I thought I saw tears streaking his face, but it was too dark to tell.

He turned me around to face him and delivered a sharp uppercut into my middle. He pulled me up by my hair, opened the truck door, and stuffed me inside, pushing me to the passenger's side so he could climb in after me. I curled into the pain in my stomach and pelvis as he drove back to the wooden house. He dragged me inside and into my room, where he threw me to the floor.

Venom dripped from his mouth with every word, and spittle flew as he kicked me.

"You disgusting, filthy little whore," he said. "You dirty, disgusting slut. How could you do this to me? To us? I gave you everything. I've done everything you've asked, given you all that you asked for and this, this is how you show your gratitude?"

He spit on my curled form. Dimly, I thought of reminding him that I had asked for only two things: my freedom and books. I had only books. In fact, he had given me only one thing I'd asked for. I thought it went without saying that I would give any amount of books for my freedom.

"You're disgusting," he said, his voice husky and moist.

He bound me hand and foot and left me tied to nothing, lying in a spit-soaked heap on the bedroom floor.

He did not return for several days.

When he returned, he was crying. Like a small child. He sprawled on the floor and pulled my head into his lap. He poured water over my lips, and I tried to drink it as fast as it came but ended up choking on most of it.

He stroked my face and hair and rocked me back and forth. "I'm sorry, my sweet Lynn," he said. "I'm so sorry. I should not have blamed you. It's my job to keep you safe and I didn't. It's all my fault."

"What are you talking about?" I said, my voice only a whisper.

"I've made it right," he said, rocking, rocking, rocking. "I've made it right."

"I don't know what you're saying," I said.

"I've done it," he said. "I've made it right. You'll see."

He carried me into the living room, my small body crushed against his, my head lolling like the broken stem of a heavy flower on his shoulder. He lifted my chin gently and turned my head toward the front door so I could see what he'd done. He had to gather me up like a pile of falling leaves when the dry heaves set in.

"I've made it right," he said softly, lowering me to the floor.

Rudy had been bludgeoned to death. At the sight of his body, I swayed back and forth on my hands and knees. My stomach had nothing in it to expel. My body tried to turn inside out. Then the room expanded so that everything in it seemed miles away. It snapped back, slingshotting toward me and knocking me to my side. I felt the boulder of panic crushing my chest. There was no air, but there was blackness. I let it take me.

Rudy took his place in the backyard next to Sarah. I watched the dirt cover his body, one shovelful at a time until all that was left was a slightly raised mound of freshly turned earth. Now in my hell I had my own private cemetery of people whose lives had been taken in my name. A fictitious name, a name given to me by a man who had taken by force everything that mattered.

Each night I sat in the darkness—forehead pressed against my window—and held vigil over the two unmarked, unconsecrated graves.

I could never go back. I understood that finally.

I had a new fantasy. In it, my captor left for work, or wherever he went when he was not devising innovative ways to twist my soul and body around his depravity. He did not return. Ever. Though I would have no way of knowing, I still imagined that he was killed in some random disaster. A car wreck, a fire, earthquake, flood, or some freak occurrence like being struck by lightning.

I hated him with an intensity that rocked my entire being but knew I could never kill him myself. I could never do what he did so easily and without compunction. Having seen the things I had, I knew that taking a life, even one as abhorrent as his, was not within my capabilities.

Each time he left the house, sometimes leaving me locked in my room but no longer binding me, I willed him not to return. I would pass my days reading and rereading the books he had brought. If I got out of the room, I would nourish myself until the house was emptied of its contents. Then if I were lucky, I would die. Maybe after a while someone would find me, and the mystery of my disappearance would be solved to some degree.

My family could lay me to rest, and they would never have to know all the things I knew. Perhaps they could live peacefully in that way. The bodies in the back might be found and identified, more mysteries finally laid to rest. Their own families could give them proper burials, and no one would know my part in their demise.

CHAPTER

TWENTY-SEVEN

Connor didn't believe a single thing Irene Geary had told him. He doubted she had knowledge about Claire's abduction, but she was definitely hiding something. He'd have to put a call out to the Phoenix PD in order to see if they could spare someone to make a house call. But first he dialed Noel Geary's number.

She answered on the fourth ring. Connor identified himself, explained that he was investigating the disappearance of a woman named Claire Fletcher and the possible connection between her and a former tenant of Irene Geary, who'd lived at 1653 Larkspur Road in 1995.

"A tenant?" Noel said. "We never had any tenants. Who told you that?"

"Your mother," Connor replied.

Humorless laughter, sharp and derisive filtered through the phone line. "Is that what she's telling people now?"

Connor leaned his elbows on his desk and pressed the receiver close to his face. "You did not have a tenant at that address at that time?" he asked.

"He wasn't a tenant," Noel said. "He was her boyfriend."

The spiral of excitement that had fizzled when Irene Geary hung up on him suddenly exploded, sending a buzz through Connor's body.

"Her boyfriend?"

"Yeah," Noel said. "One of many. He was a freak, a real weirdo, that guy. I never saw him again after we moved, but it wouldn't surprise me if he did something disgusting to some unsuspecting female."

"Do you remember his name?" Connor asked.

"Sure," Noel said. "It was, uh, Rod something. Rod . . ." She trailed off. "Shit, I can't remember his last name, but I could probably think of it if I tried."

"Ms. Geary, would you be willing to meet in person?" Connor asked.

"Sure," she said. "There's lots I can tell you about that perv. But I gotta work tonight. You could come by tomorrow at like, noon."

"That would be great," Connor said.

"You got my address?" she asked.

"Uh, yeah," Connor replied.

"I'm on the second floor, number twenty-nine. Just knock."

"Great," Connor said. "I'll see you then."

Connor felt like he might be propelled right out of his chair by the adrenaline coursing at warp speed through his body. Whatever Noel Geary knew could very well break the case wide open. Connor tried to quell his excitement. Yes, Noel Geary could break the case, but it was also possible that the lead could go nowhere. Plus he had a whole day to kill before he met with Farrell.

Connor spent the day at his desk. He tried Irene Geary several times, but she did not answer. He threw himself into paperwork. It wasn't nearly as exhilarating as what he normally did in his capacity as a detective, but it kept him occupied. He left the office at six. Night closed in as he pulled into his driveway.

Connor locked his car door. He heard a noise coming from the back of his house. The impending darkness cast dusky shadows over the street. Connor stood perfectly still and listened. He heard something muffled and quick, but he could not identify it. Normally he would have dismissed it as a neighbor's escaped dog or cat, but tonight Claire's words hung heavy on his mind.

You might be in danger.

Slipping his hand inside his jacket, he drew his gun and stepped quietly to the side of the house. He lifted the latch on the wire fence and opened it wide enough for his body to slide through. He stayed off the cement path that led to the backyard, padding his steps in the grass. He kept close to the house, gun held in both hands, pointed slightly downward.

It was darker toward the back of the house, and Connor paused long enough for his eyes to adjust before turning the corner into his backyard.

There was a figure cut from the shadows, tall and solid. The man's back was turned to Connor. He peered through the sliding glass doors, seemingly unaware of Connor or the gun trained at the center of his back. Connor took two steps forward and said, "Turn around with your hands in the air."

The man's hands shot up over his head, and he turned immediately. "Parks, it's me," he said.

Connor squinted. "Mitch?"

"I'm stepping toward you," the man said.

Connor backed up one step, and out of the shadows stepped Mitch Farrell, hands held aloft, grinning. Connor sighed and lowered his weapon. "Farrell, what the hell are you doing? I could have shot you."

Farrell looked as relieved as Connor felt. He put his hands down and shook his head. "I'm too old for this shit," he said. "You almost scared the piss out of me."

Connor holstered his weapon. "I scared you? Farrell, I thought you were breaking into my house. I could have killed you."

The two men walked around to the front of the house. "I just got here before you. I told you I wanted to check out your security measures," Farrell explained.

Connor let them in the front door and flicked on the living room lights. "By skulking around in the dark and peeking in my windows?"

Farrell trailed Connor into the kitchen. "Sorry," he said. "But you know this place really isn't that secure."

Connor opened his fridge. He handed Farrell a beer before popping one open himself and guzzling down nearly half of it in a single gulp. He looked at Mitch. "Not that secure? If I had put a bullet in you, you'd be singing a different tune."

Mitch rolled his eyes and took a drink. "Yeah, a funeral dirge. I'm serious, Parks. You don't even have a security system. Anyone with half a brain could get in here."

Connor took off his jacket and hung it on the back of one of the kitchen chairs. "Without alerting me?" he said.

Mitch held a hand up in the air. "Since you're the one with the gun, I'm not going to argue with you, but I'm going to call the home security outfit I use and have them come out here."

"You really think that's necessary?"

"We don't know what we're dealing with here," Mitch said. He frowned and looked at Connor from under a thick furrow of brows.

"What is it?" Connor said.

"I checked out Teplitz, Speer, and Randall today," Mitch said.

The statement held no trace of menace, but Mitch's tone was foreboding enough to make the hairs on the back of Connor's neck stand up. He gulped down the rest of his beer and retrieved another from the fridge.

"I found out something today too," he said. "Come in the other room."

Farrell followed him into the dining room. He gasped when Connor flicked on the lights, taking it in. "Wow," he said. "You're a one-man task force."

Connor managed a grin. "I know."

They sat at the table, and Mitch fingered the pages from Claire's file spread before him. Connor rolled up the sleeves of his shirt and put his elbows on the table. He took a long drink before looking at Mitch. "What did you find out?" he asked.

Mitch cocked his head to one side. "It doesn't look good," he said. "I couldn't find any of them, but I found their next of kin."

Again, Connor felt icy fingers stirring the hairs on the nape of his neck. "Next of kin?"

"Teplitz disappeared two days after visiting the Fletchers, almost a week after he reported spending the night with Claire. He was living in an apartment just outside the city, working for some computer place. He went to work, drove home, parked his car out front, and was never seen or heard from again.

"Apartment was undisturbed. Didn't look like he'd even been in there after work. The door was still locked. The employer called his emergency contact when he didn't show up for work three days in a row. His mother drove up there, had the super let her in. Nothing. Filed a missing persons report, asked around, but no one reported seeing anything suspicious or out of the ordinary. Nothing in or on the car. He just disappeared. Vanished. No sign of him for the last eight years."

Connor's limbs felt chilled. He wasn't sure he wanted to know any more but asked anyway. "Martin Speer?"

Mitch took a long sip of beer. "Speer's house burnt to the ground two months after he visited the Fletchers. He was asleep in his bed. The cause of the fire couldn't be determined, but arson could not be ruled out."

"And Randall?" Connor asked, swallowing hard over the lump that had formed in his throat.

"Another vanishing act," Mitch said. "Three weeks after he went to the Fletcher home, he disappeared. Left his house, told his roommate he was going to the bar, never got there, although his car was found in

136

the parking lot. No one in the bar saw him. No one remembers seeing him in the parking lot or seeing anyone else around that time. Car was fine, no sign of a struggle, assault, or homicide. When he didn't come home after three days, the roomie calls his work to see if he showed up there. They hadn't seen him either. Roomie calls the family; they file a missing persons. Nothing turned up."

"You didn't hear about any of this before?" Connor said.

Mitch shrugged. "Hey, I interviewed them, turned them over to the guys who worked the original case. With the exception of Speer, who was older, they all cleared as suspects immediately. They produced no real leads, and I couldn't be sure that the woman they'd met was really Claire. It didn't seem important to follow up."

Connor ground his teeth together and closed his palms around the cool, sweaty beer bottle in front of him. Farrell was right about the three men producing no leads. Even if he had followed up before and the men had been around to talk to him, it was doubtful Farrell would have discovered anything useful; however, the fact that now two of them were missing and one was dead seemed rather significant.

Mitch studied Connor over his upturned beer bottle as he drained the rest of the fluid from it. "Bet that home security outfit doesn't sound like such a bad idea now, huh?"

Connor rubbed his face with both hands and then swept them through his hair. "Holy shit," he said.

He tried to think clinically, like he would on any other case that did not personally involve him. "So we have three guys, all meet Claire, spend the night with her in a motel. She leaves the address, they go to the house, find out she's missing. They talk to you, talk to the police. Once they're in the clear with the authorities, they go on with their lives, probably wishing they'd never heard of Claire Fletcher. Next thing anyone knows is they're gone, either missing or dead."

"Yep," Mitch said. "I think we can assume that now we know what Claire meant when she said you might be in danger."

"How does this guy know who she's seen?" Connor said.

Mitch shrugged. "Who knows? Maybe he's keeping an eye on her or maybe he is keeping tabs on the Fletcher family residence. Maybe both. Who the hell knows? I think you should come stay with me till we figure this thing out."

Connor shook his head. "No. No way. I'm staying put."

Mitch leaned over the table and pointed a finger toward Connor. "Whoever this piece of human garbage is, he's smooth. Either he's the luckiest damn criminal in the world or he knows what the hell he's doing. We shouldn't be taking any chances."

"Duly noted," Connor replied. "But I have an advantage those other poor schmucks didn't. I know he's coming. I say we rig the house and let the bastard come."

Mitch grunted. "Don't be an idiot, Parks. I want to get this guy as much as you do, but I don't want to get killed doing it, and I don't want you to get killed either."

"Farrell, I'm a professional. I deal with this kind of scum every day."

"Not the kind that knocks on your door," Farrell pointed out.

"I'm firm on this," Connor said. "I'm staying put. Besides, after tomorrow, we might be able to knock on his door."

Mitch's eyebrows shot up. "Tell me," he said.

Connor recounted his phone calls to the Geary women and told Mitch about his appointment with Noel Geary at noon the next day.

"I'm riding shotgun," Farrell said in a tone that brooked no objections. "Did you run the area for addresses belonging to guys with the first name Rod?"

Connor sighed. "Yeah, for the better part of the day. I tried Rod, Roderick, Rodney, every variation I could think of and got nothing. But I think we'll have a better handle on it after we talk to Geary."

Mitch nodded.

"Where'd you get with the phone records?" Connor asked.

"I have a call out but it's going to take some time," Farrell said. "Then again, the way things are shaping up, we may not need it. We could break this whole thing wide open by Monday."

Connor nodded, then frowned. "Monday," he groaned.

"What about it?"

"The review board. I'm going on the spit," Connor said.

He told Mitch about the shooting two weeks prior and about the case that led up to it. As he spoke, the memory of Claire in his arms, soft and intoxicating, asking to hear the details of the gruesome crimes teased his brain.

"Well, it's not the best case of officer-involved shooting," Mitch said. "But you might be okay. Just act properly remorseful. You took a human life. Justice should never reside in the hands of a single man, even if he is an officer of the law. The guy had rights. He should have had his day in court. Protect and serve and all that crap."

"Guy evaded arrest twice, had a long list of priors—which included possession of illegal firearms. He was hiding in the closet, which meant he was already aware that the police were on the premises. He went to draw a weapon, you made a call, it just happened to be the wrong one, et cetera. Show them you're sorry, and they ought to cut you some slack."

Connor nodded along with Farrell's suggestions, thinking that none of Farrell's words coming from his lips would be a lie. It felt good knowing that the rapist was off the streets forever. No chance of acquittal or appeal on some technicality. No chance of parole. He would never hurt another person. A small part of him felt gratified—the part that still had nightmares about the battered faces of the victims, the horrible accounts of their ordeals told from trembling lips wet with tears. On the days that he thought about those women, whose trust in everything safe and good in the world had been shattered, whose bodies seemed to be made up more of fear than of flesh and blood, Connor felt good about the shooting.

But those moments were not as plentiful as the ones in which he felt guilty and ashamed.

Mitch looked around the room and sighed. "You want me to stay here tonight?" he asked.

Connor shook his head. "No," he said. "I appreciate the offer, but I'm okay for tonight."

They talked for another half hour before Connor walked Mitch to the door. Mitch turned to him before leaving. "Sure you don't want me to stay?" he asked.

Connor smiled. "Thanks, but no. I'm a big boy, Farrell."

Clearly uncomfortable leaving Connor alone, but realizing that he couldn't change the younger man's mind, Mitch rolled his eyes. "Fine. But that's a standing offer. You have my contact information."

"Yes, I do. I'll see you tomorrow at eleven a.m. sharp," Connor said.

As Connor closed the door behind him, Mitch called over his shoulder, "Lock that door!"

Connor laughed and turned the lock. He moved through the house, straightening up and mentally ticking off the questions he'd ask Noel Geary the next day. He tried to focus on the upcoming interview, but the thought of Teplitz, Speer, and Randall all having left the world in one way or another shortly after meeting Claire kept creeping back into his mind.

"Protect yourself," Claire had said.

Although Connor knew more about crimes, both random and premeditated, than anyone should have to know, he wasn't one of these safety nuts whose home security measures teetered past the line of good sense into paranoia.

All Connor had were the locks on his windows and doors and his guns.

"I need a dog," Connor muttered to himself.

He'd always wanted to get a dog. A big one that he could count on to deter burglars and other unsavory characters, but Denise had never liked dogs. For now, he'd have to settle for guns and knives. He had two handguns he used for target practice, and a rifle, which he placed strategically around the house in places that would not be readily observable to visitors. He would keep his department-issued Glock 9mm on him when he was in his task-force room or bedroom.

He had a few hunting knives he had purchased over the years mostly as collector's items, but he figured they would pierce an intruder just as easily as they did a FedEx box if such an occasion presented itself. Connor used Denise's old Tupperware to fashion sleeves, which he nailed to the undersides of four pieces of furniture. The knives fit easily into the plastic sleeves, handles protruding from the edge of the sheaths for easy access. He placed one sheath on the underside of the dining room table, one on the underside of the kitchen table, another on the underside of one of the bathroom shelves, and the final knife he secured to the underside of his bed. From where he slept, he could roll over and easily draw the knife, if necessary.

An overzealous German shepherd would probably have been less complicated, but Connor did take some perverse satisfaction in shredding Denise's Tupperware.

Finally, Connor set his alarm clock and lay down to rest, his Glock on the nightstand within easy reach. He had worried that he would be unable to sleep after hearing Mitch's news, starting at every sound, afraid to drift off lest an attacker materialize out of the shadowy corners of his bedroom and kill him while he slumbered, but he was exhausted and dozed off within minutes.

CHAPTER
TWENTY-EIGHT

The edge of the counter dug into my hip as I peered through my kitchen window. I had turned off my lights hours ago. Now I stood in the dark listening to the symphony of mockingbirds nestled in the trees around the property. Across the road, there was no shuffle in the curtains. No sign that either of them was watching.

Silently, I padded to the door and slipped through a narrow opening so I didn't unleash a creak from its rickety frame. In black, silent increments, like the stealthy growth of a plant, I made my way across the street. Earlier that day I had chosen markers, places to crouch and wait to see if the lights in the wooden house flicked on or if a pair of eyes appeared in the corner of a window. I counted, watching the house so intently that whirling dark shapes seemed to surround it. Then I moved slowly to the next marker.

After an eternity, I stood at the side of the house, beneath a living room window. I did not move. My ears were tuned to any sound within. My body melted into the darkness of the night. The rhythm of my breathing fell into time with the steady, imperceptible motions and sounds of the wilderness.

I had watched them the last few days, the ugly sensation in my stomach building inexplicably. Twice more they had argued on the porch of the wooden house. Twice more he had flown off in a spray of dirt and gravel, leaving Tiffany half pouting, half scowling after him. Still I could not hear what they were saying.

Earlier in the day he had been outside, circling his car. Then he began the meticulous cleansing ritual he had specially crafted for the inner sanctum of his vehicle. His obsessive-compulsive tendencies were in high gear. I could not fathom what it might be, but between his recent behavior and Tiffany's pouting, I knew something was going on in that house.

I didn't know for sure whether Tiffany had witnessed me come and go the night I met Connor. I had to be certain. So I waited until after dark to creep across the road and spy, but after a half hour, I'd heard nothing.

Using my markers, I returned to the trailer in the same fashion I had left, periodically glancing behind me in case one of them woke and looked out the window. Once safely inside my trailer, I dropped to the floor and sighed. I thought about confronting Tiffany again but knew it would only make her more suspicious and more likely to rat me out—even if it was for something she made up.

For many years, Tiffany had been both a curse and a blessing.

CHAPTER
TWENTY-NINE

1998

During the third year of my captivity, Tiffany came to the wooden house like a new bride. He had been gone for several days, and when he returned, she followed him through the door, lapping at his heels, questioning my presence and shooting me looks of disdain.

From the streets of Portland, where she had lived since she left home at eleven, she came to rule his house like a queen. She was a tiny queen. Much smaller than me. In spite of starvation, beatings, and malnutrition, I had grown taller and begun to fill out. The soft places on my body became harder, angles making themselves known. My breasts grew, full and round. Had I had the courage to look into the mirror he had put in my room, I would have seen that I had become a woman.

Perhaps that is why he went in search of her. She was his crowning achievement. A pet he did not have to chain, beat, starve, or drown. She was thin with the gangly movements of adolescence. Her body had not yet relinquished its awkwardness, though she feigned womanhood at every turn. Tiffany was not her real name. He had christened her with a new name as he had me.

She did not seem to mind. A new name for a new life.

He had not bothered to wash the dirt or grime from her, and it caked in every slim fold of her skin. Her hair was stringy and oily, a lackluster brown. She arrived wearing a small green shirt that exposed her pale stomach and cutoff khaki pants that retained little of their original color, darkened by muck and filth. Her skin was sallow from lack of nutrition, and it stretched taut across her bones except for the two small buds where her breasts had begun to develop.

She stood over me, clutching a green canvas bag, her thin mouth coiled. She talked about me as if I were a deaf mute or a piece of furniture that was not to her liking.

"Who is this?" she said. For him, she reserved her most whiny tone.

He smiled. "This is Lynn," he said.

"Who's she?"

"She's your sister."

"I don't have a sister."

"You do now."

"You said it would just be the two of us."

He put his hands on her arms and smiled lovingly. "Oh, darling, it is the two of us. Lynn won't be any trouble at all. You'll see. You'll be sisters. We're going to be a family."

Her dark eyes looked down on me once more, beady in the baby-fat roundness that hugged her face even at her thinnest. "This isn't what we talked about," she said.

He bent down and kissed her, his tongue probing her small mouth, making loud, wet sounds that turned my stomach. When he pulled back, her face was flushed, and she smiled at him. He touched her cheek.

"Oh, my Tiffany," he said. "I am going to make you happy here. You'll see. You just get settled in. This is your home now. I'm going to make you something to eat."

She watched him leave the room.

"What's your real name?" I asked.

"What's it to you?"

I shrugged.

"So what are you—like his girlfriend?" Tiffany asked.

"Hardly."

She thrust her chin out and crossed her arms. "Yeah, well, I'm his girlfriend now, and if you know what's good for you, you'll stay out of my way."

"Where are you from?"

"Portland, not that it's any of your business."

"You left your family for him?"

"No. I was living on the street. How 'bout you? You ever hook?"

"Hook?"

She rolled her eyes. "Are you dumb or something? You know, have sex for money."

"You're a hooker?"

"No, I only do it when I need something."

"How old are you?"

"What's it to you?"

"You seem really young."

"I'm not that young. I mean I'm thirteen. I'm not a little kid, you know."

But she had the face of a child. Dirt-smudged and gaunt but still the face of a child. I stared at her. "Is he paying you?" I asked.

She smiled. "No. He asked me to come home with him."

"Why?"

"He's in love with me. He told me."

"No. Why would you come home with him?"

She shrugged. "Why not? He treats me good. I get a whole house, and I don't have to work. All I have to do is fuck him sometimes."

I leaned forward and vomited on her sneakers.

She jumped back and shrieked. I was still retching when he flew into the room. She pointed at me. "That fucking bitch threw up all over me," she cried.

Pulling me by my hair, he dragged me to my room and thrust me inside, locking the door. I fell to my knees, my body still heaving. When the nausea finally subsided, I got into bed and burrowed under the covers.

In the hollow place carved out of my insides, a germ of shame began to grow. It grew outward in concentric circles and multiplied. It was obvious to me that Tiffany would never be an ally. In her I would find no comfort, no solace, no escape, and no commiseration. But she did offer me something. Something that shamed me to my core, filling in the places he had pared down and whittled away to nothing. She diverted his lascivious attention away from me.

For the most part, the reign of Tiffany turned me into another kind of prisoner. I was now in solitary confinement. I lived in my little room with the fading flowery comforter and piles of books, which she liked to tear and burn in the grass outside of the house when she was most fitfully agitated by my presence. Any glance at me or smile or any small gesture from him that Tiffany deemed inappropriate earned me days in solitary confinement.

She had talons, long and sharp, and she dug them into the charred mass of his soul, seeking to possess him entirely. This was the salvation that shamed me. During the nights I heard them through the walls. She slept in his bed, a willing partner in his perversity, and sometimes I wept with relief that it was not me.

CHAPTER THIRTY

Noel Geary's apartment building was in a less effulgent part of the city where the streets were unkempt and usually deserted during daylight hours. It filled up after nightfall with club hoppers and a melee of young people—college students and professionals looking to relieve the day's tension and find someone to take home for the night. The building was a three-story brick structure that lacked decor. A single set of steps led into a cramped foyer with two walls of metal mailboxes.

There was no elevator, so Connor and Mitch took the stairs to the second floor. Mitch knocked on the door to twenty-nine. A female voice yelled, "Just a minute."

Almost five minutes later, Noel swung the door open and said without preamble, "Page. That was his last name. Rod Page."

She looked from Mitch to Connor, her wide brown eyes taking him in from head to foot. "Who's your friend?" she said, directing the question to Mitch.

Mitch too looked at Connor. Connor smiled and raised a hand. "I'm Detective Parks," he said. He pointed at Mitch. "This is my associate, Mitch Farrell."

Noel did not take her eyes from Connor's frame. "Well, I'm a lucky girl today," she said. Then she spun on a bare heel and walked into the apartment, crooking a finger over her shoulder. "Come in," she said.

In spite of themselves, both men watched the pointedly seductive sway of her rear, which was barely covered by a pair of cutoff denim shorts that showed off her long tan legs. Connor pushed Mitch inside the apartment and closed the door behind him before Noel could turn around. Thick blonde hair cascaded down her back, and when she turned, her breasts bobbed under a tank top that left no doubt that she wasn't wearing a bra.

Noel was the kind of woman who could turn heads wearing a muumuu—and she knew it. She smiled at the two men and gestured to a ratty maroon couch propped up against the wall. "Sit," she said.

The living room was cozy. Connor and Mitch took up most of it. They situated themselves side by side on the couch, which faced a long, oval coffee table and a makeshift entertainment center composed of a small dresser, television, and VCR. Noel carried a green plastic lawn chair from one of the other rooms and placed it across from them. She sat in it as if it were a velvet-cushioned throne and crossed her bare legs, revealing a firm expanse of bronze-colored thigh.

"Sorry about the furniture," she said. She waved a hand, indicating the rest of the apartment. "This place is a shithole. I'm trying to finish school, but I have to pay the bills too."

Mitch cleared his throat. "What are you studying?" he asked.

"Communications," she said. "I want to go into journalism."

Connor looked at the strong lines of her face, high cheekbones, and pouty lips. He could instantly picture her as a news anchorwoman, her face pasted on city billboards advertising some channel's hot nightly news team.

"Mind if I smoke?" she asked.

Connor shrugged. "It's your place," he said.

She smiled at him as if they'd just shared a private joke. Mitch shot Connor a sideways glance. When Noel went to the kitchen to retrieve her cigarettes, Connor looked at him and shrugged helplessly. Mitch simply shook his head.

She returned to her chair and from under a pile of mail and magazines fished an ashtray from the coffee table. "So," she said, lighting up and inhaling deeply without taking her eyes from Connor. "What do you want to know about Mr. Rod Page?"

Mitch pulled out a notepad and pen to take notes while Connor took the lead with questions. "We'd like to hear everything you can tell us about this guy," Connor said. "Let's start with the first time you met him."

Noel nodded. "Well, he was my mom's boyfriend. I never knew my dad. My mom had this habit of finding the most vile and abusive men within a fifty-mile radius and then letting them move in so that when they beat her one too many times or cheated on her, we'd have to move just to be rid of them."

She took another drag on her cigarette and flicked ash into the ashtray, bending just enough to reveal her ample cleavage. "Those types aren't easy to get rid of. They're like roaches," she said. "I was twelve when she met Rod. I don't remember where they met or anything. I just remember he started coming around a lot. She thought he was the greatest thing she ever set eyes on. He would buy her flowers, come by and fix things around the house. All that shit none of those other assholes would even think of doing.

"Anyway, he was really creepy. I mean he looked normal enough, kind of nondescript—brown hair, brown eyes, about five nine. He was thin, just average if you know what I mean."

Both men nodded and Mitch jotted the description down.

"Did he have any identifying features?" Connor asked. "Birthmarks, moles, tattoos, piercings? Anything like that?"

Noel shook her head. "No. He was just plain. Plain as the day is long."

"What was it that made him creepy?" Mitch asked.

"I don't know," Noel said, grinding the butt of her cigarette into the ashtray before lighting another. "He was just weird. He was a little too quiet. He didn't talk much, and when he did, he always talked in the same tone. A monotone, I guess. Like nothing upset him or got him riled up. I never even heard him raise his voice. Oh, and he never laughed. He would smile this tight-lipped, creepy little smile, but he would never laugh. I think the thing that creeped me out the most was that he was always looking at me."

She crossed one arm under her breasts, jostling them upward against the thin fabric of her shirt. "Especially when my mom wasn't really looking or wasn't in the room. He'd just stand there and stare at me."

"You said he wasn't a tenant," Connor said. "But he lived with you?"

Noel rolled her eyes. "Biggest mistake my mom ever made," she said. "Yeah, he moved in after they were dating for like three months. My mom was all excited at first, but then after a while she got kind of depressed."

"Depressed?" Connor echoed.

"Yeah, well apparently they weren't having sex anymore. I heard her telling one of her friends on the phone that he couldn't get it up for her." She shuddered and hugged herself tighter. "Turned out it wasn't some physical thing like erectile dysfunction that could be fixed with pills."

Connor honestly didn't want to hear what came next, just as he never liked hearing the worst parts of the stories of victims he interviewed all the time, but he steeled himself. Someone had to listen to their stories and promise to do everything possible to deliver justice. Most days Connor was glad he could count himself among that group of people—but he still hated hearing the horror stories.

"What happened?" he asked.

Noel's coffee-brown eyes turned darker and her full lips twisted in on themselves. She looked away from Connor finally, and he was so intent on her words that he forgot to be relieved to be free from the heat of her gaze.

"He was a pervert," she said. "A pedophile. He could only get it up for little girls. Maybe for little boys too. I don't know, but he sure as hell got it up when he started sneaking into my room at night."

"What did he do?" Connor asked. Most of the time he would have taken a less direct route to finding out details, since victims of sex crimes were often reluctant to relive the horror of their ordeals, and rightfully so, Connor thought. But Noel seemed as if she wanted, maybe even needed, to talk about it.

Now she looked at Mitch, who held her gaze thoughtfully, compassion tempering the usually military affect of his face.

"Well, he started out climbing into bed with me and just touching me," she said. "He'd wait till my mom was asleep and he'd creep in and get under the covers with me. I never slept after the first time. I was always up, waiting to see if he would come or not. I didn't have a lock on my door. After a few times, I figured out how to wedge a chair under the knob and that stopped him for a while. He would just slip his hands under my pajamas and rub me—you know, my chest and between my legs."

Noel made a face of disgust. Goose bumps rose along the flesh of her arms and legs.

"Did he say anything?" Mitch asked.

"No," she said. "Not then. I kept pushing him away and telling him to stop. Back then I didn't know a whole lot. It wasn't something I was prepared for." She lowered her eyes, ashamed. "I kind of didn't know what to do."

Mitch nodded. "That's very common, Ms. Geary."

She gave him a shy smile, which lasted only until she spoke again. "Plus, I felt really dirty and gross, you know?"

Mitch and Connor nodded in unison.

"I mean it just felt so . . . dirty." She used the word *dirty* again as if it was a curse, her voice low and throaty.

"Ms. Geary," Mitch said, his voice soothing, as if he were speaking to a child. "You have nothing to be ashamed of. You were a child. What he did to you was wrong and certainly not your fault. Most children do not know how to respond to such things and that's okay—children are not supposed to find themselves in that situation."

"Yeah," she said, as if she wasn't quite sure she believed him.

"So when you started putting the chair beneath the doorknob, did the abuse stop?" Mitch asked.

She shook her head. "For a while. Then it started again when my mom was at work. She didn't get home for about two hours after I got home from school—and he was there. He was always there. I don't remember him ever having a job. Anyway, he would corner me in the living room or bedroom. He would take my clothes off and touch me. He kept saying he was doing it because he loved me and he wanted to make me feel good, but all I ever felt was disgusting. I told him I was going to tell my mom and that she would make him stop, but he said that she wouldn't believe me.

"He said he was the best guy my mom had ever gone out with, and I knew that was true 'cause she said it all the time. He said she would never believe that he would do anything untoward to me. That's the word he used. *Untoward.* I had to look it up in the dictionary."

Her eyes narrowed. "He was a real fucking sicko," she said. "He kept saying that we had to keep our love a secret because other people wouldn't understand—like I wanted him to grope me and stick his nasty fingers in me. I told him that my mom would believe me, even though by that time I wasn't totally sure. I was almost as afraid of telling her as I was of him molesting me all the time because I kept thinking, *What will I do if she doesn't believe me?* I couldn't face that."

"It's a tough spot to be in," Mitch said. "Unfortunately, there are many parents who don't believe their children or choose not to believe them when faced with the prospect that someone they love, someone

153

they have welcomed into their home, is hurting their children in the worst possible way. That doesn't make it right, though."

Noel smoothed her hands over her thighs. Blonde locks fell over her shoulders, partially blocking her face. "Yeah," she said. "I knew this girl in my school back then who said her pastor was screwing her—she was my age. She told everyone and nobody believed her. Nobody. Not her parents, not her grandparents, not our guidance counselor, or any of our teachers. All that guy had to do was deny it and everyone bought it. Five years later, the police caught him doing some eleven-year-old girl in the back of his car and he went to prison. Then all of a sudden, everyone realized that that girl might have been telling the truth."

"Did you ever try to tell anyone?" Mitch asked.

"No. Well, I tried to tell my mom a few times, but I didn't know how to say it. I was so afraid she wouldn't do anything that I never really got past the words, 'Mom, I have something to tell you.' So it kept happening. He went from touching me to touching himself while he touched me. He didn't have any problems getting it up when he was being a big, disgusting pervert. After a while, he would make me blow him. That was the worst. I had heard girls at school talking about it, although I don't think any of them had actually done it at the time. There I was, thirteen and having to suck this guy's dick when I got home from school. Then my mom would come home and he would be all sweet and pleasant with her like he couldn't do a thing wrong."

"Did your mom ever walk in during one of these incidents?" Mitch asked.

Noel smiled, a delightfully wicked smile. "Better," she said. "The day he actually tried to fuck me, she came home early from work and saw him on the couch, trying to stick his cock in me. He was rock-hard too, so it was pretty clear at that point why he couldn't get it up for her. He liked kids."

"What did your mother do?" Mitch asked.

"She beat the shit out of him. I never saw her like that. I mean all those assholes she dated before used to knock her around, and she didn't do a damn thing but take it and then cry all night long. But that day, she didn't even put down her bag. She was on top of him so fast I barely had a chance to get off the couch and away from him. She just kept hitting him and hitting him. It took him a few minutes to get her off him. Then she just stood there, looking like a wild animal. Her hair was all messed up, and her clothes were rumpled. She told him to get out.

"Then he started in on this thing about how him and I were in love and we were going to be together forever and she couldn't stop it—all this really sick shit. She didn't buy a word of it. She told him to get out again, and he said he wasn't leaving without me. Then she broke a lamp over his head. He laid there moaning while she got me dressed and then we left."

"Where did you go?" Mitch asked.

"For the first couple of nights, we went to a hotel. It seemed like she didn't know what to do. She asked me a few questions, like how long it was going on, and why I didn't tell her and all that shit. I know she went back there a couple of times to try and get him to leave but he wouldn't. So then we went to stay with one of her friends until she could get him out of the house."

"Your mother never called the police?" Connor asked, feeling it was safe to rejoin the conversation now that the worst parts were over.

"No. Never. I thought she would, you know? But she didn't. At the time, I didn't really care. I was just happy to be away from him. But looking back, I wish she had. I mean it wasn't right. God knows what he's done since then, how many other girls he's done things to."

"What did your mother tell her friend when the two of you moved in there?" Connor asked.

Noel shrugged. "I don't know, but I know she didn't tell her about him being a pervert. She made up some story. We really never talked about it after that, not to each other, not to anyone. Anytime someone asked her what happened with that guy, she made up some story."

"Did you ever go back to the house?" Mitch asked.

"No. I never did. He lived there for almost six months, though. She couldn't get him to leave. Finally, when she told him she was selling the house and people would be coming by to look at it, he took off. Just like that. There one day, gone the next. She went, got our stuff, and we moved to Arizona."

"Do you get along well with your mother?" Connor asked.

Noel laughed. "Not so much," she said. "I moved back out here for school to get away from her. I mean we still talk on the phone, but I'm happier when she's not around."

Connor and Mitch asked her a few more questions about Rod Page, Mitch taking notes furiously. They thanked her for her time and for talking with them, especially since the subject matter was not easy for her to speak about. The session seemed to take something out of her, cast a pall over her buoyant mood. She was quiet as she walked them to the door.

Connor turned to her once more before leaving. "Ms. Geary," he said. "Would you be willing to sit down with an artist and come up with a composite sketch of Page?"

Noel shrugged. "Sure. Why not?"

Connor handed her his card. "Thanks. I'll be in touch. Call me if you think of anything else."

CHAPTER

THIRTY-ONE

Outside, the two men stood on either side of Connor's car. They stood by their doors but made no move to get in. Connor looked at Mitch from across the vehicle's roof.

"That's quite a woman," Mitch said. "And I don't mean the way she looks."

"Yeah," Connor agreed. "I think that may be the first time she's ever talked about what happened to her."

Mitch frowned, deepening the lines in his face. "You think this is the guy who took Claire?"

Connor ground his teeth before answering. "He's looking pretty good. He was close by. I checked the address out the other day, and they had a garage. He would have been alone there for months. The car fits. Plus, the minute he heard people would be coming to look at the house, he left."

"And he was a grade A sicko."

Connor sighed and leaned his arms atop the car. "Well, Geary said that he thought they were in love with each other. That's what he told the mother. So the mother takes her away and he freaks out."

"That's probably what triggered it," Mitch said, placing his arms on the top of the car to mirror Connor. "He decided to go get him a new girl, one he could keep."

"Which would explain why he didn't kill Claire," Connor said.

They looked at each other, both distinctly uncomfortable. Mitch's eyes were watery, and for a moment Connor thought he might cry. "What he must have done to her," Mitch murmured.

Connor swiped a hand through his hair. "Yeah," he said. "You know, even if she could have come home, maybe she didn't want to. Not that she didn't want to get away from him, but maybe she was ashamed to face her family."

He thought of the victims of the rapist he had killed. He knew that for some women who suffered through sexual assaults or sexual abuse, facing the world again could be as traumatic as enduring the abuse.

Many times their families and friends, coworkers, and other acquaintances no longer knew how to act or what to say to them. Many rapes went unreported because it was just too difficult for the victims to tell their stories over and over again to hospital staff, police, attorneys, and then in court. Many victims who did go through the process of seeking justice described it as being raped all over again.

"But her family wouldn't have cared," Mitch said.

"It changes you, Mitch," Connor said. "I deal with rape and sex abuse victims all the time. It changes you. It's not pretty."

Mitch waved a hand. "I know, I know," he said.

"Do you? You worked homicide, right?"

"For a long time, but I worked my share of sex crimes."

"Well, I know this is hard to wrap your mind around because it's Claire—and she was like a niece to you—but I don't think this guy kept her for ten years just to look at her."

"You think he's still, you know, abusing her?"

Connor squinted. "I don't know. She's probably too old for him now. But obviously he still has some control over her, some claim on her, or she wouldn't be calling me to tell me to protect myself."

"You think he's got another girl now?"

"I don't doubt it. These guys don't stop. He snatched Claire and so far he's gotten away with it. There's nothing stopping him from doing it again."

"Man, this is a real shitstorm." Mitch tapped the roof of the car. "We should check out missing persons for girls between twelve and fifteen. You wanna try and find this guy while I do that?"

"Yeah," Connor said. "I need to get an artist out to Geary's place too."

"You know any forensic artists?"

Connor grinned sheepishly. "No. Can't say I do. There is someone the division uses now and then. I could find out who."

Mitch waved a hand. "Nah. I know someone. It's gonna cost close to a grand, though. Could be more. I doubt your department is going to pick up the tab on this since you're not even supposed to be working this case."

Connor shrugged. "I'll pay for it."

"Really?"

"Yeah. I'm a divorced workaholic. What do I have to spend my money on? It'll be a small price to pay if it helps crack the case."

Mitch stared at him for a long moment, a smile playing at the edges of his mouth. Finally, he said, "We'll split it then."

"All right," Connor said. "You check on missing girls and get me an artist. I'll see what I can dig up on Rod Page. I'll drop you off at your car, and I'll come by your office later when I've got something."

CHAPTER

THIRTY-TWO

1998

After our first conversation, I tried to pity Tiffany. I tried to imagine her as a baby, a toddler, a preschooler, unspoiled and rife with promise. What had happened to her that sent her down this ugly path to his bed?

As time wore on, I found I could no longer pity her. I hated her. I hated her not for reasons that she surmised, which had mostly to do with jealousy over him, but because she had chosen freely to live the life I had been forced into. I hated her because she had thrown away a girlhood I would have died to recapture.

I became a ghost in the house, only conjured back into form when the two of them needed me to cut a path through the mire of their bizarre liaison. When she felt his attention slipping away for even a moment, she would tune into my presence long enough to blame me for some transgression against her, for which he would punish me. My punishment placated her and jerked him back to her.

After a while, she discovered that refusing to fulfill his sexual fantasies was even more powerful than putting me in the cross fire between them. On those nights, he would suddenly remember me. He came to my room and tried to force himself on me. I had become stronger with growth and months without physical abuse so that, finally, I was able to fend him off. I think he came more to make her jealous than to fulfill his degenerate needs.

They professed their love for each other relentlessly, but their connection thrived on the warped, writhing entrails of jealousy more than anything else. It was music they danced to, a theater in which they acted out a tedious melodrama. I had only cameo roles. Mostly, I did not even speak.

I embraced my life as a sentient ghost. I endured their summons from a place far away, aware of them only as vague annoyances. I kept watch over the two graves outside my window and read what books Tiffany had left me again and again until the pages were dog-eared and the bindings loosened.

Still, Tiffany was an irritant. Like getting an eyelash in your eye. She was a paper cut on your index finger that wouldn't heal. She was the incessant twang of an alarm clock that you could never turn off. Sometimes she was a hot burner you accidentally placed a hand on. No amount of cold water could cool her.

She tested even his patience. I saw in his face sometimes that he questioned the decision he'd made to bring her home with him. In a way, I had been easier for him to deal with. I could be beaten into submission and chained to him. Tiffany, however, had to be placated. If he tried once to hit her, she would leave, and she fulfilled his ultimate fantasy—the child bride wholly in love with him.

Her campaign to exile me from her kingdom began almost the moment she arrived. One evening, the three of us sat at dinner. I ate silently and did not look at either of them.

"What's the matter with her?" Tiffany asked him, looking pointedly past me as if I were merely air, an unpleasant odor, or a stain on her tablecloth.

He set his fork down. "With whom?"

She stabbed her own fork in my direction. "Her. She don't say nothing."

He smiled. "Oh, Lynn has always been very quiet."

He didn't mention my litany of protests, my howled entreaties to be returned home, or the hours I'd spent screaming so long and loud that I could no longer tell when I had stopped.

"Is she dumb or something?"

"No."

"Retarded?"

"Tiffany," he said, gently admonishing.

She did not lower her eyes. "Well, she acts like it."

She resumed eating, shoveling forkfuls of food into her mouth as if at any second the feast before her might be snatched away.

I pictured her eating from a garbage can. He reached over and touched her forearm. "Slow down," he said. "From now on you will have all the food you could ever want."

At this, she was humbled. Her face was like broken glass when she beamed at him. "I want chocolate," she said.

"Anything you want, my darling." His words dripped saccharine over her sour demeanor.

He lavished her with anything she asked for. He would not allow her to leave the house, though she begged to go everywhere with him.

In the three and a half years he'd held me captive, he had never had a television. Now he installed one nearly the size of Tiffany. When he was gone, she languished in front of it, making lists of things she wanted, which she gleaned mostly from commercials.

One day I spied her latest list:

Sneekers
Wakman
Beretts
Makup
Joolree

She caught me standing with the list in my hand. She snatched it from me.

"What the hell do you think you're doing?" she asked.

I looked at her blankly. She settled onto the couch with her blanket and a box of half-eaten chocolates.

"I could teach you to spell," I said.

"I don't need you to teach me anything," she replied haughtily. "Besides, what do I need to spell good for?"

I shrugged.

"You think you're smarter than me 'cause you read all the time?"

Finding no response that might suit her mercurial nature, I shrugged again.

"Only retards stay in their room with their face in a book all day," she said.

She stretched, catlike, and smiled wickedly. "You can't even talk," she said. "How could you teach anyone anything?"

Still, I said nothing.

She picked a small, square chocolate from the box. Holding it between two fingers, she licked the edges of it. Then, eyes narrowed at me, she threw it. It pinged off my chest and fell to the floor. She laughed. Then her face hardened abruptly.

"Pick it up, retard," she commanded.

"What?" I said.

Her face creased. "I said pick it up, retard. I swear you're totally deaf sometimes."

"No," I said.

She plucked another brown square from the box and popped it into her mouth. She worked it around in her mouth, cheeks wiggling furiously. She spit it at me with a swift *tooft* sound. This time it left a dark-brown smudge on my shirt. She smiled, satisfied with her ingenuity, as though she had just created a new game. I suppose she had.

I turned silently and went back to my room. Later, she lamented to him that I had called her dumb. She also claimed that I had stolen her chocolates and ground them into the carpet one by one.

Sure enough, after I was chastised for being cruel and hurtful toward my sister, I looked at the carpet and there were big brown flaky splotches ground into its shabby orange fibers.

As he lectured me, I thought only of how Sarah's legs had dangled uselessly over the carpet, kicking the side of the couch with muted thuds as she fought desperately for air, eyes locked on mine in our mutual death.

Prior to the chocolate incident, I had thought only of her eyes, death opening her face into a wide yawn. Then the dirt filling her putty-thick mouth and clinging in tacky misshapen globules to her pupils.

That day I began to think of her feet. They were much smaller than mine. Dainty in perfectly white, virginal sneakers and white anklet socks circled by a black stripe. He had killed someone in this spot, and now he was worried about chocolate.

At Tiffany's insistence, he ordered me to clean the carpet, but I refused, even after he slapped and punched me and pressed my nose into one chocolate lump. I was confined to my room for several days, and when I was finally allowed back into the rest of the house, the stains were gone.

CHAPTER

THIRTY-THREE

Connor went directly to the division after dropping Mitch off. He held the piece of paper Mitch had given him with the name and descriptors of Rod Page. Not that Connor needed it. He wasn't likely to forget anything about the case.

Boggs and Stryker sat at their desks facing each other, both their heads bent over reports.

"Boy, you girls work a lot," Connor said as he approached.

They looked up at him in unison. "The same could be said for you," Stryker said. "For a desk jockey you sure are out a lot."

"You worried about the review board?" Boggs asked.

Connor had almost forgotten about it. "Yeah, I guess," he said.

"Fuck 'em," Stryker said. "Let those suits go storming a house one time looking for some asshole who'd shoot his own mother. They have no idea."

Boggs looked pointedly at Stryker, who was at least fifteen years Boggs's junior. "Checks and balances, Stryke. Checks and balances. Someone's gotta make sure we're not out there shooting off our guns like vigilantes."

Stryker looked appropriately admonished. Boggs turned to Connor. "What time does that start?"

Connor shrugged. "Nine, but I don't have to be there till noon. They're debriefing the other guys first."

Boggs looked serious. "We'll be there, man."

"Yeah, we'll be there," Stryker chimed in.

"Thanks," Connor said, encouraged by their support.

Connor sat at his desk, booted up his computer, and rolled up the sleeves of his white dress shirt. He and Mitch were both working on the assumption that Rod Page was still living in the state. If he wasn't, it would be far more difficult for Claire to come to the city in search of unwitting men and disappear before the night was through, particularly if Page was still monitoring her.

In addition, Mitch had pointed out that if Page had been kidnapping other girls since he'd snatched Claire, he might not want to risk taking them over state lines because then he'd be looking at federal charges.

Not that Page seemed particularly concerned about getting caught, Connor thought. He'd already molested Noel, abducted Claire, and in all likelihood murdered at least two of the men Claire had been with in the last ten years. Connor had an ugly, creeping suspicion that the fire that had killed Speer was not an accident either, which would make three murders. Besides that, if Noel had not been his first victim, who knew how many girls Page had victimized before he moved into the Geary household.

Connor worked for three hours before driving over to Mitch's office. They locked the front door and went to Mitch's back room, settling on the leather couch and spreading their respective printouts on the table.

"I have good news," Mitch said, bobbing up and down with excitement, like a large dog. "My artist friend is between jobs. She's over at Geary's place now working on a composite."

Connor smiled and patted Mitch's shoulder. "That's great. As soon as you have it let me know. We can talk about how best to use it once we've got a sketch."

"Sure thing," Mitch said. "What about you? What have you got?"

Connor frowned. "You're not gonna like it," he said.

Mitch's upper body sagged. "It's an alias, isn't it?"

Connor shrugged. "Hard to say, but I'm thinking yeah." He handed Mitch a sheet of paper. "There are two Rod Pages in the state. One is black so that rules him out. The other is only twenty-one. I pulled up both their driver's license photos and neither one fits the description."

He handed Mitch another sheet of paper. "There's one Roderick Page and one Rodney Page. Roderick is eighty-six years old, and he lives right here in the city. No good. Rodney Page is fifty years old, which is probably within the age range—Noel said her Rod Page was in his midthirties at the time she knew him, but she couldn't be entirely sure."

"So what's the catch?" Mitch asked. He was looking at the sheet Connor had just handed him with Rodney Page's driver's license photo on it. "He's a little gray but he fits."

Connor handed him another sheet. "No, he doesn't fit. The guy is a big research doctor for a pharmaceutical company on the south side. He's highly visible. He has a wife and two kids, and he's lived in the same house for more than twenty years. I checked back in the company's press release archives, and he was receiving some award in New York the week Claire was abducted. He's too stable."

Mitch frowned. "Okay," he said. "So the guy wasn't using his real name, which means he's probably got priors. Anything?"

Connor shook his head. "No. I checked the whole state for the last thirty years looking for priors on everything from forcible rape to indecent exposure for guys who would have been in his age range. I got nothing. But I did find this."

He handed Mitch a final sheet of paper. "This guy died in 1992. His name was Rod Page; he was thirty-three. Car accident."

"You think our guy was cruising the obits?"

"Claire's abductor? Probably. He may have had priors in other states or maybe just arrest records under his real name or other assumed names. He might have moved here about '92, looking for a new identity. The real Rod Page died in '92, and I'm betting Claire's abductor took over his identity."

"If Claire's abductor took over Rod Page's identity, then he might have tried to get a driver's license with it," Mitch said, eyes widening with excitement.

Connor shook his head and grimaced, extinguishing the flicker in the older man's eyes. "I already checked. Claire's abductor never renewed the driver's license in Page's name, so I couldn't get a photo. The DMV sent out a renewal form to a post office box registered in the city, but he never got the photo taken. But he did file taxes as Rod Page from the post office box until 1994."

"So we can find out where he worked," Mitch said.

"Yeah. It might take a couple of days to find out and interview the employers, but we're not dead in the water yet."

Mitch studied the sheets of paper Connor had given him. He pursed his lips, then spoke. "This guy has got to have priors," he said. "Why else do you go looking for a new identity? I mean, he moved in with Irene Geary in 1994, so he probably wasn't planning on abducting anyone at that time."

"He already had a twelve-year-old girl right there at home," Connor agreed.

"Did you check the violent crime database?" Mitch asked.

Connor nodded. "ViCAP? Yeah, but I haven't got any results back. But what about you? Find anything on missing persons?"

Mitch slid two sheets of paper across the table. "Okay, in the last ten years, there have been seven girls between the ages of twelve and seventeen." He tapped a finger midway down the list. "Now, two of them were thirteen, but they're listed as custodial interference, and the parent who took them is listed along with them. One was twelve and one fifteen, but those two are custodial interference as well.

"These two," Mitch continued, tapping a finger at the bottom of the list. "Sixteen and seventeen, are listed as probable runaways. Both had a history of running away, drug use, trips to juvenile court, and dropping out of school—what you usually see with runaways. This last one . . ." Mitch indicated the first name on the list. "Seventeen-year-old Miranda Simon disappeared eighteen months after Claire was abducted. She drove to cheerleading practice, worked out with her team, stayed after to talk to her coach, walked back to her car, and was never seen again. She lived about twenty miles northwest of the city."

"Seventeen," Connor said. "That's a little old for our guy, isn't it?"

"Yeah, I was thinking that too, but I don't think we should rule it out."

"All right," Connor said. "What's that?" He pointed to the last sheet of paper lying in front of Mitch.

"Oh yeah." Mitch slid the paper over to him. "This wasn't in my search parameter, but I think it's relevant. It's been all over the news the last month."

"The Ward girl?" Connor asked.

"Yeah, Alison Ward. Eleven years old. Went missing a month ago. Walking home from school. Never made it. No one saw or heard anything."

Connor studied the photo. It was a school picture. In it, Alison Ward showed off a toothy grin. Her long, shiny brown hair was partially pulled back, her thin arms resting in front of her in an artificial pose.

"Where was this?" Connor asked.

"It was over in Rancho Cordova," Mitch said, referring to a nearby city in Sacramento Valley. "I'm sure your department was contacted on this one."

"Yeah," Connor said, still looking at Alison Ward's photo. "We were. I know a couple of guys who went down there and helped search.

I didn't go because I've been swamped with cases, although I might have all the time in the world after tomorrow."

"What time is the review board?" Mitch asked.

"I have to be there at noon," Connor said. He flashed the missing persons flyer at Mitch. "You think this could be our guy?"

"I don't know," Mitch said. "Anything is possible. I wouldn't rule it out. But we're working on a theory here."

"That the guy who took Claire lived nearby."

"Yeah, which led us to Rod Page, who fits in a lot of ways—the description is similar, he had access to a similar car, he was a pedophile, and now it looks like he was using an alias. All very suspicious, but if the theory is wrong, we're way off track."

Connor nodded. He knew that in the same way a case could be solved by looking into the smallest detail, it could also be hindered when an investigation focused on the wrong detail for too long and went on from there. He looked at Mitch. "I think we have it right, though," he said.

"Yeah," Mitch said. "Me too. We still have a lot of work to do. We'll see what ViCAP turns up. In the meantime, assuming that Claire's abductor was using the Rod Page identity, we can try to get his tax records from '93 and '94 and see where he worked. Then we can go down there and start asking questions."

Connor nodded. "You still have a call out on those phone records?" he asked.

"Yeah. It's gonna take a few days, though."

They sat silently for a few minutes. Connor felt exhausted even though it wasn't quite evening yet. He also felt disappointed. He'd known the odds of actually finding and catching Claire's abductor that night hadn't been great but in a way, he really wished they had. He'd have to go home to his empty house again, worrying about an intruder or a fire, spend an hour looking at the phone, wishing Claire would call, and try not to think about the review board. It wasn't a night he was looking forward to.

"Wanna get something to eat?" Mitch asked. "My treat."

Connor smiled. "Sure," he said. "My last meal."

Farrell waved a finger at him, brow furrowed. "Don't joke about that, son," he said.

Connor rolled his eyes. "I meant my last meal as a detective."

"Oh. Well, don't joke about that either. You'll do fine."

CHAPTER

THIRTY-FOUR

1999

Tiffany put on weight in the months after her arrival. By the time the chocolate incident was over, her arms were thick and pudgy, and small doughy rolls of stomach announced themselves beneath her too-small shirts. I sat in a chair across from her permanent station on the couch. She did not look at me. We sat in silence for a long time, the television babbling endlessly at a lowered volume as the sunshine waned outside.

I saw only her profile, which looked morose and slightly bored. She sighed loudly and flipped through the channels, finally returning to the one she'd been watching in the first place.

"Where do you think he is?" she said abruptly, not turning to look at me.

"What?" I said.

"Where do you think he goes when he leaves?" she said.

"I don't know."

She glanced at me from the corner of her eye. "Well, he has to go somewhere," she said.

"He's probably out raping young girls," I said.

Now she looked at me. "What?"

I looked straight into her eyes. "He's a pedophile, Tiffany."

"A what? What's that?"

"A sicko, a pervert, a child molester. He likes little girls."

She crossed her arms in front of her. "That's stupid," she said. "You're lying."

"No. It's true. Why do you think he brought you here?"

"He loves me. That's why. He told me so."

I laughed, short and hard. "He loves any girl under fifteen. The only thing he loves about you is that you let him do things to you. He should be in prison."

She snorted. "You're just jealous because he doesn't want you anymore."

"Why do you think that is?" I asked. "I'm too old for him now. That's why you're here. He needs a little girl to satisfy his sick sexual fantasies."

She glowered at me. "I'm not a little girl," she said.

"Why did you leave home?" I asked. I expected her to tell me it was none of my business, which was her usual response to any questions I asked that were personal in nature.

Instead, she said, "It was easier on the street. I got to do whatever I wanted. I didn't have to take care of anyone's babies, and I didn't have to get beat up every day."

"Who beat you up?"

"My mom. She was a real bitch. Real stupid too. She just kept getting pregnant, and men would always leave her because she was so stupid. So I had to take care of all those stupid babies all the time while she watched TV all day."

Sitting in front of the television with boxes of candy piled up around her, Tiffany did not see the parallel.

"What about your dad?" I said.

"I don't even know who my dad is," she said. "Like I said, she could never keep a man around. She used to keep me home from school a lot to take care of her dumb kids. I hated them. I think she used to be nice to me before she had them."

She told her story carelessly, as if it had happened to someone else: Her mother had gotten in trouble with Child Protective Services after sending Tiffany grocery shopping alone at seven years old. Tiffany had lived in a foster home for a while before being placed back with her mother. Her mother started going to church and taking better care of Tiffany and her siblings, but by that time Tiffany had no patience for all of her mother's new rules.

"So you just left?" I asked.

"Yeah, well there was this other girl I knew at school who was running away. She was like thirteen and still in the same grade as me 'cause she kept getting held back. She said she had some boyfriend in the city and she was gonna go live with him. She said I could come with her, so I did. But that guy lived in a fucking car. He did all kinds of drugs, and when we got there, it turned out he just wanted us to hook so he could make money to buy drugs. After a while, I left. I figured if I was doing all the work, I should get to keep the money. So I found some other people to hang out with and went with them."

"Where did you live?"

"Oh you know, we didn't really live anywhere. All we had to do was find a place to sleep where the cops wouldn't bother us."

It was the most she had ever said to me without spewing insults. Her entire existence was alien to me. I had grown up with a loving family. I had never once dreamed of running away.

"What about you?" she asked. "You're here."

"He kidnapped me," I said.

She laughed. "Yeah, right," she said.

"He did. He kidnapped me and kept me tied up. He raped me." It was the first time I had spoken the words. Said them aloud to another person. I felt suddenly vulnerable, as if all the nerves in my body were exposed. I felt skinless.

"I was raped once," Tiffany said. Her cavalier tone scraped against my raw, armorless nerves.

"I had a family," I said. "I loved them."

"So why didn't you just leave?" she asked.

"I tried. He caught me every time."

"So go home now," she said, her face scrunching up, her tone annoyed as if she were tired of this discussion. "You're not tied up."

"I can't," I said.

She looked at me. Her eyes narrowed as the bud of an idea bloomed in her head. "You can leave. You just don't want to. You like it. You're just mad because he loves me now."

"That's not true," I said.

"Yes it is. You're just jealous. That's why you said all that stuff about him being a pervert. So I wouldn't love him anymore and I would go away. Then you could have him all to yourself. Well, forget it. You'll never have him. He's mine now. You just watch. I'll make him get rid of you." Her smile was a scowl as this latest scheme took root in her mind.

"Be my guest," I said, although she was right—I did not want to go home again.

I couldn't. How could I tell my family what he had done to me? How could I tell them about the dead bodies in the backyard? Then there would be police. They would want to know what he had done to me. They would make me tell it all, over and over again. They would make me talk about watching Sarah die. They would want to know why I had done nothing as he choked her with his belt. I had broken from my bindings before to escape, but I had not been able to do it the night of her death. They would blame me. They would blame me for all of it—the rapes, the torture, Sarah, and Rudy.

I dreamed of being free but not of going home. I was not the Claire Fletcher who had left for school that day—my head full of boys and a science test, of the weekend, and my mother taking me and Brianna to the mall. There were living nightmares in my head, and I could not share them with my family.

That night at dinner—despite my misgivings about going home—Tiffany cracked my death-infested eyes open to the last bastion of my strength, and this I held on to for a very long time.

The three of us sat together at the dinner table, as we did on the nights when I was free to roam the house. A perverse family. I said nothing, as usual, while she chattered to him incessantly about shows she had seen on television and things she wanted. Her wish list grew endlessly long. He smiled, beamed, and grinned at her, making small sounds of acknowledgment and occasionally closing his eyes as if he were listening to a fine symphony.

I only noticed that she had changed the subject when the pitch of her voice went up. I looked up from my plate to her scowl.

"She was saying mean things about you today. She said you were a pervert and a child molester. Then she said you kidnapped her, and that she wants to go back to her real family."

He shifted in his chair, looking decidedly uncomfortable. He looked at me. "Is this true, Lynn?"

I stared back at him, my face a blank slate.

"I don't know why you would say such hurtful things," he said, looking wounded.

Tiffany's body lurched upward. "I wouldn't say those things," she said. "I didn't believe them either when she told me."

He turned back to her. She put a hand on his arm. "I love you," she said. "She doesn't care about all the things you do for us but I do."

"Thank you, Tiffany," he said.

Her eyes brightened with his attention. "I would never want to leave you. You're my family now. I just want to make you happy."

She pulled his hand to her and kissed it. "Do you want me to make you happy?"

His voice croaked. "Y-yes."

She stood up, tugging him along with her hand. "I want to make you happy right now," she said.

She led him away, turning back toward me once to smile. What I saw in her eyes was almost as frightening as the look in Sarah's eyes as she asphyxiated. In Tiffany's eyes, I saw pride and smug satisfaction, coupled with ambition. She enjoyed it. She embraced it for reasons that may have been equally as sick as his were in pursuing her affections.

I shuddered. In four years I had never once felt anything remotely kind toward him. Even when he starved and deprived me and then showered me with bare essentials that seemed like priceless gifts at the time, I could not muster enough gratitude to thank him. I hated him.

If I had spent one hundred years in his house, I don't believe I would ever succumb to him. I could never feel anything resembling affection toward him. Had I resigned myself to this fate, I might have turned into Tiffany. The only thing that made us different was my resistance to the life she embraced.

There was still something left of Claire Fletcher after all.

CHAPTER THIRTY-FIVE

It was 8:30 p.m. when Connor arrived home, his stomach full and his mind racing. As he pulled into his driveway, he saw Brianna Fletcher sitting on his front stoop. She sat with her back curved, her arms curled around her drawn-up knees. She stood as Connor pulled in, glaring at the car with a look that could have broken the windshield.

She was dressed in jeans and a sweatshirt, her short hair styled and giving her a more feminine look, although it did not soften the angry lines of her face as she crossed her arms and regarded Connor. As he approached, he took a scan around the immediate area.

"You shouldn't be here," he said.

"Why not?" She thrust her chin toward him. Compared to her tiny mother, Brianna was a giant. The Fletcher children must have gotten their height from their father's side.

"It's not safe," he said, brushing past her and unlocking his door.

She turned. "Well, I'm not leaving."

He sighed and extended a hand into the open doorway. "Come on in then."

Wordlessly, she moved past him into the house, one shoulder brushing against the doorway so she would avoid touching him.

"Straight ahead," he said, indicating the living room. "There's a switch on your left."

Connor locked and dead bolted the door. He followed her into the living room and motioned to the couch. "Sit," he said.

Narrowing her eyes at him, Brianna took a seat in the living room. Connor tossed his jacket on the empty chair beside her and settled onto the couch. She glowered at him, arms still crossed tightly across her middle. Connor waited for her to speak, which didn't take long.

"Just what the hell do you think you're doing?" she said.

"You'll have to be more specific," Connor said.

She rolled her eyes. "You know damn well what I mean, Detective." She spit out the word *detective*, as if it were a dirty word. "Why are you carrying on with this, this"—she waved a hand in the air angrily—"with Claire's case? I know my mother came to see you. What are you trying to do?"

Connor held her eyes, kept his voice calm and even, as if he were talking about the weather. "I'm trying to bring Claire home."

Brianna made a *puh* sound of contempt. "You really think the woman you met was my sister?"

"I know she was."

"Fingerprints?" Brianna said dismissively. "Hardly reliable."

Connor smiled. "Well, if the criminal justice system has been relying on them for the last fifty years or so, I'm gonna go ahead and make the leap that fingerprints are a pretty sure thing."

"The computer could be wrong," Brianna pointed out.

Connor nodded slowly. "Yeah, it could," he agreed. "But I don't think it is."

"Why are you doing this?" she asked, seeing that she would get nowhere arguing with him over fingerprints.

"It's my job," Connor said simply.

"Your job is torturing my family? Giving my mother false hope? Starting this whole ordeal over again? In ten years, no one has even come close to finding out what happened to my sister. What makes you think you can find out the truth? Who do you think you are? How dare you come into our lives and disrupt everything again. We've had enough."

Connor leaned forward. "We've had enough?" he asked. "Or you've had enough?"

Brianna looked shocked, as if he'd just slapped her across the face. "You have no idea what it's like," she said.

"No, I don't," Connor agreed calmly. "So why don't you tell me? I know it wasn't easy."

"Easy?" she said, the word lodged in her throat. "Easy? It wasn't. You know, maybe I'm a selfish bitch for feeling this way, but when that bastard took my sister, it ruined my life. It ruined everything. My whole family may as well have been abducted that day because they were gone.

"My mom forgot about my senior prom because there was some lead on Claire's case. During my high school graduation, my parents spent more time looking at their watches than the ceremony because they couldn't wait to get home to man the phones in case a detective called with news about her. Tom had to move me into college my freshman year because my parents were too busy or too upset. Nothing was ever happy again. Nothing was ever the same. Then my parents split up. It was horrible. Nothing that happened to any of us after that meant anything. Nothing could compare to the loss of Claire. Nothing could compete with the possibility that she might still be alive somewhere and might still come home."

She was no longer looking at him, her eyes drawn to the floor. Tears streamed down her face. With each revelation, her tight posture loosened a bit until her shoulders slumped forward and her hands rested loosely in her lap. Connor let her go on, wondering if she'd ever really talked to anyone about Claire's abduction before.

"When my sister disappeared, it tore my family apart. My mother is like a different person. The not knowing was the hardest those first two years. Every time the phone rang or there was a knock on the door, we hoped it would be news of Claire. My father and I, we couldn't live like that, in limbo all the time. Never moving forward, always waiting for a day that would never come. We had to believe that Claire was dead."

"Why?"

She shrugged and wiped the tears from her cheeks. Her voice squeaked. "It's just easier. I know that sounds horrible but you don't understand. You can't understand. I mean how likely was it that Claire was really still out there somewhere, alive? It's extremely rare. And if she was—" Brianna paused, sucking in air, holding down a sob. "What was he doing to her? What has he been doing to her all this time? If she came back, she wouldn't be my sister. She wouldn't be Claire."

"Ms. Fletcher, there are all kinds of things in life that change us, that change who we are, how we act, how we conduct our lives. Whatever Claire has been through, she will be changed by it, she will be different. But she is still your sister," Connor said.

Brianna hugged herself tightly again. "Look," she said. "All I'm asking is for you to not put my family through this again. Every so often something turns up, like those other men, and it gets my mother all caught up in it again. When nothing happens, it's like watching her die. The disappointment is too much, and every time it gets worse. She doesn't come out of her room. Doesn't eat, doesn't talk to anyone.

"My father and I have moved on, but my mother is stuck. Every time something like this happens, she gets further and further away from living a normal life. What if this woman is a hoax? What if it is

Claire but you can't find her? I can't watch my mother be destroyed again."

Connor took in her words and let them hang between them for several minutes while he formulated a response. Contrary to her words, Connor didn't think Brianna had moved on at all. Had she, she wouldn't be sitting across from him this very minute asking him to back off the case.

He did understand her position regarding her mother, however, and if he had not had any solid leads, he might have agreed to back down. But he had a name, a suspect who fit the profile—a man who had the means and the deeply twisted motive to have kidnapped Claire. As he discussed with Mitch, they could very well be barking up the wrong tree, but Connor felt in his gut that he was on the right track. And if he was, he was closer to finding Claire than anyone had been in ten years.

But most of all, he simply could not walk away.

He didn't want to.

"I'm sorry," he said. "I'm sorry that this is difficult for you, but I can't leave it alone. I think the girl I met is your sister. I think she's in trouble. I think that if I were to walk away from this whole thing and pretend that I never heard of Claire Fletcher, I wouldn't be able to look at myself in the mirror every day. I think it would be an insult to her, to you, and especially to your mother. I think I have a fair chance of bringing her in and I am going to try to do just that. You're just going to have to find a way to deal with that."

Brianna sighed and squeezed her eyes shut. When she opened them, she smiled wanly at him, her energy depleted. Her tone was sarcastic. "You want to be a hero?"

"No," Connor said. The image of a dead rapist bleeding out on the floor of a broken-down bedroom in a broken-down house that had seen more than its share of violence burst over the screen of his mind. "I just want to do the right thing. That's all."

He must have sounded as weary as he felt because Brianna had no biting response. She stared at him for a long moment as silence descended between them. Her fingers worried an imaginary piece of lint on her pants. Finally, she stood to go.

"I guess there is nothing left to say," she muttered.

Wordlessly, Connor walked her to the door. He unlocked it and held it open for her. She stepped out onto his front stoop and turned back toward him, her voice heavy with unshed tears. "I just hope you're right. For the sake of my family, I hope you can do this."

"Me too," Connor said.

CHAPTER

THIRTY-SIX

I dreamed of Connor, his musky male scent filling my senses so that when I woke, I thought I could still smell him. I gathered my blankets tightly around my body and smiled without opening my eyes. In the nowhere place between sleeping and waking, it was easy to imagine that I was lying in his bed, at his house. That he had gotten up to use the bathroom and would return to bed at any moment and wrap me in his arms, as he had done the night I met him.

I remembered the feel of his long, lean body against my own, his breath in my hair, tickling my neck. Never had I fantasized about a man in such a way. There remained a small ache inside me—desire. Curled in my tiny trailer bed, I sighed and imagined spending a whole day with Connor. I drifted back to sleep with his smile languishing in my head.

A series of loud, angry bangs woke me moments later, reminding me of my reality. I opened my eyes. Fear crept into my thoughts of Connor. An image of my captor beating a prone Connor flashed in my mind, and I pushed it back.

With a blanket wrapped around my shoulders, I took my time answering the door. Tiffany stood outside, her shiny, emaciated face crumpled, as if she smelled a very foul odor. I didn't invite her in.

"What do you want?" I asked.

"I need milk," she said.

"Are you kidding me?"

Her sigh was exaggerated. One hand found its place on her hip. "No, I'm not kidding you. You have milk. Give me some."

In the doorway, I stood a foot taller than her. I studied her skeptically. She had not graced my door in two years, and she had never turned up for something as benign as milk. "What's going on?" I asked.

Frustrated, she threw her arms in the air and turned to leave. "Nothing," she muttered. "You're so paranoid."

"With good reason," I called after her. "Get the pervert to buy you milk."

Pausing at the edge of the road, she turned. "You know, even if there was something going on, I wouldn't tell you."

"Oh yeah, right. But you have no problem spying on me all day and night and telling him every little thing I do."

She stared at me and for once, she had no retort. Finally, she spun on her heel and stomped across the road, slamming the door to the house loudly. I stayed in the doorway for a few minutes, watching the inert structure across from me, holding all his secrets with utter silence. I wondered if something was going on over there and whether Tiffany's request for milk was just a ploy to get me to talk to her so she could unload and get whatever was bothering her off her chest.

If so, I had spoiled my opportunity to ferret out an explanation for all the strange goings-on at the house and the stomach-churning unease I felt lately. I shut my door and placed the chair under the knob. In the kitchen, I boiled water and made tea. Getting information out of Tiffany might not have been that easy. Her loyalty to him was unyielding. I was better off keeping silent with both of them, as I had for years.

CHAPTER
THIRTY-SEVEN
1999

After the night she led him away from the dinner table, proving herself more worthy of his affection, I said as little as possible, quiet as always. I had never spoken to him except to ask for books, plead for my freedom, protest his advances, and beg for the life of a girl I did not know. With Tiffany working diligently to turn him against me, there seemed even less reason to speak. Anything I said could be used against me later, and even though I was starved for stimulation, I could not muster the energy to respond to her taunts or tricks.

On the day he came home and announced we were moving, however, I spoke loudly and firmly. I did not want to leave. It wasn't that I had grown attached to the place. Some of the most demoralizing, desperate hours of my life had taken place in that house. I did not want to leave Rudy and Sarah alone in the backyard. The thought of being separated from their invisible presence ripped away the hazy gauze of numbness I'd wrapped around me.

He was in a great hurry to leave. He had brought piles of boxes for us to pack our things in. Tiffany was excited. For her, it was a new adventure, and I could see visions of a palatial estate welling up in her eyes.

"I'm not going," I said, when he began packing up the kitchen.

"Good," Tiffany said. "No one wants you around anyway."

He turned to me, body half bent over a box. "You're going whether you like it or not," he said.

Beside him, Tiffany pouted. "I don't want her to go."

"I'm not going," I repeated.

He straightened. Tiffany tugged at his shirtsleeve. "She doesn't want to go. Let's just leave her here."

"Lynn," he said. "You are going. You don't have a choice in this matter."

"That's rich," I said. "I haven't had a choice in any matter since the day you kidnapped me."

He was momentarily stricken. Tiffany tugged harder on his sleeve and stamped her foot. "Leave her here!"

He strode across the room and slapped me hard across the face. But I was almost as tall as him now and much stronger than I had been. Sucking the blood from my teeth, I raised my eyes to him once more.

I slapped him back with as much strength as I had. His head snapped to the side with the satisfying *thwap* of my palm. Tiffany gasped.

"I said I'm not going." Dimly I wondered if anyone had ever hit him before.

He touched his hand to his cheek, which had gone pink. His voice rose up from his bowels, a high, shrill keening. "You bitch!" he shrieked.

He flew at me with his fists. I managed to avoid only one or two before ducking my head and barreling into him with the entire weight of my body. I knocked him back several steps. He tripped on a chair and fell on his behind. I toppled with him, my hands curled tightly into fists, hitting, hitting, and hitting. I swung blindly, hitting anything that felt like him.

Again I had the sensation of having left my body. I floated upward and hung as if suspended from the ceiling, watching it all. Tiffany stood a few feet away, too stunned to react. Her arms hung slack and useless at her sides. Her thin mouth was agape. I had straddled him and my fists swung wildly at his face, which he covered with his hands. He was gasping and bucking his hips weakly. It occurred to me that I had knocked the wind out of him when I sent him crashing to the floor. I was yelling something in a voice I barely recognized as my own.

It was no longer a girl's voice but a woman's voice. My disembodied self strained to make out the words.

"You fucking bastard. I hate you. I hate you. You took everything from me. I hate you. I hate you. I wish you were fucking dead. You piece of shit, pervert, sicko, pedophile bastard."

Every curse word I knew, every derogatory thing I had ever thought of calling him spewed from my lips in a fury of bloodred spit.

Finally, he caught his breath. He reached up between my flying hands and grabbed a handful of my hair. He yanked hard to the side, freeing himself. My hands kept flying, and when he pulled me to my feet, I kicked and stomped, my limbs searching for solid mass.

My disembodied self braced for his retaliation, for the possibility that he might beat me to death as he had Rudy or strangle me as he had Sarah. Perhaps he would drag me into the bathroom and drown me again. My body was beyond caring, so caught up in its visceral rage. But he did none of those things. Instead he dragged me to the threshold of my room and half pushed, half threw me inside, slamming the door swiftly behind me.

My body had gained such momentum that for several moments longer, it beat its arms and legs against the door, still screaming obscenities and working until its arms and legs were bruised and bleeding and several of its toes broken.

When the body pulled me back, it was exhausted and sore. But I had found my rage, a geyser of it, a wellspring. I resolved to hold on to it—keep it coursing through me until he came back.

He must have sensed this because he did not return for a very long time. It became impossible for me to stay awake, much less fuel my blessed fury for the next encounter. When I woke, I was still on the floor. I had curled up on the carpet, next to the door, hoping to spring at him when he opened it. I had failed.

There was a plateful of food on the table beside my bed and a large glass of water. My first instinct was to hurl it into the wall and resume my battle with the door. Then I realized that I would need my strength if I was going to best him again. I ate and drank and soon after, a familiar feeling spread throughout my limbs.

I was suffused with warmth, my body so relaxed that I could hardly move. Lazily, my mind sifted through memories of my captivity, seeking to identify this feeling and the last time I'd had it. I was in the first place he had kept me, tied with one hand to a bed, wearing the shorts and T-shirt he'd given me, which had almost caused me to weep after so many weeks of being naked and cold. There too was food on the bedside table.

"Oh no," I groaned, although I was no longer entirely sure that I had spoken the words aloud or merely in my head.

The last time I felt like this, I had woken up here, in this house.

My mind tried to keep me awake, alert. *The food*, it said, *the food*. He put something in the food. As though this belated realization might make a difference. I drifted off thinking of Sarah, Rudy, and finally, for reasons I could not articulate, my mother.

I woke for a short time what must have been days later. I was in my bed but not in the same room. Not in the same house. My right arm was bound again to the bed, giving me a jarring sense of déjà vu. Surrounding the bed were boxes marked "Lynn." My mouth felt as if it were stuffed with cotton. A cloudy image of Tiffany's face pressed against a car window flickered in my mind. I drifted back into sleep.

The next time I woke, Tiffany was sitting on the edge of the bed, filing her nails with an emery board. I shifted and moaned. She glanced at me.

When I began to sit up, she spoke. "He said if you don't be good, he's going to keep you like this."

"Like what?" I said. My voice was a hoarse whisper.

"Drugged. Tied up."

"Where are we?"

"You sound like a frog."

I reached up and untied my hand from the bedpost. He had used only rope. My wrist was raw, the skin cracked and scabbed.

"How long have I been here?"

"Three weeks. He doesn't want to see you. He made me take you to the bathroom." She made a sound of disgust. "It was totally gross."

I flexed my legs and moved into a sitting position, resting my dizzy head against the headboard. "Where are we?"

"Some shitty place in the middle of nowhere. It's worse than the last place even though it has more rooms. He said if you ever hit him again, he'll kill you. He said it like he really would too."

I had no doubt that he meant it. "How long did it take us to get here?" I asked.

She continued filing her nails. She had not looked at me once since we began talking. "What the hell do you care? You're in a lot of trouble, you know."

"Just tell me," I said. My voice was raspy and my throat felt like sandpaper.

She rolled her eyes and blew on her nails. "I don't know. Like a half hour."

"Have I been sleeping the whole time?"

She shrugged. "Mostly. Sometimes you were like a zombie. Like you could walk and eat and stuff but you weren't really there. Why does he care so much if you leave or not?"

I rubbed my hands over my face. "Because if I leave, he knows I'll go to the police and turn him in."

She looked at me finally. Her face was blank. "So what you said is true? He kidnapped you?"

I nodded. I tried to swallow but it hurt. "I need some water," I said.

Her brow furrowed, lines creasing her face. "I don't believe you," she said. "You weren't even tied up when I came. You want to stay. I don't know why he cares so much about you. You're just dumb anyway."

Her entire body seemed to pout. She looked at her feet.

"Please just get me some water," I said.

"I hate you," she said softly, her voice sounding sad, lacking the malice she usually reserved for me.

I closed my eyes. "I know," I said. "Tiffany, please. Water."

She made a sound of exasperation and the bed shifted beneath me as she stood. My mind was working far too slowly to take everything in. All I could think about was water, and when she finally handed me a glass, I drank it down in one long series of gulps. I held it out to her again. "More," I gasped.

Wordlessly, she left and returned with a full glass. I drank more slowly, and she settled back onto the bed.

"What do you want?" I said, my voice starting to sound more normal.

"Look," she said. "I'm tired of taking care of you like you're a cripple or something. It's gross anyway. I'm just supposed to find out if you're gonna be good or not so I don't have to take care of you all the time."

I sighed. Living death was almost too good to turn away from. I had lived for at least three weeks in a windowless sleep, a life with no memory, no images to haunt me, no effort, and neither pain nor hope to assail me. I could live that way. Drugged. Asleep. Until one day I didn't wake up. It seemed better than my present circumstances.

Then I remembered the small piece of Claire Fletcher that lived in me. Just a tiny ember, barely visible even when exposed to air yet real and still harboring the smallest bit of heat. I didn't know what it meant or if I could ever fan it enough to turn it into a flame, but I wanted it. I wanted to keep it. I owed the girl I used to be at least that. Not to mention Sarah and Rudy, whose lonely bodies I'd had to leave behind.

"Fine," I said. "I won't hit him again."

"You'll be good?" she asked.

"I said I wouldn't hit him again, didn't I?"

She stood up. "The bathroom is across the hall. You should take a shower. You smell."

CHAPTER

THIRTY-EIGHT

Connor loosened his tie and paced back and forth in the fourth-floor hallway of the police administration building. He hadn't slept well. As he lay in his bed the night before, all the conversations, events, and the stress of the last two weeks had played out in his mind in a jumbled mess. He thought about what he was going to say to the review board the next day, a day that had been coming faster and faster, leaving him with no hope of rest. He still had the blanket he'd shared with Claire, and throughout the night he pressed it to his face, trying to smell her. But the scent was fading and with it his sense of calm.

Now he stood nervously in front of the door, waiting for his name to be called. Boggs and Stryker sat on a bench beside the door, each one sucking on a lollipop since they couldn't smoke in the building. They sat side by side like two small boys waiting outside a principal's office, their heads moving in unison as they watched him pace back and forth.

Finally, Stryker pulled the lollipop from his mouth and said, "Relax, Parks. It's not like you've never been to one of these before."

Connor looked at him and realized he had been too nervous to even make fun of Stryker and his red-stained mouth, glistening with the preservatives of a cherry lollipop. "Yeah, but I've never had to go in there and defend my own actions," he pointed out.

Like Stryker, Boggs pulled a grape lollipop from his own mouth and waved it in the air in time with his words. "Stryke is right, Parks. Relax. You're not gonna lose your badge. Now sit down 'cause you're making us dizzy."

With twin motions, the two of them popped their treats back into their mouths. Connor stood between them. With grunts and rolled eyes, they shifted so he could sit between them. Connor looked at his watch and drummed his fingers on his knees.

"Knock it off," Stryker said.

Connor folded his arms in front of him and sighed.

"Try not to look so nervous," Boggs offered. "They'll think you meant to do it."

"Now don't tell him that," Stryker said, leaning across Connor to look at Boggs. "He's nervous enough as it is. He's giving me motion sickness over here with the way he's goddamn twitching."

Boggs held up his hands. "What? I'm just saying he shouldn't go in there wound up like a damn meth addict."

"Well, you're not helping," Stryker said. "Just keep your fucking mouth shut."

Boggs scowled. "Hey, you ever been to one of these?"

"I don't need to have been to one to know not to freak the dude out fifteen minutes before he goes in there," Stryker replied.

Connor was about to intercede and tell them both to shut the hell up when a booming voice said, "Well, just look at you kids. All lined up like you just got caught fighting on the playground."

Connor looked up to see Farrell grinning and Jen Fletcher trailing behind him, dwarfed by Mitch's heavy frame.

Boggs bolted up from his seat. "Jenny Fletcher!" he said, removing his lollipop.

Connor watched in disbelief as Boggs lifted Jen off the ground into a tight hug. He set her down and she smiled up at him, her eyes twinkling. "Danny Boggs," she said. She looked at his lollipop. "You finally quit smoking?"

Boggs looked to the floor, suddenly bashful. "Nah," he said. "I can't smoke in here. Gotta do something."

Connor stood and shook Mitch's hand before Jen pulled him down into a quick hug.

"You two know each other?" Boggs asked.

Connor looked at him with arched eyebrows. "I could ask you the same thing."

"Boggs looked over the case for me a few times since Claire went missing," Jen explained.

Boggs shrugged. "I remember when it happened. I did some work, but I wasn't the lead investigator at the time. Couldn't forget this little lady, though. She called almost every day for five years."

Jen nodded. "Connor's doing some work for us." She winked at Connor. "Nothing much since he's on the desk right now, just looking over the case file."

Connor turned to Mitch. "What are you doing here?"

"Well, we thought you could use some moral support is all."

Jen slid an arm around Connor's waist. "You've been a big help," she said. "We just wanted to do something to repay you."

From his spot on the bench, Stryker spoke up for the first time. "Give him a sedative," he said. "That'll help."

"Shut up, Stryke," Boggs said. The two started arguing again but stopped abruptly when a uniformed officer poked his head out of the door and said, "They're ready for you, Detective Parks."

All eyes were on Connor. He looked down at Jen, who gave him a squeeze, and then at Mitch. "You guys gonna stick around?" he asked.

Mitch nodded.

Boggs and Stryker stood up and flanked Connor, patting him heartily on the back. "Good luck in there, man," Stryker said.

Connor nodded, took a deep breath, and straightened his tie. He flashed a smile at his ragtag group of supporters and walked through the door.

CHAPTER
THIRTY-NINE

1999

The new house was one story, although it could hardly be called *new*. It looked as if someone had slapped together a few pieces of plywood and called it home. Paint on the walls peeled and chipped. The floors were not level, causing most of the furniture to tip to one side or the other. The pipes running just beneath the floors groaned and banged whenever a faucet was turned on, and it took a full five minutes for hot water to work itself up to the spigot. There were old tiles in the kitchen and bathroom, white turned brown with age and chipped around the corners. And throughout the entire house, there was a persistent smell as though some animal had crawled beneath the place to die.

Just outside the front door was a low porch with floorboards that were rotted on one side. Beyond that was a stretch of grass—where he parked his car and the old truck, which he'd spray-painted green after he killed Rudy. Trees dotted the edge of the property, and just past that was a narrow road. Across from us was an old trailer, which sat unused and creaked when the wind was strong.

For many days I sat on the porch, a book open and unread in my lap, and waited for cars to pass. The road was hardly ever traveled; when cars passed, they sped by as if they were racing toward a finish line.

I did not bother to unpack my things. I lived from the boxes, rifling through them when I needed something. He left the house less often, but he did not speak or look at me. I needed new clothes. The ones I had did not fit well. When I asked him for new clothes, I did not say please and he did not acknowledge me, but a few days later, a pile of new clothes appeared on my bed.

I was able to roam the woods around the house and even across the street by the trailer. Tiffany kept a close eye on me and always reported to him when I had taken a walk. He said nothing. I walked as far as I dared through the trees in every direction and even along the road but did not see any neighbors. I didn't know what I would do if I came upon someone else. It felt good to be outside, the quiet broken only by my feet over downed branches and fallen leaves.

Most of the time, I stayed on the porch, counting the cars that passed. Tiffany stayed inside, periodically appearing in the window to see if I was still there. Sometimes she came outside and sat on the opposite end of the porch, pointedly ignoring me.

One day, she left the porch and returned with a long branch, which she held in her hand as she got down on her belly and probed underneath the porch.

"What are you doing?" I said.

"I hear something under here. I'm getting it out."

"It's a skunk. Leave it alone."

"How do you know?"

"I've seen it. It's not hurting anyone. Just leave it."

Her head popped up, eyes narrowed at me. "What if I don't want a skunk living under the porch? They're gross." She resumed poking beneath the floorboards, her stick scraping against them.

"It's going to spray you," I said.

"No it won't. Skunks only spray at night."

I laughed. "Who told you that?"

"I just know it. Besides, it's probably not a skunk at all. You probably just said that to scare me. It's probably some weird animal you keep under there as a pet, and you just don't want me to scare it off."

I said nothing. The skunk, who apparently found Tiffany no less annoying than I did, promptly sprayed her. The pungent smell wafted up over her shrieks. She ran from the porch, but the skunk did not emerge. She ran in circles, arms waving, face pale and scrunched up. I stood and walked slowly into the house. I went into my room and pushed a box up against the door.

I went to sleep and woke to the sound of their raised voices. Apparently she had showered and taken up residence on the couch, but the smell lingered and now it was strong and heavy in the house.

"What were you thinking?" I heard him say.

"Well, that bitch in there told me there was something under the porch and I should get it out or you would be pissed" came her high-pitched reply. Then there was an audible pout. "I didn't know it was a skunk."

A sigh.

A moment later, he knocked on my door but did not enter. I heard him through the door, the first words he had spoken to me in three months. "Lynn, I'm getting tired of these little games." I heard footsteps—Tiffany's. "I can't leave the house for even a few hours without you two getting into trouble." A sound of disgust. "Get into the bathtub and don't get out until I come back," he said.

Whining. "Where are you going?"

"To get something to rid you of that awful smell. Now go."

I heard no more after that, though when I emerged the next day the smell was fainter. The couch had been tossed out into the front yard, and Tiffany was holed up in one of the empty rooms.

That evening he called us both to the dinner table. Tiffany and I sat on either side of him. She glared at me, eyes narrowed to dark slits. He looked tired. His eyes were rimmed with black circles, his expression weary.

Finally, he spoke. "This has got to stop," he said.

Tiffany immediately piped up. "Well, if she would just leave me alone. I don't do anything to her. She hates me."

He raised a hand to silence her. "Lynn," he said. "You have to stop fighting with your sister."

"She picks on me all the time," Tiffany blurted.

"Lynn?" he said, waiting for my response.

I raised my chin. "Go to hell," I said.

Tiffany gasped. He lowered his eyes and shook his head with disappointment. "We've talked about this," he said.

"About what?" I shot back.

"About you being a good girl. If you're not going to be a good girl, I'm afraid—"

"What? You'll kill me? You've tried enough times, why don't you just finish the job this time?"

Tiffany's eyes widened. He looked up at me sharply.

I smiled without humor. "What? You think I care what you do to me anymore? Do you honestly think that death could be worse than this?" I waved a hand around the room. "Just do what you have to do," I added.

"You said you would be good," Tiffany said.

"Oh, shut up," I told her. I turned back to him. "And stop talking to me like I'm five years old. I'm nearly twenty. I'm not a girl anymore."

"You ungrateful bitch," he said. He threw his fork down, and it clattered on his plate. He stormed off to his bedroom and did not come out the rest of the night.

Two weeks later, I found a newspaper article taped to the inside of my door. It was a small piece, cut from the metro section of the city paper:

LOCAL RESIDENT CRASHES INTO STOREFRONT

Thomas Fletcher, a local businessman, crashed his car into the large storefront window of Starbucks at 4:00 p.m. yesterday. Fletcher was driving down Ninth Street when the brakes on his Chevrolet Lumina failed. Fletcher was taken to Memorial Hospital and released later. Police say Fletcher's brake lines had been cut, and they are investigating the incident.

"We fully intend to prosecute," said DA Pamela Williams. Fletcher, though shaken by the incident, is glad no one was injured. "It was terrifying," he said yesterday afternoon from his Bell Street home. "I'm just glad no one was killed. I have no idea who would want to do something like this."

Police too are baffled by the incident but will continue to investigate. "This was attempted murder," said Detective Daniel Boggs. "We can't have citizens afraid to drive their own vehicles. This is very serious, and we're looking into it with all of our resources."

There was no photo. Hands trembling, I pulled the clipping from the door and held it to my chest. Had he really tried to kill my brother? My throat felt thick. I tried not to think of my family often. It was too painful. I liked to imagine them living their lives, happy and fulfilled, doing all the things I could never do. He may have held me captive and ripped me away from them, but in my mind my family was untainted, unspoiled by his evil hands. Now he was a threat to them.

I slid to the floor, holding the article to me as if it were Tom himself.

CHAPTER FORTY

Two hours later, Connor emerged from his meeting with the review board, smiling, his body slick with sweat under his suit jacket. Boggs, Stryker, Mitch, and Jen stood in a half circle in the hallway and looked expectantly at him.

"Well?" Mitch said.

"Six months on the desk, no active investigating, no time on the street," Connor said, sighing with relief, as if he'd held his breath the entire time he'd been in there.

Boggs and Stryker high-fived him and hooted. "See," Stryker said. "It's all good, man."

Boggs gave Connor a sideways hug over the shoulder, jostling him roughly. "You'll be back on the street in no time," he said.

"Yeah, and in the meantime, you can type up all our reports," Stryker added.

Jen rose on the tips of her toes to kiss him on the cheek. "I'm glad," she said.

"You wanna get lunch?" Mitch asked. "You can buy since you still have your job."

Connor laughed. "Yeah. I'm starving." He looked at Boggs and Stryker. "You two wanna come?"

Boggs shook his head. "Nah, some other time."

"We got work to do, man," Stryker added. "Riehl will pop a vein in his forehead if three of us are MIA today."

Connor thanked them for coming and watched them walk down the hall toward the exit, already bickering over something.

At the restaurant, Mitch ordered a round of drinks and three shots. Connor peeled his jacket off and rolled up his sleeves.

"So what did you tell them?" Mitch asked.

"The truth," Connor said. "Just the truth. I figured I had a fifty-fifty chance of keeping my job. And then I thought if I lost it, I could always go into private practice. You've got an opening, right?"

Mitch laughed. "Yeah, for you? Could be. I don't know, though. You'd have to really bone up on home security."

"Cute," Connor said.

Jen leaned forward from the other side of the table. "Was there a lot of press over this case?" she asked.

"Well, there was some, but something else happened the same weekend so I was bumped back to the last page of the metro section," Connor said. "Which might have just saved my ass."

Jen nodded. "Yes. I know a thing or two about the press. They either make things much better or much worse."

"No," Mitch said. "It's not so much the press as the unthinking masses who take everything they read to heart."

The waiter arrived with everyone's drinks. Jen held up her shot glass. "A toast," she said. Connor and Mitch quickly grasped their own shot glasses and waited for her to speak. "To Connor getting to keep his job," she said.

"Yeah," Mitch added. "To a damn fine detective."

Connor looked at Jen and held her gaze for a long moment. "To your daughter," he said. "And bringing her home."

Tears filled Jen's eyes as they clinked glasses and knocked back the shots.

They chased the shots with long gulps of beer. The waiter returned to take their order, and then Mitch got down to business. He pulled out a file from under his jacket, which he'd brought from the car, and handed it to Connor.

"I've got the composite," he said.

Connor flipped open the file and pulled out the sketch of the man who had abused Noel. Connor was immediately struck by how ordinary Page looked. He had thin features and slightly wavy hair, but for the most part, he was unremarkable. He was the guy you bought your morning coffee from every day, whose name you wouldn't be able to recall even if your life depended on it. He was the neighbor on your street you waved to each morning on your way to work whose physical description you'd never remember in enough detail to recognize him elsewhere. He was a thousand men whose faces were blank spots in your memory.

"He looks like a regular guy," Connor commented.

Jen spun the sketch around so that she could study it. "He looks like my old pharmacist," she said.

"He looks like our waiter too," Mitch pointed out. "That's the problem with composite sketches. But this is the best we can do in lieu of a photo right now, so what should we do with this?"

Connor frowned. "I have an idea but it involves some risk."

He looked at Jen, who held his gaze without flinching. "Tell me," she said.

He held up the composite. "We take this to the press. Tell them there has been a break in the case and that this man is a person of interest."

"What about Claire?" Mitch said. "What if he kills her? If he thinks he's close to getting caught, what's to stop him from killing her and getting rid of all the evidence, as it were?"

"If we didn't know she was alive and we had this lead, what would we do with it?" Connor countered.

"We'd go directly to the press," Jen said.

Connor nodded and looked at Mitch. "He's not going to kill her. It's been ten years. She's still alive."

"You don't know that for sure, though," Mitch pointed out.

Connor sighed. "No. I don't," he conceded. "But I think this is a risk worth taking. Someone might recognize this guy right away. We don't know what will happen, but this is a solid lead."

They both looked at Jen. Mitch reached across the table and slid a meaty hand over hers. "It's your call, Jenny. She's your child."

She nodded, her blue eyes steely. "We go to the press," she said.

Mitch turned to Connor. "Well, I guess we need to have a conversation with your captain."

CHAPTER
FORTY-ONE

1999

After finding the clipping about my brother, my sole activity in his house was to avoid Tiffany. Any interaction could lead to me being blamed for something, and I was not so sure I could keep my mouth shut if he chastised me one more time, imploring me to be a "good girl."

I was frightened for my family, but I was also angry. He had already killed two people because of me. If he was so displeased with me, why didn't he just kill me? I knew he had it in him. I had seen it firsthand. It was as if he enjoyed this special sort of torture. Keeping me alive but ignoring me. Keeping me in his house with indirect threats but acting as if I was no longer there. It seemed I served him no purpose, yet he held on to me. If his concern was that setting me free would cause him to go to prison, he could easily have silenced me with death, yet he didn't.

I was on the brink of giving up entirely. Then one day, two weeks after I found the article about my brother taped to my door, he found me in the kitchen. I was standing at the sink, washing dishes and staring idly out the tiny window above the sink. I did not hear him and was only aware of him for a split second before his hand was on the back of my head.

He snapped my head forward, driving my forehead into the windowsill. My vision was filled with fuzzy dark circles. The pain split right down the middle of my skull. He pushed my face toward the sink but I braced myself, hands on the edge of it, so that my head did not submerge in the sudsy water.

This was it, I thought. The rest of my body slackened with relief. It would be over. He was going to kill me.

But he didn't. Instead, he yanked my pants down, fumbling with his fly. He tried to force himself into me, but he was limp. I could feel his hand working furiously between our bodies, his flaccid penis pushing against the back of my thighs. His breath was labored. He pressed harder on the back of my head as I tried to get my bearings.

Abruptly, he stopped. He let go of me with one more push to the back of my skull. Then he said, "Get out."

He left. I stayed there, bent over the sink. Blood dripped into the dishwater from the gash in the middle of my forehead. I watched the drops fall and diffuse into the water. I listened to my breathing, tried to squeeze out the throbbing, echoing pain in my head. My arms ached from holding my upper body over the sink. After a few moments, I stood upright and straightened my clothes. Blood dripped warm and slow down my nose. I used a towel to stop it.

He had told me to get out. Just two weeks ago, he had tried to kill my brother. Now he was telling me to get out. Could I just walk through the front door and leave? Flag down the nearest car and tell them I was Claire Fletcher, the fifteen-year-old girl who'd been abducted four years ago? Or would that cost me a family member? Would he wait for me to leave and then sneak up on me, drag me back to this shack, and torture me into compliance?

Anger swelled inside me enough to match the throbbing in the center of my head. I was weary of his games. I strode into the hallway and burst through his bedroom door without knocking. He was not standing by the window, watching for my escape. Instead he sat on the edge of the bed, pants undone, Tiffany's head working furiously in his lap. His head snapped in my direction, but Tiffany did not even pause.

"What are you doing?" he asked.

"What did you just say to me?" I responded, holding the towel to my forehead.

"Get out," he said, his tone low and menacing.

"Right now?"

"Yes." He glanced down at the top of Tiffany's head. "I'm in the middle of something."

"You want me to leave? Just walk right out of here? Go home?"

He sighed and pushed Tiffany away with a single thrust. She fell on her back with a small cry.

He stood and zipped his pants. "You can't stay here anymore," he said, facing me. His face was red.

"What?"

"I said—"

"I heard what you said. What does that mean? I can just go home?"

"Home?" he said.

"Yes. To my family. You know goddamn well what I mean."

He took a step toward me. His fingers played nervously with the buttons on his shirt. "Your home is with me. You know that."

"You just told me to get out."

"You can't live here anymore. I've arranged for you to live in the trailer across the road. You're free."

I threw one hand up in the air, resisting the strong urge to slap him once more. "I'm not free, you shithead. What if I don't want to live in your stupid trailer? What if I walk out of here right now and never come back? Then what?"

He donned his most serious look. "Then you know what happens to the Fletchers."

Tiffany, still lying on the floor like a wounded doe, said, "Who's the Fletchers?"

We ignored her. "Just what the fuck am I supposed to do over there?" I said.

"Lynn," he said. "Sooner or later, you have to grow up. I've arranged it all. You'll have papers, and I will supply you with a modest income for your needs."

"Papers?"

"Yes. A driver's license in your name, social security card, that sort of thing."

"My name is Claire Fletcher."

"Your name is Lynn," he replied, as if talking to a recalcitrant child.

"Why are you doing this to me?" I asked. It was a question I had asked in the first days of my captivity, through tears and pleas, that he had never answered. Now, as the question issued forth from me once more, I realized I wasn't asking why he did the things he did. I was asking the impossible question: Why had this happened to me?

His motives were simple. I had fulfilled a need, a desire for him. His reasons for keeping me long after I'd ceased to satisfy his sick urges were practical—if he did not either keep me or kill me, he would surely go to prison.

The question of why my life had taken the bizarre twist it had that day on the sidewalk was the one that truly plagued me. It was as useless as asking: What is the meaning of life? There was no answer that would satisfy me, that would make the years of torture, abuse, isolation, and separation from my loved ones justified.

He chose not to hear me. Instead he walked to his dresser, opened the top drawer, and dangled a set of keys before me. "Here are the keys to the trailer," he said. "Why don't you go have a look?"

The moment he told me to get out, I should have taken those words for what they were. I should have just walked down the road until I could flag down a car and ask the driver to take me to the nearest police station. But part of me feared that he would harm my family, even if I did not return to them. What he really offered me was pseudo-freedom. A place of my own where my comings and goings would be carefully monitored. I was still a prisoner with an invisible tracking device strapped to my ankle.

I went to live in the trailer, which was small and not well suited for bad weather. But for the first time in my life, I was alone. There was a lock on my door. The silence into which I slipped so easily went uninterrupted. For a time, he delivered food and toiletries, carrying a brown bag across the road every few days.

When I had not attempted any escape, he decided to test my new-found independence. He arrived with a thick manila envelope, which he handed to me as we stood in the trailer's small kitchen.

"You need to start doing things for yourself," he said, as if he were a father figure instructing a child.

"What's this?" I said, fingering the envelope but not opening it.

"In there you will find identification items. You will also find directions to the nearest town. Since you made it clear you are able to drive, I've included the keys to the truck, which you may use only to go to town and purchase necessities." His eyes bore into me, adding emphasis to the word *only*. "I've also included some money to get you started. This is a big step for you, Lynn."

"Don't call me Lynn," I said.

He ignored me. He moved closer. I felt his breath on my face, hot and rapid. He fingered the buttons on his shirt. "Don't disappoint me," he said.

I held the envelope in front of me like a shield. I held a breath, waiting for his hands to slip around my throat or grab my hair and jerk me across the room, or for his fists to fly at my face. Some kind of warning. A beating for good measure. Something to assure me that if I breached his protocol, I would pay.

But he stepped away without touching me. Before he stepped outside, he turned to me. "I will be watching you," he said. "If you betray my trust, there will be consequences. Do not forget that."

When he was gone, I opened the envelope and spread the contents over the kitchen table, which extended from the wall, sandwiched between two vinyl-cushioned benches like a restaurant booth.

I placed each sheet of paper side by side, lining them up until the surface of the table disappeared. There was a birth certificate, social security card, and a temporary driver's license all in the name of Lynn Wood. According to the documents, I was twenty-two. My birthday was August 23, and my eyes were brown, not blue.

I was considering whether there had been a real Lynn Wood whose life I was taking over, and whether he had killed her, when I spied an item he had not specified. My heart jumped as I picked up the neatly clipped newspaper article.

It was not much larger than the one about Tom. This one involved my parents and the house I grew up in. The kitchen, which was at the rear of the house, had caught fire in the middle of the night while my mother and sister slept upstairs. The kitchen was a total loss, but the rest of the house and those in it were saved by a next-door neighbor who was awakened by a noise outside.

He thought he saw a prowler and phoned the police. By the time they arrived, the kitchen was ablaze. Despite police protests, the neighbor had turned his garden hose on the blaze until the fire department arrived.

Investigators could find no evidence of arson, nor could they rule it out, but the neighbor remained firm on the source of the noise that woke him—a prowler.

Here was my warning. Subtle, silent, and far more effective than any physical pain he could have inflicted on me.

That night I slept with the clipping beneath my pillow, as if I could protect the members of my family by keeping them tucked safely in my bedding. I dreamed that the girl I used to be was entering her sopho-more year of college, studying veterinary medicine. My father helped her move into a dorm room, he and my brother hefting boxes and a few small pieces of furniture up stairs and down hallways rife with young, beautiful people. The girl I used to be hugged and thanked Tom and my father. They made plans to meet at my parents' house for a Labor Day barbecue the coming weekend. All three of them were happy, their faces intact, unbroken by tragedy, loss, or uncertainty.

CHAPTER

FORTY-TWO

Captain Riehl held the composite sketch in one hand and stared at it. He hadn't spoken for a full minute. Connor knew because he had watched the second hand on the conference room clock above Riehl's head. The only sound in the room was Stryker cracking his knuckles. Boggs nudged the younger detective and Stryker stopped. They all looked at Riehl, waiting for a response. Twenty minutes earlier, Connor had arrived at the division after his lunch with Farrell and Jenny and gathered the three men in the conference room.

Connor had started at the very beginning and told his colleagues everything. He told them about meeting Claire, spending the night with her, and finding only her name and address the next day. He told them how he'd shown up unsuspecting at the Fletchers' front door only to be stunned by the revelation that the woman he'd met had disappeared ten years ago. He recapped his meeting with Farrell, calling in a favor with Lena Stark to get a fingerprint confirmation, and every lead he and Farrell had followed up since.

"Cap?" Boggs prompted.

Riehl sighed and looked at Connor over the top of his reading glasses. "You were supposed to be on the desk."

"I was! Cap, I met her in a bar—"

Riehl held up a hand, silencing Connor. "Now you want to take this to the press?"

Connor nodded.

Boggs cleared his throat. "Cap, this could actually be a good thing for us."

Riehl raised a skeptical eyebrow but said, "Enlighten me, Detective."

"If Parks solves a ten-year-old case—a missing persons no less—it makes him and the department look pretty damn good. That rapist he shot? Old news. No one will care about that anymore."

"Yeah," Stryker chimed in. "This is Parks's way of redeeming himself."

Riehl's expression did not change, but the fact that he had not immediately dismissed the idea of putting Connor's name out in the press boded well for Connor.

"The other three guys you mentioned—the ones who saw this woman—they're all dead?" Riehl asked.

"Speer is dead. The other two are missing."

"Seems to me someone"—Riehl waved the composite sketch in the air—"is keeping an eye on this woman's activity and getting rid of anyone she comes into contact with. Either that or he keeps an eye on the Fletcher home and who comes to visit. You think this guy will come after you?"

Connor shrugged. "I don't know. I'm hoping someone will recognize him. But if he does come after me, I'll be ready."

Riehl shook his head. "I'm not sure we have the resources to keep you out of harm's way. You got someone you can stay with for a few days?"

Connor swiped a hand through his hair. "That would defeat the purpose of flushing this guy out if he *is* spying on the Fletchers or keeping a tight leash on Claire."

Riehl handed the composite back to Connor and folded his arms across his chest. "I don't like it."

"Cap, let's say we had no idea these other three men either disappeared or got killed—what would we do with a lead like this?" Connor asked, using the same argument he had used earlier with Mitch and Jenny.

Riehl stared at Connor for a very long moment. Connor held Riehl's gaze, unwavering. Boggs and Stryker watched them, Stryker shifting his weight from foot to foot.

Finally, Riehl gave another heavy sigh. "The best I can do is send patrols past your house a few times a night."

Connor smiled, resisting the urge to high-five Stryker and Boggs. "All right," he said.

Boggs looked at his watch. "Well, let's get some reporters on the line. We should still have time to get on the eleven o'clock news and make tomorrow's newspaper."

CHAPTER
FORTY-THREE

I heard them arguing. They weren't even on the porch yet, and Tiffany's unintelligible squeals were audible across the road. I went to the trailer door this time and flung it open, standing in the open doorway. His voice answered hers loudly, sending a shiver through the center of my body. In ten years, I had only heard him raise his voice a handful of times.

An instant later, he came flying out the front door, stumbling over the decaying floorboards, Tiffany's hands on the backs of his shoulders. Her face was streaked with tears, nostrils flared angrily. She stood with fists clenched at her sides, chin raised defiantly as she waited for him to turn around.

She didn't move when he raised his hand and slapped her hard across the face. Without conscious thought, my feet skittered backward, my stomach clenching. I felt the slap all the way from where I stood, as surely as if it had been my face he'd reddened and stung with his palm.

He'd never hit Tiffany.

Never.

In the seven years they'd lived in their own sordid bliss, he had never been violent with her. Slowly, I closed the front door and stepped backward until my body met with the wall. In that moment, none of the beatings or rapes I'd endured flashed in my mind. Only images of Sarah suffocating, her legs kicking uselessly against the couch like a marionette, and Rudy's bloated, unrecognizable body lying on the living room floor. The news clippings.

Then a new image, more horrible than the others. An image that brought tears instantly to my eyes and caused a snake of fear to coil around my lungs, forcing the breath from my body. Connor, dead and badly beaten, lying on the carpet right in front of me, my captor's latest insurance policy, assuring my silence and the continued ruse that Claire Fletcher was dead.

Clearly, my captor's interest in Tiffany had waned or they wouldn't be arguing every day. She would have no second thoughts about revealing my recent nightly trips away from the trailer, but she had never seen firsthand what he was capable of. She had never seen him kill, never seen the dead body of someone she'd slept with hemorrhage and leak brain tissue onto the carpet. She had no idea.

I stood shivering in the trailer, though it was not cold. My mind raced. I could not get away to call Connor or to spy on him and make sure he was okay—at least until the next day. But I might have to risk it again. The constant arguing between Tiffany and my captor may have been about something unrelated to Connor or my breaches of *trust*—my secret outings—but I could not quell the creeping, nauseated fear that whatever was happening in that house was wicked enough to warrant my efforts.

CHAPTER

FORTY-FOUR

The next day, I arrived back at the trailer from work smelling heavily of wet dog, which wasn't wholly unpleasant to me. Every Wednesday, I was responsible for washing and combing whatever animals were in residence at the hospital. Today the hospital was populated almost entirely by dogs, some of whom raucously objected to being bathed.

I glanced across the road to see the rustle of a curtain in the front window. He was not home, but Tiffany was watching. She was the eyes in the back of his head. I would have to wait hours before sneaking out to determine whether Connor was safe.

I locked the door behind me, stripped off my clothes in the bedroom, and turned the shower on. I waited for the water to turn lukewarm, standing outside the tiny cubicle, marching in place and hugging my nakedness.

Afterward, I threw on a pair of jeans, a T-shirt, and a sweatshirt. I felt a chill that had nothing to do with the balmy air in the trailer. I couldn't get warm. I checked the window from the bedroom. The house stood as always, appearing slightly off-kilter as if it might collapse in a heap of particleboard at any moment. His car was still not in sight. But

Tiffany's beady eyes remained in place, zeroed in on the trailer. I put on two pairs of socks and went to the kitchen to make tea.

I didn't hear him come in, but he broke the latch on the door and bent the frame like a partially crushed soda can. He was on me before I could react. I had never seen his face so red with fury. His entire body thrummed with anger, a high-pitched buzz that seemed to make the small room tremble around both of us. He hit me square in the stomach and I doubled over, my body falling as if it were tumbling through a hatch in the floor.

He reached down and tangled one hand in my unruly curls. He jerked my head back so that he could look at my face and then punch it. I felt the insides of my lips split against my teeth, which felt loosened by the strike.

"How could you do this to me?" he said.

I was trying to breathe in deep enough for my mind and body to acclimate to the situation. He hit me again, and my left eye exploded in a thousand pinpricks of pain and one long, stabbing throb that radiated the length of my jaw.

"You fucking bitch," he added.

I tried to stand. He let go of my hair, flicking me away as if I were something slimy and germ-ridden that he'd accidentally put his hand in. He kicked and his sneaker-clad foot made contact with my hip bone as I squirmed to protect my center, my kidneys. My legs went out from under me like they were made of air. I collapsed onto the tile floor, gasping for breath and clenching my teeth against the assorted pains in my body.

I did not know which pain to attend to first—the one in my hip, my kidney, or my face. Using my hands, I gathered my stunned legs into me and curled into a ball. He kicked again, this time hitting my forearm.

"Stop," I said, but the word came out raspy and barely audible.

"You will never learn. Will you?" he said.

He paced back and forth in front of me like a cat with its hackles standing on end, waiting for the right moment to spring in for the kill, looking for just the right piece of flesh to sink its teeth into. He kicked thrice more, and my body made a clipped sound like that of an animal caught in a snare. It was involuntary.

"Stop," I said again.

"How could you do this to me? To us?"

I tried to catch my breath. My eyes watered. I raised my head to look at him, and he took that opportunity to kick once more, again jarring my skull as his foot rocketed into the left side of my face. The skin around my left eye was swollen, tightening and burning.

Again he paced. His hands clenched at his sides. His jaw hardened into an angry line. "I don't understand," he said. "After all this time. All I've given you. I tried to give you freedom, a place of your own, a life. It's never enough for you, is it?"

"What are you talking about?" I said. I leaned forward and spit blood on the floor. I tried to swallow but couldn't. It just made me cough. The coughing alerted me to the stabbing pain in my rib cage. Neither was pleasant.

He stopped dead center in the room and stared down at me. "You know what I'm talking about, you fucking whore."

"No," I said.

"Why would you go to the police after all this time?"

In spite of what might happen to my face, it snapped upward toward him. "What?"

From inside of his jacket, he pulled a folded section of newspaper, which he threw at me. It glanced off the side of my head and fell beside me. From my right eye, I struggled to find the item that had sent him into such a rage, the likes of which I hadn't experienced for years.

Officer Cleared of Wrongdoing in Shooting of Suspected Rapist Opens Cold Case

"No," I said. The shock filled the back of my throat, causing me to choke. I coughed violently. The pain of it made my eyes water again and my nose run. I did not need to read the article to know. I needed only to see the photo of my former face smiling back at me to know that Connor had been found out.

"Did you fuck him?" he said.

"What?"

"You heard me, you fucking bitch. Did you screw him? Like the others? You haven't learned anything from the past, have you, Lynn?"

Then he smiled. Panic woke inside me. I half crawled, half squirmed toward him, a begging stance. "Don't," I said.

He turned to the table and snatched up the jar I kept the sugar in. It wasn't overly large; it just fit into the curve of his hand. But it was heavy and the ceramic shell was hard.

I shielded my head with my arms, hands at the back of my skull. He beat me until sugar flew from the jar, raining down on me, an onslaught of white crystal sheets. He beat it against my body until the jar broke and he was sweating with exertion. He beat me until I passed out on the floor, my last image not of him—face red, hands raw and swollen from his work—but of Connor and his lopsided smile.

CHAPTER
FORTY-FIVE

The composite got a fifteen-second spot on the eleven o'clock news. Disappointed, Connor wondered if they should have held a press conference, but the morning paper had much more in-depth coverage. He picked up a copy of the *Sacramento Bee* on his way to the division and read it at his desk. Beside a large copy of the composite sketch was a smaller set of pictures of Claire—one of her school photograph and an age-progression photo, which didn't do her justice. The headline read, "Officer Cleared of Wrongdoing in Shooting of Suspected Rapist Opens Cold Case."

The article named Connor and recounted his involvement in the recent botched arrest during which he'd shot and killed a suspected rapist. While on the desk, he had reopened the case of Claire Fletcher, a local teen abducted ten years before. It asserted that Connor had fresh leads, was very close to solving the case, and that he believed that Claire Fletcher was alive. At the end, a lengthy review of the case was given, and the phone number for the Major Crimes Unit was listed in the event that readers had any tips.

Before lunch, Connor fielded two tips, one of which was from a man who claimed to have abducted Claire, killed her, and cut her body up into pieces. Connor sent a patrol car out to the guy's house in case he had cut someone into pieces. The second was a woman who worked at a pharmacy near the Fletcher house and claimed a man matching the composite had worked there between 1996 and 1999 as a pharmacy technician. She couldn't remember the man's name but promised to get Connor copies of the man's personnel file.

He met Jen and Mitch for lunch for the second day in a row to go over their leads. The waiter returned to take their order, and then Mitch pulled a file from under his jacket and handed it to Connor.

"Tax returns," he said.

Connor flipped it open and found himself looking at tax returns and W-2 forms for Rod Page, dated 1993 and 1994. "How did you get these?" he asked.

Mitch smiled at Jen, who said, "I have a friend, a very good friend, who works for the IRS."

Connor looked at both of them. "This is illegal," he said.

Jen arched her eyebrows. "It's been ten years," she said. "I just want my child back. Now that I know she's alive—that she really is out there somewhere—that is my only priority. I'm a little past worrying about what's legal and what's not."

"All right, then," Connor said. He looked at Mitch. "Just so we understand each other, Mrs. Fletcher, neither I nor Mitch ever saw these documents. We didn't get them from you. You didn't get them from your friend. Your friend could lose his job and go to prison over this."

"Her job," Jen corrected. "Yes, we understand each other."

"So," Mitch said. "This guy worked for the National Park Service. Summers only. Basically drove around making sure no one was starting unauthorized campfires, cleaned up trash, kept the roads and walking paths clear. Things like that."

"He didn't make much," Connor noted.

"No, he didn't," Mitch agreed. "Unless this guy is doing some serious work under the table, he must already have money."

"You think?"

"What else would give him that kind of mobility? If he's using an assumed name, which we can pretty much guarantee since the social security number on those belongs to a dead man, he would be able to hide a modest savings. He may have had some kind of insurance settlement he's living from or something like that."

"True," Connor said.

"It could be anything," Jen said. "Some civil lawsuit or insurance settlement. It wouldn't surprise me if this guy took out a policy on his own mother and then killed her for the money."

"There was a man who worked with Rod Page," Mitch said. Before Connor could open his mouth, Mitch went on, "I already talked to him. He didn't remember much, but he said he remembered Rod Page because Page wasn't memorable at all. He said Page was quiet, kept to himself. Didn't talk much. The only thing that might be of use is that Page once told this guy that he was originally from Texas."

Connor met Mitch's eyes across the table.

"We'll run a search for arrests and warrants in Texas for peepers and flashers," Connor said.

The waiter set their drinks down on the table. Jenny took a sip of water and asked, "Did the composite generate any leads yet?"

"As a matter of fact, I got a call this morning from a woman who works at a local pharmacy. She said a man matching the composite worked there as a pharmacy tech between 1996 and 1999. But that was all she had. She couldn't remember the guy's name. She's supposed to get a personnel file and get back to me."

Jen's hand flew to her chest. "Oh, my God. Are you telling me this guy worked at my pharmacy after he took Claire?"

"Didn't you say yesterday that the composite looked like your old pharmacist?" Mitch pointed out.

Jen's face paled. She looked like she was going to be sick. "Yeah. Maybe the woman who called you is thinking about the same guy."

"Well," Connor said, "we don't know if the pharmacy guy is Rod Page or not, although it is possible. I still have to check it out. And I also want to check out the Texas angle."

After lunch, Connor returned to the division. He took six more calls about the composite that afternoon, but none of them seemed promising. Texas yielded nothing. He'd gotten the ViCAP results back, but there were thousands of cases to sift through, leaving him to wonder if three-quarters of the country's population was sexually deviant. By the end of the day, he was no closer to finding Rod Page.

He left the division later than usual, but didn't go home right away. He dreaded going back to his empty house with its concealed weapons tucked about. He drove by the Fletcher home on Archer Street. The living room lights glowed behind gauzy curtains. He sat across the street in his car for several minutes, watching as a light in one of the upstairs rooms came on.

He felt a twinge of unease, although he couldn't say why. Perhaps it was his constant undertow of worry for Claire, who was still out there in parts unknown. The last time he'd heard her voice it had been heavy with tears.

He thought about stopping by Farrell's office, but instead he went home. As he walked up to the front door, he scanned the perimeter for anything amiss but found nothing out of the ordinary. The flowers along his walk swayed, as if in welcome. He closed and locked the door behind him.

The last thing he remembered was reaching for the light switch in the dining room.

CHAPTER FORTY-SIX

When I woke up, pain coursed through my body like the rhythmic booms of a car stereo playing so loudly you could feel its vibration in your teeth as the car passed on the street. I was bound to the thick column beneath the kitchen table in my trailer.

The chain, a personal favorite of his, was one he had fashioned himself years ago and had used often on me. It looped around the metal column beneath the table, fastened with a padlock, which he had begun employing when he figured out I could easily undo the metal clips he originally used. From the base of the table, the chain extended three or four feet. He had attached handcuffs to the end of it, the tiny chain between them inexplicably threaded through one of the links on the larger chain. He had my wrists cinched so tightly that the metal of the handcuffs bit into my skin and pressed mercilessly into the bones.

My left eye would not open. I lifted my hands and felt the side of my face, which had swelled disturbingly large in the wake of his beating. My skin was the texture of a grapefruit peel, and I imagined it looked like I had a grapefruit growing out of the side of my face. Dried blood crusted the edges of my mouth.

My right eye searched the kitchen and locked on to the object I was looking for. He had left it on the floor where he'd thrown it at me. Using my legs and squirming erratically, I used my feet to pull the newspaper to me. On my knees, I bent my body toward the floor, my face inches from the page, and read the article with my good eye.

I was shocked to see the composite and wondered where in the world Connor had gotten it. It was a good likeness of my abductor, although in it he looked much younger than he was now. The article named Connor directly but even if it hadn't, I believed my abductor would have found him. My captor was all-knowing, all-seeing, or so it had seemed these many years.

The night I left the trailer and found Martin in an upscale city bar, bedding him at a nearby hotel several steps up from the motel in which I'd first given my body up to another man, I'd thought for sure that my captor would have no way of finding out whom I'd been with.

I had known that Tiffany watched from one of the windows as I left in the truck. When I returned, he was still not there. I knew she would tell him I had been gone for almost an entire night, but I figured he would only beat me, maybe revoke my newfound privileges, or maybe kill me.

But I thought for certain he'd have no way of really knowing where I'd gone or whom I'd been with. Martin was dead two months later, and like the newspaper clippings in which my brother and mother and sister were almost killed, a new one had been taped to the inside of my trailer door. One in which Martin had no nosy neighbors to call the police before the fire blazed out of control, burning him alive.

With Jim, I'd been far more careful. I'd studied my captor's schedule. When the time came for me to sneak away, I'd put the truck in neutral and let it roll down the road as far as I could get it before starting it. I was gone only six hours, and the house was dark when I returned. Again, I turned off the truck and let it roll to its place behind the trailer. Neither he nor Tiffany alluded to the fact that they knew I had even left. It was months later—when something I said or did displeased him—that he stopped by and dropped Jim's wallet on my kitchen table.

I didn't know how long he'd had it. Whether he had actually done anything to the man or if he'd just pilfered the wallet to use later as a way to intimidate me. All the same, it had worked. It worked because no matter what I did, he found out. I had no idea how. It had been almost three weeks since I'd met and slept beside Connor Parks, nestled in the warmth of his arms, against the lovely smooth skin of his chest.

I realized my captor had not known about Connor. Otherwise he would not have flown off the handle when he discovered the newspaper article. Seeing the composite, it was no wonder he believed I had gone to the police. Tears blurred the vision in my right eye. I tugged uselessly against the chain. Connor was a police officer. A detective. He'd shot and killed someone the day I met him. Surely he could defend himself against this man.

I sat upright, flexing my body, testing this way and that for pain that might hinder any escape I made. I had no idea how much time had passed, but outside, the world was dark. The small lamp I kept on the table was lit. I'd turned it on before he entered, anticipating a cup of tea while I sat there and read a book, waiting until I could sneak out to check on Connor.

I took several deep breaths and shifted so that I could brace my feet against the base of the table. Pulling with my hands and pushing with my feet, I tried to break the chain from its vise around the column. I was not thinking clearly. Pain in my ribs screamed and my body went limp, gasping for air.

I shifted again, this time bracing my feet awkwardly against each of the benches on either side of the table. I pushed against them and pulled with the chain, trying instead to dislodge the column from the table so that I could slip the chain over it. It did not give.

A sob rumbled up from the back of my throat. Tears leaked slowly out of the slit that was my left eye and burned my face as they slid down to my chin. They flowed more freely from my good eye.

I stood up, though the length of the chain did not allow me to straighten my body completely. I used both hands to pull at one corner of the table, but the effort caused too much pain. I found myself back on the floor.

I looked at my hands and the flesh of my wrists blooming on either side of the metal rims of the handcuffs. I pulled at my right hand. I could easily dislocate my thumb again. At least I could easily deal with the pain of it. I had done it twice before in desperation. But now the cuffs were flush against my bone, and my hands seemed much larger than they had before. There was not even room for the cuffs to scrape the skin away.

My mind raced. There had to be some way. There had to be something I could do to free myself. I looked around the kitchen for anything I might use, and my eyes fell on Tiffany, standing just inside the trailer door, silent and staring at me.

She looked sad. I had no idea how long she'd been standing there. When she spoke, her voice held none of its usual malevolence. It was hollow and flat.

"Now you've really done it," she said.

CHAPTER FORTY-SEVEN

Tiffany walked into the kitchen and gasped when the circle of light illuminated the full injury of my face.

"Wow," she said.

"Get me out of here," I said.

She put her hands on her hips and stared at me. Her face was slack and all the more disturbing because it was not twisted in the sneer that she usually directed toward me.

"Come on," I said, pulling at the chains and offering my hands up to her as if in prayer.

She ignored me, sitting on the floor in front of me and folding her legs into a triangle, bony knees jutting out from her shorts. As if we were two teenage girls at a slumber party, sharing secrets atop a sleeping bag in the middle of the night.

"I don't understand it," she said. "I don't understand you. You always want to get away, but you never leave. He's obsessed with you. No matter what I do, it's not good enough. It's never good enough. You treat him like shit, and he still has to know everything you do, every place you go."

She picked at the hem of her shorts, face bent downward, and her thin brown hair fell across her cheek. "I thought it would be so great after you left, and it was for a while. Then he started going out more and staying out overnight. He told me he didn't mess around with other girls, but still it seemed like he never wanted to be with me. We still had sex all the time, well, at least till last year. Now he hardly touches me. It's like I'm ugly or something."

"Tiffany," I said. "Listen to me. You have to get me out of these chains."

She looked at me, and her eyes were sorrowful. "Why should I? You ruin everything. You've totally ruined everything after tonight."

"Oh come on," I said. "He's angry. He'll get over it like he always does, and the two of you can go back to doing, oh I don't know, whatever sick, bizarre things you do over there. But you have to get me out of here right now. He's going to do something bad. He's going to hurt someone I care about if I don't stop him."

Her face pinched. "See? You don't care about me. All you can think of is yourself. You're not even listening to me. No one listens to me. You don't care how I feel." She said the word *feel* as if it were the first time she'd uttered it. It peeled off her tongue like a foreign word.

"I do listen to you," I said. "You think he cares about you but he doesn't. If he did, he wouldn't have made you his sex toy when you were only thirteen. Someone somewhere cares about you, about how you feel, but it's not him."

Her eyes flashed: a familiar emotion in the flatland of her face. "You're wrong," she snapped. "He's the only one who ever cared about me. You think my mom cared about me? You think those stupid social workers cared about me? You think my grandparents or those snotty people at that dumb old church cared about me? No one did. No one gave a shit about me until he came along. Now everything is ruined."

I moaned. "Fine. Fine. Whatever. But it's not ruined. Look, he's held on to me this long, do you really think he's going to send you packing now? Just get me out of these chains. I have to stop him."

Again, the flat quiet settled over her. She resumed picking the thread from the hem of her shorts. "No," she said. "It doesn't matter what I do. He'll keep you or he wouldn't have chained you up. So what if you go after him. That's probably what he wants. But he doesn't care about me anymore."

I struggled with the words, not wanting to say them but seeing no other way to coax her to help me get free. "Yes, he does. Of course, he does. Don't say that. Just help me out of here."

Again, I offered my hands in supplication. "No, he doesn't," she said, more sharply. "He's already got someone else."

All the throbbing, stabbing pain in my body was sucked into a single point in my stomach, like a whirlpool pulling it down to some dark place I never wanted to see again. "What?" I croaked.

"He brought her home a few weeks ago. I didn't know she was in there right away until I realized he'd started locking the door. I only saw her once. I don't know why he likes her. She's small, and she doesn't even talk. All she does is cry all the time. She's a big, stupid baby."

On my hands and knees, I crawled as close to her as the chain would allow. My voice held a new intensity, desperation. "Tiffany," I said. "You have to help me get out of here. Now."

She shook her head.

"Please," I said. "This is very, very important."

Again, she shook her head.

Then, an idea. "I'll take her away," I said. "Help me get out of here, and I'll take her away and she'll never come back."

"Yeah right," she mumbled. "Then he'll just be mad at me even more 'cause I let you go. Forget it. I wish you would go away."

"I will. Let me go and I will. I'll go away, so far away you won't be able to find me, and you'll never see me again."

"No way," she said. "Like I would believe anything you said. You're a big, fat liar."

She sat, staring at the floor, slowly unthreading her shorts. I resumed my struggle with the chains, gasping, squirming, pushing, pulling, and nearly screaming with frustration. When I was spent once more and the pain in my ribs had become too much, I stopped and faced her again.

I watched her for a long time, my mind working through countless words I could use to convince her to help me. I shifted so that I could rest my back against the side of one of the benches. I tried to even out my breathing.

"Could you at least get me some ice?" I said. "For my face."

She looked at me and then rolled her eyes. "Fine," she said.

She went to the freezer and took out a tray of ice cubes, which she dumped into a kitchen towel. She gathered the ends of the towel up in one hand and brought it to me. She held it out. I took it with both hands and pressed it to the side of my face. She took up her position across from me once more.

After several minutes, I held the makeshift ice pack out to her. "Could you hold it on my face for a while? It hurts when I keep my arms up like that. I think he broke some of my ribs."

She rolled her eyes again but shimmied over and took the ice pack from me. As she reached up to press it to my face, I swung my arms over her head and looped the chain around her throat. I pulled her into me with both hands and the chain tightened, its length fully expended. She choked and spluttered. Her hands flew to her neck and dug into the skin above and below the heavy links of metal. Her legs shot straight out.

I steeled myself against the awesome pain in my ribs, pulling and pulling until she slackened a little. I loosened the chain slightly, and her breath emerged in small bursts of air.

Into her ear, I hissed. "Now you listen to me. You're going to get me out of these chains or I am going to kill you. I'm going across the street, I'm taking that girl, leaving with her, and you aren't going to say a fucking word. Do you understand?"

She gave no indication so I jerked furiously on the chain. This time, her back arched, and her body danced helplessly, like a branch caught in a storm. After several seconds I released my hold again, allowing her to breathe. Still, she clutched at her neck.

"You think I won't kill you? You think I don't have it in me? Well, I do. I'll pull this chain until all the breath is squeezed out of you. I'll keep pulling until you suffocate. Did you know it only takes four minutes for a girl like you to asphyxiate and die? I learned that from him."

With my last words, her body seized again, as if I had pulled the chain tight across her windpipe once more.

"That's right," I said. "I watched him do it to someone just like you. If you think for one second that I won't do the same to you, you're dead wrong. You will get me out of these chains and you will let me go—with the girl."

Nothing. I began to tighten the chain again, but then she began nodding furiously. I let go but did not remove the chain from her neck. She turned on her side, coughing and choking into my lap. Tears leaked from her eyes onto my pants, and a long thread of spittle dripped from her mouth. She rubbed her throat.

I jangled the chain. "Are you going to help me?" I asked.

"Yes," she said, her voice throaty and raspy. "Yes. Yes. Just stop."

"Do you have the keys?"

She shook her head, and I gripped the chain again. "No. Wait," she breathed. "He took them with him. But I can do something. I don't know . . . something."

The effort of speaking wore her out. I glanced at the padlock. "Get a hammer," I said. "Do you have a hammer?"

She nodded.

"Go," I said.

Stumbling, her legs not working quite right, she ran from the trailer. Minutes later she returned, breathless, wielding a hammer, its head rusted over with age. I pointed below the table with both hands. "The padlock," I said.

She dropped to her knees, ducking her head under the table and made several feeble attempts to smash the lock. "Give me that," I said, pushing her aside. She dropped the hammer on the floor and moved out of my way. She sat with her back against the opposite bench, kneading the skin at her throat and breathing irregularly.

I put my legs on either side of the column and gripped the handle of the hammer with both hands. I could not raise it above my head for momentum because of the table, although it would probably have hurt far too much to do so anyway. I swung as hard as I could. I swung again and again until sweat poured down my ruined face, burning my eyes. The hammer clanged angrily against the lock and the column. As it started to mangle, I increased my efforts, adrenaline dulling the pain in my body.

Finally, it broke loose. I scurried out from under the table and tossed the hammer into Tiffany's lap. She jumped, and her eyes widened at the sight of me. I flattened my palms against the floor, pulling the small chain between the cuffs taut.

"You have to break this," I said. "I can't drive like this."

She stared at me blankly.

"Tiffany," I said. I reached up and pushed the hammer against her thin chest. "Goddammit. Right now."

She took the hammer, and I flattened my palms again. "Aim for the center of the chain," I instructed.

She raised the hammer to face level and brought it down with a dull thud. I looked up at her. "You're going to have to go harder than that," I said. "Come on, I don't have much time."

After several half-hearted tries, she began to bring the hammer down hard, its impact on the chain making a high-pitched ping. Then she swung a little wildly and hit my left hand. I howled in pain, and she backed away as if I might attack her. I put my hands back on the floor. The throbbing had to wait. "Again," I said. "Use the other end."

She turned the hammer over so the pick end faced downward. As she raised it above her head, I said, "Do not hit me again."

It took three tries, and the small chain broke. I bolted to my feet, toward the door. I fell down the three front steps of the trailer, swearing and kicking up gravel and dirt as I stood again. Tiffany watched dumbly from the doorway. I held my left hand in my right as I made my best attempt at a sprint across the road toward the house.

I barreled through the front door, using only my shoulder, again falling on the hardwood floor and scrambling back to my feet. I searched the rooms until I came to the locked door. This too was padlocked.

"Son of a bitch." I turned to see Tiffany watching me. "Go get the hammer," I said.

Wordlessly, she left. I began kicking at the door with as much force as my injured body could muster, which was not much. Even given the age of the house and poor quality of the door, my kicks were ineffective. Tiffany returned and held out the hammer. I took it in my right hand. I tried to wrap my left hand around it, but that hand had gone almost completely limp. With my right hand I swung downward, driving the hammer into the lock and grunting with my efforts. Finally, the lock fell to the floor with a clang.

With my foot, I pushed the door open.

CHAPTER

FORTY-EIGHT

Connor opened his eyes to darkness. For a moment, he thought he was dreaming. Then he wondered why he didn't remember going to bed. As his eyes adjusted to the dark, he realized he was on the floor of his bedroom, and then it came back to him. Not that it was very much. He knew he'd been hit on the head, mostly because it hurt so damn much.

He reached up to touch it and saw that his hands were bound together with heavy rope. He felt a thick, sloppy fluid matting his hair. Blood. He winced as he ran his fingers clumsily along the gash. He lifted his head yet saw nothing but the dark, familiar shapes of his bedroom. His feet were bound as well. He pulled his feet up toward his head and tried to untie the rope.

He sensed rather than saw the black figure flying at him from his left side. Instinctively, he rolled away and a heavy foot landed in his back. He rolled back and grabbed the figure's foot, sweeping the man down to the floor with him. He pulled on the leg and squirmed toward the man, trying to get on top of him. Another foot hit Connor in the shoulder.

The man was on top of Connor, on his knees, fists raised high above his head. Connor covered his face and took most of the blows on his forearms as he planted his bound feet on the floor and lifted his rear end to buck the man off. As the attacker toppled to the side, Connor reached above his head. He knew the bed was there, and he hoped he was in position to grab the knife he'd stowed.

As his fingers slid over the homemade sheath, the man came at Connor again. Connor grabbed the edge of the bed for stability and turned his body, swinging both legs out and again knocking the attacker to the ground. He drew his legs in to cover his body and once more reached for the knife.

Silently, the blade slid from its sheath. Connor gripped it and flipped onto his back like a landed fish. As the attacker came at him again, Connor swung, slicing through the man's pant leg but hitting nothing save the fabric.

The attacker descended on Connor, both his hands covering Connor's in an effort to control the weapon. He kneed Connor heartily in his upper abdomen, and Connor instantly felt his breath leave him. Had he enough wind to curse, he would have. The attacker wrenched the knife from Connor's hands.

Connor tried to recover, willing his breathless body to move. Somewhere in the back of his mind, a perfectly calm voice mused, *This must be what panic attacks are like.* He'd known hundreds of people in his career who were plagued by them after being victims of violent crime. Even a handful of his colleagues had fallen prey to panic attacks after seeing one too many gruesome crime scenes—the worst ones involving children.

Flat on his back, unable to breathe, bound and weaponless, Connor braced for death. The knife plunged into his right thigh. Connor howled, and his body automatically curled toward the pain in his leg. The calm voice in his head instructed him to pull the knife out of his leg, and he reached for it.

The attacker's hands covered his once again, and they struggled for control of the knife. It had gone deep, and the wound burned as

Connor pulled it from his leg. Without conscious thought, he swung at his attacker, aiming at center mass. His breath returned, and he flipped onto his side where he could move more freely with his hands and feet tied.

He felt the blade of the knife clang against bone and saw the dark shape of the man fall to one knee, clutching at his ankle. Gripping the knife so hard his hands ached, Connor withdrew and rolled to his knees. He drew his hands back and arced the knife downward, felt it plunge into flesh, and heard the man drop onto his back with a yelp.

Again Connor rose up, falling on the man and bringing the knife with him. The attacker let out a horrendous sound that made goose bumps rise along Connor's arms. Grabbing just below Connor's hands, where the blade met his flesh, the attacker pushed Connor, who fell to the side with the knife still in his hands.

The man rolled away from him and crawled quickly toward the bedroom door. Connor shrimped his body wildly in pursuit, but the man was too fast. He heard glass breaking, then feet hitting pavement; Connor slumped, breathing hard, still gripping the knife as if his life depended on it.

CHAPTER
FORTY-NINE

It was no more than a large closet, empty except for a bucket and a very young girl huddled in one corner. The sight of the bucket brought me to my knees. My body tried to vomit, but the pain in my ribs would not allow it. For several moments, I fought back the heaves.

Two large brown eyes stared at me from beneath dirty brown hair. She was naked, hog-tied, curled in a corner. As I approached her, she squirmed crazily, inarticulate grunts and whimpers punctuating her wild movements. Her fingernails scratched the wall as if to escape. I crawled toward her, and the closer I got, the wider her eyes became. I suddenly realized how I must look to her. Grapefruit face. I held out my good hand.

"It's okay," I whispered. "It's okay now. I won't hurt you."

She stopped struggling but not whimpering. I glanced behind me. Tiffany stood in the doorway, the flat stare still covering her face. "Get her some clothes," I said.

"From where?"

"Goddammit," I said, my voice rising in pitch and volume. "Just do it. Now."

Tiffany's shadow receded from the doorway. I looked again at the girl and inched closer toward her. I could see, feel her body tense up.

"It's okay," I said again. "Come here. I'm going to help you."

She shook her head rapidly and pressed herself against the wall.

"My name is Claire," I said. "I'm here to take you home."

At the word *home*, she stilled. I nodded at her. "Yes. Home. I'm going to take you there, but you have to come with me right now. We don't have much time."

She stared at me, brown eyes glistening with fear and hope. Tiffany appeared in the doorway again, holding out a T-shirt and pair of sweatpants. "They'll be too big for her," she said.

I snatched them from her and moved toward the girl. She held out her hands, which thankfully were tied with only rope. It took several minutes for me to undo the knots with one hand injured and swollen. When her hands were free, I looked her in the eyes. "I need your help," I said.

She seemed to understand instantly and deftly untied her feet, throwing the ropes aside. I thrust the clothes at her, and she pulled them on with trembling hands.

"Can you walk?" I asked.

She shook her head. She crawled toward me, swaying. He had probably starved her. Made her even weaker than her small body would allow against someone bigger, stronger, and crueler. My right eye blurred again with tears.

I saw it then. I saw what he had done to me in its entirety. How he had stripped away every single thing and left a hollow paper shell where Claire Fletcher used to be. I pulled the girl to me, and she wrapped her arms around my neck, her legs around my waist. She fit her body to mine like a soft barnacle, and I stood, stumbling under her weight.

Adrenaline and the thin, cool feel of her against my body propelled me. Passing Tiffany in the hall, I barked for her to retrieve the truck keys. She pulled the extra set from a drawer in the kitchen, handed them to me, and stood in the open door of the clapboard house as I lurched across the road to the truck, a young, trembling girl fused to my body.

When we reached the truck, I tried to push the girl in through the driver's-side door, but she would not let go of me. Her whimpers turned to a high-pitched wail. I talked in her ear, stroking her hair with my right hand, which also held the keys. They jangled against her scalp.

"Shhh, it's okay. It's okay. I'm going to help you. I'm taking you home, but you have to get in. You have to help me."

Reluctantly, she disentangled herself and scurried across the seat. I got in, swung the door closed behind me with my good hand, and started the truck. She moved back across the seat so that her body pressed against my side.

"Shit," I said, as I threw the clutch into reverse.

I'd have to steer with my left hand, which was practically useless. But then I realized it would be far easier than having to shift with an injured hand. I let up on the clutch and punched the gas. The truck roared backward, cutting an uneven path to the road.

It stalled and I started it again, shifting into second as I picked up speed. I put the headlights on and glanced at my companion. Her head rested against my shoulder, and her eyes searched my face.

"It's okay," I said.

CHAPTER FIFTY

Connor lay on the floor for several minutes, trying to catch his breath and decide what to do next. He could feel blood oozing from the wound in his leg, hot and fiery. When he was certain his attacker was not coming back, he reached down between his legs and sawed through the ropes with the knife.

He tossed the knife aside and stood unsteadily. Collapsing on the edge of the bed, he picked up the telephone receiver from his nightstand. Gingerly, he put it in his lap and dialed 911. When he heard the ringing, he cradled it in his hands and pressed it against his ear.

When he got through to a person, he gave his address. "Officer down," he said. He repeated his name and badge number twice. The dispatcher wanted him to stay on the line until help arrived, but Connor could no longer hold on to the receiver. He slid down to the floor and closed his eyes, waiting for the beautiful harmony of sirens in the distance.

Minutes passed like hours, and then suddenly light blasted Connor's vision. Paramedics stood over him talking, asking him questions. He tried to answer as best he could. They moved him onto a board, and immediately one of them cut away his right pant leg and began working at the knife wound. The other staunched the bleeding from the gash in his head.

Uniformed officers appeared as the paramedics hoisted and strapped Connor onto a stretcher. They wheeled him down the hall and out the front door. As they moved out of the house, down the driveway toward the back of the ambulance, Connor looked up at one of the paramedics.

"Let me out of this thing," he said.

They stopped just outside the ambulance. The paramedic looked down at him. "Mr. Parks, you're badly injured. You need medical attention as soon as possible."

Connor struggled against the straps. "Detective Parks," he corrected. "You give me medical attention right here and let me up."

"You need to get to a hospital," said the second paramedic.

"Yeah, yeah. I'll go, but you let me up and let me talk to those officers first. I'm not gonna bleed out or I'd be dead already."

A uniform, whose name badge read Baxter, laid a hand on the shoulder of the first paramedic. "Let him up," he said.

Clearly disapproving and shooting both Connor and Baxter looks of contempt, the paramedic unfastened the straps. Connor sat up and swung his legs over the side of the stretcher.

Officer Baxter, a stocky man in his thirties with a moustache and bright blue eyes, held up a hand. "Whoa there, Detective. You just sit there for a minute. We checked out the perimeter. Perp is gone."

Connor accepted an ice pack from one of the paramedics and held it to the side of his head. "You're going to need stitches," the man said, but Connor waved him away and addressed Baxter.

"I need you to call detectives Boggs and Stryker with the Major Crimes Unit and tell them to get their asses down here right now. And Mitch Farrell. He's a PI, he should be in the book."

Baxter scribbled in his notepad, which he'd pulled from an inside pocket. "The Crime Scene Unit is en route," he said. "And I think your buddies are too."

Connor glanced beyond Baxter. Two police cruisers sat at the curb, lights flashing. One uniformed officer stood outside the door of the first car, talking to dispatch with the radio extending through the open door. Another stood at Connor's front door, ensuring no one entered the house.

An unmarked vehicle screeched to a halt in front of Connor's driveway, blocking the path of the ambulance. Boggs and Stryker emerged.

"What the fuck?" Boggs said, looking Connor over.

Stryker took Baxter aside, the two men talking in hushed tones. One paramedic changed the dressing on Connor's thigh. The other wrapped long strips of gauze around Connor's head.

"How did you know?" Connor said.

"News travels fast, my friend. Someone heard it on the scanner. We were still at the office. Now you wanna tell me what the fuck is going on?"

Connor winced as the paramedic finished dressing his head. He waved a hand toward the house. "He was already inside when I got home. I didn't even see him."

"Start at the top, Parks," Boggs said.

"Came home, went inside, locked the door. Guy suckered me. Woke up in the bedroom tied up. There's a knife in there that probably has his blood on it. You'll need to bag that."

"You let me worry about the scene," Boggs said. "Who is this fucker?"

Connor raised his eyes to meet Boggs's. "Claire Fletcher's kidnapper," he said.

Boggs arched an eyebrow. "Wow. He works fast. Guess that composite worked."

"I stabbed him," Connor said. "Two, three times—I don't remember, but I got him. There's probably blood in there."

Stryker walked up as Boggs was about to tell Connor once more to let them worry about the evidence. "Holy shit, Parks. You're a regular fucking sideshow. You all right?"

Connor pressed an ice pack to his head and nodded. "Call Farrell," he said to Boggs.

"You're going to the hospital," Boggs said.

CHAPTER
FIFTY-ONE

Her name was Alison, which was the only word she uttered during the entire drive. We drove fast, sometimes in fits and starts. I steered mostly with my left wrist, and she grabbed the wheel to help me navigate turns. It was a half-hour drive. I had not given any thought to where we would go, but as I pulled onto the street in the direction of a house I'd been to only once before, I realized where we were headed.

CHAPTER

FIFTY-TWO

Much to their irritation, Connor waved the paramedics off twice more as he waited for Boggs to finish talking to Stryker.

Someone shouted as an old green pickup truck careened down the street—going entirely too fast—and plowed into one of the parked cruisers. Everyone froze and stared. A puff of white smoke, turned red and blue by the flashing lights, materialized from the hood of the truck. The driver's-side door opened, and a woman got out. She paused at the door, revealing another figure in the cab of the truck.

When she came around to the sidewalk, they saw that the second figure was a young girl, and she was wrapped tightly around the woman's body.

Connor jumped off the stretcher and limped a few steps. "Claire?" he said.

She looked around frantically. Half her face was distorted from what must have been a very hard blow. Baxter and another uniform approached her warily from either side, hands resting on their pistols. They called out to her, but she did not look at them.

Connor limped another couple of paces. This time he yelled. "Claire?"

She saw him, and he swore he saw a smile of relief in her good eye. "Connor," she mouthed.

Neither of them could run, but they closed the distance between them as quickly as possible. They crashed into each other, the young girl's body between them. Claire's left hand was cushioned between the girl and her own body, but with her right hand she reached up to Connor's face.

He pulled her to him and rested his hands on her shoulders. They both spoke at once, not giving the other time to speak.

"My God, are you all right?" Connor said.

Claire touched his cheek. "I thought I was too late."

"What are you doing here?"

"What did he do to you?" she murmured.

Connor ignored her question and studied her mangled face. "You need to see a doctor."

"I didn't know what else to do. Who to go to."

Then another voice, not their own: "Hey."

They turned and saw Boggs standing two feet away, staring at them. When Claire turned her head, Boggs's face paled. He stepped forward and peered at her as if she were an apparition. "No," he murmured.

Stryker walked up beside Boggs and looked at each of them in turn. "What the hell is this?" he said.

Boggs reached up and pushed a mess of curls back from Claire's forehead. "It's Claire Fletcher," he said. "Fuck me, it's Claire fucking Fletcher."

Stryker cocked a thumb toward Alison. "Dude, there's a kid right here. She can hear you. You're the one always telling me not to swear in front of *your* kids."

Claire explained Alison's presence as quickly as possible to Boggs and gave him directions to the house. She warned him about Tiffany, trying to explain the girl's complicity to a baffled Boggs. She gave him the name of her captor—at least the name he had been using since they'd moved.

She wouldn't be separated from Connor, so they rode together in the ambulance, sitting across from each other. Stryker followed in one of the cruisers, leaving the unmarked for Boggs, who was already on the phone to ten different people. The paramedics tried to pry Alison away from Claire in order to check her over, but she screamed so loudly, it echoed off the walls of the ambulance, rivaling the siren atop it.

"It's okay," Claire said, hugging Alison to her with her right arm.

Quietly, she listed her own injuries for them, and one of them cleaned her face as she stared across the narrow divide at Connor. He looked like a wounded soldier. He held the side of his head; blood soaked through the dressing on his leg. He smiled at her, and Claire wept.

CHAPTER
FIFTY-THREE

The ER was packed full of people. It was disconcerting. The last time I had seen so many people in one place was at an assembly in high school. Nurses and doctors bustled, strode, and ran. A child wailed loudly from behind a half-open door. I was grateful that we invited no stares. Those around us were nursing various injuries, faces haggard with pain, waiting to be seen.

With a flash of his badge and some fast talk, the plainclothes detective named Stryker arranged for the three of us to wait in a private room. A stout nurse wearing blue scrubs looked annoyed but ushered us to a small room nonetheless.

Alison clung to me, arms clasped tightly around my waist. She blinked rapidly against the harsh fluorescent lights like a baby animal entering the world for the first time. As she buried her face in my shoulder, it occurred to me that she had spent an indeterminate amount of time in darkness, locked away in a closet.

I shivered with the remembered knowledge of that darkness. I had spent years trying to forget it, banish it from my body's memory. Through the thin frame of her body, I felt its cloying presence, the cold of it and the stark embrace of its terror.

The adrenaline that had allowed me to threaten Tiffany's life, move through the crush of a hammer blow, break down a door, and rescue this girl began to seep away. It left a stunning multitude of pains throughout my body.

I struggled helping Alison the short distance to the exam room, past bloodied and bandaged bodies and scrambling medical staff. Connor, in spite of a heavy limp and the fresh blood trickling down his bare leg from beneath a dark-red dressing, held me up. He helped me step up and sit with Alison on a gurney. He took a chair beside us.

Until that moment, all thought was lost in my physical efforts. Now I was seized by panic. My spine slammed ramrod straight, muscles tensing in spite of exhaustion.

"My family," I said.

Before Connor could speak, Stryker intervened. "Relax, Ms. Fletcher. Detective Boggs took a unit over there himself right after we left. In fact, I imagine your family won't be far behind us."

A new panic took hold. I hadn't thought this through, hadn't thought at all. I had to face them now. After all these years. There was no going back to my hell, which, while torturous, held all of my darkest, most humiliating secrets.

Every part of me would be bared. I would be naked again, but this time the audience would be far bigger, their eyes probing me for all the great and small indignities, the humiliations I'd endured. I could not go back into hiding. They would want explanations, and I would have to offer up my shame for everyone to see.

Stryker studied me, perhaps sensing my panic. He used a soothing tone that clashed with his macho demeanor. "Right now you need to be seen by a doctor," he said. "We can start by getting those cuffs off."

I held up my left hand, which was so swollen the metal ring cut off my circulation. It was a deep purple.

"Stryke," Connor said. "Has anyone called Farrell?"

Stryker nodded. "Yeah. He's on his way. Now let me go and see if I can light a fire under someone's ass around here before you lose a pint of blood. Sit tight."

Stryker pulled the door closed behind him, leaving the three of us alone. I looked at Connor. The deep-blue eyes I'd seen so many times in my dreams during the last few weeks were alive before me now, an oasis.

I was full of a million words. Novels, volumes to tell him. An encyclopedia of explanations.

"Not now," he said as I opened my mouth to speak. "Later. Right now I just want to look at you."

My laugh was throaty and thick. I shook my head but he smiled.

"Believe me," he said. "Nothing has ever looked better to me."

I sniffled. "Connor?"

"Yeah."

"Whatever happens, don't leave me alone."

His smile widened to a grin. "You're stuck with me now, babe," he said.

The medical staff descended on us in a fury. Nurses, doctors, Stryker, and even a female uniformed officer who tried to coax Alison away from my body, but she refused to budge. Together, we squeezed our eyes shut as they sawed the metal bracelets from my wrists.

Both Connor and I required X-rays and we went together, Alison too—our bodies close together, making it clear we would not be separated. Stryker fielded all comments and complaints from the staff. The three of us returned to the exam room. As a doctor stitched Connor up, the gentle coaxing for Alison to free herself from me began again. She would not move.

A half hour later, Alison's parents arrived. Her mother burst into the room, tears streaming down her face. She called her daughter's name, and Alison raised her head warily. She stared at her mother for a moment as if she didn't quite believe the woman was real. Then she twisted away from me and opened her arms.

Her mother scooped her off my lap, enveloping her until she disappeared into her mother's trembling form. Until they were one. I felt empty, bereft without my burden. The mother opened her eyes to me over Alison's head. She saw past my bruised melon face and looked right into the place where Claire Fletcher, the girl I used to be, still lived. Her penetrating eyes caused a lump to form in my throat.

"Thank you," she said.

The father approached me tentatively. He moved as if to hug me but stopped, afraid of hurting me. With my good eye, I met his wet gaze head on.

"It's okay," I said.

He gathered me in his arms gently and squeezed me. His whole body hiccupped with sobs, which were muffled in my hair. He kept saying, "Thank you. You just don't know . . ." But he could not finish the sentence. I let him pour his grief over me, taking his sobs like ocean waves rolling over my body.

The moment Alison and her family left, I was placed on a stretcher and whisked four floors up to surgery. Connor lurched madly along beside me. Before they could operate on my hand, I was called back to the ER. With her parents on either side of her, Alison allowed the staff to examine her, but she would not consent to a rape kit unless I was there.

It was just the two of us, one female doctor, and one female nurse. They told me Alison was eleven and this was her first pelvic exam. I sat by her head. With my right hand, I stroked the hair gently from her face. I turned her head so she was watching me.

"Just look at me," I said. "It's okay."

That is all I said, and gazing at her, I knew it was all I needed to say. There was a tacit understanding in her eyes. She knew without being told that I too had been in that closet. Now, if I showed her that submitting to this invasive exam was necessary, she would trust me. She would endure it because she knew that I knew that few things were worse than the darkness that had been visited upon us.

Connor waited outside the door for me, having kept his promise not to leave. Once more, he followed as I was shipped back upstairs for surgery. I was brought into a small room, and the nurses began stripping my clothes away. One of them asked Connor to step outside, but he placed himself in front of the doors, arms crossed over his chest.

"No," he said.

Before the nurse could object, I touched her arm. "It's okay," I said. "He can stay."

Once I was garbed in a flimsy hospital gown and the anesthesiologist pumped several different medications into my veins, Connor asked the staff for a moment alone with me.

The drugs worked quickly. I could hardly lift my head from the pillow as he approached. It was so silent now. Connor touched my shoulder and his face came into view, floating above me.

"Just don't go," I managed.

He leaned down, and I felt his dry lips on my temple. "I'll be right outside the door."

"They won't let you come in, will they?" I mumbled.

He laughed. "No, I think I'm pushing my luck as it is. But when you wake up, I'll be here."

I wanted to say more, but my lips didn't work. My body was heavy with sleep. The last thing I felt was Connor's hand sliding into my good one.

CHAPTER

FIFTY-FOUR

Connor watched as two nurses and the anesthesiologist wheeled the gurney with Claire on it through the double doors to the operating room. He stood for a moment. The doors flapped and Claire's sleeping form receded, finally disappearing into another room. He turned and nearly knocked Farrell to the ground.

Mitch steadied himself. "Watch out, kid."

"Where's Boggs?" Connor asked.

"On his way up," Mitch replied. "Jenny's here."

"What took so long?" Connor asked.

"Press," Mitch said.

Connor swiped a hand through his hair. "Shit."

"Yeah, it's pretty bad. She was talking to Boggs when I left her. She'll be right up. Brianna and Tom won't be far behind. I talked with Rick. He's booking the first flight out."

Connor's head snapped up, causing a wave of nausea to sweep upward from his stomach. He put one hand on the wall and bit back the bile rising in the back of his throat. The attending physician in the ER had given Connor industrial-strength painkillers for his leg. Thankfully, the stab wound was not serious enough to warrant surgery, but Connor would be on a heavy-duty course of antibiotics. His body wasn't used to the drugs. Silently, he cursed himself. Had he realized at the time that they'd make him woozy and light-headed, he would have refused them. At least until Claire's abductor was in custody.

"Did they get anything?" Connor managed.

Mitch shook his head. "I don't know. Boggs will be up shortly to brief you. I brought you some pants."

Mitch pulled a folded pair of khakis from under his arm. "They'll be a little big, but your house is still a crime scene, so they'll have to do."

Connor smiled and took them under his own arm. "Thanks," he said.

Mitch jammed his hands into his pockets. The two men looked up and down the halls, waiting for Jenny and Boggs. Connor briefed Mitch on the night's events while they waited.

"You want to sit down?" Mitch asked.

"No," Connor said. He knew if he sat down, he might not get back up. He wasn't feeling much pain, but his limbs were starting to feel like they were made of lead.

A moment passed in silence, and then Jen Fletcher came running down the hall toward them, her sandals flapping against the tile floor. Her gray-brown hair had come loose from its tie and fluttered wildly around her head. Boggs walked behind her, head down, cell phone pressed to his ear.

Mitch seized the khakis from Connor's hand a split second before Jen nearly knocked him to the ground with her embrace. She pressed her face into his chest and squeezed him hard. Connor regained his balance and wrapped one arm around her, the other still pressed against the wall for support.

Jen looked up at him, concern flooding her eyes. "Oh, am I hurting you?"

Connor laughed. "No. I'm fine." He turned his head and lifted the gauze so she could see the four-inch gash the doctors had sewn shut earlier, after shaving the hair away. "Just here and my leg," he said.

Jen's lips pressed together as she surveyed his wounds. "Good Lord," she said.

Connor rubbed between her shoulder blades. "I'll live," he said.

Jen reached up and pulled his face down to her so she could kiss his cheek. "You brought my baby back," she said.

"Actually, she came back on her own," Connor said, exchanging a glance with Mitch.

Jen's eyes glistened. "I don't care. She's here. That's all that matters. If it weren't for you . . ." She choked. Connor pulled her into him, letting her wet his T-shirt with her tears and rubbing her back as she sobbed.

Boggs reached them, flipping his cell phone closed and dropping it into his pocket. He glanced warily over his shoulder. "Goddamn nurses are all over me," he said.

"Cell phone?" Mitch asked.

"Yeah."

"Can't have them on in here," Connor said.

Boggs raised his eyebrows. "Yeah, well, I'm on official police business here. How is she?"

Connor glanced back at the double doors. "She's in surgery now. Could be a few hours."

Boggs nodded. "How 'bout you? Think you'll make it?"

"Yeah. They want to keep me overnight. Said I was lucky, the knife sliced clean through my leg without hitting anything important."

"Good. They're still combing your house over, taking video and photos and all that. Should be finished about now, but you won't be able to get in there till tomorrow sometime. We'll need statements."

"Did you get him?" Connor asked, one arm tightening around Jen's shoulders. She raised her head from Connor's chest and looked at Boggs.

"No," Boggs said.

Connor, Mitch, and Jen all deflated at once. "Did you find the house? Where he was keeping the other girl?" Connor asked.

"Alison Ward," Mitch supplied.

"Yeah, but we were too late. Looked like he flew back there, packed a few things, and took off. There was blood. I don't know how far he's gonna make it wounded. We did a perimeter search around your place, and then we went to the Fletchers' in case he got the idea to go there. Nothing."

Connor sighed. "I doubt he's sticking around."

Boggs nodded. "Well, Cap wants a guard on the door here tonight, especially with the press all over this. We've got patrols all over the place. Claire didn't happen to mention what he was driving, did she?"

"Son of a bitch," Connor said. He hadn't thought to ask Claire. He wasn't thinking like a detective. He had been too busy looking at her, assuring himself she was real, trying not to cringe as he surveyed the damage her abductor had done to her.

"Forget it," Boggs said. "It's okay. We'll work with what we have." But his mouth pressed briefly into a hard line. Connor knew Boggs was frustrated that none of their detectives had thought to elicit that small detail. A detail Connor knew could make the difference between catching the guy and letting him disappear without a trace.

"I'm putting a guy on the door once she's out of surgery. Yours too. I'm not sure you're ready to go another round if he decides to pay a visit. If he survives, that is."

"You shot him?" Jen asked, looking up at Connor.

Connor grimaced. "No," he said. "I stabbed him. Two or three times, I'm not sure. It was kind of crazy. Boggs, did you get anything on that name Claire gave you?"

"No. Another alias. This guy is a regular Houdini. I'm betting when we finally do nail him, there's gonna be a long line of unhappy people waiting to extradite him for priors."

Jen shuddered in Connor's arms.

"But we have his blood, DNA, and they're getting prints right now. Stryke is already on it. We'll get him," Boggs assured them.

The sharp beep of Boggs's cell phone startled them all. Glancing around to make sure no medical staff were nearby, Boggs flipped the phone open and pressed it to his ear. Connor knew by the way Boggs's body tensed ever so slightly as he barked clipped "yeahs" into the receiver that something was happening.

Boggs hung up. "They're out a few miles from the house where he was keeping Alison Ward. Local patrol spotted a white Ford Taurus with a male and female in it, driving erratically. They tried to pull it over but the driver took off."

Connor glanced at Mitch. "It has to be them."

"I gotta go," Boggs said.

CHAPTER FIFTY-FIVE

Two hours later, Connor sat in a chair outside the operating room, his head falling and snapping back to attention as he fought off sleep. Jen was on one side of him and Mitch on the other. Across from them, Tom and Brianna were side by side. Tom had dozed off, but Brianna sat stiffly, arms folded across her thin chest. She glanced alternately at Connor and her mother. She had said little to Connor since she and Tom arrived, greeting him only with a tight smile. A uniformed officer paced back and forth in front of the entrance to the suite of operating rooms, exchanging dirty looks with medical staff who had to answer his questions before they were admitted to the surgical unit.

A radio sat atop the officer's right shoulder, and every so often he barked into it. No one listening would be able to make much sense of the litany of numbers continually called out over the frequency, but for Connor, it was a second language, and he listened absently for updates on the pursuit while he dozed. Jen nudged him awake as Boggs got off the elevator. Across from him, Brianna whispered softly in Tom's ear, waking him. They all straightened up and stared expectantly at Boggs.

Connor could tell from the set of Boggs's shoulders that they hadn't caught Claire's abductor. Before Connor could ask, Boggs said, "We chased him until he crashed his car. He had another girl with him. They left the car wrapped around a tree and took off on foot. We lost them about twenty miles away from the house Claire said he was living in. It's all wooded out there. We're still looking. We've got the dogs out there now and we're working on getting a helicopter up there."

All three of the Fletchers seemed to deflate, their bodies slumping in disappointment.

Mitch leaned over and caught Connor's eye. "Any idea just how badly you wounded him?"

Connor sighed and swiped a hand through his hair. "I don't know. It happened so fast. I know I hurt him because he howled, but I have no idea how deep or how serious his wounds are. I would think he'd need stitches, but I couldn't see anything—it was dark."

"So he could conceivably get away?" Jen asked.

"He's not getting away," Boggs said firmly. "I gotta get back out there, but we'll keep you posted. He's not getting away."

A half hour later, they were ushered two floors up to a private room where Claire had been situated after her surgery. Mitch went for coffee as Connor, Jen, Tom, and Brianna slid into the room. Connor watched the steady, slow rise and fall of Claire's chest. Her left hand was secured with a splint and Ace bandage, and it lay on a pillow at her side, elevated to prevent swelling. The left side of her face looked as if someone had run over it with a truck. Connor knew that she bore many more bruises on the rest of her body, some in the shape of shoe prints.

It didn't matter to him. She would survive all of the injuries. What mattered to him was that she was there and she was finally safe. He wanted to touch her, to assure himself that she was really there, but didn't want to interrupt the Fletcher family's first moments of reuniting with her.

Connor stood by the door as Jen approached the bed. Tom and Brianna stood behind Jen, holding hands, their fingers laced together. Connor wasn't sure which one of them gasped first, but Jen's hands flew to her face as she looked upon the child she'd lost ten years ago, now a woman, battered and bruised.

"Oh my God," Tom whispered. "What did he do to her?"

Tears shone in Tom's eyes, and Brianna pulled him into a hug, letting her brother sob into her shoulder. She was the only one whose emotions were in check. She reached out a hand and placed it between her mother's shoulder blades.

Connor bent his head as Jen's thin shoulders shook and heaved. She pulled a tissue from her pocket and blew her nose. Then she moved away from her older children, rounding the bed and perching on the side of it. She took Claire's good hand and pressed it to her mouth. She raised her wet eyes to Connor's.

"Mitch told me she looked bad. He said she—I had no idea," she whispered.

Connor grimaced. "She'll heal, Jen. The important thing is she's here. She's with you now."

"She'll be okay, Mom," Tom said encouragingly as he separated from Brianna and moved closer to the bed. Brianna hung back, taking up position at the foot of Claire's bed.

Jen stroked Claire's hair back from her face. Her voice was heavy with emotion when she spoke again. "It's really her," Jen whispered. "It's really my baby."

Connor smiled. "I know."

He watched Jen weep quietly over her child while Tom and Brianna looked on, and then wordlessly he inched out the door, leaving the newly reunited family alone.

One hour and two cups of coffee later, Connor slipped back into Claire's room. He breathed a sigh of relief that she was still there, chest still rising and falling evenly as the IV dripped medication into the crook of her right elbow. Jen remained in the same place as when he'd left her. Brianna and Tom had pulled chairs up to the other side of

Claire's bed and sat watching their mother drink in the sight of the child she'd spent the last decade searching for.

Jen turned when he entered, eyes wide and questioning. She mouthed, "Did they catch him yet?"

Connor shook his head. Jen's shoulders drooped as she looked back at her daughter.

"Where did he go?" Brianna asked. "What's taking so long?"

"They're doing everything they can," Connor responded.

Brianna opened her mouth to speak, and from the scowl that darkened her visage, Connor guessed her next words would not be pleasant. He was relieved when Tom silenced her with a shushing gesture. Brianna met her brother's eyes, and Connor saw the unspoken conversation between them. Tom's eyes darted to their mother and back as if to say, "This isn't the time." Brianna sighed and leaned back in her chair, avoiding Connor's gaze.

A long, silent moment passed. Connor watched Jen study Claire, her eyes roaming her daughter's face as if Claire might vanish the moment Jen looked away. Connor saw her bite back the tears that glistened in her eyes. Lightly, she ran her fingers over the right side of Claire's face.

"Look what that bastard did to my child," she said in a whisper laced with anger. "She looks so . . . her face . . ."

Connor stepped closer to the bed. "She'll be okay."

Then Claire's voice, thick and dry. "Mom?"

Jen jumped as if the bed held an electric charge. She peered into her daughter's face. Claire's right eye opened slowly. For a long time she looked at her mother. "Mom?" she repeated.

Jen nodded, unable to hold her tears back any longer. They fell from the end of her nose onto the bed. "I'm here, honey."

"Dad?"

"He's not here yet, honey. He's on his way. But Tom and Brianna are here."

The siblings stood and leaned over the side of the bed, peering into their sister's battered face, murmuring their greetings.

"Where's Connor?" Claire asked.

Connor stepped forward, taking up position beside Jen. "I'm right here, Claire."

She closed her eyes again, and Connor watched as she squeezed her mother's hand.

CHAPTER

FIFTY-SIX

I woke from a morphine coma, sleep hanging thick and heavy on my limbs. It reminded me of the times my captor had drugged me in order to transport me from one house to another—from one prison to another—each time taking me farther away from my family and the life I had known. I opened my right eye and looked around, a slow panic rising from my gut as my brain tried to orient itself. It took a long moment for me to remember where I was and how I had come to be there.

The hospital room was semi-dark, the first light of dawn glowing beyond the windows and the lamp above my head illuminating my family members asleep in their chairs. My mother had pulled her chair as close to the bed as possible, and she slept with her upper body resting on the side of it, my good hand gripped tightly in her fingers. My brother and sister slept sitting up on the other side of the room. Brianna's head lolled on Tom's shoulder, and my brother's head reclined on the back of his chair, his mouth yawning open. One of them was snoring, but I couldn't tell which one.

I remembered waking earlier when Connor was in the room. My family's faces had floated above me, seeming disembodied, trying not to look too shocked at the sight of my injuries. Even in my drug-induced haze, I had momentarily wished that they would leave and come back later, when I looked less like a set of tire tracks and was alert enough to greet them. But perhaps it was better to be reunited with them while I was still in a semi-comatose state.

I was frightened of their faces, their arms, the tears they would shed, and the questions they would surely ask. I had always been afraid to return—afraid my family would see me the way I saw myself. Dirty, used up, and weak. Like I was covered in a filth that could never be washed away. I felt branded by all the years of rape and abuse. And as long as I stayed with him, in the small, carefully controlled world he'd made for me, those memories were at rest, silent, and existed only to me.

I always believed that if I returned, my family would demand that I share those memories, and then every sordid thing that had been done to me would become a part of them as well. My ordeal would become like another family member, shared by everyone, ever present, a constant reminder of who I had become.

"Claire?" My brother's voice startled me out of my reverie. I turned my head in his direction, the shift causing my mother to stir and sit up.

"Tom?" I croaked.

The three of them were inches from me then, and as I struggled to sit up, my mother's able hands guided my upper body forward. Tears streamed down Tom's face, and his body shook with sobs. He leaned over the side of the bed and gathered me in an awkward hug.

"I'm so glad you're home," he whispered.

He made room for Brianna, but her hug was stiff and awkward. "I can't believe it's you," she said, stepping quickly away from me.

I felt her distance like a knife in my heart. I could see the questions in her mind, crowding out everything else. It wasn't the time to ask questions, but Brianna had never been very patient. Still, she held them back, and I had a feeling that things between us would never be easy again until I answered them.

"How do you feel, sweetheart?" my mother asked.

I started to answer her but was interrupted by a sharp knock at the door. We all turned toward it as it opened. I expected Connor or Stryker, but instead a man I hardly recognized stepped into the room.

"Rick," my mother said.

He had aged considerably, his hair a salt-and-pepper mix where it had once been a lustrous brown. He was still handsome, but I estimated forty pounds lighter than when I'd last seen him a decade ago. His gray suit hung on him, making him look much smaller than I remembered.

His whole body twitched, hands fidgeting and trembling. His eyes were wide and undone as he stared at me, his body going utterly still. He swallowed two or three times and strode over to the bed, Brianna and Tom quickly making way for him. He leaned in and touched my face. His fingers moved along the contours of skin and bone, like a blind person searching for something.

"Dad?" I said.

He tugged my good hand from my mother's grip and pressed it to his cheek. He closed his eyes and took several long, deep breaths. Without opening his eyes, he said, "It's really you."

Tears burned my eyes. I watched him breathing in my existence as if I truly had returned from the dead, and I felt the last years I'd spent in the trailer—too afraid, too ashamed to come home. They felt heavy and wrong. Had I done this to my own father? Turned him into an old man withered away to a loose sack of bones?

A terrible wave of guilt, tempered with shame—a new kind of shame—engulfed me. Why hadn't I trusted him or my mother—my family—to receive me once more with love and relief? I was fifteen when my abductor smashed my head in and stole me from them. I was old enough to realize that my parents loved me unconditionally—that all I'd seen and endured would mean nothing to them just so long as they could hold their child again.

My experience had overwhelmed me, it had become the sum of my parts, who I was, and I hadn't deemed myself fit to return to those who loved me.

"I'm sorry, Dad," I squeaked.

His eyes snapped open. He looked at me, shock and alarm dancing in his eyes. "No, no, no," he said. "No, honey. I'm the one who's sorry. I'm so sorry, Claire."

With that, he broke, dissolving into a weeping mass, his body draped over the side of the bed, head in my lap. Hesitantly, I placed my right palm on his scalp.

He shook. "I'm sorry I doubted you," he said.

I breathed.

"Me too, Dad. I'm sorry I doubted me too," I said.

CHAPTER
FIFTY-SEVEN

At 5:00 a.m., Stryker called the hospital to give Connor an update and check on Claire's status. Connor took the call at the nurses' station down the hall from Claire's room. As he listened to Stryker, he watched the uniformed guard continue his even pace back and forth in front of the door. The man was like a metronome. He had only been interrupted once, by the arrival of Rick Fletcher. Farrell was dozing in a chair next to Claire's door.

"Nothing," Stryker said into the phone. "We been lookin' all night. Even got an FBI helicopter up here with fucking floodlights and everything. We got Feds, Staties, locals, and division people combing half a county and we got nothing. It's like this guy just vanished into a puff of smoke or something."

"Any sign of the girl he had with him?" Connor asked.

"Nope. Everything shut down about an hour ago. We're chasing our tails out here in the goddamn dark. We're gonna recharge and start again at first light. We got technicians dusting for prints at the car and the house. I'd like to get an ID on this guy, but it may take a few days." Stryker sounded as bone tired and weary as Connor felt.

A nurse rounded the other side of the station counter and set a disposable coffee cup in front of Connor. The smell of coffee wafted up to his nostrils. He gave her what he hoped was a smile, and she winked back at him. She pointed down the hall toward Claire's room where one of her colleagues stood, handing a second cup of coffee to the uniformed officer. The nurse peeked into Claire's room, glanced at Mitch, seated just outside the room, and set a carrier in the chair next to him with two additional cups.

Connor almost forgot he was on the phone. Stryker's voice faded out and then back in loudly. "Parks? You there?"

Connor blinked and picked up his coffee. "Yeah, yeah. I'm here."

"I said what's the fucking deal with this guy?"

Connor's brow puckered as he sipped the burning liquid. He thought about the day he'd stood outside Strakowski's house and pieced together the abduction and how the guy had managed to pull it off in broad daylight during a busy morning with the police crawling all over the place five minutes later.

Connor sighed. "I'm sure he planned for this. He probably had a couple of escape routes picked out in case something like this happened," he told Stryker. "Keep me posted."

"Will do. I'll be stopping by within the hour to check on you guys."

Connor watched as Jen emerged sleepy eyed from Claire's room. She shook Mitch awake and spoke softly to him. A moment later, Brianna and Tom followed.

"Stryke," Connor said.

There was a long silence on the other line, then he answered, "Yeah, I'm here."

"We have to find this guy. We just—we just have to."

CHAPTER
FIFTY-EIGHT

Between the drugs they gave me to soothe my anxiety and the ones to ease the pain of my injuries, I slept through most of the next three days. My sleep was broken up by faces and voices—nurses, doctors, my parents, Tom, Brianna, Mitch, and Connor, who stayed faithfully outside my room most of the time. I wanted to ask him questions, but I couldn't get my mind or my mouth to work. He said nothing, occasionally sitting in the chair beside my bed with his leg elevated and a big strip of gauze wrapped round his head.

When my mother was there, she lifted the covers and snuggled beneath them, cradling me in her arms the way she had when I was a small child. I shrunk in her arms, filling my lungs with the scent of her, which was still familiar to me after so many years. With each breath I grew smaller and smaller until I was compact against her, an infant again, secure in the comfort of her body. A body I'd longed to curl into for ten long years. A body of love, denied to me by a monster whose sick appetite superseded all else.

Her unconditional acceptance was as much a salve to me as the drugs the doctors gave me to heal my wounds. She was a sort of buffer against the rest of my family, all of whom sat by my bedside for hours each day but were still tentative with me, unsure how to approach me or talk to me. I sensed in her that nothing I could tell her about the ten years I'd been gone would matter. I need not tell her at all if I chose, and she would continue to hold me each day as long as I required it. This fact consumed me and birthed a great guilt in my core. So many years I had been afraid, ashamed to return home. Even as I drove back to my life with Alison clinging to my side, I dreaded facing my family again, yet here was my mother, deep lines etched around her eyes from my absence, welcoming me without caution or reserve.

She did not ask me questions, for which I was grateful. Sometimes she talked, filling in the last ten years in a soothing voice that lulled me back into the dark oblivion of sleep brought on by painkillers. She talked about world events that had happened after my resignation to my role as Lynn, after Tiffany arrived and spent her days locked in front of the television, after I moved into the trailer and took a job at the animal hospital—when I could watch the news or read the paper.

I knew about the Twin Towers—9/11—the Christmas tsunami, the space shuttle *Columbia* disaster, the war in Iraq, and the lives of United States soldiers still being lost there years later. The news—the world—was beset with unmitigated tragedies that had made my own bleak existence and the violations I endured seem trivial, silly even, in comparison.

On 9/11, I had been in the back of the animal hospital, surrounded by whining animals when one of my coworkers rushed in and flipped on the small TV we kept there. We stood for hours, frozen in place, watching the footage. The woman next to me cried, sometimes turning her face into my bony shoulder as I watched images that looked like the interior of my soul.

My mother talked about things that had happened during the first years of my captivity—time spent mostly in darkness and a terror that blotted everything else out. The things that had happened outside of my infinitesimal world. Things that seemed far worse as I listened to my mother recap those years as the rest of society had known them—the Oklahoma City bombing, the shootings at Columbine, the Heaven's Gate cult mass suicide, and the gruesome murders of Matthew Wayne Shepard and James Byrd Jr., one because of his sexual preference and the other because of his race.

I had also missed the White House sex scandal, the O. J. Simpson trial verdict, and the death and funeral of Princess Diana. My mother promised to get me history books so I could read about those years for myself. I drifted in and out of sleep as she spoke, feeling suddenly grateful to be alive and lying in a hospital bed with my mother by my side.

On the fourth day, I woke alone for the first time. My door was propped open, and I heard men's voices talking. I recognized Mitch's and Connor's voices. The other voices sounded like the detectives Boggs and Stryker.

"Man, you look terrible. You give new meaning to the expression hammered shit."

"Thanks, Stryke. I appreciate that. So anything on this guy?"

"No, but we've got the whole damn state looking for him."

"The press is all over this. Jenny and Rick want to take her home, but they're camped right outside the house."

"We're going to need a statement from her soon. You'll have to bring her down to the division."

"Shit. All right. Well, they're discharging her tomorrow. I'll talk to Jenny and Rick. See what they want to do. There was talk of them staying at Mitch's house for a while to avoid all the press."

I opened my eyes and shifted in the bed. I felt like a newborn in this sudden world of freedom, of my return to the role of Claire Fletcher. The weight of all the things to come made me heavy and exhausted. I still had many things to tell Connor, but it looked as though he wouldn't be the only person.

The thought of my captor on the loose chilled me. Connor had reminded me that he'd been wounded, and that his escape attempt

Lisa Regan

may have been thwarted by an untimely death, but I knew better. The man who'd stolen my life was invincible. In my mind he loomed large, his voice whispering in my ear, calling me by the name he'd given me, reminding me that he could go anywhere, do anything, and walk away unscathed—free.

I knew I would have to tell them about the bodies beneath my old bedroom window, even if it meant that I might go to prison for not coming forward sooner. Part of me needed to convince them of the depravity of my captor, the lengths that he would go to perfect his man-made universe. As long as he was free, I did not feel safe.

My left eye had opened again. I blinked painfully, losing track of the voices beyond my door, tuning in only to the timbre of Connor's words as they came, hearing the sound but not the meaning. I found the television's remote control built into the bedrail and flipped it on, keeping the volume low.

Connor had kept the television off, even while I slept, and now I saw why. Many stations had news of my return, of my rescue of Alison Ward. There were video clips and stills of my mother's house, Connor's house, the house and trailer where I'd spent the last five years of my life. My yearbook photo, a girl I barely recognized, flashed again and again across the screen, sometimes taking up all of it and other times floating just to the side of a reporter's head. A reporter stood outside of the hospital, speaking into a microphone, and repeating my name. Behind her, other reporters did the same for their own cameras.

I left the television on and climbed out of the bed. My legs were stronger, and a body brace staunched the sharp pain of my ribs as I moved to the window. Carefully, I made a small eyehole in the mini-blinds and surveyed the street below me. Sure enough, news vans and reporters were spread along the sidewalk, milling, standing, and some jogging to their respective vans. There were microphones and notepads, earpieces, and video cameras.

When I felt Connor's hand at the small of my back, I jumped.

"It's okay," he said. "Just me."

I gestured toward the window, swallowing hard over the lump in my throat. "They're all here for me?"

"Yeah. But don't worry about them. The press is the least of our concerns right now."

"I didn't want this," I said, turning and looking up into his eyes. Peach fuzz grew around the gash on the side of his head. "I wasn't going to come back."

Connor's voice was gentle. "Why?"

"I tried to tell you that night on the phone. I don't know if I can do this. The questions, the press, the police. All of it. You don't know what he did to me."

"Claire," he said.

Tears stung my eyes. I pulled away from him. "See?" I said. "I haven't been Claire Fletcher for ten years. That wasn't even what he called me. I'm not sure I know how to be Claire Fletcher anymore."

"No one expects you to be the same girl who was abducted ten years ago, Claire."

I shook my head, tears leaking from the corners of my eyes. I swayed and stumbled back to the bed, collapsing on the edge of it. I wrapped my arms around the front of my body. "They'll all want to know. They'll want to know the things he did to me."

Connor stepped in front of me. His voice was soft. "It wasn't your fault," he said.

My lower lip trembled. "I have to give a statement," I said.

"You were the victim of a crime. Yes, you should give a statement to the police. Especially since this guy is still on the loose. He was going to do the same thing to Alison Ward that he did to you. People like him don't stop."

"I know," I mumbled.

We were silent. I looked at Connor's hands resting at his sides. Hands that had held a gun and shot a man. Hands that had touched my body gently, tenderly, making me feel things I had never felt at the touch of a man and didn't think I could.

"There are things I need to tell you," I said.

"You don't have to tell me anything you don't want to tell me," he said.

I lifted my chin and met his eyes. "I need to tell you," I said.

"You can tell me anything you want, Claire, but it's your choice what and when you tell me." He sat beside me on the bed. His hand floated tentatively over mine, testing, waiting for a protest. When I said nothing, he took my right hand in both of his, lacing his fingers through mine. "You can do this," he said.

"You need to know," I began. I took a big gulp of air. "There are bodies."

"Rudy Teplitz and Jim Randall," he said.

I started. "What?"

"They've been missing for some time now. After the way he came after me, I think we can safely assume that he killed them. We can't change that, but we can give their families some closure, and when we catch this guy, we can make sure he's held accountable for the things he's done."

"There's someone else," I said. "A girl. Sarah."

"Sarah?"

"That's what I called her. Actually, I don't know what her name was. He strangled her. She's with Rudy at the second house—the house in the woods where he—" My throat seized up. I had never spoken to another soul about the things I had seen, about Sarah. She existed in my mind apart from the corporeal world, as if she had always been a figment of my imagination. It made it easier to deal with that way.

"Do you know where their bodies are?" Connor said, and I was suddenly grateful that he was a detective who dealt with this sort of thing regularly. He didn't recoil in horror or drop my hand as though it burned his skin. His professional mind was at work.

"Yeah," I murmured. "I mean I could help you find them, I think."

"You're going to have to tell Boggs when you give your statement," Connor said. "This is very important."

A sob rose in my throat, making my mouth feel stiff and heavy. "But I could go to prison," I said, voice rising. "It was because of what I did—things that I did—that he killed them. He killed them because of me."

Connor sighed and squeezed my hand. "Look at me," he said.

Slowly I met his eyes.

"Those people were murdered because he chose to murder them. Not because of you or anyone else. Killers love to place responsibility for the lives they take on everyone and everything around them, but it's all bullshit. You didn't make him kill Rudy or Sarah or Jim Randall. He made that choice on his own, and he's the one who needs to bear that burden. Not you."

"But I never came forward, never told anyone," I said.

"At the time, were you in a position to call the authorities or intervene?"

"While he was killing them? No, I . . . well, I didn't know about Rudy or Jim until later. With Sarah, he chained me—made me watch. I tried to get out but I—" The sob came on full force, making my body curl and my ribs ache. With each heave of my chest, pain stabbed me in the side, making me gasp and hiccup for air.

"Claire," Connor said calmly. "The DA is not going to waste their time trying to prosecute you for something you had no control over. I'm sure once they hear the whole story, they'll be far more interested in nailing this guy's ass to the wall."

I nodded, though his words failed to soothe the raging anxiety coursing through my body.

"Do you think he'll come back for me? Try to hurt my family?" I asked.

"What makes you think that?"

"He always said he would. He threatened me, my family." I told Connor about the newspaper clippings—the one about Tom's car accident and the fire in my mother's kitchen.

His eyes widened. "Wow," he muttered. He released my hand and rubbed his eyes, taking a moment to digest these facts. "Well, I think those threats were mostly to keep you there. At this point, there are so many police agencies looking for him that it would just be foolish for him to do anything retaliatory. Plus, sexual predators like him prefer to lay low if they can—that way they can keep on fulfilling their sick fantasies. The less attention drawn to them the better. At this point, I think he'll cut his losses and run. If he comes after you or your family, he's walking right into police custody. I think he's too smart for that."

My voice cracked when I spoke. "Are you saying he never intended to follow through on his threats?"

Connor's face softened. "Look at your face, Claire. The threats he made were real. You were right to be afraid. But now it's over. You're free. He's not coming back for you or your family."

I nodded. I saw the logic in what Connor said, but the fear I'd held on to for so many years was not so easy to cast off.

"Look," he continued. "Right now we need to focus on you and what you're going to do next. First things first. We have to figure out where you're going to stay when you leave here. You'll need to give your statement. Your mom and Brianna are out shopping now. We figured you would need clothes."

I managed a half smile and tugged at the collar of my hospital gown. "Really? I thought I'd start a new fashion trend," I joked.

There was that lopsided smile I loved so much. The one I hadn't been able to stop thinking about after I left Connor's house that first night. The one that made me feel tingly and nervous but in a way that was not wholly uncomfortable. "Well, the hospital gown—that's a good look for you," he said.

We smiled at one another. Connor glanced over my shoulder. "You shouldn't be watching that," he said, referring to the television.

"I know," I said. "I have a better view from the window."

Connor chuckled. "Claire."

"Yeah."

"You'll get through this. You will. You have a lot of people supporting you."

Tears sprang to my eyes again. "I don't know," I said.

Connor stood and lifted my legs back into the bed. He covered me with a sheet and kissed my forehead as his hand found the remote control on the side rail and switched the TV off.

"One thing at a time," he murmured. "First, we get you out of this hospital."

CHAPTER
FIFTY-NINE

We left the hospital the next morning to go directly to the police station. Because the press was so hungry for the smallest sound bite or video clip, Connor and I left via ambulance, wearing EMT uniforms complete with hats and sunglasses. My hair was pulled back in a ponytail, which jutted out from the hole in the back of my hat. Between the hat and the thick mask of foundation my mother had painted over my face, my bruised and swollen face was not noticeable as long as I kept my distance. The uniforms masked both our injuries well.

Less than five minutes later, we were in a parking garage beneath the police building. We took an elevator to the fourth floor, which consisted of a large room littered with unkempt desks. Men and women in smart dress clothes moved among them.

No one looked at us or stopped to stare openmouthed. Connor guided me to the back of the large room and sat me behind his desk. "I'll be back," he said.

Although my surgically repaired left hand remained in a splint, my right hand was free, and I could not stop it from trembling. To distract myself, I began opening desk drawers, peering at the contents, and closing them. I found nothing of interest until I opened the center drawer.

From it, my fifteen-year-old face smiled innocently at me. I picked up the missing persons flyer, glancing briefly at the facts I already knew. Beneath the flyer was a file marked with my name. It was almost an inch thick.

I pulled it out and set it on the desk. I didn't know what to expect. I opened it, sifting slowly through the pages until I came to Connor's handwritten notes at the very back of the file. My face paled as I read his notes about interviewing Noel Geary. Heat drained from my skin as if the floor were leeching it out from the soles of my shoes. I felt cold in the way I had for uncounted weeks in that first room—alone, naked, and unable to move.

Connor's voice startled me. I jumped and the chair slid back as if it had been hit with an electrical charge.

"You okay?" he said.

I stared at him, holding the pages of Noel Geary's interview in my right hand.

Connor limped around the desk and saw the contents of my file scattered across it. He began gathering the pages together. I held the other papers forward. "Noel Geary," I said.

Connor sighed. "I have a lot to tell you too," he said. "But right now they're ready for you."

"I wasn't the first. I mean I wasn't the only one."

Connor sat on the edge of the desk. "Well, you knew that," he said. "You were the one who found Alison Ward."

I shook my head. "No. No, I thought I was the only person he'd done this to, the only person he'd hurt until Alison."

Connor folded his arms across his chest. His eyes were dark with concern. "Claire, people like him don't sprout up out of the ground overnight. They don't develop these tendencies in an epiphany one day. Usually they nurture their sexual compulsions for years, even as adolescents. You were the first he imprisoned, that we know of, but we're betting the farm that when we figure out who this guy really is, he'll have a long list of priors with everything from Peeping Tom and indecent exposure to fondling."

"I didn't even think of that," I mumbled.

The bubble that had been my existence for so long was punctured, the air hissing out in a slow leak. I realized how ridiculous my words must have sounded. *I thought I was the first one.* I heard myself telling Tiffany he was a pedophile, out prowling the streets for young girls when he wasn't home. I'd said it to taunt her, to hurt her, never taking into account the gravity of my accusations. By that time, my entire world had narrowed to a solitary pinpoint, a singular focus—me. My survival, which most of the time had hardly seemed worth the fight.

Tiffany stayed by choice, but my mind and body recoiled from the life he'd forced on me. It did not allow room for the possibility that there were more like me—chosen specifically by him. Forced to endure his touch, his mouth, his eyes, and his anger.

"You weren't the first, Claire. If we don't get this guy soon, you won't be his last," Connor said, plucking the pages from my outstretched hand. "Are you ready?"

My jellylike spine hardened, and my anxiety morphed into a sort of resolve. How many girls came before me? How many would come after?

Even though I had dreaded my freedom and still did to a degree, a little anger lived inside me. This person took ten years of my life, possessed me entirely, and violated whatever innocence survived in me at fifteen years old. The rapes, the beatings, the starvation, the drowning, the killing, and the various humiliations I had suffered at his hands went unpunished. He destroyed lives with impunity, and there appeared to be no end in sight.

"Do you think I can help catch him?" I asked.

"Yes," Connor said. "Yes, I do."

They placed me in an interrogation room, which was scarred by cigarette burns and graffiti. It contained a table and three chairs. There was no mirror. Instead, there was a square cut into the wall facing the table. In the square was a video camera protected by thick Plexiglas.

I had my choice of either Boggs or Stryker as an interviewer. Boggs was older and he did not look quite as mean, but I chose Stryker instead, remembering how gentle he had been with me and Alison the night we returned from captivity.

He brought a notepad and a cup of coffee. He offered me something to drink, and I accepted a soda. He explained that I was not under arrest but advised me of my rights. I waived my right to an attorney.

I glanced repeatedly at the camera in the wall until Stryker informed me that they were taping the interview and that it was standard procedure. Then, for the first time since my aborted attempt to explain to Tiffany that my captor had raped me, I told my story.

CHAPTER SIXTY

Connor sat in the video room with his injured leg propped on a table. Boggs stood behind him, and Captain Riehl paced the room as they watched Claire's interview live on a large screen television.

Boggs had set a cup of coffee in front of Connor, but it stood untouched and now cold. The camera revealed only Stryker's back, but Connor could see every nervous tremor in Claire's frame as she spoke. At times, she looked at the floor, unable to meet Stryker's eyes as she recounted her story in enough detail to make Connor shudder and Boggs murmur, "Holy shit," every so often. At other times, Claire's face paled considerably and she pulled her borrowed EMT jacket tightly around herself as if she were chilled to the bone.

After three hours, they broke. Stryker called for food, and the two of them ate in silence, Claire unwilling to be left alone in the room with only the dead eye of the video camera on her.

One of the other detectives poked her head inside the video room and nodded to Connor. "Parks," she said. "Visitors."

Muscles stiff and tense from sitting still in his chair, Connor rose slowly and followed her out to the office. Mitch, Jen, and Rick stood by his desk, talking quietly. They smiled as Connor limped toward them. Jen's smile disappeared as he drew closer.

"What is it?" she said.

Rick looped an arm around his wife's waist and met Connor's eyes, worry darkening his features. "Just tell us," he said.

Connor swiped a hand through his hair and shook his head.

"It's bad, isn't it?" Mitch said.

Connor felt lines crease his own face as he glanced from Mitch to Jen and Rick. Jen looked up at each one of them and folded her arms across her chest. Her chin jutted out, mouth a thin, firm line.

"Well, we expected that, now didn't we?" she said.

Mitch nodded, and Rick's gaze swept along the floor, tears glistening in the corners of his eyes. Connor said nothing. The things he'd heard in the video room chilled him and made his hands itch.

"Well, I don't care how bad it is," Jenny said. "I have my child back and I'm going to get her through this."

As she spoke, Connor saw how Jen Fletcher must have looked to the many police officers and reporters she'd faced in the last ten years during her search for Claire. She was suddenly taller than all three of the men around her. Her presence filled up the room. Connor felt the grim, raw waves of determination rolling off her like a magnetic field, encompassing and drawing in everyone and everything around her.

"Okay," Connor said, not daring to argue with her.

A tiny smile played at the edges of Mitch's mouth. "So," he said, "how much longer?"

Connor shrugged. "I don't know. They're taking a break now. Could be a few more hours."

"We want to be here when it's over," Rick said.

"Sure thing. I'll call you once she's finished," Connor said. "She's going to need some time to decompress. She was nervous. Where to after this?"

"I've made arrangements," Mitch replied. "The press is all over this, so Jenny's house is out. They will never get any peace there."

"Clearly," Connor said, jiggling his injured leg.

"My place is about twenty minutes west of here. It's secure. We're thinking that's the place to hide out for now until things settle down."

"The kids are gathering some personal belongings, groceries and stuff like that right now," Rick added. "They'll meet us there later."

Connor nodded. "That sounds good," he said. "I'll escort you guys out there."

Boggs called to Connor from across the room, beckoning him back to the video room. Connor shook hands with Mitch and Rick and kissed Jen's cheek.

"Give me some time to talk to her afterward," he said. "I'll call you when we're ready."

CHAPTER
SIXTY-ONE

By the time the interview was over—nine and a half hours after finding my file in Connor's desk—I was exhausted. I felt as if I'd been running on a treadmill the entire time rather than talking. Sweaty ringlets of hair stuck to the back of my neck. My body was weak. My limbs shook. There were so many questions. Far more than I anticipated. I tried in vain to explain to Stryker the extreme sense of disorientation I had felt during most of my captivity.

He wanted dates and timelines, and I could not answer. He wanted the location of the second house, where Rudy and Sarah were buried, but I had no idea of the address. I explained I could probably find it again given time but could not tell him how to get there. He wanted to know Tiffany's real name and several other items of personal information, but I knew none of that. I knew only the things she had told me the rare times her guard was down and she deigned to talk to me.

Stryker assured me I had been very helpful, but I felt useless and drained. "Are my parents here?" I asked when we finished.

"I'll find out," Stryker replied.

"Can I see Connor now?"

Stryker grinned, the first smile I'd seen on his face all day. "Yeah," he said. "I'll send him in."

I waited in my chair. I'd been sitting in it for so many hours, it felt like one of my appendages. Connor limped into the room, smiling, and leaving the door ajar behind him. We looked at each other for a long while. I knew he'd been watching the interview all day, but his eyes betrayed nothing. He looked the same and looked at me the same.

I rose and walked slowly toward him. He came closer and lifted his arms to hug me, but I shook my head. I didn't want anyone to touch me so soon after discussing the rapes. I asked him for a few minutes alone, and he gave them to me, leaving the door to the room open slightly.

I paced for fifteen minutes, trying to bar all the memories from my mind. Connor poked his head into the room, and I waved him in. He stood several feet away from me. After a few minutes, I walked over and touched one of his hands. I expected the contact to repel me—he was a man like my abductor and there were parts of me that would always equate men with terror. The touch was not as frightening as I expected.

In small increments, I went from a touch to holding his hand to carefully laying my cheek on his shoulder. When he sensed I was comfortable, he put his arms around me. He held me until the tears came, riding silent on each exhale of my breath. My body quivered in his embrace, shedding the bleak horror of dredging up so many memories in one day. We stood like that for almost fifteen minutes, until the raw emotion in me wore itself out.

I followed him back to his desk. There were far fewer people in the office, but it was still busy. Again, no one even glanced at us, for which I was grateful. Connor handed me a box of tissues and explained the temporary living arrangements that had been made.

"Your family will stay at Mitch's house," he said.

"What about you?" I asked.

He smiled. "I already told you, you're stuck with me. I'll be around."

My shoulders slumped, relief easing the tension in my muscles.

"You take as long as you need," Connor said. "Use the bathroom, get a drink. Compose yourself, and then I'll call in the troops."

I nodded and wiped my eyes with a clump of tissues.

"I know you've had a long day," Connor continued. "But the worst part is over."

I wanted to smile, but my face hurt like hell. I kept my eyes on Connor's, my anchors in this new and overwhelming reality. "I hope so," I said.

CHAPTER

SIXTY-TWO

Mitch's house was twenty minutes outside of the city. My father drove my mother and me in his rental car. Connor followed behind in my mother's car, ready to head off any press that might follow us. The driveway leading to the house was marked only by a mailbox. A half mile of gravel opened up before a large one-story, ranch-style house. Mitch's nearest neighbor was a half mile away. It was the perfect refuge from the press. I had a vague recollection of being there for a couple of barbecues before I was abducted.

The first few weeks at Mitch's house I slept in the living room, ensconced between my parents on an air mattress in front of the fireplace. Sometimes Tom slept on the couch above our heads, and Brianna stretched out in a sleeping bag near our feet. It was like camping out. Nestled between my parents' bodies, I fell easily into sleep. My sleep, however, was riddled with nightmares in which my abductor found me, slaughtered everyone I loved, and took me back to a cold, dark place.

My mother or father shook me awake. I screamed and thrashed during the dreams and woke pale, trembling, covered with sweat. Together, my parents held me, cradling me in their arms the way they had when I was a small child, one stroking my hair while the other whispered soothing words in my ear.

My wounds began to heal. The bruising on my face, back, and legs faded to a dull yellow, making my skin look jaundiced. The stitches in my hand were removed, and I went without a splint during the day, though the doctor and physical therapist cautioned me to continue my home exercises. We could not go back to my old home immediately because of the press camped outside, hungry for any news or a glimpse of me. For the most part, I was able to avoid being photographed. The press had gotten one or two photos of me wearing hats and sunglasses, my face not fully visible. Tom became the family spokesperson, fielding all press requests, although we all made a point not to watch any press coverage.

When I was abducted, Tom had been a software engineer. In the last ten years, he had gone back to school and was now a financial planner. He had set up a trust fund for me made up of donations that strangers sent. It added up quickly, and I was grateful. I was uninsured, and my medical bills were already upward of $50,000. I spent many hours writing thank-you cards to people I had never met whose kindness astounded me.

My family insisted that I see a psychotherapist. I resisted at first. I did not want to tell my story to yet another person, especially a stranger. But the therapist's strategy consisted mainly of getting me assimilated into my new life. She spoke to my family about what they could do to make the transition easier for me, and they put her suggestions into action with gusto.

Tom gave me Internet lessons. My father resumed the driving lessons he had been giving me ten years earlier. My mother took me shopping for a new wardrobe with Brianna trailing along behind us, seeming disinterested. We had family dinners each night, and my family talked about all the things that had happened in their lives in the last ten years. Mitch stayed with us most nights, our unofficial bodyguard. He and

Connor mostly concerned themselves with helping us avoid the press at all times.

Connor joined us for dinner once a week. I pumped him for information about the hunt for my abductor, but there was none. Leads were still being called in to his department, but none of them had panned out. Even the fingerprints the police had taken from the house he and Tiffany had lived in did not yield immediate results. Connor said there was some problem matching the prints. I was able to help Connor and his colleagues locate the house where Sarah and Rudy were buried, but for the most part my parents tried to discourage me from discussing my case with Connor or becoming too involved in it. Still, I lay awake nights, wondering where my abductor was and if he would take another girl. Maybe he was lying in wait until he thought that police interest had waned before targeting someone new.

Again and again I was told to focus only on healing my wounds and making a new life for myself, but I was a person who had ceased to exist until two months ago. The future was a large black hole in my mind. For so long, I believed it held nothing. Now I could simply not imagine filling the black hole with anything. I was reluctant to try, knowing that *he* was still out there somewhere. Connor kept reminding me that my abductor would not return for me. It was too risky, and he would not want to draw that kind of attention to himself. But images of Alison, naked and shivering next to a bucket in a dank closet, filled my brain until I could not block them out. Her terrified face became the backdrop for everything else in my mind. There was another girl like me, like Alison, in the world right now whose life was about to be ruined by my abductor if he wasn't apprehended soon. I knew his appetites well, and they could not be satiated or suppressed.

CHAPTER

SIXTY-THREE

As the weeks wore on, I began enjoying my family again. My father stayed with us at Mitch's house, using up years' worth of unused vacation and sick time. My mother took as much time off from work as she could but eventually had to return. Still, I was almost never alone. One of them was always with me. All the fears I'd held on to over the years of returning to the fold were falling away one by one. My family had only love and concern for me. Their excitement over my return eclipsed the sadness of the ten years we had lost. Only Brianna kept her distance. I had a pretty good idea what was bothering her. One evening before dinner my suspicions were confirmed.

I heard her talking to my mother in the kitchen before I reached the doorway. Mom was cutting vegetables. I heard the sound of the knife against the cutting board. Brianna's tone was hushed. "Have you asked her what happened?"

"What? Why would I do that?"

I pictured Brianna rolling her eyes. "Mom, don't you want to know what happened?"

"I don't need to know what happened," my mother said calmly. "If she wants to tell me, I will be happy to listen, but I don't need to know."

"You don't have any questions?" Brianna said incredulously. "None at all?"

My mother stopped cutting. "No. I don't have any questions. All I care about is that Claire is alive and that she is home. Besides, the therapist said that the best thing for us to do right now is to live in the present moment. If Claire needs to talk about the things that happened to her, she is free to do so—in her own time. I don't think we should use up any more of our precious time together on the man who took her by talking about him constantly."

"You have got to be kidding me."

My mother's tone was a warning. "Brianna."

"You don't want to know what the hell she was doing with that guy for ten years? You don't want to know why she slept with those men but didn't come home? You don't want to know why she didn't leave? How can you *not* ask her? How can you not need an explanation?"

I stepped into the kitchen. My mother and sister stared at me. Brianna looked stunned, but she thrust her chin at me defiantly, daring me to answer. My mother's face was sad. "Claire," she said gently.

My hands shook. I met my sister's eyes. "I slept with those men because I hoped that if they came to the house, you would at least know I was alive, I was okay."

Saying it aloud, it sounded so ridiculous. Yes, I wanted my family to know I was alive. But I was not okay. Not at all.

"That makes no sense," Brianna said. "You wanted to stay, didn't you? Why else would you stay with that man when you were free to leave?"

I felt as if she'd punched me in the solar plexus. I backed up, leaning against the door frame for support. I tried to gather myself together inside, all frayed edges and sharp, broken things. Sometimes family hurt you far worse than any depraved stranger. I let a moment pass.

"You don't have to do this," my mother said. She rounded the table and came toward me, but I put up a hand to signal for her to keep her distance.

"I know," I choked, looking at Brianna. "Nothing about the last ten years of my life makes sense. I don't have an explanation. I . . ."

During the last few years in the trailer, I had convinced myself I was protecting my family, protecting their lives, their innocence. The newspaper clippings about Tom's auto accident and the fire at my mother's house served as harsh reminders that if I wanted my family to remain unaffected by my abductor—the delusional psychotic I knew so well from years of forced intimacy and trauma—I had to stay.

"It wasn't as simple as me walking away," I tried. "He threatened to kill all of you. You don't know the things he did."

"Then tell us," Brianna said.

"Claire," my mother said again. "You do *not* have to do this."

"He killed a girl in front of me. Seventeen years old. She was . . ." I couldn't go on. I had only dredged up that memory aloud once to give my statement to the police. I could not do it again, not even for my sister. I squeezed my eyes shut and clenched my fists. I concentrated on my breathing, counting to five, and visualizing each number in my mind.

When the hysteria inside me receded, I opened my eyes and looked at Brianna again. I swallowed and tried once more to give her some explanation for why I had stayed missing. At that moment, I saw myself as she must have seen me—inexplicable and absurd. Tiffany had arrived three years into my captivity. My brain filled with all the times I could have left. There were countless days he'd left us alone. I could have escaped. I doubt Tiffany would have tried to stop me, as she was so intent on being the sole focus of his attention.

All those opportunities.

Squandered by fear and shame. I had sat in a room I called prison or on a porch I felt invisibly chained to like a dog, paralyzed by the memory of violations that were not my fault. I let years pass by outside the realm of my abductor's clapboard wilderness kingdom, and for what?

"I couldn't face you," I said. "I was so ashamed of what he did to me."

"It wasn't your fault," my mother said. She tried to get my attention, but my eyes were locked on my older sister whose face had now gone from incredulous disbelief to a cross between pity and horror.

"You don't know all the things that he did to me. It was so disgusting. All those years." I shuddered and Brianna winced. Her throat worked as if she was going to say something, but no words came.

"I didn't want anyone to see me. I felt so dirty. I didn't think—I don't know what I was thinking," I added.

Tears streamed freely, my composure leaving me with each one. I felt nauseated.

Brianna moved to touch my arm, but I swatted her away. I didn't want anyone to touch me while I talked about it. How could I make her understand that what had happened to me had changed who I was irrevocably? Every disgusting, hurtful thing my abductor had ever done to me had changed me. The vicious assaults chipped away at my sense of self, at my soul. There was no return to a former state once something like that happened. I was irreparably damaged in my soft places. Whatever that made me, the transformation was permanent.

"I feel sick," I mumbled.

"Goddammit, Brianna," my mother said.

I turned and ran back down the hallway, reaching the toilet just in time for my lunch to come up. A moment later, my mother knocked on the bathroom door, calling my name.

"Go away," I said, instantly feeling guilty for sending her away.

"Claire, please. Let me in, sweetheart."

My mother's voice cut me. I was thirteen again, locked in my room, crying over something trivial that had happened at school, and she wanted to come in so she could hold me, soothe me, and mother me.

I had never been like Tiffany who had no one to look for her, no one to worry about her, no one to care whether she was alive or dead, safe or suffering. I had always had my mother, and she was on the other side of the door now as she had been my whole life—even while I was missing. I knew what she had done after I was abducted. Connor had told me. My mother had turned her life into a search for me, finding hope in the small nooks and crannies of lackluster evidence, and the family was torn apart in my absence. She hadn't given up the search because there was not a single thing that could change the fact that I was her child, and she loved me absolutely and without conditions. Nothing I had seen or suffered could come near her love for me.

My mother had endured my absence while I squandered years of my life, ashamed of what my abductor had done to me. Too afraid that the family I had known would never accept me after the disgusting acts he had forced me to engage in. My mother took the pain of all those years, and she did that for me. But in my hell, I could not perform a single act of love for myself, least of all the most important one—leaving.

Her voice came again. "Claire, honey. Please let me in."

I couldn't bring myself to respond. I felt an overwhelming sense of guilt. How could I have doubted the love of my family for so long? Wasted were the years I had spent in the trailer, and before that, across the road, avoiding Tiffany's snipes and taunts while the days slipped silently by.

Each day I stayed instead of ending both my and my family's pain was a sin. I had accumulated a lot of them. I felt condemned. I did not deserve their love. If I had only believed in the strength of their love for me, if I had only been strong enough to bear the burden of all I had been through in their presence, I could have returned home years earlier.

The idea of staying captive in order to keep my sordid secrets and protect my family from the truth of my experiences seemed ridiculous, just as my explanation to Brianna had sounded when I tried to share why I'd slept with Rudy, Martin, and Jim. Still, there were all of my abductor's threats and the reality of the murders he had committed in my fictitious name. The landscape of my mind had turned to rubble. I could hardly muddle through the mass of conflicting feelings and contradictory thoughts.

My mother's gentle knock came again.

"Mom, I'm sorry. I can't. Please, not right now."

She stood on the other side of the door for several minutes before turning away with a sigh. The bathroom was too small. In fact, the entire house suddenly seemed too small. I needed to get out. I waited a few minutes, and then I slipped into the bedroom where I kept my things and fished my cell phone out of one of my bags. My family had insisted that I have it even though I had no one to call. They had been with me daily since my return, and although their numbers were programmed into it, I had no need to call any of them. There was one other number that I had programmed into the phone myself. I dialed it.

Connor picked up on the third ring. "Hello?"

"Connor? Can you come get me?"

"Claire? Is everything okay?"

I swallowed. "Yeah. I just really need to get out of the house. Can you please come?"

"Sure. I'll be there in twenty."

CHAPTER

SIXTY-FOUR

True to his word, Connor pulled up in his car twenty minutes later. I waited for him at the edge of Mitch's long driveway. He got out and smiled at me. His head had healed entirely except for a gnarly strip of scar tissue, surrounded by hair that was still shorter than the rest. He still walked with a limp from the stab wound, but he moved around much faster, with far fewer grimaces.

"Where do you want to go?" he asked.

I passed my cell phone back and forth between my hands and bit my lower lip. "I don't know," I said. "I didn't think that far ahead."

"Hungry?"

I wasn't, but I nodded. I wasn't used to social interactions, and as I climbed into the car with Connor, I realized that I had no idea what I was doing. We pulled away, and as we drove, my nervousness took on a life of its own, filling up the car until the air felt thick around me. I realized I hadn't really been alone with him since the night we had met. Sure, we had been alone in my hospital room, or in the kitchen at Mitch's house, but there had always been other people around. I knew I had nothing to worry about—that Connor would never harm me—but still my feet drummed against the car floor, my knees bobbing up and down at breakneck speed. Connor pulled over. My heart raced.

He put the car in park and undid his seat belt. "Why don't you drive?" he said.

I stared at him. "What? I don't have my license yet."

"Your dad says you have your permit, though. You can drive with that as long as I'm in the car with you."

"Oh. Okay. But I don't know—"

"I'll tell you how to get there," Connor said before I could finish. His relaxed demeanor was in stark contrast to my near panic.

We switched seats. After driving for a few minutes, my heartbeat slowed. I began to feel more relaxed. Connor gave directions to a diner outside of Sacramento. We seated ourselves and looked over our menus in silence. The noise of the diner—plates clinking, the door opening and closing, patrons talking—overwhelmed me. I hadn't been out to eat since I was fifteen years old. It was just one more thing in a long line of mundane activities that I had been denied during my captivity. Anger boiled up from the pit of my stomach. It was astounding how much my abductor had taken from me—from my innocence to the simple pleasure of eating out.

I decided in that moment that even though I wasn't hungry I was going to enjoy the experience. I was free. I could go where I wanted when I wanted—as long as I kept my family apprised of my where-abouts at all times. I could eat in a diner with a friend because I felt like it. I could order whatever I wanted. Even though it was dinnertime, I chose Belgian waffles with strawberries and whipped cream. Connor ordered a cheeseburger.

After the waitress took our menus away, Connor met my eyes. "I had to shake a few members of the press before I came to get you," he said. "They're still wise to the fact that I am in contact with you and your family."

"Thank God they don't have my photo," I said. "I wouldn't be able to go anywhere."

"Yeah, at least you still have some anonymity. Your mom said you guys had managed to visit your house without being photographed, though."

I swallowed. "I couldn't go in."

"Into the house?"

"No. Into my room. I couldn't. She said she kept it exactly the way I left it. Exactly. That the pajamas I'd changed out of that day were still on my floor."

"I know," Connor said softly.

"That room in your house—your wife's room—why did you keep it that way after she left?"

The corner of Connor's mouth dimpled. "I cleaned it out after I met you," he said. "Turned it into the Claire Fletcher task-force headquarters. Ask Mitch, he'll tell you."

From somewhere, I found the strength to smile. Connor looked away momentarily, a shy lilt to his eyes. His face and neck turned light pink.

"But why did you keep it that way—before?" I asked.

His eyebrows drew together. The blue of his eyes seemed startling even though I had gazed into them many times in the last month. He looked as though it pained him to say what came next. "Because I was hoping she would come back. I hadn't—I hadn't accepted it yet—the fact that she was gone. I couldn't even go in there. Before you came over that night, I hadn't been in there in almost two years."

It was a strange admission from a man who'd killed someone. A small fragment of the tension that bound me whenever I was near men melted away.

"Why?" I asked.

Connor looked up from the spot on the table his eyes had been fixed on. "Why what?"

I shrugged, not even sure what part of his reasoning I wanted explained. "Just why?"

Connor laughed. Then he said, "I loved my wife very much. I didn't want her to leave."

"Even though she met someone else?"

He sighed and gave me a helpless look. "Yeah."

He waited for me to respond. When I didn't, he said, "It was a little different for me. You know, your mother knew you were alive all those years. I think keeping your room like that was her way of saying she wouldn't give up."

"But what if I never came back? What if he had just killed me?"

Slowly, Connor shook his head. "I don't know, Claire. People do what they have to do in order to survive."

That I knew.

"You don't have to go back into that room," Connor added.

Hesitantly, he reached across the table and placed a hand over mine. I stared at it, feeling the warmth of his skin against mine. I had a sudden flash of the night we'd spent together—the feel of his hands on my bare skin, the smell of him, his lips trailing along my neck, the safety of his long, warm body against mine, shielding me. I had felt safe.

"You okay?" he asked.

"I don't know."

"How is your hand?"

I shrugged. "Okay. I finished physical therapy. I just have to do home exercises. It feels fine."

"Do you want to talk about today?"

I shook my head and smiled weakly. "No. Yes. My family—my sister—she wanted to know what happened. She wanted to know why I didn't come home before."

Connor frowned.

"Don't you want to know?"

Connor's eyes darkened. "I was there when you gave your statement. I know what happened to you, Claire," he murmured.

"But don't you wonder why I didn't come back sooner?"

"No."

"Really?"

He gave my hand a squeeze before releasing it. The waitress brought our food, but we didn't eat right away.

"When I was fourteen, a friend of mine—Dell—was abducted," Connor said. "He was my age. A neighbor kind of went nuts and took off with him. I guess the guy had been molesting Dell for a while but decided now and then wasn't enough. So he kidnapped Dell, and they were gone for about a month. The FBI found them at a motel in Nevada."

"That's horrible," I said.

"Yeah. Well, when Dell came home he had it pretty rough. His dad couldn't look at him. Said he couldn't understand why he didn't fight the guy off. He came back to school, but the other kids made fun of him. He went from being Dell to being the kid who took it up the ass. Kids made slurping sounds when he passed in the hallways. It was really brutal."

"How awful."

Connor grimaced. "He shot himself. He was home for about six months before he couldn't take it anymore. He got his dad's gun and shot himself. So no, I don't wonder why you didn't come home."

"Is that why you became a cop?"

Connor chuckled. "No. I just didn't want to go into plumbing with my dad, and being a police officer seemed like a lot of fun."

"Is it?"

Connor shook his head and sighed. "Some days are better than others."

We ate in silence for a few minutes. I was surprised to find that I was actually hungry. Looking across the table at Connor, I realized that a great deal of the anxiety that made me call him was gone.

He glanced up from his cheeseburger and said, "What else is on your mind?"

"I still can't sleep at night," I confessed. "It's not over."

"We're going to catch him, Claire."

"He's going to do it to someone else. He's going to take another girl. He won't stop."

"Claire." Connor's eyes were steeped in concern. "No matter what it takes, we are going to make sure he doesn't hurt anyone again. We will find him."

I swallowed over a thickening glob of saliva in my throat. I studied him for a while. I wanted to hold his hand again, but I couldn't bring myself to initiate it.

The night we'd met, physical intimacy was easy for me because I had trained myself to think of it merely as a means to an end. I had learned to use my body. It was something apart from me. A tool. I had slept with those other men to get them to do what I wanted.

Now everything about my life had changed. The armor of my anonymity and narrow existence had been stripped away, leaving a woman who was made up of wreckage more than anything else. Often, even in the safety of my family's company, I felt more exposed, more vulnerable than I had when my abductor had tied me naked to the bed in that first blackened room.

Love was an exiled emotion, an amputee from my inner body—the wound staunched and cauterized with cruelty and privation. During the ten years I spent under the watchful, cloying eyes of my abductor, never once had I fantasized about love. Not with any man.

But now I was free. There was Connor, and the way he looked at me—not just with desire but with a sort of shy adoration that was completely at odds with his masculine demeanor. My mind and body writhed away from the possibility of love or romance. I had disbelieved it for so long, I wasn't sure I could handle it. What would I do with it?

"Claire?" Connor said, interrupting my thoughts.

"I'm sorry," I said. "I'm listening."

"I said we will find the man who took you."

I nodded.

A long moment passed in silence. Then Connor said, "Did you want to go right back to Mitch's after this?"

"It doesn't matter. Why?"

He smiled. "I have an idea."

CHAPTER

SIXTY-FIVE

It was almost ten o'clock by the time Connor dropped me off. I bounded into Mitch's living room where my parents sat, trying unsuccessfully to hide their anxiety. My father flipped through the channels on the television while my mother pretended to read a magazine. I had told my parents I was going somewhere with Connor. They knew I would be safe with him—but still, they were afraid to let me out of their sight. I saw the relief flood both of their frames when I walked in. I had come back. I had come home.

"Hi, sweetie," my mother said, trying to sound calm, even.

My father muted the television. He studied me for a moment. "You look happy," he said. He uttered the word *happy* like it was some rare disease that I was unlikely to contract. I suppose in my case it was.

I grinned. "Connor took me shooting."

My father frowned. "Shooting? You mean with a gun?"

"Yeah."

His frown deepened. "That's . . ." He searched for the right word, finally settling on "odd."

My mother made a sound that was half laughter, half a scoff. "Why is that odd?"

My father shrugged. "I don't know. It just seems odd. I don't really think of shooting as a primarily feminine hobby."

My mother raised an eyebrow at him. "Well, I think if more women did it, more women would enjoy it." She turned to me. "If you enjoyed it, maybe we could go together next time. I have a nice little Ruger .380 you might like."

My father stared at my mother as if she had just landed on the couch in a spaceship. "Jenny," my father began.

Her eyebrow arch grew even more pronounced. "After you left, a lot of things changed," she said pointedly.

"I did enjoy it," I said. "I mean it was scary and intimidating at first, and I only got on the target a couple of times, but it was great."

My mother beamed. My father looked back at me with an open-mouthed, dumbfounded expression on his face.

"It's been so long since I tried anything new," I gushed. "You know, just for the sake of trying something new. Just because I could. It was exhilarating."

When my father glanced at my feet, I realized I was rocking back and forth on my heels. When he looked back at my face, his eyes were wet.

"Dad? Are you okay?"

My mother smiled. "He's crying, dear, because you sound like your old self."

My body stilled. I looked from one parent to the other. "Really?"

Both my parents nodded.

I smiled. "I guess that's good."

"Yes," my mother agreed. "Yes, it is."

◆ ◆ ◆

Brianna waited in the room I'd been sleeping in, curled up on the bed, reading a book. The sight of her made my stomach fall. The high I'd enjoyed a moment earlier dissipated completely. She jumped up when she saw me.

"Claire," she said.

I didn't look at her. "Can we do this another time?"

"I'm not here to . . . I don't want to . . ." she stammered, tossing her book onto the bed and putting her hands on her hips. "I'm sorry."

Hesitantly, I met her eyes. She wore reading glasses, which she removed. Her usual hard exterior softened. She looked like the sister I had known ten years ago. I ached for the time we had lost. I saw now the way her bitterness had become like the hard outer shell of a tortoise. She used it to keep the world out—all of it.

"I'm sorry," she repeated.

I sighed and sat at the foot of the bed. "Me too," I muttered.

Brianna rounded the bed and stood before me. "I shouldn't have come at you like that. I had so many questions. I was trying to understand. Mom said to think of the worst thing that had ever happened to me and to try to imagine how I'd feel if I had to discuss it with everyone and their brother ad nauseam." She sighed and sat down next to me. A long moment passed. Brianna continued, "I've never been raped. Never been beaten. I've never even had a guy come on too strong. The only thing that came to mind was that a guy I was living with cheated on me once. The more I thought about it—about how humiliating that was—I realized I *never* wanted to talk about it or answer questions about it. I just wanted to forget."

"Bree, you don't have to explain."

"I know it's not even remotely comparable to what happened to you. I'm just trying to make a point. I am *trying* to understand what it must be like to be in your shoes. But in all honesty, the worst thing that ever happened to me was you being abducted."

I looked at her. My eyes stung with unshed tears. "I'm sorry," I said, my throat thick.

"Were you scared?" she asked, her voice low and tentative.

I sniffed. "All the time," I admitted, my voice cracking.

"I know that what happened to you was not your fault," Brianna said, taking my hand. "I'm angry and bitter, but I know that what he did to you was not your fault. I wish . . . I . . ." She struggled, looking away and then back at me, shoring herself up for what she would say next. All the years of anger had made it difficult for her to be vulnerable. "I wish I could somehow take on some of your pain, relieve you of some of it. I don't care about what happened to you. I care that you are back with us. You're my baby sister. I love you."

I nodded, dropping my chin to my chest, squeezing Brianna's hand. I couldn't hold the tears back. They streamed silently from my tired eyes, a mixture of raw emotions that could not be tamed. Relief, guilt, shame, and happiness.

"One day I will tell you," I offered. I said this because I had always shared everything with Brianna. I also knew that she was trying to smooth things over between us, but one day she would want to know. One day I might need to confide in her.

"Claire, I don't need . . ."

"It's okay," I said. "One day I will tell you. But not today."

"Okay." She hugged me hard, and I inhaled her scent. She released me and said, "Hey, wanna make brownies and watch *The Cutting Edge?*"

I laughed. It had been our ritual before I was taken. Whenever one of us had needed cheering up, we would make brownies and eat all of them while we watched *The Cutting Edge*. It was a silly romantic comedy, but it always made us feel better. I hadn't thought about it in almost a decade.

"You still have that on tape?" I said.

Brianna wrinkled her nose. "On tape? I have it on DVD."

"What's DVD?"

Her eyes widened. "Wow," she said. "Sometimes it really is like you were in a coma for ten years."

"I wish I had been," I said.

She grimaced. "Shit. I'm sorry. I shouldn't have said that."

"Don't worry about it. Really. It's fine. I'd prefer it sometimes if we could pretend that's where I was."

"Maybe we can, kind of," Brianna said. I followed her down the hallway to the living room. My parents had gone to bed. "We can come up with a code word. You just say *coma* and I'll know to pretend that's where you were."

I laughed. "Maybe," I said.

"I'm going to mix the brownies. You turn on the TV. When I'm done, I'll give you a lesson on DVDs," she said.

"Okay." I used the remote to turn the television on. I flipped through a few channels, but the same thing was on every channel. It was a breaking news report. An Amber Alert had been issued for thirteen-year-old Emily Hartman. She had been abducted six hours earlier from outside her home in Bakersfield, California. The news programs showed a photo of her. It was a candid shot, probably taken by a family member. She had a broad smile, big blue eyes, and long, curly brown hair. She looked a lot like me. Like Alison Ward. She had been abducted by a man and a young woman.

Brianna came back into the room. Her voice barely registered. "Claire? Claire. Hey, are you okay?"

Nausea rocked my body. Acid burned the back of my throat. A man and a young woman. My abductor and Tiffany.

I felt Brianna's hand on my shoulder. "Claire. You're freaking me out."

Numb, I gestured to the television. "It's him," I said. "He's taken someone else."

CHAPTER

SIXTY-SIX

"It's been two weeks since Emily Hartman was abducted. You don't have any leads?"

Connor watched Claire pace in Farrell's kitchen. She kept folding her arms across her chest and unfolding them, like she didn't know what to do with them. There were dark circles beneath her eyes. Connor estimated she had lost at least five pounds, if not more. She had already been thin. She was approaching gaunt now.

"Claire, that's really not up to us. Bakersfield PD is handling that case. That's a long way from here," he pointed out.

She stopped walking and gave him a stricken look. "But it was *him. He* took her. I know it. Have you called the police in Bakersfield? Did you tell them?"

Connor sighed. "Yes, Stryker contacted them. He suggested to them that the man who abducted you might have also abducted Emily Hartman."

She shook her head, as if disgusted with this paltry offering, and resumed her frenetic pacing.

Connor took a step toward her. "Claire, your mom said you haven't been eating or sleeping."

She stopped again and met his eyes with a serious look. She lowered her voice in case any of her family members were outside the kitchen, listening. "I can't . . . I can't do this," she said.

"Do what?"

She gestured around her. "This. Live a normal life. He's out there, he has taken another girl, and now the same thing that happened to me is happening to her. I can't . . . I can't do this."

Tears leaked from her tired eyes. Connor fought the urge to gather her in his arms and comfort her.

"I keep seeing Alison in my mind." Claire shuddered and hugged herself. "It wasn't real until I saw her. Can you understand that?"

"What wasn't real?"

"That he could do what he did to me to someone else—that he *would* do it. There was only ever me. Tiffany was there willingly. But when I saw Alison and after that, when I came home, I found out about that other girl, Noel—" A sob choked off the rest of her sentence.

Connor laid a hand on her shoulder. She didn't wince. He wanted to comfort her, hold her, but he didn't want to scare her or add to the tremulous fear he saw in her eyes. The more time he spent with her, the more Connor felt an inexplicable pull toward Claire. She was traumatized, and along with that angry, frightened, overwhelmed, and confused. But she was also Claire. There were panic attacks, nightmares, and tears. In spite of that, being with her was effortless. The whole thing was making his mind spin.

"Claire," he whispered. "This isn't your job. Believe me, the police are looking for this guy. The whole state is looking for him."

She took a moment to compose herself, swallowed, and looked up at him. Her eyes made him ache. "Do you have any leads?"

Connor cleared his throat. "Not on the photo yet, but they started digging at the house you took us to—the one where Miranda Simon was killed."

As Connor had anticipated, Claire's abductor had switched aliases from Rod Page to George Minarik and bought the property outright. Boggs and Stryker had tracked down the real estate agent who sold it. Rod Page aka George Minarik had paid cash over nine years earlier.

They had caught two breaks this time. First, because the suspect bought the house under a false name and was wanted in connection with two abductions, three counts of attempted murder, and several counts of assault and rape, they were able to get a search warrant and dig up the yard, which would add at least two murders to the man's crimes, although it had taken two weeks to get all the requisite technicians and equipment before the digging started.

The second break was that George Minarik had a recent driver's license.

Finally, they had a photo. Both Claire and Alison had positively identified the man as their abductor, and the photo was almost an exact match to the composites the police department had created in the previous weeks. The driver's license photo was released to the media, and for the last two weeks, Connor could hardly turn on the television without seeing the man's face. The department got over a hundred calls but no viable leads. Boggs and Stryker were still waiting for fingerprint matches in the national database, although Stryker had called Connor that day to say they might have something by the next morning.

Claire stopped pacing. Her face was incredibly sad, and for that, Connor felt like a failure. "That doesn't sound like very much," she said.

He grimaced. "It's not, but I promise you, my division is working on this. Look, Boggs and Stryker wanted me to come by the division tomorrow morning. They think they may have found some new leads. Why don't you meet me there and see if they've turned anything up?"

Claire sighed. Her face was so drawn and haggard. She looked like she had been through a war. Connor saw now why Jenny had called him, asked him to talk to Claire. "Fine. I'll meet you there tomorrow." She didn't sound the least bit enthused. "But Connor—" She broke off, and he saw a raw mixture of anger and fear in her eyes.

"Yes, Claire."

"Every hour that goes by is another hour that he is spending torturing Emily Hartman."

CHAPTER SIXTY-SEVEN

Claire was already waiting for him when Connor arrived at work the next morning. She sat outside the building that housed the Major Crimes Unit with a cup of coffee in her hands. He could tell she had not slept overnight. In spite of that, he felt a little thrill go through him at the sight of her. She rose abruptly when she saw him and smiled. Once again, looking into her eyes, he felt a split second of panic. This time it wasn't from the sorrow he often saw there—it was her.

He looked away from her eyes, instead studying the untamed dark curls resting against her cheek as she gazed up at him. He was completely disarmed by her, and it frightened him to think how much he had come to care for her in such a short period. The last time he'd even come close to feeling what he felt for Claire, he'd wasted eight years of his life only to have his heart trampled on. But he already knew he could not turn his back on her. It was far too late for that.

He smiled. "I heard you got your driver's license. Did you drive yourself?"

Her eyes lit up a little. "Yeah, I did. I've driven before—as you know—but not as a licensed driver."

Connor laughed and led them inside. Stryker greeted them as they got off the elevator at the division. Connor and Claire followed him to his desk. Stryker pulled out his chair and gestured to Claire. "Sit," he said.

Claire took a seat, and Connor sat on the edge of Stryker's desk. "Where's Boggs?" he asked.

"Following up on something. He should be here any minute."

Claire fidgeted with her hands and looked from Connor to Stryker.

"What have you got?" Connor asked.

Stryker sighed. He folded his arms across his chest and looked directly at Claire, his eyebrows drawn together. "Miss Fletcher," he began.

"Claire. Please, call me Claire," she said.

"Claire, what I'm about to tell you is generally not released to the public during an open investigation. A lot of it is public record, but pretty much if the press doesn't splatter it all over the front page or the six o'clock news, then people aren't aware of it."

"I understand," Claire said. "I'm not a police officer or an investigator."

Stryker nodded. "First, we found the remains of Jim Randall. At least that's the initial report from the ME. It'll take him a few days to write it up in his official report and release it to the press, but the dental records match."

Claire's face turned pasty white. One of her hands flew to her chest. She swallowed with difficulty. "Where?"

"A few yards away from Teplitz and Simon," Stryker said.

Claire squeezed her eyes closed. Connor saw a tremor move through her frame as she fought off the shock and horror of the revelation.

Stryker gave her a moment before he continued. "Second, I want you to hear this because I know a lot of victims of sex crimes who blame themselves for what happened to them. Almost all of them do at some point or another. But you gotta know that none of what happened to you was your fault. This guy was a creep from the get-go."

Claire looked at Connor. The color did not return to her skin. She radiated dread. Connor could feel it where he stood. He smiled briefly at her. He was used to this. There weren't many rap sheets or criminal pasts that surprised him. Repeat offenders made crime a lifelong habit. Many of them started out with misdemeanors and escalated into felonies. Before Stryker read off the various charges levied against Claire's abductor in the past, Connor could almost tell her word for word what they would be.

Claire blinked. "Please. Just tell me."

Stryker reached between Connor and Claire and pulled a thick file off his desk. "This guy's rap sheet reads like a pedophile's résumé," he said. "This is the reason the goddamn prints took so long. Not all of this shit was in AFIS." For Claire's benefit, he added, "AFIS is the Automated Fingerprint Identification System. It was before the technology came along. We turned up so many matches we thought the system was on the blink. Took a while to sift through them and confirm we were looking at the right guy. We've got several aliases but all their prints match up and so do photos and descriptions. He moved around a lot. He got mostly misdemeanors in a number of states—trespassing, stalking, indecent exposure, and a couple of Peeping Toms. Not all states have laws against that."

"What happened with those?" Connor asked.

"He paid the fines and they let him go. He only ever spent one month in jail, and that was in Vermont twenty-two years ago."

"So he has money," Connor said.

Stryker pursed his lips momentarily. "Oh, you don't know the half of it, Parks." Stryker pulled a sheet of paper out of the file and placed it on the desk in front of Claire. Connor saw a black-and-white photo and a summary of criminal charges beneath it on the page. Claire studied it for a moment before gasping.

"It's him," she said.

Stryker nodded. "Bradley Cullen, Minnesota. One count of sexual assault and battery against a minor. This is the first record of a more serious offense that we could find. It's pretty old. He made bail and took off. They never found him. The statute of limitations ran out but we managed to get a copy of the file thanks to our good buddies in the Minneapolis PD."

"What does that mean?" Claire said.

Connor frowned. "Well, that's a tough one. Depending where you are, sexual assault and battery can include anything from the guy rubbing himself against you to rape. It has to involve contact." Connor turned to Stryker. "What did the file say?"

"Thirteen-year-old girl. Apparently she lived across the hall from him in an apartment complex. He let her come over to his place to watch television. One day he starts fondling her. Kid starts screaming to high heaven. Parents called the cops and he was arrested that day," Stryker said.

"What else?" Claire interjected before Connor could glean more information on the case from Stryker.

Stryker pulled out another sheet of paper similar to the first one. Again, he placed it in front of Claire. "Meet Timothy Bush. Virginia. One count of sexual assault and battery. Same story. He made bail and took off."

Stryker placed another sheet in front of Claire. "Jem Nebesky. Tennessee. One count of statutory rape, two counts of sexual assault and battery. Makes bail, takes off. Next, we have Henry Kreisher. Florida. This is where our guy got a little smarter. He hooked up with a single mother. She had a twelve-year-old daughter. He ended up with six counts of aggravated sexual assault. Made bail, took off. Then he went to Colorado. Called himself Doug Spellings. Hooked up with another single mom who conveniently had a thirteen-year-old daughter. Three counts of aggravated sexual assault. Four counts of statutory rape. Made bail, took off. Next thing we hear from him, he's living with Irene Geary."

With each printout Stryker placed in front of Claire, her abductor's face looked older and older. "These are the ones we know about," Stryker added. "Although they're all about three to four years apart, so I don't imagine he'd really have time to slip much in between all the moving and identity switching."

"Oh my God," Claire murmured. She shuffled through the pages with trembling hands. "They're all him," she said. "All of them. It's him."

She looked at Connor, her eyes wide as saucers. "He's been at it a long time," Connor said.

Claire shook her head. There was an angry set to her jaw. She shuffled through the papers again, this time more frantically. "I can't believe this," she said. "I don't understand. How could he just keep doing it? So many of them."

She was close to hysteria. Connor stepped toward her, but Stryker leaned in and caught her eye. "Claire," Stryker said. "We're going to nail this piece of shit." Despite his words, Stryker's tone was soft and soothing. Connor had seen him do this several times with panicked or frightened victims.

Most of the time, Stryker looked like he might pull your heart out through your rib cage if you looked at him the wrong way. He intimidated the hell out of suspects. But then there was this. A firm touch to convey comfort, determined eyes, and the slight downward turn of his mouth that made him less intimidating. He'd talk in that voice—confident, calm, even. Connor had seen his colleague talk a lot of witnesses and victims from absolute terror to relative calm in a matter of moments.

Claire didn't look up, but she nodded and stopped the mad shuffling of her abductor's rap sheets. Stryker turned her chair around and crouched down in front of her. "Hey," he said. "You need to know that what happened to you and to all of the other people this guy hurt was not your fault. He's a predator. He was a predator before you were even born. Communications were limited for a long time from one state to another. That's probably one of the reasons he got away with everything for so long. But now we can look things up on a computer and keep track of scum like him. We are going to nail him."

Claire wiped tears from her cheeks. Connor leaned over Stryker's shoulder and handed her a tissue. Stryker continued, "Claire, I want you to remember one thing, and you keep this in the front of your mind every day until that bastard is behind bars. You saved an eleven-year-old girl from all of this." He lifted a hand and spread the pages across his desk. "Because of you, Alison Ward is at home with her family. She's safe. Because of you, we have a shot at this guy. We can put an end to all this once and for all."

Stryker watched Claire intently. She stared at the floor, tears coursing down her cheeks. "Hey," Stryker said. "You got that?"

Connor could practically feel Claire dismissing the idea of herself as some kind of hero, even if it was only to one girl and her family. He knew the way her mind worked, the ways in which her abductor had warped it in order to remain blameless for all the horrific acts he committed. Connor knew Claire felt guilty for having stayed his captive for so long, even after she had opportunities to go home. But it was an indisputable fact that Claire had saved Alison from a fate as terrifying as her own. Connor watched her, expecting her to protest as she always did, but instead she nodded, acquiescing to Stryker.

After a moment, she squeaked, "But Emily is still out there. I know he has her."

Stryker frowned. "I know. We're working on it. The whole state is working on it. Claire, we will find him."

Stryker stood and gathered the pages to put back in his file. Connor moved behind Claire and put his hands on her shoulders, grateful that the tension in them dissipated instead of escalating. "So who is he?" Connor asked. "What's his real name?"

Boggs's voice boomed across the room. "Hey kids," he said. He was grinning from ear to ear. Connor felt a flutter of excitement. It had to be good because Boggs rarely smiled. The older detective waved a piece of paper in the air as he approached them. When he saw Claire, his face fell. He looked from Stryker to Connor. "You told her," he said. It wasn't a question. "You okay?" he asked Claire.

She smiled wanly. "I've been worse," she said.

Boggs plopped into his own chair across from them. "Well then, let me be the bearer of good news. We got some leads."

"The bail money?" Stryker said.

Boggs nodded, looking every bit like a cat that just swallowed a bird. He looked at Connor. "All right. Here it is. Every single time this guy gets arrested, he makes bail, which we thought was odd since he never had his own lawyer and had no family or close associates in any of the places he got nabbed."

"We're going on the theory that this guy has a lot of cash," Connor said.

Boggs stuck an index finger straight up in the air. "Right. But while he's sitting in jail waiting to be assigned a public defender, who is taking care of his business?"

"You won't believe this," Stryker said.

Boggs went on: "Every single time this guy gets arrested and charged with a crime, in every state in which he resided, the same law firm arranged to have his bail paid so he could walk out of there, flee the state, and never face the charges against him."

"A law firm?" Connor said.

"Yeah. The same one. A firm in Texas. Obviously they're representing someone, whether it's him or someone he knows. But all they do is front the money. No one from their office ever went to any of this guy's arraignments or bail hearings for that matter. They just kept paying and paying and paying and not a peep out of them."

"You think it's some kind of trust fund?" Connor asked.

"We don't know," Stryker said. "But it's a damn good place to start."

"Did you check for similar crimes and prints in Texas?" Connor asked.

"Yeah," Boggs said. "We got nothing. But we're gonna talk to the locals and the DA there and see what we can come up with," Boggs said.

"So who is he?" Connor asked again.

Boggs shoved a file across the desk to Connor. "Reynard Seymour Johnson of Houston, Texas, born May 13, 1958, to Seymour and Sheila Johnson of the Johnson Oil Company. He was their third child. Two older brothers, Seymour Jr. and Lawrence, and two younger sisters, Carolyn and Jane. Seymour is deceased, but the mother runs the company side by side with her eldest son. She claims she hasn't heard from or seen Reynard since he was twenty years old and left home."

"The law firm that paid his bail?" Connor asked.

"Hired by the family," Boggs said. "At least they handle most of the family's affairs. His estate money, trust fund, or whatever you want to call it—all the money goes through there. It's all handled through that office. Reynard gets in a jam, calls his contact there, and they just wire cash to wherever he specifies. That way the parents—well, now, just the mother—can claim no involvement. That they didn't know what he used the funds for or even when he withdrew cash from the estate."

"How much are we talking?" Connor asked.

Boggs shrugged. "Don't know for sure, but it's a lot of money. A bottomless pit of cash. The family is wealthy enough to have the state of Texas renamed after them."

Connor looked at Claire. She was pale, and her hands trembled when she took the Johnson file from his hands. As she leafed through it, she asked, "Are you sure? Are you sure this is him? The same guy?"

"It's him," Stryker said.

"It took us a while to pin him down," Boggs added. "He has no priors in his home state. But that's him all right."

"His real name is Reynard?" she said.

Stryker laughed. "Yeah, I know. No wonder he made up aliases."

Claire looked up at the two detectives. "If he had so much money, why did he keep us in such dumps? Every place he ever took me or Tiffany was practically falling apart."

"Anonymity," Connor said. "If you've committed as many crimes as this guy has, and you're holding someone against their will, you don't want to draw attention to yourself. You'd want to be out of the way, which he was, living out in the middle of nowhere, but you also want to make sure you're as indistinguishable as the thirty other people around you. If he'd bought up land out in the woods and built a palace, people would notice. People would talk. People would come around."

"That's probably how he went undetected for so long," Boggs added.

"Have you tried contacting the family?" Connor asked.

"Yeah. That's the bad news. His family lawyered up," Stryker said.

Claire looked at Connor, puzzled. "They got an attorney," Connor explained. "It means they don't have to tell us anything. We, or any other authorities, can question his family about his whereabouts but only in the presence of their attorney, who I'm guessing has already advised them not to answer any questions."

Claire's shoulders slumped.

"Sorry," Boggs said to her.

"So what now?" Claire asked.

"Well, there isn't much we can do now," Stryker said. "If the family doesn't want to talk, they don't have to, even if they do know where he is, and we don't know for sure if they do."

"Can't you get a subpoena for them to reveal what they know?" Connor asked. "It's obstruction, harboring a fugitive, aiding and abetting if they know and don't give that information to the police."

Stryker grimaced. "Yeah, we're working on it, but we have to coordinate with the local boys now. We gotta let them handle it. We're trying to get the FBI to come in on this since he's wanted in so many states, but now they're trying to decide which field office they want to work out of. It's going to take a while."

"We already have a BOLO out on him," Boggs said. "Now we have a name to go with it."

"BOLO?" Claire interrupted.

"Be on the lookout," Boggs explained. "We send out his photo and all his information, get it to as many agencies as we can, and hope someone runs into him. Now that we have a name, we get the press in on it. Son of an oil tycoon, a kidnapper, and sexual deviant? It'll go national in all of thirty seconds, and then the Johnsons will wish they had told us what they knew from the start and kept the whole thing quiet."

CHAPTER

SIXTY-EIGHT

In the months since my homecoming, my family, Connor, and Mitch had formed an unofficial committee. They liked to discuss me and what my brother had once referred to as my recovery.

"She's not a hurricane-ravaged city, Tom," Brianna had scoffed.

"Well, her reentry into the world," my father had put in quickly, coming to Tom's defense.

Brianna gave him a cutting look.

Connor, who had been sitting silently at the dinner table that night, laughed. "That makes her sound like an ex-con."

Mitch, who remained silent throughout most discussions, nodded and chuckled.

My mother threw her arms into the air, losing patience. "The therapist said we should think of it as her assimilation into her new life. Let's just call it that."

"You all know that I'm sitting here, right?" I finally interjected, drawing blank stares from them all. I popped a piece of my mother's delicious steak into my mouth and talked around it. "I like what Mom said."

Thus the unofficial committee for the assimilation of Claire Fletcher into her new life was formed. Under different circumstances, I might have been annoyed, angry even at their discussing me and my future this way, but having been robbed of ten years with the people who loved me most, I appreciated their earnest commitment to my happiness and well-being.

That's what they were really discussing—my well-being—as if I were a child they had just adopted. The day after I found out the true identity of my abductor, the committee was in session again. It was unplanned, of course. They all just happened to be there for dinner that night. They were already worried about me—my insomnia, the number of hours I spent watching news coverage of the search for Emily and googling her case. I watched a broadcast one day where a wall of people waded through a barren field in Bakersfield, moving slowly, scanning the sparse brush for any sign of Emily. I knew they were looking for her body. I also knew there would be no body. Reynard had taken her, and he would use her until there was nothing left of the girl she had been or until he tired of her—maybe both.

Connor and Mitch thought it would ease my anxiety if Mitch went to Texas and tried to scare up what background he could on Reynard, perhaps find something that might help police in California locate him and Emily. Brianna agreed. My parents and brother thought it was a terrible idea. My obsession with Emily's abduction was unhealthy, they said—I needed to move on. None of us even knew for certain that Reynard had taken Emily. What if we were just chasing our tails?

They were split—three of them for the trip, three of them against it. The next morning my therapist cast the deciding vote, and two hours after that, Mitch was on a plane bound for Houston.

I didn't sleep at all until Mitch returned. It took a few days. He got back just after dinner, and Connor was with him. It was only me and my parents that night, as Tom and Brianna were at their own homes.

The three of us went out to the deck at the back of Mitch's house while my parents cleaned up from dinner.

"So what did you find out?" I asked.

Mitch got right to the point. "Reynard Johnson grew up in rich town, USA. Huge house—a compound actually, complete with tennis courts, in-ground pool, horses, stables, the whole nine yards. Couldn't get much on family life. But I found a housekeeper who worked for the family while the kids were growing up. It cost me, but I got her to talk on the condition that she wouldn't have to testify in a court of law."

Connor shrugged. "I don't think that will be a problem. We're talking about when he was a juvenile, right?"

Mitch nodded. "Yeah. The things she told me anyway. Turns out our boy was a Peeping Tom as young as fourteen. The housekeeper said she caught him spying on his younger sisters several times. Apparently he also exposed himself to them. There was some trouble at school with him groping girls. One lady I talked to went to school with him. She said he would just kind of sneak up behind them and start touching them whenever he found one of them alone or away from the pack."

My stomach felt hollow. "My God," I muttered.

"Yeah. Sick shit. When he was fifteen, the parents sent him to an all-boys boarding school. The mother was against it, but the father insisted. I think old Mr. Johnson figured that the kid would have to stop acting on his urges if there were no young girls around."

"But he managed to find one," Connor supplied.

"More than one. The faculty lived on campus and a few of them had twelve- and thirteen-year-old girls. Johnson went back to his peeping routine, and when the opportunity to expose himself came along, he took it. Get this—the families of these three girls got together and decided to press charges. The Johnsons tried to buy them off to keep them quiet."

I wrapped my arms around my middle and rocked back and forth on the edge of my chair. It was almost too horrifying to hear. I was glad I had only picked at my dinner because what little I had eaten threatened to come back up. "No," I said.

Mitch held up a hand. "Well, the families weren't having any of that. They pressed charges and Reynard got sent to juvie for his senior year of high school."

"Juvie records are sealed," Connor pointed out. "How did you find that out?"

Mitch smiled. "People love to talk, my friend. They just love to talk. So he gets out of juvie, turns eighteen, and somehow gets into college. Family probably arranged that as well. He only lasted one semester. He stopped going to classes and started a relationship with a thirteen-year-old local girl. Claimed it was consensual. Maybe it was, it's hard to tell, but her dad found them going at it in a motel room and beat the piss out of him. The girl's father pressed charges, but this time the Johnsons were able to make it go away.

"They brought Johnson home, where they could keep an eye on him. Then he gets caught twice trying to lure thirteen-year-old girls into his car. The Johnsons paid and kept it quiet, but that was it for them. They kicked him out and told him never to come back—not to their home and not to the state of Texas. The mother convinced the father to set up the fund through the law office so he would be taken care of."

"I am going to be sick," I said.

"We don't have to talk about this, Claire," Mitch said.

I shook my head, shored myself up, and met Mitch's gaze. "No," I said. "I have to. I have to hear it."

Connor reached over and squeezed my shoulder. "So the reason he has no priors in Texas is because the parents bribed people to keep quiet," he said.

"Yeah. That was over twenty-five years ago, though. I found a lot of people who were willing to tell me the details just so long as they never had to go to court."

Connor's mouth twisted in revulsion. "So the parents knew that their son was a pervert well before he turned eighteen, and their solution to that problem was to give him unlimited funding and turn him loose on the rest of society?"

Mitch's bushy eyebrows drew together. "Yeah, just so long as he didn't tarnish the family name."

Connor stood and paced the deck. He looked every bit as disgusted as I felt. "Unbelievable," he muttered.

Reynard had ruined so many lives, and in spite of Connor's assurances that he would be caught and punished, he was free and he had taken another girl. Another life ruined. When would it end?

I took a breath and swallowed the bile that rose at the back of my throat. A plan was already half-formed in my mind. I couldn't sit idly by anymore trying to live a normal life as a raging insomniac with no appetite, sustaining myself on the scant details of Emily's case. I had to *do* something.

CHAPTER

SIXTY-NINE

I hadn't been on an airplane since I was thirteen. My father had taken us to Washington, DC, on a short vacation. As the plane lifted up, airborne on rumbles and thundering speed, my body was pinned to the seat cushions. The insistent pull of gravity caused a fleeting sense of fear, which was quickly overcome by guilt. I knew my family would be beside themselves with worry, but as they had pointed out to me repeatedly since I had come home, I was an adult now. I was free to come and go as I pleased. I had my driver's license for just that purpose. My family didn't want me to feel restricted in any way after having been a prisoner for the past decade.

Of course none of that made it okay to steal Brianna's driver's license and credit card to fly to Houston without telling anyone. But that's just what I did.

Once we were at cruising altitude, the steady hum of the engines and the off-balance sensation of flying lulled me into a warm, deep sleep. I fought it to no avail. I had planned to use the time on the flight to mentally review my plan and figure out what I would do next if I didn't get what I wanted. But I hadn't slept for weeks.

When a flight attendant shook me awake, the plane was empty. She handed me my carry-on bag, and I made my way into the bustling airport. My eyelids were heavy. I felt groggy. I paused outside the gate, looking for the signs to baggage claim. Once I made my way there, I found a rental car company.

The woman at the counter studied Brianna's license for a long time. "That was taken when my hair was short," I explained awkwardly. I prayed that Brianna and I looked enough alike that I could pass for her. Mostly, I needed her credit card. I had been reborn into the world as a twenty-five-year-old woman. I had no resources of my own other than my trust fund, which Tom oversaw for the time being, and I knew he would never have sanctioned this trip. The woman at the rental car desk looked me over, a skeptical arch to her brow. A few tense moments ensued, and then wordlessly she pushed the paperwork across the counter for me to sign.

With the key to a rented Nissan Sentra in hand, I stepped out into the thick Houston heat. I blinked against the sunlight. My eyes burned from exhaustion and the sudden brightness of daylight. I used the directions given to me by the rental car agent and found the hotel within minutes. Continental breakfast was being served when I arrived. I grabbed two croissants and the biggest cup of coffee I could find and headed to my room.

The room was airy but dark and sterile in the way all hotel rooms seem to be. It was a way station with stark white walls and a double bed. I dropped my bag on the floor and climbed onto the bed. I had purchased a map of the city at the airport. Now I spread it before me on the bed. I called Brianna and left her a voice mail explaining what I had done. I had considered not contacting my family at all until my mission was complete, but that didn't seem fair to them after all they had been through. After I hung up, I noticed I had two missed calls. One from my mother and one from Connor. My heartbeat quickened, and I felt a distinct pain in my emotional core.

I knew my family and Connor would be worried about me, but it couldn't be helped. I had wasted ten years of my life standing by and doing nothing. Now a young girl's life hung in the balance. I felt responsible for her. I hadn't been able to save myself or Sarah—Miranda. Even Alison had spent a month in the dark confines of a closet before I rescued her. But now I was free, and I could do something to save Emily.

My days of standing idly by were over.

CHAPTER SEVENTY

As he sped to Mitch's house in a department-issued vehicle, Connor tried Claire's cell phone. Just as Jenny had predicted, he got no answer. It switched over to voice mail. He didn't leave a message. His heart pounded hard in his chest, and sweat soldered his shirt and jacket to his frame.

Jen had called him twenty minutes earlier. She said Claire had gotten up early and taken her car. She hadn't left a note, and no one had seen or heard from her for several hours. Jen and Rick met him at the door. Jen wrung her hands nervously. Behind her, Rick stood stock-still, an unnatural pallor to his face. Connor imagined that this is what they must have looked like over ten years ago when they realized their daughter had been abducted.

"We're sorry," Jen said. "We didn't know who to call. She's not answering her phone. We didn't know what to do."

"It's okay," Connor assured them.

"We just got her back," Jen said, her voice cracking. Rick moved toward her and pulled her into his arms. His hands were shaking.

Connor urged them both toward the couch, where they sat down. "It's okay," he repeated. "I'm sure this is just a misunderstanding. Maybe she just doesn't realize her cell phone is off. We'll find her. Let's just take a breath, calm down, and we'll make a list of places she might have gone."

Brianna's voice reached them before she was through the front door. "Houston," Brianna said. Connor hadn't even heard her pull up in the driveway. Her short hair was in disarray, her eyes wide, and her face every bit as pale as her father's. She held out her cell phone, as if offering it to them. "She left me a voice mail. She stole my driver's license plus one of my credit cards and went to Houston."

Jen's brow wrinkled in confusion. "Houston?"

The news was like a slap to the face. Immediately, Connor thought of the look on Claire's face just two days earlier when Mitch had told her about Reynard's long history of luring and molesting young girls. He should have known. He closed his eyes, willing himself to stay calm.

"Houston, Texas?" Rick said.

Connor opened his eyes and looked at Claire's parents. "That's where Reynard Johnson's family lives. Mitch just got back from there, remember?"

Still, the Fletchers looked baffled. Brianna walked over to the couch. "She said she was going to try to find Emily Hartman," she said.

Connor shook his head. "She went after him," he said.

CHAPTER
SEVENTY-ONE

The Johnson estate was just as Mitch had described it to me. It was huge, stately, and imposing. It was a complex easily the size of the city block I'd grown up on, if not larger. A faded salmon-colored stone wall surrounded it. At the front was a locked gate with an intercom and three cameras situated in different places, triangulating the entrance with their electronic eyes.

The gate and long wall were unexpected. Coming here had been an abstract idea gaining force and momentum in my mind in the last twenty-four hours. I hadn't had the time or the foresight to figure out how I'd get in. In my mind's eye, I just appeared inside the Johnson household, confronting the first family member I happened upon.

But now I was locked out. I walked several yards west of the gate until I found a piece of crumbling wall beneath the overhanging bough of a large tree that stood on the outside of the estate.

Almost the instant I saw the tree, I decided to sneak in. I doubted anyone would let me in, and I had no time to coax or cajole my way onto the grounds. Emily had no time. The sooner I found Reynard, the sooner she would be free. I climbed the wall using the trunk of the tree for support. Dropping to the grass on the other side, I dusted my palms on my jeans and walked resolutely toward the Johnson mansion.

I was spurred on by the memory of Alison huddled naked in that closet filled with the putrid smell of fear, filth, and vomit. That had been me. That was Emily now. I didn't know her—that was true—but in a way, saving her felt like saving myself. When I reached the front door, I did not knock. I let myself in and went in search of someone who would give me answers whether they liked it or not.

The foyer was enormous with vaulted ceilings and marble-tiled floors. My footsteps echoed in the cool chamber. The floors, walls, and furniture were all swathed in muted earth tones. For a moment, I felt as if I'd stepped into a mausoleum. There were heavy double doors on both sides. A large set of stairs lay ahead of me and to the left of that, a long dark hallway. There was nothing inviting about the place. Even the still-life paintings adorning the walls were flat and unexpressive.

I wrapped my arms around my middle and looked around. As I turned back in the direction of the front door, I was startled by the appearance of a young Hispanic woman. I didn't hear her enter. It was as if she materialized out of thin air. She was dressed in jeans and a short-sleeved indigo sweater. Her hands were clasped at her waist. She was petite, shorter than me, her features small and refined. Her black hair was pulled back tightly in a bun, revealing a round face and coal-black eyes.

The woman stared at me with a solicitous expression. She was waiting for me to notice her. I wondered how long she'd stood there, watching me in silence.

"You are trespassing on private property," she said with a slight Spanish accent. Her face was a stone mask.

I stepped toward her, but she remained unruffled, like a statue. "I'm here to see Sheila Johnson," I said, and marveled at how strong and certain my woman's voice sounded when I felt nothing like that on the inside.

"Mrs. Johnson does not entertain trespassers," the woman replied. The statement sounded strange from the woman's lack of inflection. Her words were clearly scripted. "I will call the police now," she added without a hint of threat in her voice.

"Please do," I said calmly. "While they're here they can arrest Mrs. Johnson for aiding and abetting and obstruction of justice."

For a fleeting second, confusion furrowed the woman's brow and livened her dull eyes. Then she said, "Who are you?"

I lifted my chin. "Claire Fletcher. I'm here about Reynard."

The woman swallowed. She waved a hand toward the double doors on her right. "Come," she said.

She escorted me inside the large drawing room and waited for me to sit on one of the brocaded couches positioned in the center of the room. "Wait here," she instructed.

She was gone for ten minutes, and when she returned, her affect was as flat as ever. "Reynard is not here. Leave now."

My fists clenched. I stood and my legs trembled with rage. I moved within inches of her and stared down into her face. "I want to speak with Mrs. Johnson right now," I told her.

"Mrs. Johnson will not be meeting with you."

"Reynard has kidnapped another girl. You tell Mrs. Johnson I want to know where he is, and I'm not leaving until I find out."

The woman did not reply. She returned my stare. Something was working behind her eyes. Maybe she had thought I would simply leave. Maybe now she was deciding whether to return to Sheila Johnson for further instructions. A long, tedious moment passed. When she swallowed, the delicate brown skin of her throat quivered.

I broke eye contact with her when a movement behind her caught my eye. There was a crack in the double doors we'd entered through. A big brown eye peered through at me. The woman seemed unaware of the spy, all her concentration focused on my face. From the dark sliver between the doors, the eye held mine. The door cracked open a bit more, revealing the owner of the peeping eye. It was a young boy, no older than seven or eight, pale and thin with sandy-blond hair.

I opened my mouth to speak, and the boy pressed a finger against his lips in a shhh motion. He looked over his shoulder and back at me. Quickly, I cleared my throat, signaling my understanding. The door closed just as quietly as it opened. I looked back at the woman.

"Did you hear what I said?"

She didn't respond.

I leaned in closer to her, the simmering rage in the pit of my stomach making me feel menacing for the first time in my life. "I'm here to see Sheila Johnson, and I am not leaving until I do. So you have a choice. You can stare at me all day or you can go tell your boss to get her ass in here, but keep one thing in mind—every second Sheila Johnson wastes with this stupid game could mean the difference between a thirteen-year-old girl living or dying. If she dies because your boss is too much of a coward to come out here and face one of her son's victims, she will be held responsible and she will pay—trust me, she is going to pay this time."

I was exaggerating a bit. I didn't believe Reynard would kill Emily—he needed her to fulfill his perverted fantasies—but given enough time, he would murder her innocence and any chance she might have at a normal life. In the depths of the woman's onyx eyes I saw confusion and something akin to fear. "Wait here," she said before spinning on her heel and leaving the room.

Once she was gone, I counted to ten and crept into the hallway. I pulled the doors closed behind me and stood listening in the hallway.

I wondered if I had imagined the small boy peering through the door when I felt a little hand slip into mine. I had not heard or seen him approach. Big brown eyes stared up at me with solemnity. Again, a single finger crossed his thin mouth, urging me to be silent. I nodded.

I had no idea who he was—a grandchild or a child of a staff member, but his eyes told me to do as he instructed. He led me deeper into the hallway, past darkened walls and grim-looking doors. The house was both cavernous and cloying. I felt a whole-body shiver as we made an abrupt turn and entered a doorway that led to a staircase.

Still grasping my hand, he led me up the stairs. His footsteps made no noise. Beside his muted movements, my own steps caused slight creaks that sounded like thunderbolts cracking the silence. Again, I shivered and looked at the boy. For a moment, I wondered whether he was real or a ghost haunting the Johnson mansion, guarding its secrets.

We turned left at the top of the stairs. My feet sank mercifully into plush mauve carpeting. Moving down the hall, we stopped at the third door on the right. The boy rapped once and pushed it open. He released my hand.

"Go," he said.

I stepped inside and jumped when the door swung shut behind me. Another short hall lay before me.

A female voice that sounded like wind chimes called to me. "Come."

I followed it into an apartment contained within the huge house. It was a world apart from the confines of the elegant dark mansion, decorated in a southwestern motif. Colorfully braided rugs adorned the floors. Indigo beaded lampshades caught my eye. Native American shadow figures and pottery dotted the simple shelves and tables.

A wafer-thin woman with long, thick chestnut hair lay on the couch. Her skin was ghostly pale, making her dark hair and ruby lips all the more striking. She wore a long white linen dress.

"Sit," she commanded.

I dropped into a rocking chair across from her. I didn't know what to say. I stared at her. She smiled, an enigmatic curve to her pouty lips, jarringly sensual and penetrating.

"You're the Fletcher woman," she stated.

"Yes."

She appraised me, her eyes roaming up and down my body like hands. I shifted and straightened my spine.

"I'm here because—"

"I know why you're here," the woman cut in. "My mother stone-walled you."

I nodded, inwardly startled to surmise that she was Sheila Johnson's daughter. I searched her face for some resemblance to Reynard. There was nothing there save the simmering, calculated hostility that glowed in her eyes.

The woman gave a short, humorless laugh. "That's right. The Queen Mother expelled me from her loveless little womb, the same as Reynard."

Hearing her say his name was strange—there was a lilt of familiarity to it but also contempt.

"My nephew keeps me informed of all visitors of interest to me. He's a very good child in spite of this family's influence. I'm trying to keep him that way."

"By teaching him to sneak around and spy?"

She was more amused than defensive. "My dear, you do not grow up in this family, you survive it. Some things that I encourage are necessary evils."

"Where are his parents?"

"His mother, my sister, is somewhere in Europe, spending a large quantity of the family fortune on things that will never change who she is or what"—she hesitated—"happened to her. His father? A weeklong fling in Barbados. God knows what became of him."

"Tell me where Reynard is," I said.

"I don't know where he is, but I will help you. Patience, Claire Fletcher."

"I don't have time for this," I blurted out, face flushed.

"So you think he's taken someone else?"

Through gritted teeth, I replied, "Yes." She said nothing so I repeated, "I don't have time for this."

The woman's expression did not change. "What will you do when you find Reynard?"

I looked her straight in the eye. "Make him pay," I said flatly. I had no idea how I was going to make my abductor pay, but I didn't share that with her.

She smiled wide, revealing a perfect set of teeth.

"You're his sister," I said. "Which are you? Jane or Carolyn?"

"Carolyn," she said. "But everyone calls me Lynn."

I had the sensation of free-falling, my stomach suddenly defiant of gravity, floating somewhere up near my throat. My face must have paled considerably, because Carolyn—Lynn—Johnson arched one shapely eyebrow. She looked strangely pleased by my reaction, like a precocious child testing the tolerance of an adult and winning. I stared at my lap, where my resting hands trembled.

"What?" she said. "He had to start somewhere, didn't he? You know about my family, so you must have read some police files, maybe even hired a private investigator. I'm guessing that wasn't in your files."

I shook my head.

"When you were brought in with that Ward girl, it was reported that you called yourself Lynn Wood. At least that was the name on the identification he'd provided you, according to the newspapers. Are you surprised?"

"No," I said, holding my stomach. "I feel nauseous."

She swung her legs off the couch and sat up. "Yes, well so was I when it happened to me."

"How long?" I croaked, not wanting to look at her but unable to turn away.

She cocked her head to the side. "Let's see," she said thoughtfully, as if she were trying to remember what she'd had for dinner the night before. "Three years. He tried my sister out first, but there was something he never quite liked about her. Of course, the fact that she hated him never entered his mind."

"Yeah," I muttered weakly, thinking of all the times I had railed at Reynard, howling my hatred for him, only to have him coo back at me with professions of love as though I hadn't even spoken.

"Of course," Lynn continued casually, "the whole time he was forcing himself on Jane, he was cultivating a very loving, protective older-brother persona in front of me. I had no idea what he was doing to Jane. She didn't confide in me. Once I caught him . . . interfering with her, but I was far too young to realize what it meant. Before it started, he was wonderful to me. He talked to me, walked me to school, read to me before bed, showered me with gifts. I thought he was the most wonderful person in the world. He made me feel so safe. My big brother."

"Oh God," I whispered, horrified. Had it been worse for her? She would have been younger than I had been at the time he abducted me, violated by someone she loved, someone she trusted.

"It was very confusing," she added, reading my face. "Horrible, painful, disgusting." She used the same words that described my own experience, but her tone was flip, almost bored.

"Did you tell anyone?"

"Jane." Lynn laughed derisively. "Her big idea was now that it had happened to us both, we could go together and tell mother."

"She didn't believe you," I said.

Lynn's dark eyes narrowed. "It wasn't a matter of believing us. She already knew. She knew every single thing that was said and done in this house. She just didn't care. We were not to mention it to our father—ever. She talked with Reynard, though I don't know what she said. But the damage was done. He thought he was in love with me by then. He had delusions of the two of us marrying. It only stopped when he was sent away."

"I'm going to be sick," I said.

Calmly, she pointed to her right. "The bathroom is down the hall to the left."

I scrambled down the hall and into the bathroom. I had no time to close the door. Everything I'd eaten that day came up with projectile force as I gripped the sides of the commode. It left me breathless. Heaving, I let my legs go slack and plopped onto the tile floor.

Moments later, a pale hand brushed past my left ear and gathered toilet paper from the roll. "Here," Lynn said softly.

She flushed the toilet and perched on the edge of the bathtub. She crossed one long leg over the other and rested her chin in one hand, watching me. Her expression was an odd mixture of curiosity and detachment. Glancing at her, I realized that she found it very fascinating that I was sprawled on her bathroom floor, vomiting in her toilet.

"This was all about you?" I asked, blotting my lips on the toilet paper.

"Oh no," Lynn said matter-of-factly. "My brother is a bona fide pervert. A pedophile. I just happened to be the first he thought he loved."

I draped an arm over the lip of the toilet seat and rested my clammy forehead on it. "All this time," I said, unable to suppress a shudder. "All this time you knew what he was capable of. How could you just turn him loose on society? All those girls. So many girls. Your mother knew. You knew. How could you let him go into the world, knowing that he'd do the same thing to someone else that he did to you?"

Her face hardened. "How could you stay with a man who raped and beat you for ten years?" she asked quietly.

I drew my body up straighter. "That's not the same."

"Isn't it?"

"You could have stopped him. Your family could have stopped him. There were over a dozen girls before he even got to me."

"You could have left years before you found Alison Ward in that house. Why didn't you?"

I didn't answer. Tears stung the backs of my eyes. Lynn smiled again, a predatory turn to her mouth. "For someone so bold, I expected a little more."

"It's none of your goddamn business," I snapped. I stood and splashed cold water over my face from the sink. Lynn stood and handed me a towel.

Her face floated behind mine in the mirror. I was struck suddenly by our resemblance. I shivered. The heat from her thin body warmed my back. Slowly, she ran a hand through my curls, the movement half-tender, half-lascivious. She watched my face, which had a slight green tinge. "I waited for you," she said softly. "I hoped you would come."

"Why?"

She sighed and smoothed both hands over my hair, down my back. "Because now you'll do what I've always been too weak to do."

"Not too weak," I said. "Too lazy. Someone else always cleans up your messes, don't they? When something goes wrong, you people pay someone to fix it, no matter what it is or how many lives it destroys."

The luster drained from her face. Her hands fell to her sides. "For someone who wants my help, you're not so nice."

"*Nice* does not enter into this equation. I want Emily Hartman back safe, and someone in this house is going to help me find her," I said.

"I'll help you, Claire," she said. "No one else in this family will."

She disappeared. I followed her back into the living room. She motioned to the chair I had vacated earlier, and I sat. She sat on the arm of the couch and picked up the phone, dialing rapidly. "Yes," she said. "This is Carolyn Johnson for Peter Brecht. Yes."

She motioned to a box on the coffee table that hadn't been there before. "My nephew," she explained. "Take it."

It was a small wooden box with a cherry finish. It was no bigger than a child's shoe box. I opened it. A large stack of hundred-dollar bills lay inside, bound neatly with a rubber band. "I don't want your money," I said, my voice rising.

She held up one palm and turned her attention back to the receiver. "Peter? Hi, how are you? Yes. Yes. I need something from you. I need to know where Reynard is . . . well, surely you have a record of the last place you wired him money. That will do. Oh please, your firm has financed my brother's perverted crime spree for the last twenty-five years. Are you really worried about getting disbarred now?"

She smiled at me, but her eyes were wintry and lifeless. Suddenly, her voice turned icy. "Don't fuck with me, Peter. Just get me the location of the last wire transfer. I don't give a shit what my mother said. Oh really? Peter, do you remember what happened when we were together on Saturday? Good, because that will never happen again unless you tell me the location of Reynard's last wire transfer." She waited several minutes, during which she gestured to the box that shook in my lap.

"It's not a payoff," she said. "It's for your journey. To find the new girl he's taken. It's mine. Take it. My mother has nothing to do with it."

I looked at the box again and swallowed hard. Peter came back on the line. "Mmmm," Lynn purred. "That's good. That's a good boy, Peter. Yes. Yes." She picked up a pencil and notepad from beside the phone and scribbled something on it. "Well, you know where to find me," she said, and hung up.

Another sigh. "Men and their proclivities. I keep someone in the firm well compensated for times like these. Not that there have been many concerning Reynard."

"Compensated?"

Lynn rolled her eyes. She tore off the page she'd written on and handed it to me. "Really, Claire. You can't be that naive. Some things can't be bought with money."

"But they can be bought with sex," I said limply.

Lynn took my elbow and pulled me up. Numbly, I walked as she steered me out of her apartment and down the opposite end of the hallway, to another staircase. As we walked, she gave me directions for leaving the estate without drawing attention to myself. Before she shooed me outside, she kissed my cheek and whispered into my ear. "When you get there, stop at the Langdon Hotel," she said. "There will be a package waiting for you. A gift from me to you for when you find Reynard."

Then she was gone.

CHAPTER

SEVENTY-TWO

Sweat trickled down Connor's back. He'd driven from the Houston airport to the Johnson estate and found Claire's rental car parked a quarter mile away. The moment he saw it, he knew she hadn't entered the Johnson compound by invitation. Connor left his suit jacket and phone in the car. He rolled up the sleeves of his dress shirt and tried to look as inconspicuous as possible as he searched the wall surrounding the Johnson estate for an easy place to scale it. He kept his left side toward the wall so the Glock in his shoulder holster wouldn't be immediately visible to passersby. He'd been able to fly with it as long as he checked it.

Once he made it over the wall, he spent the next half hour prowling around the massive home in search of Claire. Connor felt distinctly uncomfortable breaking the law, but he pushed the discomfort into a dusty corner of his mind. He had to find Claire.

The Houston sun beat down on him with a damn-near-physical force. Connor had just breached the southwest corner of the mansion when Claire appeared. She stumbled out of a service door. Clutched to her chest with both arms was a small wooden box. Connor hurried his pace, making his footsteps as silent as possible. He still had a limp. He was only five or six feet away.

Then everything happened at once.

"Claire," he said in a loud whisper.

The door Claire had just exited from flew open, although in Connor's memory, it would always move in slow motion. Claire turned her head. When she saw Connor, her eyes widened first in shock, then in consternation.

Using his entire body, Connor knocked her to the ground and rolled onto her. Claire let out a startled cry. Out of the corner of his eye, Connor saw the muzzle flash. He didn't register the shrill crack of the gunshot. He covered the top of Claire's head with both hands and buried his own head into a mound of her curls.

The buckshot flew wide.

Connor heard the sharp creak-clack of the shooter chambering another round, and his whole body clenched atop Claire. She felt soft beneath him. Again, the sharp report of the gun shattered the air. Connor said a silent prayer for Claire's safety and braced himself for the burning, screeching sensation of pellets embedding themselves into his skin.

He felt nothing. The ensuing silence was eerie, a slow creep blotting out the echo of the two shots. It felt like hours before Connor's body responded to his mind's command to get up. He stood and turned quickly in the direction of the shooter. Without looking at Claire, he dangled a hand behind him for her to grasp on to. The weight of her body pulling on his shoulder as she stood steadied him. Once Claire righted herself, Connor tucked her behind his body.

Just outside the service door, at the trigger end of a Remington Model 870 series shotgun, stood a small, dour woman dressed incongruously in an expensive gray business suit. She held the gun on Connor and Claire. Connor wondered where exactly she got the upper body strength to handle the beast of a weapon so deftly. The woman was so short, Connor had trouble reconciling her appearance with the fact of her identity.

He knew instantly who she was from the look in her eyes. There was a cold flame in them that incinerated her moral sensibility. There was only one person she could be.

Sheila Johnson.

The matriarch's hair was short, thick, and stark white. She wore it unstyled and brushed straight back, much like a man's. Besides a large diamond ring and wedding band, she wore no adornments. Her only feminine touch was a bit of makeup, which did nothing to soften her jowly face.

"Get off my property," she snapped.

"Easy," Connor said, his right hand creeping toward his shoulder holster.

Claire stepped out from behind him. "You almost killed us," she said.

Sheila's gaze moved from Connor to Claire. "I'm still considering it so why don't y'all get the hell off my property."

"I'm a police officer," Connor said.

Sheila looked him up and down. "Not around here," she scoffed.

Claire took a step toward her. Connor was torn between pulling her back and reaching for his Glock.

"How dare you?" The rage in Claire's voice quickly drew Connor's eyes toward her. She looked taller. A white-hot rage emanated from her thin frame.

"You're trespassing on private property," Sheila replied coldly.

Claire took another step. This time Connor reached for his pistol, unsnapping the holster and slipping the weapon out. He lowered it to his side.

"One of your son's many victims trespassing on your property should be the least of your concerns right now," Claire shot back.

There was a flicker of something in the older woman's eyes, though Connor couldn't tell what.

"Like mother, like son," Claire continued, inching boldly closer. "Violence solves everything." She waved the wooden box in the air. "And when that doesn't work, you use money. What kind of person condones those sorts of things? What kind of mother lets her son run wild raping, killing, and kidnapping young girls?"

"Get off my property now or I'll shoot," Sheila said, but a faint tremor in her hands shook the barrel of the gun. Sheila was so intent on Claire that she still didn't notice Connor's gun. He wondered if he would be able to squeeze off a shot before Sheila could. Adrenaline pumped so hard through his body, he forgot whether Sheila had reloaded and chambered after her second shot.

Claire spit out her abductor's name like it was something dirty in her mouth. "Reynard threatened to kill my family if I didn't stay. He killed people, and the things he did to me—" Claire broke off abruptly.

Sheila raised her head from the gun's stock and narrowed her eyes. "What do you want?"

Claire laughed. The sound was so loud and unexpected that both Connor and Sheila jumped. Claire's head tipped backward, an almost maniacal laughter erupting from deep in her stomach. The barrel of the shotgun quivered and fell slightly. Connor brought his left hand to the slide of the Glock, ready to rack a round into the chamber.

It was then that he recognized the feeling flitting in and out of Sheila's eyes as she watched Claire—horror.

Slowly, Sheila's mask of indifference and cool disdain peeled back from her face, revealing a stark dread beneath it. Claire laughed until the older woman came completely undone. Sheila's hands shook openly now, her palsy jarring the shotgun.

Finally, Claire leveled her gaze at the woman, a malicious smile playing on her lips. "What do I want?" she echoed, her voice the sound of a nail being hammered into a coffin. Claire's face tightened into a scowl the likes of which Connor could have never imagined on the face of the woman he'd grown to love—in spite of her tragic and bizarre circumstances.

"I want those ten years back."

Sensing Sheila's moment of weakness, Claire lunged at her, barreling into the older woman. Claire used her shoulder to buckle Johnson's hips. The wooden box clattered to the ground. As they tumbled backward, Claire pushed Johnson's arm upward, using the webs of her thumbs beneath Sheila's elbow and armpit.

Once on the ground, Claire straddled the woman and slid her hands toward Sheila's wrist. With one hand, Claire grabbed the stock of the shotgun. With the other, she slammed Sheila's wrist into the ground repeatedly. In spite of her age, Sheila grunted and bucked, trying to dislodge Claire from the dominant position and regain control of the gun.

Numbly, Connor watched the entire scene. He couldn't feel his body, couldn't make it move. It was the same sensation he had in his dreams of killing the rapist and facing down Reynard Johnson. Every bit of training and instinct left him. He watched Claire wrest the shotgun from Sheila's hand finally with one vicious twist. She drove the butt of the Remington into Sheila's palm, turning it sharply. Connor heard bones crunch. A gray-white pallor took over Sheila's face. She howled once in pain and then clamped her mouth shut.

It wasn't until Claire raised the gun high over her head, the butt end pointed straight down at Sheila's head, that Connor regained his senses. He stepped forward and clasped the barrel of the shotgun with his free hand.

"Claire, don't."

CHAPTER

SEVENTY-THREE

The shotgun flew out of my hands just as my arms rocketed downward. In my mind, I saw Sheila's frigid face smashed and bleeding below me. I saw my own arms bringing the end of the Remington down into her skull again and again. I saw drops of her blood leap on to my pant legs. I felt breathless and abuzz from the violent exertion.

After Connor snatched the gun from my grip, I realized I was nearly panting even though the assault on Reynard's mother was all in my head. Silently, I stared down into her soulless eyes until Connor lifted me gently from her body and pulled me away.

He had holstered his Glock. He held the shotgun in one hand, and with the other, he bent to pick up the wooden box Lynn had given me. When he pressed it into my stomach, I took it. I held its sharp edges against me as Connor pulled me along. He crouched and moved as quickly as his injured leg would allow.

He spoke to me, but I heard nothing. Thunder roared and cracked in my ears. We reached the wall, and Connor tossed the shotgun onto the ground after using his shirt to wipe our fingerprints from it. He pushed me up over the wall, his hands fumbling, pressing unceremoniously into my rear. My body obeyed his commands even though I couldn't hear his voice.

I dropped to the other side on automatic pilot. Mentally, I was back where we'd left Sheila Johnson, using the shotgun to turn the bone of her face into grit. Connor heaved himself over the wall. When he dropped down beside me, his leg gave out. He fell with a muttered curse.

"Claire," he said.

I looked at him. His face was lined with pain. He held out a hand and I grasped it, helping him to his feet. Connor's limp was more pronounced as we hurried toward the rental cars.

"You'll have to drive," Connor said. "Leave mine here. I'll deal with it later."

I drove back to the hotel. The entire drive Connor kept looking behind us as if he expected a squadron of police cars to descend upon us in pursuit, but we made it to the hotel without incident.

Once inside the room, Connor locked the door. When he turned to look at me, the anger on his face jarred me back to the present moment. My fantasy of battering Sheila flicked off in my mind like a television channel being changed.

Suddenly, I felt my body again and in spite of having just come out of the Houston heat, my skin was cold and clammy.

"What the hell are you doing?" Connor demanded. "What are you thinking, Claire?" He advanced toward me. "Are you out of your goddamn mind? You could have been killed, and now Sheila Johnson will probably file assault charges against you. Claire, what the hell were you thinking? Your family is worried sick."

The closer he came, the smaller the room seemed. I was suddenly aware of the fact that I was alone in a locked room with a man. A low thrum—the vibration of terror—worked its way up from my toes to my scalp, constricting my throat as it passed. Abruptly, Connor froze. The angry tension in his face slackened. He glanced at the locked door.

"Claire," he said, voice noticeably softer. "I'm not going to hurt you."

I stared at him, my throat working but nothing coming out. Connor sank onto the edge of the bed and rubbed his scalp with both hands. He looked at me again.

"I would never hurt you."

I knew that was true. We'd been alone together several times. Connor had never been anything but warm and protective toward me. Most of the time, I wanted to burrow into the safety of his arms and let him hold me. The memory of our first night together remained vivid in my mind—a tactile memory complete with the heady scent of his skin. All the things that Reynard had done to me hung between Connor and me like dead weight—a pendulum that could not be budged.

Connor sighed. His voice was full of resignation. "I would never hurt you," he repeated. "I'm trying to help you, but you're not making it easy. What do you think is going to happen when you find Johnson?"

I stared at him. "I'm going to kill him," I said. The words were as much a surprise to me as they were to Connor, but in that moment I realized it was true. I wanted to stop him, and killing him seemed the surest way of doing that.

"Claire."

"I can do it. If I have to kill him to get to Emily, then I will," I said firmly, although I had no idea how I would accomplish this. I would worry about the logistics later.

Connor's eyes were sad. He pursed his lips. Then he said, "Claire, you're not a killer. You don't know—"

I thought of Miranda Simon, whom Johnson had strangled before my eyes. I cut Connor off in midsentence. "Have you ever watched someone die?"

The question stung. He looked as if I had slapped his face. "Yeah," he said quietly. "The day I met you."

I had forgotten. I looked away from him.

"I shot that guy close range, dead center in the chest," Connor added. "*Aim for center mass*—that's what they tell you in training. People think because you have a badge, you're some kind of expert marksman. They think because you're the police, you should be able to control yourself better than any common criminal. It's all bullshit. They teach you to aim for center mass because the only time you have to fire a weapon in the line of duty is when all hell is breaking loose and your adrenaline is pumping so hard you can hardly fucking think or see, let alone make a split-second decision like you have all day to contemplate it.

"When shit goes down, you aim for center mass because even if you're a crack shot, you're liable to miss nine out of ten times. I watched that guy bleed out right there on the floor while the paramedics worked on him."

"I'm sorry," I said.

"Yeah. Me too."

"I mean I'm sorry I brought it up. I forgot. I'm not sorry you killed that man."

I reached into my pants pocket and pulled out the crumpled piece of paper with Carolyn Johnson's handwriting on it. It said, "Langdon Hotel, Julian, California." I thrust it at Connor.

"I know where he is. I'm going to find him and bring Emily home. Will you help me?"

CHAPTER

SEVENTY-FOUR

The box held $3,000. Connor and I counted it before we left the hotel while I recounted my strange meeting with Carolyn. I left out her last instructions for me to pick up a package from her upon my arrival at the Langdon Hotel.

I was going with or without Connor's help, which he quickly surmised, his brilliant-blue eyes darkening as his resolve gave way. We compromised on our way to the Houston airport. The two of us would go to Julian alone. I would have one day to track down Reynard before Connor called in the local and state police, as well as the FBI.

Connor reasoned that we had a better chance of tracking Johnson alone since the two of us would invite little attention. Based on Johnson's previous success eluding capture, Connor was certain that Johnson already had escape routes and contingency plans in place to resort to at the first sign that authorities were onto him.

The only other condition of Connor's assistance was that if we did locate Reynard, I was not to pursue him myself. At that point, Connor maintained, we had to call in the cavalry. I knew Connor was not entirely at ease with the plan, in spite of the compromise. He was a police officer, and even though he'd seen and heard horrific things on the job, he could never know or understand what it was like to be hurt and violated the way I had been.

Connor's idea of justice was different from my own. He had killed a rapist, and he still lost sleep over it. Connor's regret over killing that rapist came from the same place inside him that now forced him to help me against his better judgment. He knew the only way he would stop me from going after Reynard and finding Emily would be to use physical force or arrest me. Connor had meant it when he said he'd never hurt me. He didn't have a choice. I'd backed him into a corner.

We caught the first flight to San Diego. In spite of Connor's protests, I used Carolyn's money to pay for the tickets. It seemed fitting that the money used to find and kill my abductor came from the family who had knowingly turned him loose on society, sealing my fate before I was even born. I could never use the money for anything else.

We arrived in San Diego at seven in the evening. We rented a car and drove to the Langdon Hotel. Julian was a small town nestled among the Cuyamaca Mountains. It was about an hour northeast of San Diego and a highly trafficked tourist area. Reynard would blend in easily there. By the time we arrived, it was dark. Connor insisted on getting rooms for the night, even though I wanted to start looking for Reynard immediately.

Our rooms were next to each other. Connor escorted me inside my room. He checked the locks on the doors, pulled the curtains closed, and plopped down on the edge of the bed. He used the phone to call my mother. He offered me the phone, but I couldn't take it. I was afraid if I talked to her, I would lose some of my resolve. It was enough that she knew I was okay and that Connor was with me.

As Connor filled her in, I went into the bathroom and turned on the shower. My clothes were wrinkled and smelled slightly stale. I hadn't bathed since I'd left Sacramento. My skin was filmy and moist, my teeth grimy. My curls sagged with oily buildup. All of it registered as a fleeting annoyance. Emily planted herself stubbornly front and center in my mind.

I put the clothes back on after my shower. When I emerged from the bathroom, I found Connor asleep on the bed. He sat upright, his head resting against the headboard. One of his legs dangled off the edge of the bed, as if he'd been in the act of standing when he dozed off. The other extended the length of the bed. He had tucked a pillow under his knee to elevate it. I stared at him for a long time.

He looked so peaceful. Carefully, so as not to jar him awake, I climbed onto the other side of the bed. I lay on my side and watched his face. The rhythmic sound of his breath easing in and out of his body soothed me.

After an hour, he woke. He scrunched up his face as though he'd eaten something sour. It made him look like a little boy, and I laughed in spite of the situation. Sleepily, he looked in my direction. It took a few seconds for him to remember where he was and why. His eyes widened abruptly.

"Shit," he said. He leaned forward to get up. "I'm sorry, Claire." He fished in his pocket and came up with a set of hotel keys, which he handed to me. "Those are yours. I'll go next door." His voice was still husky with sleep and his movements slow.

I put a hand on his forearm. "No," I said. "Stay."

He paused and studied me, the sleep gradually receding from his eyes. "I'll be right next door," he said.

"No. I want you to stay."

This surprised him. His eyebrows rose. "Are you sure?"

I nodded and pulled him toward me. We lay side by side, staring up at the ceiling. I snaked my hand down between our bodies and laced my fingers through his.

"Tomorrow we'll canvass," Connor said. "I've got a photo of Johnson. We'll go door-to-door if we have to—starting with businesses.

I already gave the hotel manager a copy of the photo. He said he would ask around to see if anyone recognizes Johnson."

I squeezed his hand in acknowledgment. Tension ebbed between our bodies. I closed my eyes and felt my body drawing heat from his, instinctually wanting to move closer. After several minutes Connor said, "Claire, it's really no problem for me to sleep in the other room."

I sighed. "This is silly. We already spent a night together."

"That was different," Connor pointed out. "You were playing a role, trying to manipulate me."

I jerked my head toward him, but he wasn't looking at me. "Is that what you think? That I was only trying to manipulate you?"

"Does it matter?"

"It matters to me."

"I don't know, Claire." He sounded tired, more tired than I'd ever heard him.

Tears sprang to my eyes. He had to know that I felt something for him—whatever that was—whether it was a simple crush or more definitive feelings. But I couldn't protest because as we lay there, I was manipulating him into helping me find Reynard so that I could confront him myself and kill him if it came to that.

"Connor, I . . ."

He didn't respond. His eyes were closed, but I could tell by his uneven breathing that he was not asleep.

I swallowed and tried again. I couldn't get the words out so I asked him for the thing I had wanted since I had seen him again in the ER— the thing I had also been afraid of since my return. "Connor? Could you just hold me—the way you did that night?"

He didn't speak. He looked over at me for a long moment. Then he rolled over and pulled me into him, circling my body with his arms and settling his warmth all around me. Within minutes, he was fast asleep.

I skimmed the edges of sleep, exhaustion tugging at every muscle in my body but not pulling me into sleep. In fits and starts, the endless possibilities of what Reynard might have done or might presently be doing to Emily flitted through my mind. Each one was worse than the last. Occasionally, I shivered, and each time Connor squeezed me more tightly against his body, pressing the ugly images outside the tortured confines of my mind.

CHAPTER

SEVENTY-FIVE

I was still awake when the man knocked on the door to our room. Connor snored lightly, his body limp and heavy against mine. I disentangled myself and answered the knock, stepping quietly into the hallway.

He was a local auto mechanic who had happened to eat breakfast in the same diner as the hotel's night manager that morning. He'd heard all about us and the man we were looking for. He thought he had towed a car for the man—for Reynard Johnson. There was a girl with Johnson, the man said, and they were staying in a cabin in the nearby mountains. The man's sister-in-law owned the cabins in that area and rented them out year-round—weather permitting.

I took directions from him before sneaking back into the room and delicately removing the keys to the rental car from Connor's jacket pocket. He didn't wake up. At the front desk, I gave them my name and told them I was expecting a package. The hotel manager presented me with a small box, not much bigger than the first one Carolyn had given me in Texas.

Clutching the box against my front, I hurried to the car. Inside the package, a shiny new Glock winked at me, its firm, sleek form inviting me to use it. I hadn't thought about how I would kill Reynard. I relied on the kindness of a universe that had punished me long enough to provide the manner of his death when the time was right. And it had used Carolyn to do so.

I looked around the parking lot to make sure no one watched me before I picked it up, checked its sight, and loaded it with the ammunition that accompanied it. Its cool steel was a balm to my ragged nerves. I was grateful Connor had given me gun lessons, although I knew he would not approve of my present intentions.

I put it back in its case, marveling at how Carolyn had arranged for a brand-new Glock to be purchased, packaged, and delivered to a location she specified in a matter of hours from several states away.

All that power did not prevent her soul from shrinking to a small, lifeless kernel.

Which of us had truly survived Reynard?

I started the car and hesitated. There was an acute ache inside me as I thought of Connor sleeping peacefully in the hotel room, trusting that I would keep my end of our bargain. I was suddenly glad I'd asked him to hold me last night. After today, I might never see him again, and even if I did, there was little chance he'd speak to me once I'd betrayed his trust. The prospect of losing Connor in my newfound life hurt far worse than I could have imagined. I had to put it away for now. There was time for pain and regret later, when I had privacy and quiet to listen to the wretched keening of my soul. For now, my focus was on finding Reynard.

CHAPTER

SEVENTY-SIX

It took Connor a half hour to track down the local mechanic who had knocked on his and Claire's hotel room that morning. After speaking with several hotel employees who had seen the mechanic leave before Claire, Connor eventually learned that the day manager had given the man Claire's room number after speaking with the night manager by phone, who had had breakfast with the mechanic at a local diner. A waitress at the diner directed Connor to the mechanic's shop. Every person Connor spoke to in his pursuit of Claire shrank from him. He hadn't bothered to shower or shave. He knew he looked and probably smelled frightful. When he woke that morning to find Claire gone, her scent lingering on his clothes, he had felt as frightened as everyone he talked to appeared.

In spite of his fear and exhaustion, Connor's mind still reeled with the memory of holding Claire in his arms the night before. It seemed like a dream, particularly the part where she asked him to hold her. He felt as though he had waited an eternity for the smallest signal from her that she was becoming more comfortable with him. He wanted to touch her all the time. The effort of resisting his impulses had worn him out.

He hadn't had time to think about any of that in the last three months, and now he had even less time to examine his feelings for Claire or her response to him. Again, Reynard Johnson stood between them. The instant the mechanic told him what he had told Claire, Connor knew what she was going to do.

His gut clenched. Connor's body gave way a little as the realization, accompanied by an image of Claire in prison for first-degree murder, hit him. The mechanic must have sensed Connor's anxiety. He offered Connor his tow truck, and Connor accepted.

Connor checked the magazine in his Glock before he started the truck. The mechanic stood just outside the driver's-side door, staring in bewilderment. Connor looked the man in the eye.

"There's one more thing," Connor said.

The mechanic nodded dumbly.

"I need twenty minutes. Wait twenty minutes. Then call your police chief and tell him what's going on. Tell him to call the FBI."

CHAPTER

SEVENTY-SEVEN

The cabin was small, set back on an incline from the narrow mountain road. A gravel driveway led to its front. The cabin itself was partially obstructed by foliage. The afternoon sunlight dappled the trees and weaved random designs on the facade of the cabin. I approached it on a diagonal line, threading my way through the trees and brush, remembering the stealth I acquired from all those nights I had snuck away from the trailer when Reynard wasn't home. I circled to the rear of the cabin, drawing the Glock once I was close enough to touch its exterior. There was a momentary tremor in my hands. I had driven past the driveway and parked the rental car a half mile up the road. I used the short walk to calm my rapid breathing and shut out the booming pulse of my heartbeat, which exploded in my ears.

Moving slowly, I rounded the side of the cabin. The windows were covered with curtains. I paused and listened, straining to hear the smallest sound. I heard nothing but the birds calling back and forth to each other above me. A truck was parked haphazardly in front of the cabin. It was old and dilapidated with California plates, much like the one I had crashed into a police cruiser in front of Connor's home three months earlier.

The windows in the front were open, but dark screens made it impossible for me to peek in without pressing my face against them. Silently, I climbed the steps. Again, I listened but heard no sounds from within the cabin. No television, no movement, rustles, or ambient noise. Sweat beaded along my upper lip. I took one hand from the Glock and delicately turned the doorknob. It was unlocked. I pushed it open and stepped into the darkness, my index finger serene against the trigger.

CHAPTER

SEVENTY-EIGHT

He looked genuinely stunned to see me. The cabin was sparsely but rustically furnished. Compared to the places Reynard had made Tiffany and me live in, it was luxurious. The air inside was still. I surprised him in the dimly lit living room. The Glock was rock steady in my hands, and my voice was strident.

"Where is she, you son of a bitch?"

He froze when he saw the gun, his body in a half turn. Slowly, he turned to face me, exposing his center mass. I almost smiled. Somewhere in a far-off recess of my consciousness, I was astonished by the impenetrable calm that possessed my body, my voice, the gun in my hand.

He said, "Lynn."

"Don't you dare. Don't you fucking dare. My name is Claire."

He dropped his gaze to the floor momentarily. "I knew you would come."

"Where is Emily Hartman?"

He waved a hand toward the doorway to what was obviously a small kitchen where Tiffany now stood, silent and immobile, watching us with disinterest. "I tried to replace you," Johnson said. "I should have known that you—you were special. You always demanded more from me. You were my first."

His voice was soft, almost effeminate. His eyes shone with adoration that made me want to shoot him right then, before finding out what he had done with the girl.

"I wasn't your first. Not even close."

He extended his hands toward me, palms up, a strange little smile on his face. "But you *were* my first. You were the first to stay. Don't you see? You were so special. That's why I could never bring myself to kill you. I was right—here you are. You came back."

Rage burned in my stomach. "Shut up. Shut up. You're sick. Delusional. What is the matter with you? You kidnapped me. You took me away from my family. You raped me and tortured me. You threatened my family. I hate you. I have always hated you. You make me sick."

He shook his head as if to indicate what I was saying was just plain silly. I wished I was close enough to spit on him. "Where is Emily? I know you took her. Where is she?"

Tiffany left the kitchen doorway, but I was unconcerned with her. I knew from my final escape from the trailer that she was ineffectual. Against a bigger, more fearsome opponent, she would not put up a fight.

Johnson sighed. "I wish we could talk about this, Lynn."

The rage boiled inside me, heating my skin until sweat broke out all over my body. "Fuck you. We're done talking—you're done talking. I only want to hear one thing from you, and after that, I'm putting a bullet in your head. Where is the girl?"

He hesitated. Then he opened his mouth to speak.

The sound of tires rolling over gravel outside stopped him.

CHAPTER

SEVENTY-NINE

Connor drove the truck full speed up the narrow gravel drive, nearly taking out the entire cabin before he stopped. The front tires of the truck bounced against the front steps as he braked. His body slammed forward into the steering wheel. He snatched his gun from the passenger's seat and leapt out of the truck.

He had forgotten about his injured leg, and it buckled when his feet hit ground. He held on to the truck door to keep his balance. He racked a round into the Glock's chamber and limped to the cabin door. He didn't hear anything, and he didn't know whether to be more or less afraid of what he would find inside. He raised the pistol in front of him and nudged the door open with his foot. It creaked loudly as it cleared the door frame. Connor stepped inside and aimed for center mass.

"Claire, put the gun down."

She didn't respond. Her eyes and her weapon were locked on Reynard Johnson, who looked from her to Connor with an amused smile. Connor wished he were in a position to smack the smile right off Johnson's face.

"Claire," he said again.

She didn't look at Connor, but she said, "I'm sorry. I tried to keep you out of this."

Connor held his gun on her. "Don't do this, Claire."

She clenched and unclenched her hand around the handle of the gun. "He deserves to die," she said firmly.

"Not like this."

She took a step forward but didn't lower her weapon. "You're right," she said. "He deserves a slow, torturous death."

"Claire, please."

"This is between me and him," she said.

Connor cleared his throat, keeping Johnson in the periphery of his field of vision. "You're not the only one. There are other victims."

"And they'll thank me for killing him."

"I can't let you do this, Claire."

"I thought you believed in justice."

Connor's face burned. The image of the rapist bleeding out came to him unbidden. He tried to shake it out of his head. "This isn't justice," he croaked.

"Isn't it?"

"Because if you do this, I lose you. I'll lose you for good. You'll either die from the bullet wound or you'll go to prison for murder. Either way this piece of shit comes out on top—again."

She said nothing. A single tear slid down her cheek.

"Lynn," Johnson said softly.

"Shut the fuck up," Connor said roughly. His throat felt thick. His hands itched. The muscles in his shoulders cramped. "Claire, please don't make me shoot you. Please."

She shook her head, gaze still squarely on Johnson. "When does it end? What happens? You arrest him and then we wait months, years for a trial. He could escape or worse, get acquitted."

"There are a lot of charges against him. He's not going anywhere. But he's the one who should go to prison, not you. Put the gun down. You don't want to spend the rest of your life in prison for someone who isn't worth spitting on. You have your family, Claire. They love you. They're waiting for you to come home to them—for good."

The tone of Johnson's voice was sulky. "I'm your family, Lynn," he said as if Connor were not even in the room, as if Claire wasn't aiming a pistol directly at his skull.

"Shut up," Claire commanded. Then to Connor, "My family. Look what he's done to us—to so many families. He deserves to die."

Connor kept his voice quiet but firm. "Killing him is not going to take it away, Claire."

Briefly, he saw her shoulders quiver. He continued, "I know you wish you could forget everything he did. I wish I could take it away from you, but I can't. I know you feel guilty for not escaping earlier, but killing this piece of shit is not going to take any of that away."

Another tear crept down her cheek. "Then what?" she asked, voice thick with unshed tears. "How do I make it go away?" She kept her gun raised and aimed at Johnson but squeezed her eyes shut. "I can't live like this," she sobbed. "I just want it all to go away."

Connor lowered his gun slightly and took another painful step toward Claire. "I don't know that it will ever *go away*," he said softly. "I do know that killing him is not going to help you with those things. You have to make new memories, happy memories—with your family. They're waiting for you." He paused. She lowered her pistol slightly, eyes still tightly closed. He wished he could see her eyes. "I'm waiting for you," he said.

"Lynn," Johnson interjected, voice tinged with desperation. "Don't go with him."

Claire's eyes popped open. Connor looked at Johnson to tell him once more to shut up, but the flash of a knife just behind Johnson caught Connor's eye. An earsplitting howl reverberated throughout the cabin. Johnson stumbled forward. Blood appeared on the front of his white shirt, spreading outward in a large blotch.

A thin wisp of a girl with lank brown hair stood behind Johnson. Her eyes were huge and black with fury. She seemed to be animated by some otherworldly force as she withdrew the knife from Johnson's back and stabbed again.

"You bastard!" she screamed.

CHAPTER EIGHTY

It happened so fast. Within seconds, Tiffany had stabbed Johnson in the back three times. Blood splattered back onto her. Fat, beaded drops landed in her hair, on her face. Blood streaked her arms. Reynard fell and rolled onto his back. At least one of the wounds had gone clear through to his front. His shirt was already completely stained.

Tiffany straddled him, her thin hips rocking back and forth over his in a macabre motion as she stabbed again and again with piston-like movements. Her howls had receded to grunts. I heard fragments of speech. "Lynn, Lynn, Lynn. That's all you care about is her. You never cared about me. I hate you."

Connor and I both stood struck dumb by the scene. Time slowed, stretching the mere passing seconds into hours. It was an eternity before Connor lurched toward Tiffany to disarm her. I watched as if the entire thing were taking place on television. Connor grabbed both of Tiffany's hands, which held the knife. Her unbridled fury gave her more strength than her thin body had. She pulled back, and Connor toppled over, falling onto the ground with her. Tiffany's skin was slick with blood. Connor struggled to control her hands. They wriggled away from Reynard, locked in battle, their bodies making a steeple with both their arms extended over their heads toward the knife.

I looked at Reynard. Even the pallor of his face was fading. One of his hands covered his chest. He stared straight up at the ceiling. There was nothing in his eyes. Still, his lips worked uselessly. He would die before help arrived.

I watched him take his last breath. Connor finally took possession of the knife Tiffany had used to attack Reynard. He subdued her using an armlock, his knee pressed into the center of her back. He looked around for something to tie her up with, but without the knife, she ceased to struggle.

Reynard's bloody form settled into death. I gazed, riveted by the sight I had longed for, wished for, prayed to see for years. His features drooped, pale and unrecognizable in the way Miranda Simon's were after he choked her. Nothing in his face changed; it was just masked in an odd, pallid stillness.

I waited for the rush of feeling—euphoria, relief, righteous satisfaction—but nothing came. The minutes went by, but the part of me that was rational and driven remained muted. My limbs were paralyzed. I tried to focus on the details of his brutal death, but my gaze was undeterred from the enormity of it.

Finally, Connor said, "The girl."

"In the back," Tiffany said flatly.

I raced, flying through the two rooms at the rear of the cabin, finding nothing. Out the back door and down two stone steps. I froze, scanning the trees beyond the cabin until the doors in my peripheral vision registered.

They were flush against the cabin, in the ground. *An outside entrance to the cellar,* I thought. I tossed the gun aside and dropped to my knees. When I pried the doors open and descended the short flight of steps, I saw that it was closer to a crawl space than a cellar. There was no light. I had to crouch low to move through it. I called Emily's name, searching blindly until my foot thudded against something soft.

I felt for her, finding her shoulders and hooking my arms beneath hers. Her limbs hung loosely, swinging as I hauled her back to the double doors. Her feet, which I saw were bare once we got closer to the light, dangled and dragged along the dirt floor.

"It's going to be okay now," I mumbled, pulling her carelessly up the steps and dropping her softly on the grass outside.

Her pulse was thready, but it was there.

The feeling I had waited for inside the cabin surged through me, but it had nothing to do with Reynard being dead. Tears of relief sprang to my eyes. Emily was dirty, bloodied, and bruised. Her clothes were torn. A particularly ghastly wound seeped greenish pus along the length of her right forearm.

But she was alive. I had pulled her from the darkness with my own hands.

I cupped her chin in my hand and said her name. When I got no response, I slapped her cheeks lightly, but her head pitched back and forth limply.

I pulled her upper half onto my lap and held her until the police and medics arrived. Connor handed Tiffany over to the state police. He helped me into the back of the ambulance as they loaded Emily on a gurney.

"I'm going to stay here and give a statement. I'll meet you two at the hospital in a couple of hours," Connor said.

I looked into his eyes. There were things I wanted to say to him. Awkwardly, he leaned into the back of the ambulance and kissed me lightly. A thrill chilled my body, but it held no fear. I opened my mouth to say something to him—anything—but he shook his head.

When he smiled, it brought more tears to my eyes. "Later," he said. "We have time."

CHAPTER

EIGHTY-ONE

"Are you ready to go home?" Brianna asked as she breezed into our hotel room. "I'm sick of this place, and if I don't get back soon, my boss is going to fire me."

I laughed as I packed our things into the suitcase Brianna had brought with her. "Yes," I said. "I'm ready."

The FBI had taken me to San Diego so they could question me in their field office. Connor accompanied me, and my parents drove down with Brianna to stay with me while the various law enforcement agencies who had been looking for both Reynard and Emily Hartman sorted out my and Connor's stories.

"Where are Mom and Dad?" she asked. She plopped onto the bed and turned on the television. Coverage of Emily Hartman's recovery and Johnson's murder could still be found on just about every channel.

"They went shopping," I said. I sat in the chair next to the bed and watched as she flipped from channel to channel.

"Shopping? They went shopping? I thought we were supposed to leave in a half hour."

"They should be back soon," I said.

"Any news on Emily?" Brianna asked, turning the television off.

I smiled. "She'll be fine."

Emily was a fighter. Johnson had had to beat her pretty badly in order to subdue her. The gash in her arm was infected, she had a major concussion, and she was severely dehydrated. But she was alive, and she had been reunited with her family.

The phone on the other side of Brianna's bed jangled noisily. She picked it up but immediately frowned. With a noisy sigh, she thrust the receiver in my direction. "It's your boyfriend," she said.

"Bree," I hissed. I pointed to the receiver, which she could have at least covered so Connor didn't hear her. She rolled her eyes and handed me the phone.

"Where are you?" I asked Connor.

"I'm still at the FBI field office. I just called to say goodbye."

My stomach went into a free fall. It had not occurred to me that with Johnson dead and my case closed, there was no reason for me and Connor to see one another again. "What?" I croaked.

"I called to say goodbye," he repeated. "I have to stay here a few more days. I thought you said you guys were leaving today."

"Oh, right. Yeah, we're packing now."

"Well, have a safe trip. Remember to wear a hat and sunglasses. The press is even worse than they were before you rescued Emily Hartman. Just be—"

"Connor," I said, cutting him off. "Will I see you again? When we get home?"

He chuckled, and I pictured his easy smile. Warmth spread throughout my body. "Yes," he said. "You will definitely see me again. You know, I meant what I said in that cabin."

My brow furrowed. The tense moments in the cabin were somewhat of a blur. "What you said?" I prompted.

"I know you need time after all that's happened, but I *will* wait for you, Claire."

"Oh."

I glanced at Brianna, who was frozen in place, leaning over her suitcase. She craned her neck toward me in an attempt to hear Connor's side of the conversation as well as mine. Her intense stare sent a flush from my collar to my scalp. I looked away from her but couldn't keep the corners of my mouth from twitching.

"I told you," Connor added. "You're stuck with me."

The smile tickling my face burst forth. I felt dizzy and giddy with relief. I squeezed the receiver harder and sank onto the bed. From the corner of my eye, I saw that Brianna was trying unsuccessfully to suppress her own smile.

"Claire? You there?"

I cleared my throat. "Yes, I'm here."

"So I'll see you in Sacramento?"

"Yes," I said. "Yes, you will."

CHAPTER
EIGHTY-TWO

Six Months Later

The girl I used to be looks back at me from the full-length mirror affixed to her bedroom door. She studies me from head to toe as I turn several times, trying with limited success to get a good look at my rear to make sure the dress I'm wearing fits well. Tonight is my first date with Connor. There are butterflies in my stomach, and even though my mother and Brianna helped me pick out the dress I'm wearing, I've checked myself in the mirror at least twenty times.

After returning from San Diego, Connor became a fixture at my home, attending family dinners, helping my dad fix the place up, and letting Tom help with his own financial planning. We hadn't spent much time alone together, and by the time Connor worked up the nerve to ask me on a real date, I felt ready to have him all to myself.

I slide on a pair of sandals and go downstairs. My father smiles at me. "You look beautiful, honey," he says. He kisses my cheek, and a sudden warmth joins the butterflies in my belly.

"Thank you, Dad."

In the kitchen, my mother and Brianna are drinking coffee and having a heated discussion about something mundane, like our grandmother's lasagna recipe. They fall silent as I enter. Brianna whistles in appreciation.

"Twirl around for us, darling," my mother says.

I roll my eyes and clutch my purse to my side self-consciously but twirl nevertheless.

"You're gorgeous," my mother says.

"Where is Connor taking you?" Brianna asks.

"It's a surprise."

My mother sighs. "Ah, I always loved the beginning parts of a relationship. Your father was very romantic when he courted me."

Brianna laughs. "*Courted* you? Mom, you're not that old." Then she frowns. "Although I think he may be courting you again."

My mother nods. "I think you're right."

Brianna turns back to me. "You're still moving in with me next month, right?"

"Yeah."

"Good, you can help me study for the LSATs."

My mother's eyebrows shoot up, and she smiles approvingly. "You're finally going to go to law school?"

"I'm going to try," Brianna answers. She looks back at me and winks. "Besides, we might need to leave these two lovebirds alone."

I laugh, and my mother hands me an envelope. "This came in the mail," she explains. She and my sister exchange a knowing smile. The return address belongs to UC Davis, one of the colleges I applied to after getting my GED. I hold my breath and tear open the envelope.

As I stare in shock at the letter, Brianna says, "The thick envelope gives it away every time."

I am so dumbfounded, I forget to smile. We hear a knock at the front door. My father calls, "I'll get it."

Moments later, Connor and my father join us in the kitchen. I look up from the acceptance letter, and my breath catches in my throat. Connor looks more handsome than I've ever seen him. Instead of the suits he wears to work each day, he's donned khakis and a short-sleeved polo shirt that clings to the firm musculature of his chest and arms. He hands me a bouquet of flowers.

A small worry line creases his forehead as he watches me. Brianna winks at him. "She got in to UC Davis," she explains.

Connor grins. "I knew it," he says.

Still, I cannot speak. "Well, we're going to the perfect place to celebrate," Connor says.

Somehow, I am ushered from the kitchen outside and down the front walk to Connor's car. My family hugs and kisses me goodbye for the evening. As Connor opens the passenger's-side door for me, I catch a glimpse of the girl I used to be in the reflection from the window. She smiles at me.

With every day that passes, I see her more and more. I want to stop and watch her, but I don't. Her eyes tell me not to—her eyes tell me that one day I'll look in the mirror and see only myself, and that woman will be beautiful and not broken.

ACKNOWLEDGMENTS

I'd like to thank my parents for nurturing this dream without hesitation or exception from the time I was old enough to put letters on the page and for not letting me give up: Donna House, William Regan, Rusty House, Joyce Regan.

The following people have always had my back, inspiring me and showing me incredible support, and without them I would be lost: Sean House; Kevin and Andy Brock (my brothers); Dot Dorton and family; Melissia McKittrick; Kerry Graham; Laura Aiello; Mike Debelle; Michael Infinito Jr.; Carrie A. Butler; Tajare Taylor; Robert Tomaino; Joanne Smith; Dr. Danny Robinson; Dr. Julie Vandivere; Dr. Elaine Atkins; Bill Baker; Julie, Kirk, and Grace House; Marilyn House; Amy Schoenfeld; Kitty Funk; Helen Conlen; the late Walter Conlen and the rest of the Conlen family; the amazing Regan family; the Funk family; the McKittricks; the Nova family; the Tralies family; and the rest of my wonderful in-laws.

Thanks to Stephanie Kuehn for helping me find the essence of the book finally. Special thanks to my close friend, alpha critique partner, and writing soul mate, Nancy S. Thompson. You mean the world to me, and I would not be here were it not for you! Thanks to Jeanie Loiacono, Amy Lichtenhan, and Katie Henson for believing in this book from day one and giving it its first shot! Thank you to Jessica Tribble, Scott Calamar, and the entire team at Thomas & Mercer for breathing new life into this story! I am so grateful.

Finally, thank you to my husband, Fred, and daughter, Morgan— you are my world!

ABOUT THE AUTHOR

Lisa Regan is a bestselling suspense novelist and a member of Sisters in Crime, Mystery Writers of America, and International Thriller Writers. She has a bachelor's degree in English and a master of education degree from Bloomsburg University, works full-time as a paralegal, and lives with her husband and daughter in Philadelphia, where she writes books while waiting in line at the post office. Readers can learn more about her work at www.lisaregan.com.